THE CREATION
OF
HALF–
BROKEN
PEOPLE

THE CREATION
OF
HALF-BROKEN PEOPLE

a novel

SIPHIWE GLORIA NDLOVU

ANANSI
INTERNATIONAL

First published in 2024 by Pan Macmillan South Africa.
First published in Canada in 2025 and the USA in 2025 by House of Anansi Press Inc.
houseofanansi.com

House of Anansi Press is committed to protecting our natural environment. This book is
made of material from well-managed FSC®-certified forests, recycled materials, and other
controlled sources.

House of Anansi Press is a Global Certified Accessible (GCA by Benetech) publisher.
The ebook version of this book meets stringent accessibility standards and is available to
readers with print disabilities.

29 28 27 26 25   1 2 3 4 5

Library and Archives Canada Cataloguing in Publication

Title: The creation of half-broken people : a novel / Siphiwe Gloria Ndlovu.
Names: Ndlovu, Siphiwe Gloria, author.
Description: Includes bibliographical references.
Identifiers: Canadiana (print) 20240455266 | Canadiana (ebook) 20240460103 |
ISBN 9781487013271 (softcover) | ISBN 9781487013288 (EPUB)
Subjects: LCGFT: Gothic fiction. | LCGFT: Novels.
Classification: LCC PR9390.9.N39 C73 2025 | DDC 823/.92—dc23

Cover design: Alysia Shewchuk, based on an original design by Ayanda Phasha
Cover and interior artwork: Dumisani Ndlovu, *Migration*
Back cover letter detail: from the archival source BLG 3/373
Book design and typesetting: Nyx Design

*House of Anansi Press is grateful for the privilege to work on and create from the Traditional Territory
of many Nations, including the Anishinabeg, the Wendat, and the Haudenosaunee, as well as the
Treaty Lands of the Mississaugas of the Credit.*

 Canada Council   Conseil des Arts
for the Arts   du Canada

 ONTARIO ARTS COUNCIL
CONSEIL DES ARTS DE L'ONTARIO
an Ontario government agency
un organisme du gouvernement de l'Ontario

With the participation of the Government of Canada
Avec la participation du gouvernement du Canada | Canadä

*We acknowledge for their financial support of our publishing program the Canada Council for the
Arts, the Ontario Arts Council, and the Government of Canada.*

Printed and bound in Canada

 FSC
www.fsc.org
MIX
Paper | Supporting
responsible forestry
FSC® C103567

BY THE SAME AUTHOR

THE CITY OF KINGS trilogy, comprising:
The Theory of Flight (2018)
The History of Man (2020)
The Quality of Mercy (2022)

'Savour the extraordinary literary gifts of Ndlovu.'
– BARBARA MASEKELA, poet and former Ambassador
to France, UNESCO and the United States

'A trilogy of extraordinary literary fiction.'
– HELEN MOFFETT, author of *Charlotte*

'Siphiwe Gloria Ndlovu's trilogy of novels reimagines
the history of a country much like modern Zimbabwe.
Through her multiracial cast of characters (with weighty
inheritances) and their fantastical comings and goings,
she realizes unpromised futures.'
– SEAN JACOBS, faculty at The New School
and Founder-Editor of *Africa Is a Country*

'*The City of Kings* trilogy is a deep ocean with many tides
that carry you away. Ndlovu manages to hold a host of
complex characters and painful histories with compassion,
insight and tenderness. Her writing is never strained, even
when telling of devastating horror and pain that cuts to the
quick. [...] This trilogy is beyond words in its scope and depth.
It is essential reading for anyone who wants to better
understand history, humanity, redemption, or be swept
away by magical and utterly compelling storytelling.'
– BRIDGET PITT, author of *Eye Brother Horn*

To those who came before me: MaNdhlovu, Mme Mokoena, MaThebe, MaMoyo, MaNgwenya, MaDube, Mme Malope, and all the other misremembered, misbegotten and forgotten women in my matrilineal line. Keepers of the Flame. Ngiyalibonga. Kea leboga. Ndaboka. Thank you for the guiding light.

AUTHOR'S NOTE

For the most part, I have reproduced archival materials as they appear in the original sources without correcting 'errors', or imposing consistency in terms of spelling, style and layout. I have, however, replaced the original name of the city with the *City of Kings*, to be more in keeping with the language of the story. I have also fictionalised the interiority of two historical figures, and have therefore given them other names while keeping their original correspondence intact. A list of Archival Sources is given on page 359.

Readers should be aware that, for purposes of historical accuracy, racially demeaning/offensive terms and sexist/misogynistic language and sentiments appear on occasion, both in the archival materials and in parts of the narrative. I am well aware of the pain, violence and damage that such terms, language and sentiments have caused in the past and continue to cause in the present. It is my hope that confronting the past allows us to learn from its mistakes and become better people.

In the beginning, there was erasure.
He came. He saw. He wrote.
And she became Gagool.

Anonymous

PART I

She did not fall at once.

DAPHNE DU MAURIER – *Rebecca*

THE ANONYMOUS WOMAN

1985–PRESENT

There was a time before this. I did not always live in the attic.

There were moments in my childhood that were happy and there were moments in my childhood that were not happy. Somewhere in between, I lost my name, but there will be time to tell of this later. What matters now is that I left that childhood, with its moments of happiness and moments of unhappiness, in the Old Country when my mother took me to live with her in the New Country.

Without that journey to the New Country, my life would have never taken the turn that led me to John B. Good IX. I was twenty-one years old when I met him, and it is because of that meeting that I am here now. I had had five relationships by then – one relationship's ending seamlessly blending into another's beginning – and perhaps because of this, because of the *ease* of transition, I felt worldly enough to enter into a relationship with a man almost ten years my senior.

I was on a Fulatha scholarship, successfully finishing my last year of university when I received an invitation from the Good Foundation to what they called a Futures event. I knew that by 'Futures' the Good Foundation meant an opportunity to work for them. An internship that would hopefully turn into an entry-level position at the Good Foundation seemed like the best (if not obvious) way forward for a Fulatha scholar, and so I attended the event to which the Foundation had invited all its current scholar-ship recipients, secure in the knowledge that previous Fulatha scholars had used it as a stepping stone towards positions of power and influence the world over.

Although our families had once been connected, it had never occurred to me that I would one day meet John B. Good IX in person. He was a world-renowned photojournalist, had won two extremely prestigious awards before the age of thirty, had been on the cover of *Time* magazine at twenty-five, and his most lauded photograph – that of a man who had just been shot by a child soldier, reaching his hand out towards his killer – had been on the cover of *Third World News Today*. Everyone seemed to appreciate the way the photographer had been able to capture both supplication and forgiveness in that moment, that one gesture.

If there was a civil war somewhere in Africa, John B. Good IX was sure to be there with his camera, shooting the most heart-wrenching photographs. The adjective 'courageous' was attached to his name in almost everything written about him. He had the kind of easy charm that got him in and out of places, which was how he managed to do his job as a conflict photojournalist so well. But what mattered most to me when I first met him at twenty-one, when he attended the Futures event, was that he was a man possessed of an almost impossible beauty. And so when he walked up to me and said, 'What an exotic creature you are,' I felt fate was smiling down on me for possibly the first time in my life. It all seemed so very fortunately fortuitous that I never thought to examine what it was I was actually feeling. I took it to be something I had never felt before: romantic love.

The incredible discovery was his: I became the exotic creature.

As I got to know John B. Good IX better, it became obvious to me that he was an emotional tourist – and I did not care. He saw me when he saw me, and loved me when and if he could – and I did not care. Once, in the early days of our knowing of each other, he took me to a club where the paparazzi took photographs of us leaving, and one of the pictures made it onto the front page of a popular tabloid. In the image we were holding hands, he was averting his face, and I was staring straight at the camera, startled into a new reality. The photograph was captioned 'Who Is That Girl?' I was not the first 'That Girl' attached to John B. Good IX, I would not be the last – and I did not care.

John B. Good IX had a name. I had none.

The first time he beat me, I understood why he had done it. He had a very stressful job and what he needed when he came to see me, in the times he deemed it necessary, was peace and quiet and every need met, not a woman who had been waiting for him with longings and expectations of her own. The second time he beat me, I accepted it, and did not even raise my hands to soften the blows. Some things you learn before you meet the man. He died before he could beat me a third time.

I am glad it cannot happen twice, the fever of first love. For it is a fever, and a burden, too, whatever the poets may say. They are not brave, the days when we are twenty-one.

It surprised me, him, and everyone else, when we were still together five years after that initial meeting at the Futures event. By then I had been working at the Good Museum for four years, and John and I seemed to be making our way towards something that, if not lasting, could at least hold together for a while. Eventually, John B. Good IX believed sufficiently in what we had to invite me to meet the rest of the Good Family.

What became an intricate and intimate relationship with the Good Family was more than I could have hoped for. My mother had created and then severed the first link to the family, so that I, like most people, only got to know of the Good Family and their good works through stories and books and through the events I would attend as a Fulatha scholar. I had been fascinated by the Good Family for most of my life because they in turn, for over a century, had been fascinated with the African continent: the place of my birth.

Before its fascination with Africa, the Good Family had been part of the landed gentry of their country for centuries. It may seem surprising that in all those years – generation after generation – there had never been a son named John. That oversight on the part of the family was corrected in 1815 when the first John B. Good was born. This first John did absolutely nothing to distinguish himself, but was directly responsible for all the many John B. Goods who came after him; and because of that, history has chosen to remember him and retroactively christen him John B. Good I.

The second, and probably the most famous, John B. Good, John B. Good II, was born in 1835 and as an adventurer, visited Africa in the latter half of the nineteenth century. A decade or two before his African adventure, while a captain in Her Majesty's navy, he had met a woman in Plymouth, believed himself to be in love with her, allowed things to progress in their natural way, and had then left Plymouth ... and the woman. He had kept the woman in his heart and mind until he had met another woman at another port, believed himself to be in love with her, allowed things to progress in their natural way, and so on and so on. The woman in Plymouth, however, had not forgotten him, and when she gave birth to a son nine months after she had allowed things to progress in their natural way with Captain Good, she had made it a point to name the son after his father.

This was how John B. Good II, the adventurer, begat a son, John B. Good III, who became a member of the British forces and took part in the Benin Expedition of 1897. The British-forces-son begat a son, John B. Good IV, who became a hunter and came to Africa as a member of Theodore Roosevelt's Smithsonian-Roosevelt African Expedition of 1909–11. The hunter-son begat a son, John B. Good V, who became a missionary and was sent to establish a mission station somewhere along the Zambesi River in the 1920s, but found, once he got there, that he was less interested in saving African souls than he was in saving African artefacts.

The missionary-son begat a son, John B. Good VI, who became an archaeologist and excavated the Ruins of Gedi in East Africa in the 1940s. The archaeologist-son begat a son, John B. Good VII, who became an anthropologist who, fascinated by the oral traditions of Central Africa, wrote many books about them in the 1960s. The anthropologist-son begat a son, John B. Good VIII, who became a historian; although trained as a Marxist whose work was supposed to focus on South Africa, he spent most of his career writing best-selling biographies of his forefathers. The historian-son begat a son, John B. Good IX, who became a world-renowned photojournalist, and who one day met me and called me an exotic creature. When I met him, the photojournalist-son was yet to beget any children of his own.

Of course there was other issue in the Good lineage, but the genealogy of the Good Family has since 1815 primarily focused on the John B. Goods.

Collectively, the Good Family used the considerable accumulated wealth and knowledge of the John B. Goods to further the study of Africa by creating the Good Foundation and building the Good Museum and the Good Library. The Good Museum and the Good Library situated, along with the Good Foundation, on the evergreen campus of a prestigious university, house the greatest collection of artefacts and manuscripts from and about Africa in the world. As a way of giving back to a continent that had given them so much, the Good Family established the Foulata (later known as Fulatha) Scholarship for students from the African continent who wanted to obtain their higher education overseas. The scholarship itself is liberal, and nothing much is asked of the scholars except that they excel in their chosen studies and emulate the generosity and self-sacrifice of the woman for whom the scholarship is named: Foulata. Foulata gave her own life for that of the second John B. Good.

Needless to say, the myriad contributions and many good works of the Good Family are unsurpassed.

As I have already mentioned, my connection to the Good Family predates that fateful meeting at the Futures event. My mother had met John B. Good VIII, the historian, while he was researching his missionary forebear at the National Free Library of the City of Kings. She had done everything the world asked of women in the 1980s: she had got herself an education and obtained a degree – from the then only university in her country; she had married a man – my father; she had had a child – me; she had secured a job – as a librarian; but for some reason, none of these things had made her feel the way she thought she should feel. And then she met John B. Good VIII.

John B. Good VIII loved my mother's need for order and cataloguing so much so that within six months of knowing her, he made her his research assistant. A year later, she divorced my father. Not long after that, we left for the New Country. The world was suddenly what my mother had always hoped it would be for her. However, almost as soon as my mother and I arrived in the New Country, she learnt that John B. Good VIII was married and had two children – and that he had found himself a new research assistant. Seemingly unperturbed, my mother severed all ties with the man who had managed to coax her away from my father, pursued a Master's degree in Library Sciences, became an archivist, and continued her love for ordering and cataloguing the world.

I had always been a problem for my mother, neither this nor that, or too much of this and not enough of the other, or whichever phrase could contain all of her dissatisfaction in me. So when I got the Fulatha scholarship, more than anything else, I think, she was relieved that someone somewhere had found something to value in me. When she learnt of my relationship with John B. Good IX, my mother expressed no emotion, and I chose to take her non-response as her sanctioning of our union. I now realise she had always meant to avenge herself on John B. Good VIII, and that I played ever so nicely and ever so easily into her plan. But what I did not know then cannot hurt me today – not where I am.

Now back to where I was, working at the Good Museum and still, much to everyone's surprise, in a relationship with John B. Good IX. I enjoyed working in the museum because it was just so full of wonderful and awe-inspiring things: in the main museum – artefacts, bronzes, paintings, precious stones; and in the Curtis Collection – elephant and rhino tusks, trophies, skins of various animals and reptiles, jars filled with life (at various stages) preserved in formaldehyde. Although I have never seen them, I know there are human skeletons and skulls in the basement of the museum.

A few of my favourite things are housed in that museum:

◈ A gigantic tapestry, titled 'Killing of an Elephant', hangs, larger than life, from the ceiling – the blood gushing out of the wounded and trumpeting elephant is of a red I have never seen anywhere else.

◈ The elaborately and intricately carved magnificent throne of some forgotten chief whose rule, whether benevolent or despotic, inspired amazing artistry and dedication – the minutely etched carvings of talking heads seem to speak volumes.

◈ The fascinating face of Foulata, which forms the threshold of the museum and is made up of thousands of tiny beads of every colour under the sun – the effect as you walk over the thick glass that protects her, is that she looks up at you with eyes made large by her never-ending sorrow and love.

◈ And, my most favourite of all, a giant pair of silver wings
(source unknown and value indeterminate) acquired by
the museum in 1960 – the only way to fully appreciate the
exquisite splendour of the wings is to see them for yourself.

Dear reader, please note that as I write this, the giant pair of silver
wings no longer resides in the Good Museum.

One day, as I made my way to the museum, I noticed a group of people gathered outside it. Two of them held a banner that read, 'Give Us Back What Is Ours'. Who was 'us' and what exactly was 'ours'? I wondered as I entered the museum and looked down at Foulata's never-ending sorrow and love. When I turned back to look at the protestors, I saw that standing among them was a venerable woman with sagacious eyes. She wore beads and a skirt made of cowhide, and seemed to belong to another place and time. She looked at me; I looked at her. Something, I no longer remember what, made me look away from her, and when I looked back at the small crowd, the venerable woman with sagacious eyes was no longer there.

Another person, a normal person, would have been relieved and shrugged it off as some trick of the imagination. But I am not a normal person. I have seen many visions in my life, and I could not feel relief.

Over the weeks, the protests grew until the Good Foundation decided to hold a public meeting. During the meeting a lot of things were brought up by the protestors, and the Good Foundation promised to take all the proposed solutions to their grievances under advisement. The entire Good Family – Dr Good, Mrs Good, John B. Good IX and Johanna Good – was present, putting forward a strong and united front. I was there as well, sitting with the Good Family, wanting so much to feel like I was one of them.

All seemed to be going as the Foundation had planned, and the protestors appeared to have been appeased, when a cocksure student, whose view of the world and the people in it was still uncompromised, stood up and asked John B. Good IX about his most famous photograph: the one of the man who was reaching out, with both supplication and forgiveness, to the child who had just shot him. 'Why didn't you intervene?' the self-assured student asked. John B. Good IX looked at the student and smiled before answering. I did not hear what he said because, before responding to the question, he had taken my hand in his, and all I could think was what a momentous thing it was for him to do in the open for all to see.

My elation did not last long, however. That evening, after the meeting, John B. Good IX beat me for the second time. The next morning he flew with his trusted camera to some conflicted distant land. I was left black and blue. A few days later, his mother called me. She had never called me before. When she delivered the bad news – that John B. Good IX had fatally shot himself in a two-star hotel in the middle of nowhere – for some time after, all I could hear was the sound of an animal being taken to slaughter, its fear a tangible thing in the sound it made.

It was only afterwards when I was in a private room of a private hospital and they told me I had screamed until I had no voice left that I realised I was the one who had made that godawful sound. I was the one who had been consumed by the unforgiving horror and terror of death. I was the one who had become an animal afraid of its slaughter. My wrists were secured to the bed because my mother had told the doctors and the Good Family that, after receiving the news, I had thrown myself against every possible immovable object. Whether the doctors or the Good Family suspected what my mother and I knew to be the truth of the situation, I will never know.

When I was finally released from hospital, the Good Family took me and put me in their attic.

It was during my initial night in the attic that I first experienced it. The scratching sound. Something sharp repeatedly scraping against the surface of something dry ... skin? Paper? Wood?

Another person, a normal person, would have been afraid and shut their eyes to the pitch darkness of the room, clenched their teeth, gripped the sheets tight, allowed their flesh to goosebump and their hair to stand on end. But I am not a normal person. I have seen many visions in my life, and so I watched as the shimmering silver writing appeared on the wall:

babylon   between starshine and clay   something has tried to kill me

In retrospect, I am not sure if it was how I screamed upon hearing the news of John B. Good XI's death, or how I remained silent after the bruises on my body were explained away: all I know is, whatever I did, it convinced the Good Family (now reduced to Dr Good, Mrs Good and Johanna Good) of something they had long doubted – that I truly loved John B. Good XI; and that John B. Good XI, in turn, truly loved me. It was this new discovery that led them to offer to take me into their home to recuperate.

The attic has a view of the not-so-distant ocean and a glimpse of a path that leads to the garden and the front of the house. It may not be the room with the best view of the ocean or the garden, but it still produces a picturesque vista. The ebb and flow of the crashing ocean waves create a calming and lulling effect that the Good Family members believe is good for me. They repeatedly assured me that it was because of this – the beauty and tranquillity the room provides, and not because it is the most secluded and secret room in the house – that I was placed in it.

I believed them. In fact, I was grateful to them for their generosity and kindness. After they found out yellow is my most-loved colour, they covered the attic walls with the prettiest yellow wallpaper, ivory stripes running down it in even, vertical lines, creating pleasing parallels throughout.

The stay with the Good Family had been conceived as a short one – 'until you find your feet,' Mrs Good had said. But then my mother had come to visit, and after paying her respects and saying her condolences and mentioning repeatedly how well I looked and how much at home I seemed to be, and how it was such a tragedy that John B. Good IX had been cut down in his prime before he could begat John B. Good X, and … She did not have to say more after that. Grief was listening and would faithfully go down the path she had charted. But she did say more. She was a woman creating a new order, and she needed to make sure that things happened exactly how she wanted them to. 'If only there was some way to bring John B. Good X into this world,' she said. Grief made the Good Family turn to look at me. 'It is what John would have wanted,' she – who had met John B. Good IX only once before he died – said with authority. Grief found a way to change its parameters so that what it contained was something the Good Family found easier to manage.

'It is what John would have wanted' became the Good Family's chosen refrain. It made them think John B. Good IX had sacrificed himself for the good of the rest of the family – to bring them together and make them stronger, closer, better. Thinking this way helped them overlook each other's sins and shortcomings and focus instead on the bigger picture. It made Dr Good feel brave enough to occasionally look my mother in the eye when he spoke to her, silently asking for forgiveness which she, equally silently, seemed to grant. It made Johanna believe the on-again-off-again A.J. Quatermain was the best man for her and made her find ways to tie him securely to her; and A.J., for his part, allowed himself to be securely tied. It made them all see a future in me, the woman who truly loved John B. Good IX, and whom John B. Good IX, in turn, had truly loved.

My verbal agreement was not really required in what was decided; perhaps because Mrs Good could still hear, ringing in her ear, the sound of the animal being taken to slaughter, or, perhaps, because my eyes had been made large by what seemed like never-ending sorrow and love. What was decided, what I was not required to voice my agreement to, was that John would have wanted a family – and that he would have wanted it with me.

You may very well wonder how it could be possible to have Good children issue out of me when John B. Good IX was already dead. The solution, although surprisingly simple, was not without its fair share of alchemy. Johanna, who has no intention of ever bearing children of her own, graciously donated some of her eggs; and A.J., who has children he has sired without ever fathering, donated some of his sperm; and in a private room of a private hospital, a fertilised egg was inserted into my uterus where it implanted itself. One time. Two times. Three times. Because that is what John would have wanted.

And that is how it came to pass that seven years after John B. Good IX shot himself, I was a mother of Three Good Children.

My mother, worried that I did not care for the children as I ought, moved into the house better to order the life in it. Her history with Dr Good, she kept a secret. But I have erred here, for my mother has no secrets; instead she calls what she has pride keepers – things you store within yourself in order to preserve your pride.

Johanna's love for the Three Good Children took her by surprise; it was so strong it moved her back into the house. A.J. Quatermain, missing his best friend, and seeing much of him in the Three Good Children, spent almost as much time in the house as he did on the safaris he runs.

It was because of the Three Good Children that we all came to live in the Good House, bringing with us our various secrets and pride keepers. It was because of the Three Good Children that John B. Good IX's self-sacrifice for the good of the rest of the family was fulfilled. It was because of the Three Good Children that the family was brought together and made stronger, closer, better.

It was because of the Three Good Children that I continued to live in the attic eight years after first entering it.

Now that you understand all this, the story can begin in earnest.

D ream or memory. I do not know what it is. The cusp of an image I am trying to hold on to as I get out of bed. Sleepwalking almost, I am *following a phantom in my mind, whose shadowy form has taken shape at last. Her features are blurred, her colouring indistinct, the setting of her eyes and the texture of her hair are still uncertain, still to be revealed.* The lips, however, are upturned. A smile. Unexpected and divine. Warm and full of promise. She is not me, then. When was the last time I smiled a genuine smile?

It is this smile that makes me do something I have not done in years. I prepare to write. The smile has taken me to my half-moon table. I reach for my pen and notebook and jot down the six words that will either be my salvation or my damnation, depending on how you choose to look at it.

In the beginning, there was erasure.

This is the sentence that will take me to Holdengarde Castle: the place from which I will never return.

I am not aware of this future fate as I struggle to hold on to the dream-memory of that smile.

There is a knock on the door. Luckily, I have the presence of mind to open the demilune table's drawer and hide both pen and notebook inside. Some things I have learnt to keep my own. There is another knock, louder this time. I scurry across the floor, trying not to make a sound. By the time the door is opened, without my having given permission to enter, I am already back in my bed.

My mother stands on the threshold of the opened door holding two children, boys, by the hand, one on either side of her: John B. Good X and Henry C. Good.

'Boys,' I say. My voice is grainy, but tries to contain within it the loving kindness I think a mother must feel for her children.

'Mother,' the boys respond, in unison.

A shiver runs through me.

My mother does not let go of the boys' hands. She looks at me the way she has ever since that business with the scissors. No, that is not altogether true; I first remember her looking at me that way the morning I woke up with the Lady Doctor next to me, and asked her if she could smell tobacco in the air. The Three Good Children had taken away that look in my mother's eyes, and the scissors had brought it back.

'Were you out of bed?' my mother asks. She seems suspicious both of why I got out of bed in the first place, and of why I got back in when she knocked on the door. Her eyes search the room for a clue.

'I told you I am getting stronger … better,' I say. But, really, there is no need to dissemble. The truth is something she no longer expects from me. I choose not to look at her, to look at the boys instead. I smile at them and they smile back at me: shy, unpractised smiles that probably mimic my own. My mother still will not let go of their hands, still will not let them come to me. 'Have Johanna and A.J. returned?' I ask.

My mother looks at me with eyes that will probably never forgive me for disordering her world.

'Say "goodnight" boys,' she instructs.

'Goodnight,' the boys say in unison.

'Goodnight,' I say. 'Johanna and A.J. will be very sorry to have missed the boys' bedtime,' I add for good measure.

Even as the boys turn away, they are still expectant. I can feel it – the full weight of their expectation. They want a mother out of me. I know that feeling … that want … that yearning: that absolute need for what we are born thinking mothers are supposed to give.

'I will be back shortly,' my mother says.

The older boy, John, momentarily braver, turns to me and waves his free hand. I wave back. We both try and fail to smile. It is the younger boy, Henry, who shuts the door without looking back at me.

My boys. I catch on too late. I should have said, 'My boys,' and flung my arms wide open. She would have let go of their hands, allowed them to run to me and allowed me to hug them, if only I had said something to claim them as my own. The use of the possessive would have convinced her; after all, love is supposed to be something you possess. 'My boys': that would have made me seem repentant for the scissors and what I did with them.

My mother returns. She enters the room without knocking. In her hands, she holds a breast-pump and some baby bottles. A handful.

She plops the bottles on the bed, and without ceremony or consent, exposes my breasts and attaches the pump. Milk squirts out of my body in fits and starts. Mother's milk is supposed to flow freely, be abundant. I imagine mothers, happy ones, all over the world, attaching breast pumps and babies to their breasts and sighing with contentment, blissful in the knowledge of providing so vital a function. The pain one feels in moments like these is just a part of it, I am told.

'How is she?' I ask.

'She has a name,' my mother says.

She has *my* name. As always, when I think of this, I am overwhelmed by sadness. I turn my head away so my mother will not see my tears.

'I thought you said you were getting stronger.'

'I am getting stronger,' I say. I am. But what can one feel when a child is named after someone whose name was taken away?

The child, for obvious reasons, was supposed to have been

called Johanna (pronounced Jo-Hanna. I probably should have mentioned this earlier because how you say a person's name is important: a name is at the heart of a person's identity.). However, when it looked like both the baby and I might die during childbirth of complications from undiagnosed preeclampsia, Grief, in the guise of my mother, spoke to the Good Family, and they listened. The decision was made to name the child after me. It is what John would have wanted. Although I am not so sure that that sentiment survived the sway of sorrow when both mother and child survived the birth.

The pump stops. My mother has taken all the milk she needs for the time being. I cover up my breasts. I expect her to leave, and so I prepare a smile. She does not leave, however. She touches me. A gentle touch on my hand. I look at her hand in wonder because it is such a rare thing. Her hand on mine. Its gentleness.

'The Good Family loves you. They want you to be strong ... better. Please do not disappoint them.'

She mentions nothing of her love, her need for my strength and improvement ... her disappointment.

My smile, long prepared, spreads thinly on my lips. She seems embarrassed by our closeness and gets up, taking the breast pump and the full baby bottles with her. A handful. She leaves with everything she came with and more. She even takes my smile with her, and repays me with no smile of her own.

But it is not my mother's smile I miss when the door closes, it is the dream-memory smile. There is something wonderfully warm and self-assured about that smile.

I must fall asleep with a vision of that smile because the next thing I know, Johanna is stumbling into the room, trying to be quiet and failing. There is new light in the sky that lies beyond the window curtain. Dawn is breaking. Johanna is still in an evening dress, stilettos hanging from her right hand as she tiptoes across the floor, her eyes doing their best to adjust to the letting-go darkness of the room. I pretend to be asleep as she plops onto the bed besides me. She smells expensive. The perfume she wears and the alcohol on her breath are things not easily afforded.

She and A.J. have been going to a lot of green events lately. The Quatermains have been in the safari and African game-hunting business for more than a century, and A.J. is at great pains to show that what the Quatermains have really been in for a century is ecotourism. He even gives talks with slide presentations to prove this point.

I see that Johanna has placed an arm around my waist and snuggled close to me. I see this closeness, but do not feel it. Instead, I catch a whiff of tobacco, its cheap smell overpowering the expensiveness in the room. I hear a tobacco-cured, throaty laugh. I look back over my shoulder, and it is not Johanna lying there; it is the Lady Doctor. She is not looking at me, she is looking at the corner of the bed, where the laughter is coming from. I look at the corner of the bed, too. A woman, black and beautiful, is crouching there, smoking from a long and curved pipe.

It is happening again.

'You were something else, Strawberry,' the Lady Doctor says to the crouching woman. 'You killed the first one, released the second one, and kept the third one.'

Both women laugh, and for some reason their happiness makes me irredeemably miserable with longing. The crouching woman with the smoking pipe looks at me, and I feel the Lady Doctor's hand, softened by Beetham's Larola, wipe the tears from eyes I do not even know are crying. The comforting touch of her hand falls me to sleep.

'I love you,' I hear Johanna mumble into my hair. 'I need for you to be strong ... to get better. Please be strong for me ... for us. You have to be strong for the children.'

The Three Good Children: two boys named after famous men and a girl named after me.

As I teeter on the edge of dream-memory, I know one thing for sure; I will disappoint Johanna.

I was right. I have disappointed Johanna, for here I lie in a bed in a private room of a private hospital with both wrists shackled to the bed frame. I must have done some violence I no longer remember. Who did I hurt? Myself? My wrists are not bandaged, so I did not commit that kind of violence this time. Maybe, remembering the spray of crimson arcing its way across the erubescent yellow wallpaper when the scissors' sharp edge struck an artery the last time, I had opted for a less messy end this time. An overdose of the already overly prescribed sleeping tablets, perhaps.

A woman, with time and patience firmly folded into her sleeves, enters the room with a look of kindness I am certain she only uses when dealing with people like me – people who have wished for an ending they did not receive.

'How are you feeling?' she asks. She stands by the bed, touching the raised railing, but not touching me.

'Fine,' I lie.

Her kindness crinkles the corners of her eyes before she says: 'Do you remember what brought you here?' She speaks with a dulcet accent.

'No,' I say. 'No, I do not remember the violence.'

A frown furrows her forehead. 'Violence?' she asks.

If not violence, then what? Is what I did too big or too small for such a word? Before I can ask her what I did, she places a hand briefly on my shoulder. 'My name is Isabella Van Wagenen,' she says. 'You and I will be working together on ways to make you better.' She gives my shoulder a gentle squeeze, 'Get some rest,' she says and then is gone.

What did I do? The pristine sterile whiteness of the room holds no answer. The rhythmic beep of the monitor holds no answer. The steady drip of whatever they are pumping into my veins holds no answer. My slow slide into sweet sleep holds no answer.

Days must pass because when I become aware of my surroundings again, the monitor still beeps, there is still a needle in my veins, but the shackles have been removed from around my wrists, and the pristine sterile whiteness of the room has morphed into a yellow wallpaper with sunflowers splotched all over it.

The woman – Isabella Van Wagenen – enters the room with her kindness. She draws up a chair and sits by the bed. 'I am told yellow is your favourite colour,' she says. 'I hope this room is to your liking.'

'It is. Very much,' I say.

'Have you remembered what brought you here?'

I do not remember remembering anything, but I feel if I tell her this, she will be dissatisfied with me. I do not want to fail Isabella Van Wagenen.

She smiles at me, obviously understanding everything. 'I work with women like you. You can tell me anything. You can trust me.'

'Women like me?'

'Misremembered, misbegotten and forgotten women,' she says.

'Misremembered, misbegotten and forgotten women,' I echo, my voice a whisper.

Her kindness crinkles the corners of her eyes, makes her reach out and touch me, touch the jagged ugly keloid scars on my left wrist. 'It is painful, I know. But memory is the most important thing,' she says.

'Memory is the most important thing.' Another echo.

Without warning, there is an unwelcome guest. The scratching sound fills the room. Something sharp repeatedly scrapes against

25

the surface of something dry. Not here. Not now. Not in front of Isabella. I could shut my eyes. I could turn my head away. But I do not want Isabella to know the kind of woman that I really am, and so I nonchalantly watch as writing etches itself onto the wallpaper:

i had no model   i made it up   everyday

Isabella looks at me for a very long time, realising or recognising something. The touch of her hand grows warm, almost familiar. 'We are on the same mission,' she says. 'I believe we are kindred.'

'Kindred,' I echo, this time my voice strong.

Days must pass because when I become aware of my surroundings again, the sunflowers are still splotched on the yellow wallpaper, but there is no beeping monitor or needle attached to a vein.

My mother walks into the room. Her left arm is in a sling. A doctor, armed with a white coat, stethoscope and digital tablet, walks by her side.

'We have lowered the dosage considerably and that should help with her memory,' the doctor says to my mother.

My mother pulls up a chair and sits next to the bed. She scrutinises my face as though looking for fault lines.

'Mother,' I say. 'It is good to see you after so long.'

'I was here yesterday,' she says and leans back in her chair. She seems satisfied to have found what she was looking for.

'Yesterday?' I say. Feeling a sudden panic, I ask, 'Where is Isabella?'

'Isabella?' the doctor asks.

'Yes, Isabella Van Wagenen. She visits me regularly.'

The doctor checks the digital tablet, and it is obvious from the questioning look on her face that she is not finding what she needs to find.

'Where is Isabella?' I ask, my voice suddenly much too loud for the small and sterile room. Both my mother and the doctor start.

'I thought you said she was getting better,' my mother says, accusation plain in her voice.

'She was ... she is,' the doctor says, rapidly typing something onto the digital tablet.

'Please. Can I see Isabella?' I say in a softer voice. I want her kindness. I want her kindness. We are kindred. I want Isabella.

'You pushed me down the stairs,' my mother says, in an effort to make me focus on what she believes matters.

I remember no such thing.

'You were crouching ... *crouching* at the top of the stairs, and you came at me like a ... like a ...'

'Like a what, Mother?' I prompt. I know she has the exact word for it, but she does what she has done all my life: she manoeuvres around it.

Madwoman. Like a madwoman. A handful. I do not have the privilege of skirting the reality of my life.

The doctor stands there, not knowing what to do or say. She has obviously spent quite some time in my mother's company. She looks at me, trying to give me something, but is not sure what to give.

'Does this happen to you ... often?' the doctor asks. The name badge pinned to her white coat reads 'Dr Patel'.

'Does what happen to me often?' I ask.

'Do you often ... see people?' Dr Patel asks, her confidence petering out.

My lips form to say the word 'yes', but before I can answer the doctor, my mother says, 'You can leave us now, Doctor.'

My mother looks at me until I nod. It has been this way between us since I was a child – we turn to silent communication when words prove dangerous. Dr Patel stands there, uncertain. I nod to her as well. It always amazes me how so simple a gesture can be so reassuring.

Dr Patel, somewhat relieved, leaves the room.

'Why?' I ask, my voice deceptively strong.

'Why what?' my mother says, her eyes scanning the room and evidently finding fault with the sunflowers.

'Why would I push you down the stairs?'

'I hardly know why you do most of what you do,' she says, her eyes coming to rest on my face. I can tell she is rearranging it to suit her better. 'You have never managed to be good and normal. Always that darkness about you.'

'Did we fight?'

My mother looks at me, affronted. 'We never fight.'

She is obviously in pride-keeping mode. 'You were crouching at the top of the stairs. Lying in wait. I was on my way to express your milk and as soon as I put my feet on the landing, you pushed me down.'

I try to remember the moment, but I cannot.

'You were in the shadows. Hiding. So quiet. So very quiet. I had no idea ... no suspicion. I could have broken my neck. It is a lucky thing I did not.'

Lucky for who? I wonder before I realise how ungenerous a thought this is. I wait for the guilt to arrive. It does not.

I do not remember crouching in the shadows, waiting to hear my mother's step. I do not remember pouncing on her like a madwoman and pushing her down the stairs. I do not remember the look of fear and fright that must surely have entered her eyes when she began to fall. I do not remember the sound of her fall – its thump, thump, thump.

But ... I do remember a sense of victory.

Days pass. I am aware of their passing. I am aware of the nurses who come in at different times: to give me food and make sure I eat it, to change the bed linen and make sure I have not soiled it, to escort me to the bathroom and make sure I do not get too creative in there, to give me medication and make sure I take it, to check in on me and make sure I have not stared at a particular spot on the wall for too long.

My mother comes at the same time every day. Johanna comes twice a week, or, at least, tries to. A.J. comes once and pumps his left leg up and down until he makes me so nervous I have to ask him to leave. He stands up quickly, and then hesitates. 'I love you,' he says. And I do believe he means it as much as A.J. can mean such a thing. He kisses me on the forehead. There is that hesitation again. He kisses me on the lips, briefly. 'I need for you to be strong … to get better. Please be strong for me … for us. You have to be strong for the children,' he adds. We are both relieved when he leaves.

The Three Good Children never come to see me. My mother thinks it is best this way, and Johanna agrees.

Dr Good and Mrs Good are in Africa doing research for his latest biography, and cannot come to see me – although they would really love to. Mrs Good says seeing me in hospital like this will remind her too much of the time John B. Good IX killed himself, and she does not think this is what John would have wanted. He would have wanted us to heal and to be happy. She needs for me to be strong, to get better … for me … for us as a family … for the children … especially the children. It is what John would have wanted.

I seem to be giving in to ungenerous thoughts lately. I think Mrs Good – who was Dr Good's original research assistant, who forewent her own Master's degree so she could not only help him research but also type up his first biography, who had his two children while he went out gallivanting, who has probably known the truth about the long procession of research assistants (my mother included) that came after her – has decisively decided not to allow Dr Good any further temptations.

Dr Patel enters the room armed with a white coat, stethoscope and digital tablet. She has come after my mother's daily visit. I think this is intentional. She sits down on the chair next to the bed.

'My room at the Good House is also yellow,' I say by way of greeting.

Dr Patel looks at the splotchy sunflowers on the wall. 'Johanna told us you love the colour yellow,' she says. 'And so we made this happen for you.'

'My room at the Good House has the sound of the ocean in it,' I say. I will not tell her that it is an attic.

'We wish the hospital was close to the ocean. It would be wonderful for our patients,' Dr Patel says.

'That is alright,' I say. 'The sound of the crashing waves can be too … seductive sometimes.'

This makes Dr Patel frown. 'Can you tell me where or when you remember being happiest?' she asks.

'That is easy,' I say. 'I was happiest with the Lady Doctor.'

'The Lady Doctor?'

'She was my mother's mother, but not really.'

'Not really?'

'My mother was born in what used to be called a mental asylum. I know there is a kinder word for it now, but at this moment I cannot remember it,' I say. I can see Dr Patel wants to write something on her tablet and is restraining herself, with great effort.

'Her mother was deemed mentally unsound and was therefore considered unfit to parent a child,' I continue. 'So my mother was placed in an orphanage and stayed there until the Lady Doctor adopted her.'

Dr Patel nods. 'What made your time with the Lady Doctor happy?'

'Guaranteed sweetness,' I say.

'Guaranteed sweetness?'

'I like things that have a guaranteed sweetness. Like peach mangoes. They are yellow, juicy, small, stringy and sweet. Very, very sweet. Always. Every one. Sweet. There was a peach mango tree that grew in the Lady Doctor's orchard, and when the rainy season came in December we ate the mangoes, still warm from having been kissed by the sun. The juice would run down from our fingers to our elbows, and we would giggle and giggle, because what else can you do when mango juice trickles from your fingers to your elbow? We did not care about the mess, the stickiness, and the strings that got stuck in our teeth. We cared about the guaranteed sweetness.'

Dr Patel nods as though she too has such a memory.

'Mangoes here cannot even compare to the peach mango.'

'My family is from India, so I know a little something about mangoes,' Dr Patel says with a smile. 'So that was your happiest time ... December spent with the Lady Doctor?'

'Every day I spent with the Lady Doctor was happy. We listened to "All Kinds of Everything" on the radio. We plaited each other's hair. We shared everything. We drank condensed milk straight from the can. She had a green thumb, and grew a garden and cultivated an orchard. I do not have a green thumb, so when she was busy tending the flowers, vegetables and fruit, I would play in the small patch of maize that always grew in the corner of her yard. I invented stories about the cobs, based on the different-coloured corn silk – blondes with sweet tempers, redheads with fiery attitudes, brunettes with conniving and cunning spirits – and told them to the Lady Doctor as she worked. She would laugh and laugh … she had the best laugh. She was laughing when she died.'

'When she died? Where were you when she died?' Dr Patel asks.

'I was sleeping next to her.'

'You discovered her …' Dr Patel begins, but cannot finish her thought. She cannot restrain herself any longer, and types something on her tablet. 'And your mother, where was she?'

'With Dr Good, helping him with his research.'

'So it was just you and your grandmother, the Lady Doctor, in the house when she died?'

'Yes,' I lie. I have long since learnt not to tell the truth about this, to not speak of the presence of the woman, black and beautiful, crouching at the corner of the bed, smoking a long and curved pipe that filled the air with the scent of cheap tobacco. The tobacco was as comforting as the Beetham's Larola the Lady Doctor applied religiously to her hands even years after the ointment had ceased to be manufactured. It did make her hands as soft and smooth as advertised. People always remarked on her youthful hands. They were her pride. I was her pride as well. She told me so, and I believed her even though I had not done anything as remarkable as making wrinkles disappear.

'Do you wish your mother had been there?'

'No,' I respond. Too quickly. 'My mother did not know how to be happy with the Lady Doctor. She was happy with Dr Good, I think. And now she is happy with the Three Good Children,' I say.

Dr Patel nods as though understanding more than what I have said. 'About Isabella Van Wagenen,' she says slowly. 'We have no record of anyone with that name coming to visit you.'

'I see.'

'Does she still come and visit you?' Dr Patel asks, making sure to make eye contact.

'No,' I say. It is the truth.

Dr Patel looks reassured as she jots something on her tablet. I let her have her assurances.

I know I will see Isabella again. I know Isabella is not like the crouching and pipe-smoking woman with a tobacco-cured laugh. Isabella is not like the woman in white I saw at Holdengarde Castle, walking amongst the staggered white rocks with mud on her hem and blood on her hands. Isabella is not like the woman with an English-rose-coloured, high-collared dress with matching parasol and gloves I once saw where my reflection should have been when I looked into a shop window. Isabella is not like the women I have been taught to fear. Isabella Van Wagenen is kindred.

It is only after I return to the attic that I become aware that the conversation with Dr Patel has been shared. My mother and Johanna are in my room, whispering. They think I am asleep and I let them think that. It is so much more peaceful this way.

'A mental asylum,' Johanna whispers. 'We had no idea, no idea. Were never told of this, this *history* of mental illness – I mean mental health issues – that runs in your family. We thought the suicide attempt was an isolated incident, completely isolated. And then there was her unprovoked attack on you. Pushing you down the stairs like that. And now this, this information about your mother … and you being born in a mental asylum. If we had known …'

'If you had known …?' my mother whispers back, encouraging Johanna to walk into a trap.

'Then – then – then we would have done all we could to help her … sooner,' Johanna says, cleverly retreating.

'My daughter has given you three children,' my mother says, no longer bothering to whisper.

'Yes, yes … of course,' Johanna says, also speaking in her normal voice. 'But if only we had known sooner … it was our right to know.'

'He used to beat her, you know,' my mother says, punctuating her conquest. 'John used to beat her.'

'He always had a temper,' Johanna says matter-of-factly. 'Ever since we were children.'

'Until she was black and blue,' my mother emphasises.

Johanna accepts her loss. 'We love her. We just need for her to be strong … to get better,' she says.

34

Black and blue. Black … and blue. Black … and … blue …

I remember now.

My mother is capable of many things. She is particularly good at culling, hollowing things out, removing what is inside.

I had taken a stroll by the beach. It had been the kind of day that wanted you to walk at the water's edge. I had enjoyed the feel of the warm sun on my face and the cold, wet sand beneath my feet. I had collected some interesting-looking stones and put them in my pockets for later … for just in case. It was rare for me to be allowed to go near the ocean after the incident with the scissors. I revelled in the feeling of unbounded freedom even as I placed the stones in my pockets.

I thought my mother was beginning to trust that I was indeed getting better and feeling stronger. I thought that was why she had let me venture out on my own towards the seductive pull and call of the ocean.

It was only when I got back to the attic from my walk that I realised my mother had not trusted anything, not even for a moment. As soon as I walked into the room, I smelled it. At first I thought it was happening again, that I was smelling the cheap tobacco that always came before the sound of the throaty laugh. But the scent in the air was not as comforting as the tobacco smell. It was acrid. It made me want to sneeze and cough at the same time.

Something had been burnt in my room, and yet everything seemed to be as I had left it … until my eyes came across the half-moon table and I noticed that the drawer was open.

The six words I had written in the notebook! *In the beginning, there was erasure.* I rushed to the demilune table, and confirmed my suspicions. The notebook and the pen were not there. I went over to the fireplace and found scattered ash. She must have torn the notebook before burning it.

I crept out of the room and down the stairs. When I entered my mother's room, it was obvious that she was expecting me, expecting the confrontation. In her room, everything was immaculate and in its place. Order. Always order.

'Why did you burn it?'

'I knew you were up to something,' she replied coolly. 'I always know when you are up to something.'

'It was just words on paper,' I said.

'When is it ever just words on paper with you?'

I did not know what to do. I did not know what to feel besides anger. My body shook with it. 'What do you want from me?'

'You need to be happy ... contented with what you have. The Good Family has been so good to you. So very kind.'

'How does my writing threaten that in any way?'

My mother just looked at me. 'You take the things you have for granted,' she said. 'That has always been your problem. No, that is not it; your problem is that you destroy the good in your life. You cannot help it. You cannot help yourself. A good man loved you ... a good family loves you ... good children love you – and you want to destroy it all. You have no idea, no idea whatsoever what it feels like to be truly alone. You think it is freedom. It is the very opposite of freedom.'

'He used to beat me,' I almost screamed. 'The good man you speak of used to hit me until I was black and blue.'

My mother blinked at me. 'You had other relationships when he was away,' she charged with venom. 'You slept with men ... and women. You were with John B. Good IX – someone both famous and respected – and he was not enough for you. You were always searching for something else, as though you could do better. You should have been chaste and contented.'

'He saw other people too,' I said. 'We understood that about each other. That was not the problem between us.'

My mother scoffed. 'You wanted to make him jealous. You dangled your affairs and dalliances. You made your proclivities known. You provoked him and when he was provoked, you acted as though you did not know why he was doing what he was doing.'

'You are saying I wanted him to beat me?'

She sighed. 'You have a good life here. You just do not know how good you have it.'

I realised I had been fooled by the gentle touch of her hand on mine into thinking that she loved me. I had been willing to overlook the reality of our long knowing of each other so I could believe she loved me. I had tried to unremember how ungentle her touch could be.

My mother had hit me three times in my life. The first time was after my school returned from an outing to Holdengarde Castle, and I told her of the woman in white I had seen there with mud on her hem and blood on her hands. The second time was after I told her about the woman, black and beautiful, who appeared during the Lady Doctor's final moments, smoking from a long and curved pipe and laughing a throaty laugh. The third time was when I did not tell her that while walking along Abercorn Street, I had looked into a shop window and seen a woman with an English-rose-coloured, high-collared dress with matching parasol and gloves where my reflection should have been.

The problem for my mother was not so much that I had seen these women, but that I had shared what I had seen with someone else: the first two times with her; and the third time with my English teacher, in a composition I had written for class. My teacher so loved how I had brought to life the woman in the English-rose-coloured attire that she affixed a golden star to the page of my exercise book. My mother so hated how I had told of having seen these women as reality and not as fiction ... as a flight of fancy ... as a trick of the imagination. She rewarded my belief in the veracity of what I had seen by making me black and blue. Black ... and blue. Black ... and ... blue. For good measure, she bent my right hand backwards until my wrist broke. I felt the words and the images empty out of me then, until I was light as air.

My mother is capable of many things. She is particularly good at culling, hollowing things out, removing what is inside.

It is a bloody business.

But apparently I am capable of many things, too. I am capable of crouching at the top of the stairs and lying in wait. I am capable of pouncing out of the shadows and pushing someone. I am capable of listening to the thump, thump, thump of a fall. I am capable of having a feeling of victory wash over me as I look down at my mother lying at an odd angle at the bottom of the stairs.

I see myself the way my mother must have seen me then, as *a strange, provoking, formless sort of figure that seems to skulk about;* something she could not manoeuvre herself around.

I am capable of creeping down the stairs to where my mother's body lies. I am capable of standing in the warmth of her pooling blood. I am capable of doing absolutely nothing to help her. I am capable of dipping my finger into her blood and writing on the wall: *In the beginning, there was erasure.* I am capable of crawling back up the stairs, entering my room, looking back and seeing the bloody prints I have created, tell-tale signs between my mother's body and mine. I am capable of closing the door, getting into my bed, and falling blissfully asleep as my mother lies dying.

I remember now.

You are probably wondering where my father is in all of this, and so the time has come for me to write about him. Most of what I know about him is sketched together from the little my mother has told me; from my own, often painful, recollections; and from a family-album-cum-scrapbook my mother once tried to throw away, but that I salvaged and secreted away.

At the very moment my mother and my father met, they were already moving away from each other; they just did not know it yet. This is why I can only make sense of my father in retrospect.

My parents met at the then only university in the country in 1980, during its heyday. The country was newly independent, students from all races and all walks of life were attending the university in droves. If you were white and able to stomach such change, then you had every right to think of yourself as a liberal – and that is exactly what my parents did.

My parents – wearing bell-bottomed trousers, rainbow-coloured headbands and tie-dyed T-shirts – saw themselves as finally free enough to do the things they believed they would have done in the late sixties and early seventies had they been old enough. After they graduated from university, they travelled the country in a Volkswagen van that they spray-painted with a peace sign and on which they wrote the words 'love' and 'understanding'. They smoked marijuana using a Tonga gourd pipe and listened to The Who, The Band and The Byrds. My mother cooked their meals, washed their laundry, and mended their clothes. My father whittled things and then sold them wherever their travels took them. They lived in the van, but they were not homeless. There were homes they could have gone to and lived in; they both just chose not to.

My parents were both running away from their pasts – pasts that, although secret, they had divulged to each other when they thought they were being free, pasts that made them run together for a short while at the point of convergence, pasts that would eventually make them run past each other and look back with accusation.

My father was born to Italian immigrants. In 1956, his father, a civil engineer, had left Italy under the employ of Impresit Construction Company. He emigrated to what would come to be known as Kariba Town to build a dam on the Zambesi River that would come to be known as Kariba Dam, and which would provide much-needed hydroelectric power to two colonies. It had been my paternal grandfather's intention to return to Italy after his contract had ended, but the spectacular display of ochre, blood-orange, mauve and deep purple that accompanied the sun's gradual dip over the river at every sunset made him fall in love with this new land.

My paternal grandfather decided he would never leave the little slice of heaven he had found, and set about building a whitewashed villa with earth-red terracotta tiles that he intended to call home. He wrote a letter to his mother inviting her to visit. She did not visit, but sent a young woman in her stead with a letter saying that she would only visit him once she received word he had married the letter bearer, and was living a good and Christian life in deepest and darkest Africa.

My paternal grandparents were married within two weeks of having first met.

My paternal grandfather was so happy in his marriage and in the small town that had been constructed above the Zambesi River that he never got to write the letter for which his mother was eagerly waiting. In 1958, while she was pregnant with my father, my paternal grandmother received news that her husband, along with ten of his countrymen (and natives whose number the government had not bothered to tally) had become trapped in the dam wall during a catastrophic flood that had inundated the land of the BaTonga, wreaking death, destruction and decimation not only upon the people who lived on the land, but all the biodiversity that made up that habitat. The government decided that instead of trying to extract the men, they would just entomb them in the wall. My paternal grandmother went into premature labour before she could give her formal consent. My father was born.

My father loved his mother very much, especially the sparkling blue of her eyes and genuine blonde of her hair that would make her the pride of Kariba Town for many years. My grandmother, prepossessing as she was, refused to remarry, refused to stop wearing widow's black, refused to move away from Kariba Town: she wanted to be forever close to the man she had crossed an entire continent to marry.

In Kariba Town, and the country as a whole, those eleven Italians who had lost their lives became heroes. So, although my father had never met his father, he had spent his entire life in his shadow. How could he ever compete with a man who had sacrificed his life for the betterment of two colonies?

When my father's chance came to be a hero – to fight terrorists in his country's civil war – instead of receiving a call-up notification, he got a letter saying his father had already sacrificed his life for the country, and that he, his son, would be exempt from conscription. The government showed how much they appreciated his father's sacrifice by giving my father a scholarship to the then only university in the country.

The war was defining my father's generation, and he was not

allowed to be part of it. He became restless and resentful. His resentment filled him with deep shame that threatened to swallow him whole. And that is how, without realising it, my father started running: away from Kariba Town with its whitewashed villas with earth-red terracotta tiles, away from Kariba Dam with his father entombed in its wall, away from his lost shot at being a national hero like his father, away from his mother in her forever widow's black. He ran towards the university, towards my mother, towards the van, towards being a father, towards anything that would not return him to Kariba Town, towards anything he could explain to his mother as a viable reason for his non-return.

My mother, for her part, was born in the White Section of Ingutsheni Hospital, a few months after my father was born. Had my father not been a premature baby, they might even have been born on the same day. Before being removed from her deemed-of-unsound-mind-and-therefore-not-fit-to-parent mother and taken to the orphanage, my mother was not afforded the chance to suckle on her mother's breasts, or the chance to be held by her mother, or the chance to open her eyes for the first time and look upon the curious creature that had created her.

At the orphanage my mother suckled on the breasts of a native wet nurse, was held and consoled by that wet nurse, opened her eyes for the first time and looked upon that wet nurse. When the Lady Doctor came to adopt her nine years later, she was already too late. My mother was already running: away from the White Section of Ingutsheni Hospital, away from the curious creature that had created her, away from the native wet nurse who had beheld her. In time, she would also run away from the Lady Doctor as she ran towards the university, towards my father, towards the van, towards being a mother, towards anything that would prove that *she* did not belong in the White Section of Ingutsheni Hospital.

I was born with the sparkling blue of my paternal grandmother's eyes and the genuine blonde of her hair and the saccharine sweetness of her temper. There is a photograph of me that proves this – in the picture, I am looking at the camera and gurgling with laughter. My father happily named me after his mother. Life was good. But, when I was about three years old, I began to change; and by the time I was five years old, I was completely not what my parents had expected. For the first time in their adult lives, they stopped running. Confused, they looked into each other's genealogies for something or someone to blame.

My father believed the White Section of Ingutsheni Hospital evinced a weakness of mind. He began to suspect that weakness of mind may have led to weakness of body and soul as well. How else could my mother explain the change I had undergone? He demanded to know who my real father was. He suspected every man – the till operator whose hand had allegedly lingered too long while giving her back her change; the bus conductor who had kept looking in her direction; the baker who always kept the warmest loaf of bread set aside for her – of having fathered me. His conjectures landed on my mother's body, and she did absolutely nothing to shield herself from them. A man who had always loved beauty, my father never hit my mother in the face. He hit her on places she could cover up with clothing, which allowed her to walk out the door with her head held high: with the very pride that made the till operator careful with her change, the bus conductor repeatedly look at her, the baker wish only the warmest things for her.

My mother, for her part, said she was not surprised that my father thought this way. Was he not the one who had told her of the kindness the postman, the milkman and the policeman had shown his mother after she started wearing widow's black? But my mother knew more than he had told her, especially about the milkman's kindness, which was rumoured to have preceded the widow's black. And was it not also whispered that his mother had left Italy already expecting him, hence the quick journey to the altar?

My father laughed bitterly at this, and said he could not expect any better from someone who had suckled on the teat of a native wet nurse.

The close living – the rough and tumble of it – would probably have made them begin to examine and find fault with each other eventually, but I was the reason they started questioning everything: their pace, their tempo as they ran making the distance between them grow, the gap forever widening between them. There was no escaping it. The change in me had trapped them in a vicious cycle, and I was trapped along with them until the Lady Doctor came to take me away.

My mother could be suspected of many things, it seemed, as long as being a bad mother was not one of them. She left the van and came to live with the Lady Doctor and me. Soon she was working for the National Free Library, falling in love with ordering and cataloguing things, waiting for her life to take another turn, and thus, without knowing it, waiting for John B. Good VIII to enter it.

When my mother told my father about John B. Good VIII, he was filled with such an impotent rage that instead of clenching his fist, he simply got in his van and began a journey that would take him as far away from us as possible. My father, although still living and travelling in the van, was no longer running. Running requires an aim, a destination, a finish line. My father was aimless, lost.

He communicated with me only once after he left. He wrote a letter telling me that he was taking back the name he had given me because it was his mother's, and I did not deserve it. He told me to tell my mother to ask my real father to name me. In this way, my father took from me more than he ever gave.

I can only make sense of my father in retrospect. He is a man who proudly gave me his mother's name; and, when I turned out not to be what he expected, he took that name from me and then travelled with it to places far, wide and unknown – places to which he knew I would never follow him to reclaim what I then felt was rightfully mine.

I would never have been able to articulate so well what lay at the heart of my parents' failed relationship had I not become aware that the vague searching and yearning feeling I had felt since the Lady Doctor's passing was my own desire to run ... to escape. I never felt like my parents' child until I grasped what lay at the heart of me.

I remember once watching a short film about an empty plastic bag blowing this way and that, going wherever the wind chose to take it. I remember crying, sobbing actually, making everyone in the darkened theatre uncomfortable. Then I had no idea why I was crying, but now I realise it was the emptiness of the journey – the strong desire to be elsewhere when elsewhere is unknown – that broke my heart, because I understood and felt it so deeply and implicitly.

In my life I have tried to travel towards a familiar, if not desired, destination; to be like my mother and fall in love with ordering and cataloguing things; but, really, I have always been like my father: aimless and lost. I understand now that running with no direction – when I met John B. Good IX, when I got the job at the Good Museum, when I moved into the attic of the Good House, when I birthed the Three Good Children – has propelled my life into stagnation.

I would like to say I have arrived at this self-awareness on my own, but I have not. I have had help from a very unlikely source.

One day I am woken by the scratching sound. Something sharp repeatedly scrapes against the surface of something dry. I wait for the writing to appear on the wall; it does not. In the morning light,

I find I am not alone. The venerable woman with sagacious eyes I saw all those years ago at the protest outside the Good Museum: she is in the attic with me. She does not immediately notice that I am awake as she runs her fingers along the wallpaper.

'No wonder it has been difficult for you to receive inspiration,' she says without turning to look at me. Perhaps she has been aware all this time that I am awake. She speaks a language I should not understand, and yet I find that I do.

I clear my throat as though readying it to say something, but I do not say anything.

'Some things have come through, have they not?' she asks. 'You have seen the words.'

It takes me a moment, but I nod. The venerable woman with sagacious eyes smiles.

She walks towards me, sits on the bed, takes my hands in hers, and without further ceremony we are sharing a vision. First, we see six men – three white, two black and one mixed-race – in the act of killing an elephant. I recognise all the men from the 'Killing of an Elephant' tapestry. The elephant dies only after it kills one of the black men. Next, we see the five survivors entering a cave and discovering a dead white man. One of the men – the mixed-race one – dies in the cave.

After this, we see the four survivors involved in a battle with many black warriors. One of the white men, the one with the golden hair, fells a black warrior's head with an axe. The beheaded man must have been the king because the surviving black man takes his place, and is immediately coroneted. And then we see the three white men enter a cave. The venerable woman with sagacious eyes is with them, as is a young woman whose eyes are heavy with never-ending sorrow and love. The venerable woman with sagacious eyes points her finger towards something that glimmers in the distance.

The three white men walk and then crouch and then creep and then crawl as they move into the darker recesses of the cave. They look like half-broken things as they scurry their way towards the glimmering light in the distance. The glimmer is made up of an abundance of glinting objects. Once they reach the glinting objects, one of the men starts filling his pockets with them. The next thing we see is the three white men escaping from the cave, leaving, dead behind them, both the venerable woman with sagacious eyes and the young woman with eyes of never-ending sorrow and love. The last thing we see in this particular vision is one of the white men sitting at a desk, pen and paper in hand, writing what follows:

> I am going to tell the strangest story that I know of. It may seem a queer thing to say that, especially considering that there is no woman in it — except Foulata. Stop, though! there is Gagaoola, if she was a woman and not a fiend. But she was a hundred at least, and therefore not marriageable, so I don't count her. At any rate, I can safely say that there is not a petticoat in the whole history.

The venerable woman with sagacious eyes lets go of my hands and the vision ends.

I know this story! *King Solomon's Mines*. My mother used to read it to me most nights after the Lady Doctor passed away, and before we came to the New Country. There must have been some sign – something I did without being fully aware – that made her think that I enjoyed the book.

'He could not even be consistent about the name. Sometimes it was Gagaoola, most times it was Gagool,' the venerable woman with sagacious eyes chuckles without mirth. 'I am the woman written as Gagool,' she says.

I want to tell her that she cannot be Gagool. I know Gagool.

The Gagool I know is a 'wizened, monkey-like figure' who creeps around 'on all fours', is 'shrunken' and has a 'most extraordinary and weird countenance' that is 'made up of a collection of deep, yellow wrinkles' and has a 'slit' for a mouth. I know these details by heart because whenever my mother went over them, a shiver would run through me. In my mind, Gagool was the most frightful thing the world had ever seen. Now that I think about it, that is probably why my mother read the story to me over and over. She liked seeing me frightened.

'Not my real name, of course,' the venerable woman with sagacious eyes continues. 'Just something that sounded ghoulish enough, I suppose. Gagool. Gagaoola. Gaga: the unintelligible sound babies make, so there was the nonsense of it as well. My real name, the one my mother gave me, need not bother you; at this time it is mine to know.' Her sagacious eyes inspect me and I feel dissected, seen through. I know she knows the image I have of Gagool.

She takes both my hands in hers, and I see myself sitting at a table in an unbelievably opulent room, pen in hand, lots of paper all around me as I write the words:

> In the beginning, there was erasure.
> He came. He saw. He wrote.
> And she became Gagool.

I try to see more of what I have written, but I can only make out one word: Daisy. I want to stay in this vision for ever and ever. I look out of the window of the opulent room and see staggered white rocks on top of each other – a familiar sight. I know this place. I have been here before. Holdengarde Castle.

'You need to go back to where it began,' the venerable woman with sagacious eyes says.

I see the woman in white walk towards me with mud on her hem and blood on her hands. I was not afraid of her as a little girl, I am not afraid of her now.

'You need to listen to what she has to tell you,' the venerable woman with sagacious eyes says. 'You need to listen to all three of them.'

I see the black and beautiful woman smoking a long and curved pipe and laughing a throaty laugh materialise and walk beside the woman in white. The woman with an English-rose-coloured, high-collared dress with matching parasol and gloves also appears next to them.

'They have been waiting a long time for you,' the venerable woman with sagacious eyes says.

She presses my hands firmly and suddenly I am in the Good Museum, standing right in front of the giant pair of silver wings I love so much. I put them on and fly away, fly across an azure sky, fly through gentle white clouds, and descend only when I see the staggered white rocks.

The venerable woman with sagacious eyes looks at me for a long time. 'You know what to do?' she asks.

'Yes,' I say. My voice sounds artificially strong in my ears because I am afraid she will not believe me.

She does believe me, however, for she smiles … and then is gone.

Another person, a normal person, would be relieved and shrug it all off as some trick of the imagination. But I am not a normal person. I have seen many visions in my life. I know what to believe.

I look around the attic, my home for the past eight years. I now see the ivory bars of the Good Family's yellow wallpaper for what they really are. A gilded cage is still a cage.

There is this reaching part in all of us, and all it wants is to survive.

The time has come for me to find my way out: to run towards a destination, to escape.

The protests outside the Good Museum have been swelling steadily ever since the protestors came to realise that the Good Foundation had not taken any of the solutions to their grievances under advisement. At first, mainly due to the fact that the protestors remained mostly peaceful, the Good Foundation remained largely unperturbed. The Foundation had been here many times before, and knew that protests always died down after talk of concessions.

But then the seemingly peaceful protestors had turned unpeaceful one day when they stormed the museum en masse: some of them attempted to break the glass that protected Foulata's face at the museum's threshold, while others attempted to burn the 'Killing of an Elephant' tapestry; still others attempted to topple the giant elephant tusks that stood sentry over the entrance of the Curtis Collection. The ensuing altercation with the university police unfortunately turned violent. The Board of Trustees had a lot to say, and the Good Foundation had no option but to listen and finally do something.

To appease the protestors, the Good Foundation had, at first, removed the giant elephant tusks that stood sentry over the entrance of the Curtis Collection, with its thousands of trophied animals and reptiles and other preserved flora and fauna. When the protestors said their demands had still not been met, the Good Foundation decided to temporarily close the Curtis Collection altogether. It fully intended to reverse these concessions because it knew that people tend to forget and then remember and then forget, again and again. The cycle always repeats itself.

The only other time the Good Foundation had felt genuinely threatened was in 1968, when students had been adamant about bringing about real change. First, they had demanded that the name of the Foulata Scholarship be changed to the Fulatha Scholarship, in keeping with the Bantu origins of the name. Next, they had demanded that at least half of the faculty in the newly created African Studies department be African. Then they had demanded that anyone doing African Studies had to be proficient in at least one language from the region they were studying. When their requests were not heeded, the students performed a sit-in at the Good Foundation. When they were forcibly removed, they broke all the windows on the ground floor and threatened to burn the building to the ground. The Good Foundation had been so shaken by the fervour and the fury of the students that it had decided to have its Golden Jubilee in 1970 take place thousands of miles away at Holdengarde Castle in the City of Kings.

Having worked with the museum and its archives, I have long known what happened in 1970. Now, after the visit from the sagacious woman with venerable eyes, I see how I can use my knowledge to my advantage. I plan my next moves carefully.

The Good Family is not a united front. They do not mind the fact that I want to get back to work. They do not mind that I want to work at the Good Foundation – they agree that the job at the museum was too physically demanding for me, and they think keeping my mind occupied but not too strained might be a good thing for me. However, they do worry that what I am planning to do may prove too taxing for me. Johanna and A.J. trust I am well enough to do what I am proposing. Dr Good and Mrs Good are not sure I am quite ready for the mammoth task I will have ahead of me. The keloid scars on my left wrist and the *history* I am sure Johanna has told them about: these give them pause. My mother, who must count as a member of the Good Family by now, is dead set against it. The Three Good Children are deemed too young to have an opinion.

But I have been on the losing side often enough to know exactly how this game is played. 'I think it is what John would have wanted,' I say. And for good measure, I add: 'He always wanted the Foundation to be more ... present on the continent.' What else can the family do except agree to that?

And so I prepare my escape.

Once the Good Family members have got used to the idea, they begin to speak of it as though it is their own. Of course Holdengarde Castle would be the perfect place for the Foundation's centennial celebrations. There is already the precedent of the 1970 Golden Jubilee. Holding the celebrations at the castle would help establish a tradition. The Good Family loves the very idea of traditions. And who else is better suited, when you really think about it, to continue the Good Family's traditions than the mother of John B. Good IX's Three Good Children?

By the time I suggest that, in order to showcase how good and deep the Good Foundation's relationship with Africa is, I want to ship a few things from the Good Museum to Holdengarde Castle – among them the giant pair of silver wings – there is no objection. Except from one person.

My mother comes to the attic for a private conversation.

'I cannot comprehend how you could do such a thing,' she says.

'Do what?'

'Leave the Good children without a mother.'

I do not say to her what I would really like to say to her, which is that the Three Good Children – two boys named after famous men and a girl named after me – have never been my children. They occupied my womb, but they have always belonged to the Good Family. 'They have you,' I say, wanting more than anything to keep the peace.

'Yes, they do,' she says. She leaves the room, but stops in the doorway. 'And so do you,' she adds, before closing the door behind her.

Now why should her words make my blood run cold?

I write to Holdengarde Castle, and a woman named Daisy
responds almost immediately. She addresses me as 'Dear
Madam' and tells me the castle will be happy and honoured to
host the Good Foundation's centennial celebrations. Her style of
writing is so formal and business-like that I imagine her wearing a
very conservative white blouse, a navy-blue or black pencil skirt,
a matching blazer (when the occasion requires it), skin-coloured
stockings and sensible black shoes with a one-inch heel. I imagine
her as the sort of person who goes to the bathroom at least twice a
day to right their appearance in the mirror.

Holdengarde Castle, evidently no longer the ruin I remember
from that school trip many years ago, is now the prime wedding
venue for the affluent denizens of the City of Kings. Daisy informs
me that the castle is already fully booked for most of the year.
Fully booked, she stresses even as she promises that she will see
what she can do. Maybe something can be arranged for July,
during the middle of the week. July, the coldest month. For a brief
moment, I suspect this might be a veiled request for a bribe. That
is what the Good Family laments most about Africa: its descent
into corruption. But then I remember Daisy's sensible shoes, and
feel guilty for even suspecting her motives.

When next we correspond, Daisy has managed to arrange
things so that the Foundation can hold its week-long celebrations
in the middle of October. October, the hottest month. But also
the month the jacarandas are in bloom, Daisy reminds me. She
understands that the Foundation will probably want to source its
own caterer for the event, but she would like the Foundation to

know that the castle is more than capable of providing fine dining for the occasion.

By this point in our correspondence, I do not want to disappoint Daisy and her sensible shoes in any way, and so I agree to the castle handling all elements of the centennial celebrations.

Daisy thanks 'Dear Madam' and the Good Foundation for our business.

It is only then, at what should be the end of our correspondence, that I inform Daisy that I will be arriving at the beginning of the year, in February, to oversee the planning.

Daisy wishes I had apprised her of this sooner. She is so professional that she does not make this seem like a reprimand. While Holdengarde Castle does boast of containing a five-star boutique hotel, the hotel is, unfortunately, currently closed for renovations. But she will see what she can do. A few days later she writes to me and informs me that there is a fully furnished room, long unoccupied, yet comfortable, in the castle. She feels, however, that I might object to the room because it is a solar – a Great Chamber – quite secluded and not conveniently placed for guests who want to have an easy time of going in and out of the castle.

I do not object to either the location of the room or the ease it curtails.

If she is surprised, Daisy does not express it. Her sensible shoes will not let her.

I imagine her as the kind of person who will open the room for a guest, look over it briefly to make sure everything is in its proper place, step aside to let the guest in before sweeping her arm with practised pride through the air and saying, 'Here you are, Madam. I hope you enjoy your stay with us,' then leaving the room unobtrusively and closing the door behind her. I imagine her rehearsing what to say in front of the mirror in the bathroom and opting for the precise 'I hope you enjoy your stay with us' over the clunky 'I hope you will feel this is your home away from home.' I imagine her not once focusing on the ugly scars on my wrist: Daisy, used to being the soul of discretion, will be too professional for that.

In all my imaginings of Daisy, I do not imagine that she can hurt me in any way, that she is capable of holding me captive, that she will be the reason I never leave Holdengarde Castle. I do not know, as I respond to her 'Dear Madams' and eagerly book my flight for 1 February 2020, that I best beware.

I've got out at last.

I'm rushing through a busy airport when who should I come across but Isabella Van Wagenen. She has so many people following her, hanging onto her every word, that I think she won't see me. But just as I'm about to turn the corner, her voice booms: 'Kindred!' I turn around to see her smiling at me, her eyes crinkling with kindness. 'I knew you too were on a mission,' she says.

'Misremembered, misbegotten and forgotten women,' I say.

'Misremembered, misbegotten and forgotten women,' she echoes, her voice filling the space between us before she is swallowed up by her followers again.

I feel anointed.

I arrive in the City of Kings after the rains. It is afternoon, the glorious sun is shining, and there is a full rainbow in the sky. It is easy to experience my homecoming as a beautiful beginning – until I realise that Daisy has not come to meet me. I don't know why I should feel so disappointed that those sensible shoes aren't making their way towards me. My shift in mood doesn't last long because just then a liveried chauffeur wearing a spectacular red-and-black uniform approaches me, tips his elegant hat, and offers his name: 'Evans.'

The chauffeur, sensing my disappointment, adjusts his brilliant smile. It breaks my heart to see it, and so I beam my brightest smile at him. 'I left the City of Kings when I was a child. This is my first time back,' I say, hoping this explains my shifts in mood. 'It's so good to be here.'

'Home,' he corrects.

'Yes. It's so good to be home.'

He nods his understanding and his old eyes twinkle as he relaxes back into his smile. He takes my luggage and leads me out of the airport. The scent of hot earth that has just been rained on – the comingling of decaying things and things coming to life – fills the air. Petrichor. I breathe in deep. Some things you forget to miss when you are in the New Country. I breathe in deep again. Evans chuckles as he places my bags in the boot of a red-and-black 1934 Citroën Traction Avant with the words 'Holdengarde Castle' stencilled in golden letters on both sides. Such a gorgeous car. The Lady Doctor was something of a car enthusiast, and together we used to collect model cars and test each other on makes and models. Some things you don't forget to miss when you are in the New Country.

'Home is always home,' Evans says as he helps me into the back seat of the car. 'Home is always home,' he repeats as he enters the driver's side of the car. The car is in tip-top shape, and in no time we are driving away from the airport, down a road bordered on both sides by not-in-bloom jacarandas. It must be a delight to drive down this road in October.

Not long into our drive, we come across a police-manned roadblock. A policeman, wearing a neon reflective vest, indicates that Evans needs to stop the car. The policeman claims to be checking that the registration disc on the car's windscreen is up to date, but he seems more interested in me.

'I see Holdengarde Castle has managed to fool someone into being a guest,' the policeman says, only half in jest.

'She's with the Good Foundation,' Evans says, looking straight at the road ahead.

'The Good Foundation?' The policeman can't help but sound impressed. He touches his cap and addresses me directly. 'I hope you enjoy your stay in our wonderful City of Kings,' he says, smiling like a mischievous schoolboy.

'I'm sure I will,' I say, with a smile of my own.

The policeman, instead of indicating to his fellow officers to lift the boom and allow the car to pass, rushes to do this himself.

In the car, Evans laughs as he drives through the roadblock. 'He wanted you to quake in your boots. Now he is eager to please you.'

I hear the policeman tell his fellow officers with awe and pride: 'She's with the Good Foundation.'

All the officers manning the roadblock smile and wave. I feel like royalty as I smile and wave back.

'Thirty minutes ago when I drove through the roadblock, they all but ignored me. Now look at them,' Evans laughs, looking at the police officers through the rear-view mirror. 'Welcome to the City of Kings.'

The City of Kings is not as I remember it. As we drive through the city on what used to be Grey Street, a street that is also bordered by not-in-bloom jacarandas, I notice that the glory of the city seems to have leached out, and the beauty it once had has been bleached by the sun. Everything – the roads, the walls, the houses, the business buildings, the people – seems weather-beaten. Evans looks at it all fondly as he manoeuvres the car around severely potholed streets. In some places, tar seems to have become a distant memory.

Paradoxically, the city teems with busy life bustling every-where you look. The road is a territory everyone and everything wants a part of: space is a commodity. Women selling fruits and vegetables on the pavements spread their produce onto the road as well – their chatter and their haggling never cease; men pushing Scania pushcarts, convey their wares, their eyes never looking behind, but always forward, ahead, already seeing their destination; young men with darting eyes stand at junctions and street corners making almost-imperceptible hand gestures, selling drugs I think at first, but Evans informs me they are buying and selling foreign currency; dumps of donated clothing are heaped for sale and obscure shop windows and their displays of sunburnt mannequins, with dulled eyes and old-fashioned hairstyles, posed at impossible angles; queues upon queues form serpentine lines outside Post Office Savings Banks where people don't save money, but collect it from relatives in the diaspora who send it via Western Union, MoneyGram and Mukuru – money, everyone needs money here, Evans tells me; drivers of every make of car under the sun drive impatiently, often ignoring the not-always-working robots, going over islands and pavements if need be. You take your life into your own hands in a city full of deadly splendour like this.

'Home is always home,' Evans says as he looks at the mayhem around him. He obviously loves the city as it is.

I am not sure what I feel.

My head begins to throb at my left temple, the first sign of an impending migraine. My palms itch. Somewhere on one of the potholed streets, there is a castle, long out of time and place, and I have arranged for the Good Foundation to hold its centennial celebrations there.

What have I done?

What am I doing?

The policeman had said that Holdengarde Castle had fooled me into coming here. But it wasn't the castle that had fooled me: it was Daisy and her 'Dear Madam'.

Storm clouds gather. Out of the blue, the sky is an angry grey. Lightning rips the air. Thunder roars. The streets become even more chaotic as people try to find cover before the downpour arrives; most are not fortunate.

The car turns onto a road that temporarily brings hope. The road takes us past the National Free Library, the place where my mother's running came to a stop and the love of ordering and cataloguing took hold of her. This road, evenly paved, is also bordered by not-in-bloom jacarandas, and secreted behind the verdant trees and mighty walls are splendid suburban homes. I know this place well. It was the first suburb built when the City of Kings was established and it is simply called Suburbs. This is where I used to live with the Lady Doctor. The jacarandas, when in blue-purple bloom, create comforting canopies over the avenues, and you feel as though you could walk under the dappled light of their generous shade forever. I can't wait for October, the month that Daisy wanted me to arrive.

The reprieve is short-lived. Soon, too soon, the car turns onto a street that is pockmarked by potholes. Wild grass grows taller than any man on either side of the road. The street sign has been rusted to near illegibility – I can barely make out the words 'Percy Avenue'. Even though there is a clear sign that has 'Holdengarde Castle' written in red, with an arrow pointing the way forward, it is easy to be apprehensive as to where and to what the road leads. We drive parallel to a long grey wall that does its best to look and remain august. There are so many walls in this city.

'Here we are,' Evans says. Two guards, dressed in the uniform of the foot guards at Buckingham Palace – scarlet tunic with dark-blue collar and gold buttons, white leather buff belt, and dark-blue trousers – stand on either side of the gate that forms the entrance to Holdengarde Castle. Even in a city known for its heat, they wear the traditional bearskin caps. As the two guards salute before swinging the gate open, I make brief eye contact with one of them, and it is clear that he is gauging whether I am the sort of person who deserves to enter such an esteemed place. He nods and smiles at me; I obviously pass muster.

The car drives on a cobbled driveway ... past a red telephone box ... past a family of monkeys that look at us with guarded interest ... past a confusion of guineafowl that the car has to let cross before proceeding on its journey. I can no longer be certain of where I am in time and space. I can no longer distinguish clearly between what is real and what is imagined. I am not sure what to believe.

At the top of the drive, lined up in two curved rows that lead to the foot of concrete stairs, I see the uniformed staff of the castle. Twenty people at least, all awaiting my arrival. There is a red carpet draped over the cobbled stones, over the concrete stairs and the entrance to the castle itself. This is all too much, too grand for a woman who doesn't have a name.

I feel overwhelmed and unprepared. For a mad moment, I wish I was back in the attic with its yellow wallpaper and seductive call of the ocean waves. I am so lightheaded that I lean heavily on poor Evans as he aids me out of the car. I must make a very sorry sight. Not at all what they expected. They are all probably wondering how the Good Foundation could have sent someone like me to represent it.

And then I see them. Standing at the top of the stairs, looking at me, before making their way down the red carpet. They wear a black newsboy cap, a white shirt with the sleeves rolled up, black suspenders, tweed derby breeks, and laced-up black boots with impractical four-inch heels. Those boots! The ensemble would look incongruous, perhaps even ridiculous, on any other person in the world, but it is just right on this person. What time and place do they belong to … in? Are they a vision? Does it matter? Probably not, this person … this vision … would look exquisite in any time, in any place.

'Dear Madam,' they say, not extending their hand for a handshake. 'Welcome to Holdengarde Castle. We've been expecting you.' They smile, and I can't help but feel that there is a warmth meant just for me in that smile.

Daisy … *my* Daisy. Definitely not as I imagined.

'She, he or they?' I ask, offering my hand for Daisy to shake. Another time, another place, Daisy would have bowed and kissed my hand, of this I am certain. We touch for the first time as we shake hands. The hand is soft, but its grip is firm.

If the question offends, Daisy doesn't let on. I was at least correct about that – very professional.

'She,' Daisy says as she lets go of my hand. 'But she my way.'

Just then I see someone … something … walking down the red carpet behind Daisy. It is the woman in white. I look at the mud on her hem and the blood on her hands. To the left of me, I hear a tobacco-cured throaty laugh; to the right of me, I see the twirl of an English-rose-coloured parasol.

Not now. Not here ... not in this moment ... not in front of Daisy. Please. Not in front of Daisy and her impractical boots.

The scent of tobacco fills the air.

It is happening.

I cannot stop it.

The woman in white is now standing next to Daisy. She opens her mouth to speak, but I can't hear what she says because just then comes a flash of lightning followed by a clap of thunder. I faint into Daisy's arms.

It's only when she is holding me, making sure I don't fall all the way to the ground, that I realise that all I wanted was to make a good first impression – and that I have not.

I'm aware of the gentle care I receive from the hands that are soft as they cool my brow, and strong as they grip me and hold me up while my clothes and bed linen are being changed. I'm aware of the steadiness of the voice that coaxes me to take just a sip of some ginger tea, of some flavourful broth, of some creamy porridge. The sound of impractical boots walking over floorboards begins to sound like comfort to me.

But I cannot seem to stay in this world. I keep journeying to a very hot place. I see a headstone, grey, simple, with black letters etched into its surface. I see my mother and the Three Good Children – two boys named after famous men and a girl named after me – standing by the headstone. I see Johanna and A.J. clinging to each other for solace. I see Dr Good and Mrs Good looking at the headstone in dismay – this is not what John would have wanted.

I feel like I'm trapped under the earth, crouching. Everything is so hot here, it is difficult to breathe. Dr Good and Mrs Good walk away. Johanna and A.J. walk away, still clinging to each other. I need someone to help me, to get me out of here. 'Look at the end you've created for yourself,' my mother says. 'You could have been good ... normal. But here you are.' My mother and the Three Good Children walk away. No one will help me.

I read the black letters etched on the headstone: Beloved Mother. And all of a sudden I am fighting to make my way out of this hot place, out of my uncomfortable crouching position. I need to stand ... I need to rise up ... I need to breathe.

67

It isn't so much that I'm not beloved. I have always known that I'm not. It's that the girl I used to be is nowhere in that epitaph.

The girl who'd visited the ruins of Holdengarde Castle and seen the woman in white who walked with mud on her hem and blood on her hands: she isn't there. The girl who'd loved fruits that had a guaranteed sweetness – isn't there. The girl who'd giggled long into the night with the Lady Doctor – isn't there. The girl who'd woken up the following morning to find the Lady Doctor dead beside her and had been struck dumb with longing and pain for an entire year – isn't there. The girl who'd, instead of her own reflection, seen that of a woman with an English-rose-coloured, high-collared dress with matching parasol and gloves – isn't there. The girl who'd seen visions and believed in them enough to write about them – isn't there. The girl who'd suffered a broken wrist – a lesson meant for her to associate writing permanently with pain – isn't there. There is just a woman who lived in an attic, and none of the history of how she got there.

Why is everything so hot here? Why must I crouch? Why can't I get up? Why can't I breathe? I need to stand … I need to rise up … I need to breathe.

Out of the ether, they arrive and stand where the Good Family recently stood: the black and beautiful woman with her long and curved pipe; the woman in white with mud on her hem and blood on her hands; the woman wearing an English-rose-coloured, high-collared dress with matching parasol and gloves.

'My name is Elizabeth,' the woman in white says. 'That is Anne,' she says, indicating the parasol-carrying woman. 'And that,' she says with reverence in her voice, 'is Sethekeli.'

I reach up my hand, and Elizabeth, Anne and Sethekeli simultaneously crouch in order to pull me up.

At long last, I can stand. I can rise up. I can breathe.

'You need to follow me into my world now,' Elizabeth says.

And I do.

When I fully return to my world, Daisy is there.

She sits on the edge of the bed wearing a seersucker newsboy cap, a sky-blue shirt and khaki trousers. This closeness is a liberty she's taken. She studies my face to see if I object to it. I don't. She smells of laundry that has just come in from drying in the sun. Such a comforting scent.

'I haven't been well,' I say. I mean it as a question, but it comes out as a statement.

Daisy smiles at me. 'You had us worried there for a moment. But you're strong. You fought whatever it was, and now here you are better – much better,' she says.

'I have been here long,' I say. Another question that sounds like a statement.

'Three days ...' She evidently has something else to say, but hesitates. It is something that I won't like. 'The Good Foundation, your mother, Johanna Good and Mrs Good have been calling. They are worried about you and want some assurance that you are safe,' she says, and then hesitates again. 'You told us not to tell them you are unwell. You were very adamant about that. So we haven't told them.'

'Thank you,' I say.

Another hesitation. 'I am sure they will expect to hear from you soon,' Daisy says.

'They will hear from me soon,' I lie. 'I need paper,' I add, covering up the lie as best as I can.

Daisy frowns at this.

'Lots of paper and a pen,' I say. 'I would like to write ... I need to write.'

70

Daisy, always the professional, nods and asks no questions. 'I'll see what I can do,' she says as she gets up.

I feel bad about having lied to her, and so I say: 'I'm not a beloved mother.'

Whatever Daisy feels about this, her face doesn't show it. 'You're here and that's what matters,' she says, and then leaves the room.

I almost believe she understands.

I look around me, taking in my surroundings. The Great Chamber is luminous and luxurious. I'm in a four-poster bed that's draped with a red-and-gold damask canopy and flanked by two side tables. The room also has a table with four matching chairs whose cushions are covered in the red-and-gold damask fabric. There's wonderfully and intricately etched wood panelling on the north- and south-facing walls. All the wood furnishings are teak. A fireplace stands opposite an ornate brass mirror. The east-facing wall is made up of twelve stained-glass panels, depicting the journey of the Magi. Behind the bed, the entire wall is covered by a painting – a replica of Simone Martini and Lippo Memmi's 'The Annunciation and Two Saints' – whose surface is kissed by an incandescent golden sheen. I lie underneath the Madonna. I can see her right hand clutching her flowing indigo cloak as her left hand keeps her place in the book she's been reading. I can see Archangel Gabriel's olive branch, the swirl and twirl of his fluttering ivory robe. I don't look at their faces.

It's a room that anticipates royalty, and so I allow myself momentarily to feel like a queen.

There's a knock on the door. I ready myself for Daisy's entrance, but it's not Daisy who comes in. I try not to feel and show my disappointment. The man who enters wears the black-and-white uniform of service, and introduces himself as Stevens. He says he's happy I'm recovering, and tells me he's brought the requested

71

pen and paper. He places them on the teak table. I'm aware that he keeps his distance. I thank him, and he leaves.

Stevens returns shortly with a man he introduces as a doctor. The man wears a white coat, carries a black concertina bag, and has a stethoscope hanging around his neck. I'm not sure what else he could be but a doctor. He seems out of place in this room that's aspiring to be medieval. The doctor, checking my vitals, tells me he's happy to see me so improved; and in seeing his happiness, I pretend to be delighted.

I catch Stevens looking at the ugly keloid scar on my left wrist. When he notices me noticing, he asks if I'd like for him to call the Good Foundation or a member of the Good Family and tell them that all is well. When I shake my head, he looks at me with not a little suspicion. I look at the stained-glass windows until the doctor tells me that he'll be back soon to check on me.

I like the doctor, but I'm glad when he and Stevens leave the room. One can pretend at happiness only for so long.

Just as I begin to notice how hungry I am, Daisy comes in carrying, on a silver tray, the most delicious thing I have ever smelled. She places the tray on the side table closest to me and lifts off the silver dome to reveal a bowl of fragrant chicken broth. I can already taste the pieces of chicken, mushrooms and water chestnuts, but all that will have to wait because next to the bowl is a plate of neatly sliced mango wedges, arranged in a crescent.

Not minding my manners, I reach for a mango slice and stuff it into my mouth. Guaranteed sweetness!

'Peach mangoes,' I declare. 'They're my most favourite thing.' I stop myself from devouring another slice.

Daisy smiles and allows this to explain my behaviour. 'I'm happy to see Stevens brought you your paper and pen,' she says. 'The bathroom is through that door,' she adds, pointing to a knob on the painted wall. Please let us know if you need anything else.'

She makes her way out of the room. I watch her leave. I look at her boots with their four-inch heels. 'I imagined you so very differently,' I say.

She seems to weigh the question before she asks it. 'When did you imagine me?'

Her slight pause has given me enough time to retreat. I busy myself with the cutlery on the tray, pretending not to have heard the question and feeling all the while like the coward that I am.

'Thank you so much for the food,' I say. 'And please thank Stevens for the paper and the pen.'

'What are you planning to write about, if you don't mind my asking?'

'A woman named Elizabeth,' I say. I'm still not brave enough to look at Daisy, and so I put the spoon in the soup.

She leaves and closes the door quietly behind her.

The real question she wanted to ask, of course, was *why* I had imagined her – and for that I have no answer.

But even though I don't understand the why of it all, I'm glad she asked me what I'm writing about, and I'm glad I told her the truth.

This desire to reach for something is a gift I have received from Elizabeth.

PART II

now there is room to crouch
and to watch the crouching others

TONI MORRISON – *Beloved*

THE MISREMEMBERED WOMAN*

1939–1979

---

* Entered the archive as Patient 925N.

Elizabeth had caught the young Mrs Chalmers totally by surprise on her way to see Reverend Carmichael about flowers for the altar. Midway up his garden path, her waters broke, and almost immediately Elizabeth started forcing her way into the world, a month or so early. Now the young Mrs Chalmers had done the right thing and taken a few steps towards home, but Elizabeth proved too determined. Two hours later, on a patch of grass near the church steps, Reverend Carmichael was holding the wailing and naked Elizabeth in his hands while one of the village women offered a white cloth from the vestry in which to wrap her. The young Mrs Chalmers was mortified: Elizabeth had made the good Reverend see things he had no business seeing.

But as soon as she held the swaddled baby in her arms, Mrs Chalmers had been ready to forgive her daughter anything. Her Liza was perfect. A skin so light as to be almost white. Eyes so incredibly blue. Hair most definitely golden. Mrs Chalmers was so contented that even when her Liza proved to be a difficult baby – crying through the night, biting while feeding, constantly crawling towards the fire – Mrs Chalmers beamed at her and marvelled at the near whiteness of her skin, the incredible blueness of her eyes, and the curly goldenness of her hair.

Mrs Chalmers knew that her Liza's perfection was all due to her mother – Mrs Benedito da Costa – and Mr Chalmers' father – Father Chalmers – who had come all the way from Scotland to settle in this part of the world. Although she had never met him personally, she thanked Father Chalmers every day for making it possible for her to live the respectable life most people in her 'circumstances', as Mrs Brown had called them, were not able to live.

Father Chalmers – as everyone referred to him even before his son was born – had had a first name, but upon arrival he had not been allowed to use it. This was because when he had settled in Ezulwini, he had done so near the mission station, and the villagers had assumed that he too was a missionary. When he introduced himself as Mr Chalmers, they promptly christened him Father Chalmers. Although the mission station was now run by the London Missionary Society, it had been started and briefly run by the Catholic Mission, and since the initial inhabitants of the mission station had asked (and not always politely or kindly) that the villagers call them 'Father', the men who came to work in it thereafter were all called 'Father' by the villagers.

Reverend Carmichael spent an inordinate amount of time, time he should have spent proselytising, trying to remedy the villager's tendency to call him Father Carmichael. He did not blame the villagers for this; he blamed the Catholic missionaries for being anything but catholic in their approach to converting the heathen hordes.

Meanwhile 'Father' Chalmers remained Father Chalmers even after he found a stretch of good green land several miles away from the mission station and settled on it. Father Chalmers he remained even after he found a good and clean woman – a native of the area – to spend his days and nights with. Father Chalmers he remained, but in a different sense, when his good and clean native woman bore him a child and had the good sense to make it a son. Father Chalmers he remained in everyone's memory when, after seventeen years, he left his stretch of good green land, his good, clean woman, and his good-sensed son to return to his home in Scotland.

Before he left – and this was why everyone remembered him

with fondness – Father Chalmers had had the goodwill to leave his stretch of good green land to his son. And so it was through Father Chalmers' goodwill that Mrs Chalmers became irrevocably respectable.

A few years after Father Chalmers left the country, his son travelled to the city and there met a pretty sixteen-year-old girl with honey-coloured skin and green eyes. He soon convinced himself, and her, that he loved her. The girl's name was Mildred 'Millie' da Costa.

When she met young Mr Chalmers, Millie da Costa was completing her studies at Mrs Brown's School of Typing and Etiquette for Unmarried and Widowed Women in the City of Kings. Mrs Brown, a widow herself, had taught Millie a few things about life, and because of these lessons Millie knew that a woman needed to be respectable; that being an unmarried woman of a certain age was not respectable; that although men had many avenues they could take to lead them to respectability – namely work and property – these avenues were not particularly open to women; and that in order to be respectable, a woman had to marry a man – and preferably one with property. Such was the lot of women the world over, but even more so for those who lived in the colonies.

The women who received certificates of completion from Mrs Brown's School of Typing and Etiquette for Unmarried and Widowed Women in the City of Kings rarely became typists, as most clerical and secretarial jobs in the burgeoning colony were held by young men who were making their way in the world. Besides being a mother and a wife, there was only one other thing a white woman could be in the colonies, and it was definitely not respectable. Therefore, Mrs Brown's school, with its focus on etiquette courses and very little instruction in typing, was the place where the City of Kings' young women came to be finished. It was the place men knew they should pay attention to when they felt they were in need of a wife.

Fortunately for Millie, men had started paying her attention. Unfortunately for Millie, Mrs Brown had told her that given her particular 'circumstances', men were not to be trusted. White men, although propertied, were not looking to make women like her respectable; and black men were not respectable themselves (with or without property), so could never make any woman respectable. Of Coloured and Indian men, Mrs Brown had nothing to say.

Millie did not know that Mrs Brown – who, upon first meeting her, had raised an eyebrow at the colour of her skin, the texture of her hair, and the fact that she came from the Portuguese and Greek part of town – had very little hope that she would find a husband and be made respectable. And so she waited, rather impatiently, for the man, neither black nor white, who would one day make her respectable. It is little wonder then that when a man with honey-coloured skin and hazel eyes, a quick smile and a way of making her feel warm inside, told her that he *owned* a piece of land, Millie smiled back at him, did not hesitate in accepting his offer of marriage, and quickly became Mrs Chalmers: an irreversibly respectable woman. Mrs Brown could not find it in herself to hide her surprise and, dare I say, dismay when Millie told her of her prospects. Mrs Brown's only consolation was that Mr Chalmers was a Coloured man.

Although she had gained her respectability upon marriage, when Mrs Chalmers saw Mr Chalmers' mother and his land, she knew she would have to work at making her husband respectable too. Mrs Chalmers could do very little about Mr Chalmers' mother, with her unfortunate dark skin, but his land she could do plenty for. The ten-acre stretch of land immediately surrounding the house, good and green though it was, was overgrown and looked like a wilderness. Mrs Chalmers demarcated a three-acre plot and immediately set about planting flowers, cultivating an orchard and growing vegetables.

This should not give the impression that Mrs Chalmers was disappointed with the inheritance Father Chalmers had left; as much as there were things to change, there was also plenty to love. The cottage was indeed small, but big enough to fill anyone who owned it with pride. It had a nice, long, ox-blood red verandah wrapped around it, and upon seeing it, Mrs Chalmers promised herself she would dedicate each morning to polishing it until it shone. There were six comfortably sized rooms, two bedrooms (one occupied by Mr Chalmers and the other by his unfortunate mother), a kitchen with a magnificent Welcome Dover stove, a bathroom with (would you believe it?) a porcelain tub, a dining room with a round teak table and six chairs at its centre, and a room the type of which she had never seen before: a library, made grand by its many leatherbound books and the surprisingly reassuring scent created by the comingling of yellowing paper, tobacco and dust.

The library was Mr Chalmers' domain, and Mrs Chalmers soon appreciated that just as Mr Chalmers had made her permanently respectable by marrying her, his father had made him permanently respectable by leaving him not only the land, but his library as well. The library was why Mr Chalmers did not find his mother unfortunate or his land wild – his library gave him an education and his education made him a gentleman and his being a gentleman made him forever respectable, and that was all there was to it.

Yes, Mrs Chalmers found plenty to love. She loved that she lived a short cart-drive away from Wilson's General Dealer, where she could procure anything that the land did not produce. She loved that the only other farm for miles around was inhabited by a relaxed old lady, Mrs Mendelsohn, who was a fountain of information about the savannah and what could be grown successfully in it. She loved that the village was both not so close to her farm as to create unnecessary camaraderie with the villagers, and also not so far as to disallow them from being of use to her when she needed them.

Best of all, she loved that every morning, without fail, Mr Chalmers would help his unfortunate mother into the carriage and, regardless of the weather, wrap her in a warm coat and drive her to Mrs Mendelsohn's farm, from where he would retrieve her every evening, without fail. This – taking his mother to and from Mrs Mendelsohn's – was the only thing he used the carriage for; for everything else there was the cart. Mrs Chalmers might have objected to this had she not found great joy in the freedom of not having Mr Chalmers' unfortunate mother in her house all day.

To show how grateful she was to Mrs Mendelsohn, Mrs Chalmers made her jams, baked her cakes and brought her the first fruits of her orchard. Mrs Mendelsohn, who had a very sweet tooth, was very grateful for these gifts. As far as Mrs Chalmers' could tell, Mr Chalmers' unfortunate mother was happy enough to spend all day sitting with Mrs Mendelsohn, crocheting, knitting or sewing, eating sweets, concocting sticky recipes, and speaking in a hybrid language only the two of them understood. Because it never occurred to Mrs Chalmers that Mrs Mendelsohn and Mr Chalmers' unfortunate mother were talking about her, she was very happy with this arrangement.

With Mr Chalmers being a gentleman in his library all day, with Mr Chalmers' unfortunate mother away at Mrs Mendelsohn's for most of the day, and with the boys from the village there to help her whenever she needed them, Mrs Chalmers was able to turn the stretch of good green land that Father Chalmers had left his son into more than just an indifferently tilled farm, and the small cottage into a house that found its way into becoming a home. Mrs Chalmers was sure anyone who walked or drove past their homestead would think to themselves: 'Good, respectable people live here.' And they would not be wrong.

And then one day, a Reverend Carmichael came to visit. He asked Mrs Chalmers if she knew Jesus Christ. She told him she did. He asked why, if she knew Jesus Christ, she did not come to church. She told him she had been kept very busy making sure the homestead looked presentable. Within this short exchange, which was carried out while they daintily sipped tea from the finest Wedgwood china, the good Reverend had come to understand what really drove Mrs Chalmers. He said, with great delicacy, 'I have no doubt that you are a good Christian woman, Mrs Chalmers. But how will people know that if you don't come to church? How will they see you for the respectable woman that you are?'

Although it was already clear to the both of them what her next course of action would be, Mrs Chalmers bit into a long-neglected Highlander biscuit patiently perched on her saucer, elegantly chewed it with the etiquette Mrs Brown had painstakingly instilled, swallowed imperceptibly, and then agreed to attend her first service at the mission church the very next Sunday.

Mrs Chalmers found that there were a lot of things she loved about the mission church. She loved the way the villagers looked at her and whispered among themselves as she made her way to the front of the church. She loved the singing, especially since she did not have to strain her voice, as others did, to sing the highest notes. She loved it that the church, with its austere bareness, obviously needed her touch. By the end of the service, she had loved enough things to know she would return. Church was a nice break from making and mending things, baking heart-warming goods, and successfully sowing seeds. She liked it that her husband did not attend church, but preferred to go fishing on Sundays. She liked it that Mr Chalmers' unfortunate mother spent her Sundays, like she spent every other day, at Mrs Mendelsohn's.

By the time Mrs Chalmers had her second child, Maria, she

had become a bona fide respectable Christian woman. Reverend Carmichael (who, because the mission school was still being built, had a difficult time finding and keeping converts) had been quick to put Mrs Chalmers to good use. Mrs Chalmers, for her part, had been quick to find her good Christian heart and use it to help the village women. The best way to help the women, Reverend Carmichael told her, was by holding a weekly meeting and using every opportunity to talk about the benefits of Christianity.

Since Mrs Chalmers was not too clear herself on the benefits of Christianity, the weekly meetings found the women discussing everything from the practicality of European forms of dress to whether or not their husbands should go to work at the nearby mine, as the District Commissioner suggested. And because Mrs Chalmers did not like idle hands, the meetings took place after the women had done various chores and duties around the church, and while they were relaxing by weaving storage and winnowing baskets.

Reverend Carmichael was sorry to hear that there was very little talk of the benefits of Christianity, but could not overlook how much he had gained from Mrs Chalmers' presence. She had transformed the church; it was now always clean, airy and often flower-filled. More people had begun to attend. Better still, the baskets the women made could be sold in the city to help build the much-needed missionary school.

Mrs Chalmers' comfortable position in their small community was cemented. The only thing that threatened it was Mrs Wilson, the general-dealer's wife. Mrs Wilson, thankfully, lived far enough away from Mrs Chalmers that her presence was rarely felt. The villagers suspected she was too afraid to venture away from her farm. Mrs Chalmers suspected she was too lazy to be of any use to anyone but herself. Afraid or lazy, Mrs Wilson did occasionally venture forth to see how her husband's general dealer store was doing, or to perform random acts of charity (that Mrs Chalmers, the true Christian, suspected Reverend Carmichael had had to flatter her into), or to simply stop by on her way to town.

Mrs Wilson did not do much; she did not need to. Unlike most in the community who bartered, Mrs Wilson had money. Unlike Mrs Chalmers and Mrs Mendelsohn who had carts and carriages, Mrs Wilson had an automobile. Unlike Mrs Chalmers' husband who had a stretch of good green land, Mrs Wilson's husband had stretches upon stretches of good green land (where Mrs Chalmers spoke in acres, Mrs Wilson spoke in hectares). But the thing that Mrs Chalmers found absolutely unforgivable about Mrs Wilson was her unequivocally white skin. Whenever Mrs Wilson ventured out, it was her white skin that made Mrs Chalmers' position in the community secondary. But since Mrs Wilson rarely left her farm, Mrs Chalmers was often happy with her lot in life.

One day, Mrs Mendelsohn's son, who lived in town and (as far as Mrs Chalmers knew) had a wife and two grown sons, came to drop off two inexplicably brown boys to keep his mother company. Even though her son had not seemed to care who had been keeping her company for over ten years, Mrs Mendelsohn took in the boys – Henry and George – without question. Mrs Chalmers saw no harm in this, and commended her neighbour for having 'a good Christian heart' even though Mrs Mendelsohn was not a Christian.

Mrs Chalmers welcomed the Mendelsohn boys forming an attachment to her daughters because she was beginning to fear that she was not going to give her husband what the village women told her he wanted most: a son. She thought Mr Chalmers would be happy, while he waited for his own son to appear, to see the Mendelsohn boys running in his yard. So she did not mind when the unfortunate one, the one with the darker skin, Henry, became inseparable from her Maria. Nor did she mind when

George, the one who was always digging around in her garden, found an enthusiastic fellow digger in her Liza.

With suddenly double the number of children to look after, Mrs Chalmers was able to convince Mr Chalmers that she needed help around the house. To this end, she employed Nonhlanhla, whom she immediately re-christened 'Pamela' because she claimed the name Nonhlanhla was too difficult for her tongue to pronounce. Even though everyone else was able to pronounce the name Nonhlanhla, Mr Chalmers had the children call the woman MaVuma, as Vuma was her last name, and he would not have any of his children call an adult by their first name.

Mrs Chalmers' 'Pamela' quickly understood the lay of the land and was soon taking care of so many things that Mrs Chalmers wondered what she had ever done without her. She particularly liked how every afternoon 'Pamela' strategically took the children to play on the edges of the orchard, far enough from the house to allow Mrs Chalmers an hour or so of much-needed rest, but close enough to let her rest in relative peace.

But soon, too soon, something happened that proved to Mrs Chalmers that she had been wrong, very wrong, to put so much faith and trust in 'Pamela'.

One afternoon, Mrs Chalmers drifted off to sleep in a house filled with the tantalising aroma of slow-cooking mutton curry. The children were playing somewhere in the orchard; she could hear their distant laughter. Just as she was about to fall asleep, she was overwhelmed by a sense of foreboding. The distant laughter did not contain within it the voices of 'Pamela' and her Liza. Mrs Chalmers sat up straight. Where was 'Pamela'? Where was her Liza? She instinctively knew that they were somewhere they were not supposed to be. She also knew they were up to no good. A mother knows these things.

She rushed out of the room and asked Mr Chalmers, who was

in his library, where 'Pamela' and her Liza had gone off to. Mr Chalmers mumbled something about the river.

She knew it! She had strictly forbidden the children from going to the river. There was never a reason to go to the river (they had a well on the homestead). She knew why the children wanted to go to the river, but felt they were too young to swim. The river was dangerous. The village women had stories about how the river occasionally took children away: sometimes drowning them in its undertow, sometimes allowing them to be dragged underwater by crocodiles, sometimes simply making them disappear under suspicious circumstances.

It took Mrs Chalmers some time to get to the river, and by the time she got there, it was already too late. There was a circle of people all dressed in white standing next to the riverbank. The people were clapping their hands in unison, creating a hypnotic rhythm. There was a man holding a staff in one hand and a book – it looked very much like Reverend Carmichael's bible – in the other hand. The man was pounding his staff on the ground, looking heavenward and chanting words in a language Mrs Chalmers chose not to comprehend. It was obvious from the dust rising that something was happening in the centre of the circle. Mrs Chalmers moved closer, recognising some of the people from the village, a few of whom attended church on Sundays. She saw 'Pamela', also dressed in white, clapping away with the rest of the circle.

It took Mrs Chalmers a moment to believe what her eyes were seeing. In the centre of the circle, there was her daughter – her Liza – dressed in white, stomping her feet in a traditional dance she had no business knowing. The song and the music reached a crescendo. The circle unexpectedly opened. Out came her Liza running towards the river, saying something about a giant pair of shimmering wings. The voice that came out of her did not belong to her, but to an old woman. The circle stopped clapping as everyone stood transfixed.

Everything stood still … the moment seemed suspended in time and space. And then Liza jumped into the river. Mrs Chalmers screamed and broke the spell. What happened next was chaos. Mrs Chalmers never knew how, but she managed to retrieve her daughter from the river – alive, if barely. Before she knew what she was doing, she was running back home with her Liza in her arms. 'Pamela' had no choice but to follow. She tried to explain to Mrs Chalmers that what she had witnessed was very much like what Reverend Carmichael did in church on Sundays. Mrs Chalmers, the true Christian, knew 'Pamela' was lying. As she made her way home, Mrs Chalmers resolved two things: no one was to ever breathe a word of what had happened to Mr Chalmers; and as soon as 'Pamela' broke something in the kitchen, forgot to wash something, or burnt something, Mrs Chalmers was going to fire her.

'Pamela' burnt the mutton curry that very evening and was promptly fired.

But the damage had already been done. The next day, while scrubbing her Liza's skin, Mrs Chalmers saw a small, dark, reddish-brown splotch on her chest above her heart. She scrubbed at the splotch, but could not remove it. The next day the splotch had slightly expanded and had become somewhat darker. Mrs Chalmers scrubbed at it, but nothing happened. The next day the splotch had grown slightly bigger and even darker – and again she scrubbed at it, and again nothing happened. This continued for a few months throughout which Mrs Chalmers was terrified that the splotch would grow to cover her Liza's entire near-white body, and that the reddish-brown colour would grow forever darker until it became, God forbid, black. Then one day the always expanding and ever-darkening splotch simply stopped expanding and darkening.

Mrs Chalmers became hopeful and waited. The splotch, which was now an even-toned brown colour, did not diminish in size or become lighter. Mrs Chalmers lost hope, but continued to wait. Nothing happened. In the end, all she could do was thank God that the splotch had appeared in a spot very few people would ever see – just above Liza's heart. Even so, there was no denying that her Liza had changed. She looked at her Liza's near-white skin and noticed that it was not a pure type of white, but a white that looked like dust had gently settled upon it. Liza's once-blonde hair was now dark brown and unruly, and her bluest eyes were now an emerald green whose vividness was somewhat unsettling. But Mrs Chalmers was still grateful that that splotch had not grown any wider or darker.

One day, when she had enough courage, Mrs Chalmers waited for the quiet of the night before slipping out of bed and going to stand in front of her full-length mirror. She sighed deeply, grateful that her husband was a heavy sleeper, and did what she rarely did in his company: she undressed fully. It took her a long moment, but she eventually looked at her reflection. There it was, as always taking her by surprise: the unfortunate dark skin that ran from her left knee all the way up to her left breast, covering it entirely. This too had once been a seemingly innocuous brown splotch above her heart before it decided to spread. She could never bring herself to touch it. She looked at it with the green eyes that she had inherited from her father, but with none of the love and compassion that his had always held. She chose to touch her collarbone instead, grateful, as always, that the unfortunate darkness had never made its way to her neck and onto her face. She supposed she had God to thank for small mercies.

As her hand touched her blessedly unblemished face, another hand travelled up her waist towards her unfortunate left breast. She would have screamed had the hand not been so gentle. It was the gentleness that let her know that the hand was not hers. She wanted to move away from the tender warmth of that touch, but instead, she let her green eyes travel up the mirror to meet her husband's hazel eyes. The love she found there took her by surprise, as always. She hated it and appreciated it in equal measure, the ability of the man she had married to know her secret and love her still. He did what she could not, and that made her love him more.

'Liza,' she said, another secret too heavy to bear.

'I know,' he said, as he kissed her temple.

'It will not be an easy life,' she said.

'I know,' he said. 'But she will have us for as long as we can hold her.'

It was Sunday after church, and as usual Elizabeth and George were playing 'Treasures' – a game that they had played ever since Elizabeth's father had come home with the head of a Victorian doll with pink cheeks, red lips, blonde hair and a winking blue eye. Well, actually, the doll had two blue eyes, but one of them was a lazy eye that always looked like it was winking at you. Her mother told her, almost daily, that she had once looked like the doll, but Elizabeth didn't quite believe her, even though her father, sister, grandmother, George, Henry, Mrs Mendelsohn, Reverend Carmichael and the villagers all attested to this fact. Elizabeth did not remember a time before the venerable woman with sagacious eyes stood on the water and spoke to her of white hills, rocks and caves, of a giant pair of shimmering wings that needed to be given to a white man, and of a boy called Ezekiel whom she would have to learn to either keep or let go.

Elizabeth dug and George excavated on the spot where Mr Chalmers had found the doll's head. George was methodical – working at a slower pace, careful not to disturb things too much, too soon – because he was certain he would find a skeleton (probably with an assegai stuck through the place where its heart had been). According to Mr Chalmers, years ago a famous battle had been fought on this spot, or hereabouts. Mr Chalmers had them call it a battle and not a rebellion, and so that is what George called it. He never told Elizabeth what he was excavating for, afraid she would end the game if she knew; for the game was hers. All the games they played were Elizabeth's.

Elizabeth was not as careful. Usually she grabbed a stick and broke the earth's crust with all her might until she was satisfied that she had dug deeply enough to find a treasure, at which point she threw away the stick, lay down on her stomach (yes, in her Sunday best – layers and layers of white that her mother had painstakingly stitched), sank her hands into the cold, damp earth, and felt around for treasures. She was really after one treasure – the body of the winking, lazy-eyed doll. She never told George what she was digging for, afraid he would not join in if he knew they were looking for the remains of a girl's doll. She needed George. Maria and Henry were entirely wrapped up in the world they were creating, and the village children did not venture far on Sundays – and so there was no one else to play with her.

Elizabeth and George had done well together: so far they had found a shard or chip of something blue, several gorgeous cowrie shells that her father said were a wonder to find so far away from the ocean, the jigsawed pieces of a shattered calabash, numerous gloriously coloured beads, a stone that looked like a diamond, but was not a diamond … and now Elizabeth was feeling something in her hand … something cold and hard. She retrieved her hand to look at the treasure. It was an odd-shaped thing. Instantly, the odd-shaped thing accustomed itself to her touch and began to grow warm and glow.

George, on first seeing it, envied Elizabeth her treasure because he thought it was a bullet, one that had been fired out of a Maxim or Gatling gun. But on closer examination (as close as he could get as Elizabeth would not let him touch it), he realised it could not be a bullet because of its colour. He was not sure what the colour was, but he was sure that because of the colour it was not a bullet. He was glad it was not a bullet because he envied Elizabeth too many things already.

As usual, now that Elizabeth had found a treasure, it was time to go home; this was, after all, her game. As they made their way home, Elizabeth and George argued about the colour of the odd-shaped thing, and when they parted, they still had not determined what colour it was. If they knew what colour it was, they felt, they would know exactly what it was. Whatever it was, Elizabeth was going to create a home for it among the other treasures in her miniature doll's house. Elizabeth kept all the treasures they found.

It was Sunday after church, and after the game of 'Treasures', as usual her mother would scrub her skin (making an extra concerted effort on the brown splotch on her chest), scrape under her finger-nails, and brush her hair hard, all the while telling her she had once looked like the doll with the winking eye.

That done, Elizabeth would sit by her father and fill his smoking pipe, which he would smoke while he read her stories from a very heavy book called *The Decline and Fall of the Roman Empire*. Elizabeth did not know this was only Volume One of a six-volume collection, and therefore listened in rapt silence. And then they would have Sunday supper, which always included chicken, probably roasted, but perhaps stewed. And then they would go to bed, and she and Maria would share ghost stories until one of them, usually Maria, became too frightened, and then they would play 'How Many Fingers?' until one of them, usually Elizabeth, fell asleep.

But this Sunday was different.

Sitting on the Chalmers' ox-blood red stoep was a boy who seemed too big for himself, so big that he had folded in over himself. He was thin but tall, too tall. His feet were big. His hands were big. Everything seemed to weigh down on him heavily, and his big, big brown eyes seemed to be the heaviest weight of all. Elizabeth felt something just looking at him, and this something made her stretch out her hand and give him the glowing treasure that was now hot to the touch. He took it. Looked at it with his big, big brown eyes, and then put the treasure in his breast pocket.

Ezekiel.

He had finally arrived.

Elizabeth walked into the house and let the rest of her life go on as it would.

For Ezekiel, it had been a day full of surprises. He had made a decision not to return home (he no longer remembered how many days ago) and walked as far as his feet would carry him. He was neither running away from something nor running towards something, so when he got to the river, he jumped into it. Perhaps he had expected to swim across it; perhaps he had known as soon as he saw it that the current would be too strong for him; perhaps he had, since the start of his journey, been willing to give himself over to something and the river was as good a thing as any. Ezekiel spent so much time in the river that he believed he had drowned, but just as he was thinking of himself as dead, there was a ray of light and a man fished him out. The next thing he was aware of was the ox-blood red stoep he was sitting on, and a flurry of white that made him catch his breath – but not from fright.

Something moved in the hibiscus hedge – white ribbons, white dress, white shoes – a wild-looking girl was climbing out of the green leaves. Just as surprisingly as she had appeared, she was standing in front of him, her hand outstretched. She looked at him and he did not look away: another surprise. He realised she was offering him something. Without really knowing what it was, he took it. It was hot to the touch, but did not burn him. He knew to put it in his breast pocket; he would examine it later. Then just as suddenly as she had appeared, she was gone. Into the house with the Fisher-Man in it. A woman's voice, slightly stern, calling 'Liza!' A man's voice, probably the Fisher-Man's, ever gentle, calling 'Elizabeth ...'

Ezekiel moved his heavy, swollen tongue to form the words 'Elizabeth', then 'Liza'. He took a deep breath, filled his lungs and settled on a compromise: 'Eliza.'

From the moment Mr Chalmers had first given Elizabeth the miniature doll's house, she had loved it, empty as it was, but had not given any thought to furnishing it. It was a proper house, and although in miniature, it was bigger in scope than any house she had ever seen, and with its three storeys, almost like a castle in a picture book. It was pretty – no, splendid – and most important of all, it was hers. No one else, not even Maria, was allowed to touch it without her permission. George and Henry were boys and would therefore break things. Ma was Ma and would therefore find something wrong with the house, and try to change things. And Elizabeth liked her house just the way it was – empty and unbroken.

It was only after she came back from playing 'Treasures' with George for the first time, carrying something blue that was a shard or chip of something much larger, a vase most probably – something blue that George had found, and that she wanted to keep safe – it was only then that she found a use for the miniature doll's house. From that day on, she furnished it with the treasures she and George found. With time, she found that she became very specific about which treasure lay in which room. And even when she moved things around, she moved them around for a reason. With the miniature doll's house now functioning as the keeper of her lost and found treasures, no one else, not even Maria, was allowed to interfere with the very precise way she ordered things.

And then Ezekiel arrived: and everything changed.

At first, all he did was stand there and look at the doll's house, a slight frown creasing his forehead, carefully examining every inch of it. Elizabeth knew her miniature doll's house was exquisite, and she was proud of her treasures, so she was not surprised by Ezekiel's open admiration. What surprised her was that he never reached out to touch the house; no matter how close he got to it, he did not touch it. She would not have minded him touching it – she even told him so – but he never did. Then one day he abruptly stopped his admiration. Just like that. He did not come to look at her miniature doll's house with its many treasures. He did not come to stand by its proud owner.

Elizabeth was understandably disappointed and when, after a week, he still showed no interest, she became angry. She did not mind many things about Ezekiel (in fact, she put up with a lot from him). She did not mind that he hardly said a word to her, even though he seemed to have things aplenty to say to Pa and George and Henry. She did not mind that although he had been with them for months, he had not made anything for her. He had made a fishing rod for her pa; he had made her ma a contraption she could use to churn her own butter (and thus eliminating the need to buy expensive margarine from Wilson's General Dealer); he had built a canopy over Maria and Henry's 'House' in the garden; he had made a wire cart for George, which George now took with him everywhere and which he would not let her touch – as though it was the only wire cart in the world. Most of Ezekiel's efforts went into making this and that for her grandma and Mrs Mendelsohn. They were supposed to use the thises and thats, but instead they chose to display them and talk incessantly about them and about how very talented Ezekiel was.

In all these things Ezekiel made, there was nothing for her. He seemed to think that she did not need anything. But the truth was that she needed something from him. Yes, she had a house full of treasures and a doll's head with a winking lazy eye, but it was not enough – not really, not when he was busy making things for other people.

Eventually, because Ezekiel no longer came by to admire her miniature doll's house, Elizabeth began to look for and find fault with it: with the one leg that had been attacked by termites, with the hinges that were extremely rusty, with its treasures that were paltry.

But then again it was *her* miniature doll's house, and even if it was not perfect, it was beautiful; and if Ezekiel knew anything about anything, he would be standing beside her, admiring it. His absence spoke for itself. He knew nothing. He did not know loveliness when he saw it. Her pa had given it to her. He had probably bought it and not 'found' it as he claimed. How dare Ezekiel look down on something her pa had given her? Yes, its hind leg had been all but destroyed by termites, but it was still the bestest present a father had ever given his daughter. That Ezekiel! He knew nothing, absolutely nothing at all.

It took her a month to find the courage to tell him just how much he did not know. She did not have to look for him. She knew exactly where he was; in her pa's tool shed, or, as everyone was now calling it, 'Ezekiel's Workshop'. He was always there, it seemed to her; building, making, fixing something for anyone who was not her. And sure enough, she found him deep in concentration, carving something out of wood. She knew he knew she was there because even though he did not look up when she entered, he shifted himself on his bench, so that his face would be facing her. And so she told him about the beauty of the miniature doll's house (wasn't it a grand house? Everyone said it was). She lied about how her pa had gone all the way to Salisbury to buy it. She told him about how she and George had worked long and hard to find the treasures. Even after she explained everything about the miniature doll's house, Ezekiel did not look up. He simply frowned. Was there something wrong?

'Do you have to keep all the treasures?' Ezekiel asked.

She did not understand the question. And he did not say anything else.

He blew the dust off whatever he had been carving – it looked like a handle – a fancy handle. If Elizabeth had known the word 'ornate', she would have used that word. As Ezekiel held the fancy handle up so as to examine it more closely, it occurred to Elizabeth, for the first time, that perhaps what he had been finding fault with was not the miniature doll's house – but her. What was it about her exactly that he did not like? She meant to ask him, but instead found herself saying: 'You do not know this, Ezekiel, but you are mine. I saw you in a vision before you arrived. You belong to me. So you might want to be nicer to me.'

He looked at her then. His frown deepened. He seemed ... she did not know what he seemed. Perhaps angry?

'Have I not been nice to you?' he asked.

'No!' she said, incredulous. How could he be so insensible as to be completely unaware of his many slights? she wondered before running through the entire litany of all the things he had not done for her.

He stood up, retrieved something from the window sill, and walked over to her. It took her some time to realise he was offering her something: something in the palm of his hand. She looked at it. It was a chair. A very, very small chair, but not like any chair she had ever seen. Ezekiel took his forefinger and gently tapped the chair – and it rocked. She looked up at him, her eyes wide with both amazement and sheer joy.

'It's a rocking chair for your doll's house. It took me some time to work out how to make it just right,' he said.

So he had made something for her after all. Elizabeth gently tapped the chair and watched it rock on his palm.

'If I give you this though, you have to give George a treasure.'

'Why?'

'Because it is only fair.'

'But they are my treasures.'

And with that Ezekiel closed his hand into a gentle fist, the rocking chair still held within it. 'Then I'll keep the rocking chair,' he said.

He seemed determined, too. He placed the rocking chair up on a shelf, which Elizabeth sadly acknowledged she could only reach with a stool. Ezekiel sat down on his work bench and continued to carve the fancy handle.

Her pa would not have made it to the work bench. He would have quickly turned around, given her the rocking chair, and made every effort to make her laugh. But Ezekiel was no Pa.

'Alright … I will give George one treasure. Just one.'

'Good,' Ezekiel said as he stood again to retrieve the rocking chair from the shelf.

And that is how George ended up owning most of the treasures he had found.

Before Ezekiel entered the Chalmers' lives and made himself so useful to each and every one of them, he had lived elsewhere; and it was his experience in that elsewhere that allowed him to be so useful to the Chalmers. That elsewhere was a minuscule house situated on a secluded and disenchanted piece of land. It stood opposite a much larger dwelling, known as The House That Jack Built. 'Jack' was the wealthy, eccentric, somewhat-reclusive collector of things and teller of tall tales, Jakob de Villiers. Ezekiel's father worked in The House That Jack Built as a master of all trades.

It was while living in the minuscule house that Ezekiel, at a very young age, came to know two things for certain about his parents: his father was inexhaustibly hardworking; and his mother was perpetually disappointed. Not knowing what had displeased his mother's mouth into a permanently stern line, Ezekiel had come to believe that he was the source of her disappointment, and so he had set out to patch up their relationship.

The journey to making amends started with the milk-white, empty vase that held pride of place on their centre table. Ezekiel had not been the one to send it crashing to the floor. The yellow cat had languidly stretched up against it and then purred disinterestedly as the vase toppled over. But he had been the one who had begged his father for the cat to be let into their minuscule home (even though his mother had said there was not enough room for a sneeze, let alone three people and a cat); and so he had to be the one to repair the vase. Ezekiel was then seven years old.

There seemed to be no end, in a home where everything wore

thin, of things that needed to be put right; and so Ezekiel took to helping his mother patch, darn, repair, mend, restore, fix and glue until the only thing he could not set to rights was the permanently stern line that was his mother's mouth.

And so it was until he came across the gold pocket watch, which was laid out on a tray of things that needed polishing and shining that his father had brought home with him from The House That Jack Built.

Another child would have been attracted to the goldenness of the pocket watch, but not Ezekiel. He was attracted to its brokenness, to the fact that the clasp wouldn't fasten. He knew just by looking at that clasp not only how he could fix it, but what he needed in order to do so. It was while he was fixing the clasp that he realised that the watch did not tick the way his father's did. Determined to find out what had gone wrong and how to make it right again, he simply took the watch apart.

And that is how his mother had found it – a beautiful thing in pieces. Ezekiel saw something appear on his mother's face, and for the first time apprehended that his mother could also feel fear. She was so overcome by the emotion that she did not even think to reprimand him. She, who seemed to trust only herself to be able to do the difficult things, was leaving this up to his father. But when his father saw the beautiful thing in pieces, he too could not act. His shoulders stooped under the weight of something that Ezekiel could not see.

For the first time since taking the pocket watch apart, Ezekiel entertained the thought that he might not be able to put it back together again. He had known, just by looking, how the mechanism worked. At least, he had thought he did. But what if he was wrong? What if the things that came from The House That Jack Built were of a different character than those he was used to? He waited for his parents to go to sleep before attempting to put the delicate device back together again. He wanted his failure, if it happened, to be a private affair.

He would only learn the names of the components years later, but he already knew the order in which they had to be assembled in order to work properly. With the greatest care he reassembled the pocket watch piece by precarious piece: mainspring, barrel, jewel, third wheel, fourth wheel, reduction gear, second wheel, jewel, fork, pallet, hair spring, escape wheel. His hands only trembled when he heard his mother approaching, but by then the pocket watch was already ticking.

It was a rather odd thing for his life to turn on, but turn it did. His parents treated what he had done as though it were some sort of miracle, rather than just another instance of his doing something he was accustomed to doing – repairing, mending, fixing. Mr Jakob 'Call Me Jack' de Villiers must have thought it was a miracle too, because Ezekiel was unexpectedly invited into The House That Jack Built, for the first time in his life.

The House That Jack Built was very different from the minuscule home that Ezekiel lived in. It had two storeys, was surrounded by an English rose garden, and had been built into the edifice of a kopje, becoming its unnatural companion for eternity. Inside the house were many rooms, among them a dining room that had a table so long and majestic it could accommodate twenty people, a ballroom whose ornate ceiling was laden with crystal chandeliers, a trophy room decorated with an impressive menagerie of wonderfully preserved wild animals, and a room filled with a collection of curious-looking automata. Ezekiel was ushered into this last room by his father, and it was there that he met Jakob 'Call Me Jack' de Villiers for the first time.

Another child would have been frightened by the eerily blank stares of the various automata, all of which had long since stopped working, but not Ezekiel. Ezekiel was determined to see them – the boy writing at his desk, the girl playing the piano, the pitch-black drummer boy, the magician's assistant with a top hat in hand, the sophisticated lady holding a fan, and the maestro conducting an invisible orchestra – animated again. Jack told Ezekiel that he had travelled the world over – New York, Chicago, London, Paris, Tripoli, Brisbane, Shanghai – in order to collect the curious things he now had in his possession. Each curiosity had its own story with which Jack regaled Ezekiel as the boy worked at reanimating the things that mattered to Jack. He liked these stories, which expanded his decidedly contained world. He liked Jack. He liked The House That Jack Built. And, for his part, Jack seemed to like him too, and to admire what he called his 'knack'.

For a dwelling that was so full of stuff, the house was very quiet. Ezekiel's father did most of the work in the house: dusting, sweeping, cleaning, cooking, washing, ironing, tending the garden, applying the Atlas range of polishes – floor, stoep, boot, shoe, silver and furniture – to various surfaces, and occasionally (but very rarely) driving Jack to a place called Town.

Jack's wife, Victoria, spent her days languidly looking out at the English rose garden whether it was in bloom or not. There was always a bottle of Sloan's Liniment faithfully resting by her side, from which she just as faithfully took liberal sips. She seemed contented, and always offered Ezekiel a placid smile whenever she saw him.

There was another resident in the house, a woman called Blue. The permanently stern line of his mother's mouth referred to her as a Hottentot. Ezekiel was never sure what Blue did in the house; all he knew was that when it was time for him to leave at the end of the day, she would invariably materialise before him, a tin of Mackintosh's Quality Street Assorted Chocolates, with its happy depiction of Regency-era life and the budding romance between Miss Sweetly and Major Quality, snuggled between her arms. She would look at him with something so far removed from disappointment that Ezekiel never found a word for it. Her smile would encourage him to take a 'sweetie', and he would. All told, his entry into The House That Jack Built brought a sweetness into his life that Ezekiel had not even known was missing.

Then, as is usually the case, things changed. The coins that he had received from Jack after reanimating all the automata seemed innocuous enough, but obviously they were not – at least, not according to his mother. She took them from him, and then did something he realised she had never done before: she walked the short distance to The House That Jack Built. Without hesitation, she knocked on the door. Naturally, his father was the one to open the door, and Ezekiel watched as his mother threw the coins at his father. He looked away as his father got down on his knees and picked them up.

'You with your silence. And him with his "Call Me Jack",' Ezekiel's mother screamed. 'I will not have the boy follow in your footsteps.'

Ezekiel looked back in time to see his father's shoulders stoop under the weight of something that he could not see.

'What kind of man are you?' his mother said, before turning to walk away.

It occurred to Ezekiel, for the first time, that his mother was disappointed in more than just him. This knowledge did not make him feel better.

His mother looked at him, and in that moment she seemed to understand something she had not before. She turned towards his father and snatched the coins from him. 'The boy will have an education. Something good must come from all of this,' declared the permanently stern line of his mother's mouth.

Before Ezekiel could even begin to wonder what an education was, he was receiving it at the Coloured School on Lobengula

Street, between Second Avenue and Third Avenue. He was ten years old and his previously contained world exploded. There was just too much of everything – people, animals, trees, machines, buildings, sights, sounds, smells – and the only way he could make sense of any of it was if he focused on the familiar things: and so he set about repairing, mending and fixing. As luck would have it, this knack of his allowed him to excel at school.

In time he came to appreciate and then enjoy reading and arithmetic too, but his teachers, who taught him how to make things, seemed more focused on his woodwork and metalwork skills – especially after he explained his abilities as simply knowing how things worked just by looking at them. His teachers nodded and said that this confirmed his 'innate' sensibilities. The Oxford Dictionary in his classroom explained to him that 'innate' meant '*a quality, feeling, etc., that you have when you are born*'. And so when this quality saw his teachers showering the things he made and produced with trophies and prizes, Ezekiel felt he shouldn't be rewarded solely for having a knack for something. He thought this until his mother attended his prize-giving ceremony and sat in the audience with her best hat perched on a head that was held high, the permanently stern line of her mouth relaxed into something of a smile. Her smile broadened when he received, as a prize, a red toolbox. When he got home, she gifted him with his very own tin of Mackintosh's Quality Street.

His mother died peacefully in her sleep soon after that prize-giving ceremony, and by then Ezekiel had come to understand that his mother loved him. That she had always loved him. Ezekiel felt the loss of her passing, but knew that she had taught him an invaluable lesson: to nurture the gifts that have been bestowed upon you.

In his third year at the Coloured School on Lobengula Street, Ezekiel was informed that a very important woman was coming to visit the school, and that Ezekiel's work would be showcased as an exemplar of the type of student the school produced. The woman's name was Mrs J. McKeurtan, and she had been instrumental in shaping Coloured education in the country. If all went well, and his teachers had every confidence that it would, Ezekiel would secure a spot and a scholarship to the new secondary school that had been built for Coloureds.

Mrs McKeurtan did just as had been predicted. She visited the school, was impressed by Ezekiel's work, and offered him a spot at and a scholarship to the new secondary school that had been built for Coloureds. That done, Mrs McKeurtan took Ezekiel aside and said, 'I know your grandfather, Jakob – or, rather, Jack, as he prefers to be called.' The genuine smile on Mrs McKeurtan's lips did not prepare Ezekiel for what she said next. 'A reclusive, eccentric fellow … knows how to tell a tall tale. Pity what he's done to your father … making his own son live in the boy's kia like that. Happy to see that you've got out – that *you* will have a life beyond servitude.'

Ezekiel saw the components of the gold pocket watch: mainspring, barrel, jewel, third wheel, fourth wheel, reduction gear, second wheel, jewel, fork, pallet, hair spring, escape wheel. Things made specifically to fit together, to move together, to work together – to belong to each other. He had had no idea until this very moment that the same kind of mechanics were at work between his minuscule home, the 'boy's kia', as Mrs McKeurtan had called it, and The House That Jack Built. He began to see the connection between Jakob 'Call Me Jack' de Villiers and Victoria … no, not Victoria, of course, not Victoria with her always faithful bottle of Sloan's Liniment, but Blue … Blue with her always generous tin of Mackintosh's Quality Street and even more generous smile … and his father … his hardworking father whose shoulders were stooped under the weight of something that Ezekiel could not see … all the many unsaid and unacknowledged things, perhaps … and his mother … his mother whose permanently stern line of a mouth he now understood had been silencing a bitter secret from the moment he was born.

But there are no secrets in an exploded world.

Ezekiel did not understand himself. How could he, who prided himself on knowing how things worked just by looking at them, not have known what he had been looking at for all those years? Had he been too close, too much a part of it, to see it for what it was? Had he who *innately* understood brokenness – and had a knack for fixing it – not been able to imagine the whole? Had he been made blind by the fact that when he joined it, his family was already a beautiful thing in pieces?

When school ended that day, Ezekiel walked not towards The House That Jack Built, but in the opposite direction. He had no idea what his final destination would be; he just knew that he needed some distance between himself, The House That Jack Built, and the too-big secret it contained. He needed time and space to understand himself anew. The Chalmers provided him with both the time and the space.

Elizabeth was absorbed, completely, with furnishing the miniature doll's house. Whereas 'Treasures' had strictly been a Sunday after-church affair, furnishing the miniature doll's house became a daily affair. She was constantly thinking of what should go where: what type of table should be built for the parlour, what should hang on the wall in the living room, what colour the library curtains should be? She was very specific about everything, even attempting to draw her most elaborate ideas for Ezekiel. And for his part, Ezekiel was steadfast. He made everything she asked for … eventually. He even made suggestions, which she welcomed because she wanted him to feel, since he was furnishing it, that the house was as much his as it was hers. And so they worked, sometimes side by side, and Elizabeth was happy.

However, whereas Elizabeth could spend every hour of every day thinking or dreaming about her miniature doll's house, Ezekiel had other things to do: go fishing with her pa, fix something for her ma, 'visit' Maria and Henry in their canopied 'House' in the garden, have tea with sticky sweet things with her grandma and Mrs Mendelsohn, go on escapades with George – and so progress on the miniature doll's house was rather slow. But Elizabeth did not mind because as long as the miniature doll's house remained unfinished in its furnishings, she could continue working with Ezekiel. And to be fair, her own progress in making the curtains and the bed linen from the scraps of material her ma had spared her over the years, was extremely slow, because Ma insisted on every crooked stitch being undone and set right.

At first Elizabeth had tried to get Ezekiel to spend more time with her – to 'monopolise' his time, as George called it. (George knew big words like 'monopolise' and 'ornate' and 'habitat' because he supplemented their missionary-school education by reading her pa's big dictionary every day.) But as hard as she had tried, she had not been able to 'monopolise' Ezekiel's time. Over the years she had gradually given up, reconciling herself to the fact that even though he belonged to her – or would in the future – she had to share him with others in the present.

Elizabeth never allowed herself to think of the moment when she would have to decide whether to keep him or let him go.

Over time, Elizabeth had become so accustomed to Ezekiel's absence that his constant presence, during her thirteenth year and his fifteenth, did not immediately make itself felt. They were furnishing the final room in the miniature doll's house: the master bedroom. Much time had passed since the gift of the rocking chair. The rocking chair was now placed by the fireplace in the master bedroom, and although it had graced every room in the miniature doll's house, Elizabeth was determined that this was to be its final habitat. The room was already well-furnished, the bed had already been crafted, as had the casement curtains and mirror; but it still needed a dresser, a wardrobe, and, Elizabeth insisted, a baby's cot. She was trying to find the perfect place for the baby's cot on her schemata – near the fireplace, next to the rocking chair, beside the bed – when Ezekiel said in a voice that seemed to be breaking: 'Do you still remember what you said to me that time?'

'What time?' she asked without looking at him, because just at that moment she had decided the baby's cot was to be placed beside the bed, on the mother's side of the bed, but not too close to the fireplace.

'The time I gave you the rocking chair,' he said as though wanting to get the words out as soon as possible.

She looked at him then. 'You mean about my having seen you in a vision?'

He nodded.

'I remember.'

He looked away, but seemed to be waiting for something.

112

Eventually he said in his cracking new way: 'You said I belonged to you.'

It was only when he said these words that she realised he had been by her side, every day, for quite some time.

She looked at him, but he was concentrating too intensely and intently on a small table he held in the palm of his hand.

'Well, maybe not belong …' she said.

He looked up, then looked away.

'But when we are older, we will love each other. I will love you and you will love me. You know, the way my pa and ma do.' She thought about this and added, 'Only better.' She smiled at him, but he was still busy examining the table in his hand.

The next question, which came after some time, was so quiet she almost did not hear it: 'And when exactly will we be older?'

'I don't know.'

'Will we be as old as your pa and ma?'

'No … not *that* old,' she said.

He looked at her then, and asked, 'So we'll be married?'

'If I choose to keep you, yes.'

He frowned at this.

'But I will love you more than anything and you will love me more than anything,' Elizabeth said. 'We will love each other more than anything, which is a very rare thing for people to do, and because of this, I think we will get married.'

He smiled a little, reassured. But it did not last long.

'I may choose to let you go,' Elizabeth said. 'I don't know what will happen to our loving each other more than anything then.'

His frown returned. 'Why would you let me go?'

'For your own good. But I don't think it will come to that.'

Ezekiel could not find the thing to say in response.

It was then that Elizabeth noticed something she had not noticed before: a bump on Ezekiel's throat. She reached out –

touched it – gently running her finger over it, and Ezekiel drew back. He left the room and left her alone. Had it been up to him, he probably would have left her alone for a very long time. But it was not up to him – not anymore.

Things would have gone according to some sort of plan had it not been for the music. Ezekiel, Elizabeth had anticipated, expected even; but not the music. It had taken her completely by surprise as it came out of the gramophone on the countertop of Wilson's General Dealer.

The store had shut for the day, and, it being a Wednesday, Elizabeth had gone to help MaVuma, who, ever since Mrs Chalmers had fired her, had been employed as the stock-boy at Wilson's General Dealer. Elizabeth made it her job to help count the stock and make sure her numbers and MaVuma's tallied – for a price, of course: a can of Borden's Eagle Brand Condensed Milk.

This particular evening, the evening of Elizabeth's first experience with the music, MaVuma seemed to have been waiting for her; and as soon as Elizabeth saw MaVuma's excitement, she knew it had something to do with the gramophone, a His Master's Voice, which MaVuma had placed on the countertop. MaVuma had explained that Mr Wilson, in a rare show of generosity, had given it to her because he had purchased the latest model for himself and no longer had any use for an older gramophone.

Now, as Elizabeth well knew, MaVuma was not the sort of woman to take gifts from men; but this was a His Master's Voice. As Elizabeth well knew, years ago a gentleman from Fort Hare, who intended to marry MaVuma, had brought her something he had called a vinyl record; and had then promised to bring her a gramophone on which to play it on his next visit. He had not brought the gramophone nor visited since making the promise.

But now, thanks to Mr Wilson's unexpected generosity, MaVuma was at last able to appreciate the gift the gentleman from Fort Hare had given her: a vinyl record made by a king, no less; a King Oliver to be exact. MaVuma proudly wound the gramophone's handle and there was music in the air. It was 'Zulu's Ball', a rhythm, both new and old, known and mysterious, joyous and mournful, that left Elizabeth with no other option but to dance ... and dance ... and dance ... until she was nothing but spirit.

When Elizabeth first heard the music, she understood it to be a language that communicated things to her that she had to express. Since she comprehended it so well, she had quite naturally thought this language was experienced the same way by everyone. But she soon realised it was – like Ezekiel – something that had been given to her especially.

Later that day, lying on her stomach, Elizabeth tried to explain to Ezekiel what had happened. She watched as his Adam's apple slowly worked the condensed milk down his throat. She enjoyed watching this. Sometimes she wished she had an Adam's apple of her own, but she knew that even if she had one, she would not love it as much as she loved his. It fascinated her. He had lived so long without it, and then one day there it was, and immediately it seemed to have always been a part of him.

For his part, Ezekiel was frowning, which she now understood meant that he was listening, really listening, to her. However, hard as she tried to explain that what she called music – the sound of what she would later learn were cornets, clarinets, saxophones, trumpets, trombones, double bass and drums – was different from what came out of the organ in church, or the 'Let Me Call You Sweetheart' or 'By the Light of the Silvery Moon' tunes her pa loved to whistle, or the six phonograph cylinders from Edison's 1500 series that her ma religiously listened to on her much-cherished Amberola, Ezekiel did not seem to understand.

'Gramophone,' he said at last, slowly, somewhere close to her left ear.

Elizabeth was disappointed. It was the machine and not the music that had made him really listen to her. She grabbed the can of condensed milk from his hand, sat up and shifted a little away from him, just in case he did not appreciate that he was being punished.

This did not deter him from explaining to her how a gramophone worked. The needle read the grooves on the black disc, the vibrations created were 'breathed' into the wooden chamber through the 'throat' at the base of the horn, and then breathed out as sound by the horn – creating what Eliza called music.

Ezekiel told Eliza that she was a lot like a gramophone. All the things that made her had a purpose, all created a delicate balance, and as such had to be handled with the greatest care. It was all about touch – the right amount – like the needle on the grooves. Everything had to be just so, otherwise there would be no breath, no vibration, no sound, no music. One wrong move – an inconsiderate word or action – and there would be nothing in response but total silence or angry, discordant sound.

Eliza, moving even further away from him, told him she did not much care for being likened to a machine.

But a gramophone was not just any machine: it was the most sublime machine Ezekiel had ever seen.

Eliza was not placated.

'I'll come to the store with you next week,' Ezekiel said.

'You'll be in the way,' Eliza said as she gulped as much condensed milk as her mouth would allow.

'Then how am I supposed to hear the music the way you hear it?' he asked, squinting up at her.

And even though she knew he was only saying this to make her happy, she let herself be very happy.

'We can go tomorrow,' she said.

'Good,' he said, sitting up and moving closer to her.

And then he kissed her – something they had only recently learnt how to do – lips sweet and slightly sticky from the condensed milk, which made them both laugh.

Years later he would be able to show her the beauty he found in the gramophone, and she would be able to communicate to him the pleasure she felt in the music – all without saying a word – and they would finally understand each other perfectly and completely.

The ending happened so fast that Ezekiel did not see it for what it was. The gentleman from Fort Hare had at last made good his promise to MaVuma. Accompanied by two other gentlemen, he had come to marry her. The gentleman from Fort Hare had not made good his second promise – that of the gramophone – but he had brought with him the honeyed voice of Miriam Makeba and the melodious harmonies of the Manhattan Brothers, and by the time MaVuma and Eliza danced to 'Baby Ntsoare', all had been forgiven.

Eliza and Maria had, quite naturally, been asked to serve as bridesmaids. On the wedding day, Mrs Chalmers, who made the yellow bridesmaids' gowns herself, glowed with so much uncontainable pride when she saw how resplendent her daughters looked, that whatever residual anger she still felt towards 'Pamela' for taking her Liza to the river all those years ago was momentarily suspended.

Ezekiel had also watched the proceedings, but, unlike Mrs Chalmers, he had not been filled with pride. He had watched Eliza, sunshiny in her taffeta dress, dance the afternoon away in yellow shoes, a marigold stuck in her hair as one of the groomsmen from Fort Hare twirled her this way and that, and occasionally threw her into the air to the sound of Louis Armstrong's trumpet and gravelly voice. 'Dinah! Dinah!'

Eliza had found only a moment to spend with Ezekiel, and in that moment all she had said to him was, 'These shoes are killing my feet.' Later, when the dancing was over, Ezekiel had watched Eliza bury her killed feet in the slightly damp sandy soil, close her eyes, turn her face up to the sun and start humming a tune in her throat … 'Baby Ntsoare'. He watched as her body gently swayed to the rhythm. Watching her from the verandah, Ezekiel contemplated whether or not to go to her. She looked so happy – so self-contained – without him.

Ever since The Three Gentlemen From Fort Hare had arrived, Ezekiel had felt a wretchedness that had started out as foreign, but soon became familiar. As he watched Eliza be content without him, he felt miserably alone, even though there were people all around him. He wanted Eliza to be thinking of him, and only him. He wished, more than anything, for her to open her eyes and look for him in the gathering until she found him.

He was waiting for her to do so when Henry tapped him on the shoulder.

'Mr Wilson is waiting for you. A car has broken down at Wilson's General Dealer.'

Ezekiel looked at Eliza again, wishing she would open her eyes and look at him, willing her to do so.

For years afterwards, as some sort of sorry consolation, he would say to himself: if she had opened her eyes that day, if she had looked at me, I would never have followed Henry. I would have gone to sit by her side. I would have buried my feet in the sandy soil. I would have let her rest her head on my shoulder. I would have kissed her and claimed her as mine, for the whole world to see.

But Eliza had not opened her eyes, and Ezekiel had got into the car with Mr Wilson who drove him all the way to Wilson's General Dealer, where he met Mrs Lewis and her companion, Caroline.

He and Caroline were introduced to each other in a carelessly casual manner that made it perfectly fine for them both not to pay particular attention to each other. Ezekiel was after all Mr Wilson's mechanic, and he suspected that Caroline was Mrs Lewis's maid, although the way she was dressed made him a little uncertain of this fact. If such a thought had been possible, he might have thought Caroline was Mrs Lewis's daughter – but that would have meant Mrs Lewis had had relations with a black man. So, unsurprisingly, the thought never occurred to Ezekiel.

Mrs Lewis was afraid of the time. She did not want to drive back to the city in the dark. Ezekiel got the impression that Mrs Lewis somehow blamed Mr Wilson, and, by extension, Ezekiel himself, for her broken-down car.

'Your man will be done soon, I hope.'

'He will if he knows what's good for him.'

Caroline looked at Ezekiel apologetically and smiled at him encouragingly.

He was determined to have the car fixed in no time. He definitely knew what was good for him, and he wanted to get back to Eliza as soon as possible. He opened the bonnet, quickly assessed what was wrong, and set straight to work.

At some point Ezekiel became aware that Caroline was giggling behind her gloved hand. He followed her gaze and saw Mr Wilson rub his cheek.

'No thank you very much,' Mrs Lewis said. The finality in her voice was unmistakable.

Thankfully, the car was soon fixed, and Mrs Lewis and Caroline were driving away in a cloud of dust.

Had it not been for Eliza, the incident would have probably gone unremembered by Ezekiel, because there had really been nothing remarkable about it. They – Ezekiel, the Chalmers Girls and the Mendelsohn Boys – were all swimming in the river Mr Chalmers had once fished him out of. Ezekiel had, after a few laps, decided his time would be better spent lying in the warm sun, chewing a blade of good, dry, wheat-like savannah grass, and thinking about the near future in which he and Eliza would be married.

Sure enough, as he had anticipated, Eliza came to join him. She sat right next to him, so close he could feel the moisture on her skin. Even though his eyes were closed, he knew that she was looking at him, and knowing this made him happy. She was silent for a long time, which was rare for Eliza. He could smell the sun gently baking her skin. With his eyes still closed, he reached out to touch the warmth of her skin.

'You remember the girl you met at Mr Wilson's General Dealer?' Eliza said.

By the time Eliza asked the question, Ezekiel was aware that a few more bodies had joined them. He did not respond, even though he knew very well that the question was directed at him, because he did not remember any girl; or, rather, he vaguely remembered several girls, but no specific girl.

'The day of the wedding. Remember?' Eliza persisted.

This time Ezekiel did not respond because he remembered the girl; or, rather, he remembered the way she had giggled behind her gloved hand, and for some reason he felt guilty for remembering her at all.

'Caroline, I think her name is,' Eliza said. 'Do you remember her?'

'Caroline?'

'Yes.'

'Yes. I remember her.'

'You have to marry her,' Eliza said as she took his hand in hers.

Ezekiel opened his eyes but he could not see Eliza – all he could see was a large bluish-black circle where she was supposed to be. He blinked. He knew he was looking directly at her, but still he could not see her. He really needed to see her. He saw instead a young woman in a pink dress with tiny white flowers on it, a veiled red hat perched on her head, a white-gloved hand covering a red-lipstick mouth as it laughed. He saw himself laughing with her at the antics of Mr Wilson and Mrs Lewis. He did not remember having laughed. He stopped trusting the memory. The woman, Caroline, said something to him, and he responded with a smile. That was definitely not what had happened.

Ezekiel tried to look past the memory that was not a memory, to see Eliza in his present. He still could not see her. Instead, he saw a wedding day: a bride in white too happy to blush as he leaned forward to kiss her beaming red-lipstick mouth. Caroline. What was this? He saw a car ride with Caroline and him in the front and three boys singing 'Let Me Call You Sweetheart' in the back: smiles all around. He saw himself and Caroline, old and grey, surrounded by grandchildren upon whom they doted. He saw himself very happy in a future he did not want.

Someone was squeezing his hand. Eliza. He tried to snatch his hand from hers. She would not let him.

'You have to marry Caroline, Ezekiel.'

If he could see her, he would know exactly what to say, but he still could not see her.

'You are a man who can have a long and happy life, Ezekiel,' she said, and then kissed him in a way that seemed to erase all talk of Caroline. 'You deserve that life. I will never be able to give it to you.'

He felt her warm body get up. He heard her walk away from him.

By the time Ezekiel could see Eliza clearly, she was already diving into the river.

Music had changed everything. Music had made Eliza dance until she was just spirit. Music had brought The Three Gentlemen From Fort Hare. Music was taking his Eliza away from him. She, who had once said they belonged to each other, was offering him Caroline as a consolation. Ezekiel did not want to be consoled; he wanted the time before the music.

Ezekiel left Ezulwini and walked as far as his feet would carry him. He was neither running away from something nor running towards something, so when he got to the City of Kings, he decided to stop there for a while. Since he was good with his hands, and was thus easily employable, he found many things to do in the city – but none of them took away his devastating desire to return to Eliza.

He should have known that his return to the City of Kings would bring his own family back into his life. One day as he lay tinkering under a bus, trying to determine what was wrong with it, he heard the unmistakable sound of his father's voice: 'Son?' He rolled from underneath the bus and found his father standing there in a faded and frayed suit with a bowler hat in his hands. 'You're alive ... you're alive,' was the only thing his father could say in the many moments that followed. Tears ran down his face, and Ezekiel felt an overwhelming love for this man who was not afraid to cry in front of other men. Although his overalls were covered in grease, Ezekiel did not hesitate to hug his father, and his father hugged him back.

He liked that they could be men like this together – father and son – for all to see. He liked that they could acknowledge their relationship publicly and not keep it hidden behind the walls of a house. In short, he liked that they could have the relationship his father had never been able to have with his own father. Ezekiel had tried to let go of the deep hurt he had felt upon discovering that Jakob 'Call Me Jack' de Villiers, the man his father worked for as a servant, was actually his grandfather. But he could not.

'We thought you were dead,' his father said, bringing Ezekiel back to the present. 'We looked for you everywhere. We had long since given up hope. Last week, I drove Mr de Villiers to the Gentleman's Club, and one of the other drivers said to me they had seen someone at Axelrod's Fitters and Turners who looked like I must have looked twenty years ago. It cannot be, I thought to myself. Not after all these years. But I promised myself I would come and see for myself on my day off ... here I am. And here you are.'

Ezekiel felt many different emotions, and he was certain that they would all remove the smile from his father's face; so he kept them to himself and just said: 'You're Mr de Villiers too.'

'I know, son. I know,' his father said, the bowler hat going around and around and around in his hands as he avoided looking Ezekiel in the eye. 'I know. As are you ... as are you.'

Why did he expect more from a man who had been a secret – something hidden – all his life? Ezekiel put a hand on his father's shoulder, not altogether sure what he was trying to reassure him of.

'Blue will be so very happy to see you,' his father said.

Imagine having to call your own mother 'Blue' all your life, Ezekiel thought. Imagine not knowing your own mother's real name because your father will only let you experience her as his creation.

'You will come to the house,' his father said, trying to make the unsure question sound like a confident statement, the bowler hat going around and around and around in hands that trembled.

'Yes ... of course,' Ezekiel said.

His father looked up at him with so much gratitude that Ezekiel had to look elsewhere for a moment.

'You do not know how happy I am to have found you,' his father said.

Ezekiel was happy to have been found.

His happiness did not last long, however. When he thought

126

of visiting The House That Jack Built, all he could think of was the room with the automata – the boy writing at his desk, the girl playing the piano, the pitch-black drummer boy, the magician's assistant with a top hat in hand, the sophisticated lady holding a fan, and the maestro conducting an invisible orchestra – and all he could see was his grandfather sitting at the heart of things that no longer worked. It would be up to him to set things to rights again. It would be what was expected. He searched within himself, and found that he could not do it. He was no longer a curious boy intent on fixing things; he was now a young man who understood in that moment that some broken things could not be fixed. He would have to disappoint his father.

His grandfather had made a choice. His father had made a choice. The time had come for him to make a choice. He chose never to return to The House That Jack Built – something was being performed there that he did not ever want to be a part of. He did not begrudge his father and his grandfather the choices they had made, and he hoped that they would not begrudge him his. It occurred to him then that there were many ways to be a man. If Ezekiel ever had a son, he would be sure to let him know this.

Ezekiel knew there was no use in staying on at Axelrod's Fitters and Turners because his father, bowler hat in hand, would just find him again. There was no use in going back to Ezulwini because Eliza would only talk more of Caroline. But he needed somewhere to be. It was time he looked for another elsewhere. As it turned out, he didn't have to look: the promise of elsewhere found him.

The man from the War Office who came to talk to the fitters and turners was particularly interested in the Coloured mechanics. His eyes, once they had landed on Ezekiel, stayed there for the duration of his evidently rehearsed speech, so Ezekiel could be excused for feeling that when the man talked about the possibility of joining up to serve in the Malayan Emergency, he was *personally* being called to duty. With nowhere else to be, the very next day he made his way to the War Office and enlisted for the Coloured Unit as Ezekiel Chalmers.

The War Office received him very happily. It had already sent the all-white 'C' Squadron to Malaya, and it was just about to send the African Rifles to Johore on the SS *Empire Clyde*. It knew that every war needed men who knew how to fix things, and the colony had trained its Coloured men to know how to fix things, so it would be a missed opportunity if they did not send them to Malaya. Of course, it needed to couch all this in more elevated language, and so what the War Office told Ezekiel and others who enlisted for the Coloured Unit was that men – men who naturally understood the inner workings of things, men who intrinsically knew how things worked together, men who innately knew how to solve problems – were needed to fight. Despite the War Office's lofty language, Ezekiel heard what they were really looking for: men who had a knack for fixing things. Ezekiel was such a man.

A few years later, as Ezekiel Chalmers lay on his back amid chaos and ruin in the middle of the tropics, it was the sight of a gramophone playing a song sung in a language he did not understand that saved him, and made him determined to find his way home – back to Eliza.

But first, Ezekiel had to locate the others: Calder and Cilliers. He sat up. He did not check himself for injuries and bruises. He could not afford to. The jeep was nowhere in sight. He struggled to get up. Something was wrong with his left arm, but he had no time to worry about that now. He found Calder and Cilliers mangled but alive. There was the sound of something moving gently, easing itself … giving way. He heard it above the music. In a normal setting, the sound would bring comfort, but in a chaotic world, he knew to suspect the calmness of that sound. He looked up, and that was when Ezekiel saw the wheel.

The jeep they had all been flung from when they drove over a landmine was smouldering on top of a tree. If Ezekiel didn't act swiftly, the jeep would come crashing down and finish the landmine's job. He helped Calder to his feet and walked him towards the gramophone. Cilliers was seriously wounded, and so Ezekiel gently placed him on a burlap sack and carefully dragged him towards the gramophone.

The jeep came crashing down and surprisingly, but thankfully, did not explode. Chalmers, Calder and Cilliers watched it from a safe distance.

'Where is the news unit when you need it, hey?' Cilliers said, his voice weak. He tried to laugh, but coughed instead.

Ezekiel laughed for all of them.

Earlier that day, before they had set out, the news unit had taken a picture of the three men. Cilliers had sat comfortably on the jeep's bonnet, leaning forward with one knee raised. On the spur of the moment, Calder had put his arm around 'Chalmers' and 'Chalmers' had let him. All three had smiled, managing to look, somehow, like they had been caught in a moment of joy, happiness and easy laughter. They seemed to know intuitively that this was what the photographer and the people back home wanted. That photograph made it onto the front page of *The Chronicle* a few weeks later. But by then, one of them was dead, and his smiling face must have seemed like cruel mockery to those who had loved him.

Now, as they waited for help, Ezekiel felt in his breast pocket for his talisman. It was still there, even in this exploded and upside-down world. He touched its cold hardness, felt around its odd shape as it began to grow warm. Even though he could not see it, he knew that it had started to glow.

Thus fortified, he pointed at the gramophone that was still playing a song sung in a language he did not understand, and asked Calder and Cilliers if they knew the language the song was being sung in. Neither of them responded. Their responses were not necessary, however, because what really mattered was that Ezekiel could hear the music.

E lizabeth, in her baby-pink tunic and soft pink slippers, was determined to bake the cake herself. As usual, she followed the recipe religiously. She measured the ingredients carefully. She turned on the oven to the required temperature. She greased the cake pans. She creamed the butter and sugar with a wooden spoon until her arm grew tired (who cared if it was a little lumpy? There was still more mixing to be done). She broke in the eggs, one at a time. And mixed. She sifted the flour (or she would have done if she had been able to find the sieve). She added the flour all at once because the time she would have taken to add the flour spoonful by spoonful had been taken up by her search for the sieve. And mixed. Batter ready, she noticed an ingredient was still unused, and added the bicarbonate of soda. And mixed.

She poured the cake batter into the prepared cake pans, painstakingly making sure each pan had an equal amount of batter. She tapped the cake pans to release any air bubbles (the matron did not understand why she did this, but she had seen her mother do this countless times, and so she did it as well). She smoothed the tops with her wooden spoon. She opened the oven door and picked up both cake pans and placed them on the specified oven shelf. She set the timer. She closed the oven door. Having burnt many cakes in the past, she stayed in the kitchen and periodically opened the oven door to check the progress of the cakes. When the timer went off, and not a moment sooner or later, she removed the cakes from the oven. They were not burnt, just a little sunken in the middle and rather lumpy on the surface. And when she felt them, they seemed somewhat dense and heavy under her touch. She was not discouraged, however, and let the two cakes cool on the window sill before she went about preparing the icing.

Just then a piece of shrapnel whizzed past her. She turned her head in time to see it cut into a man's left shoulder before sending him flying through the air. She ran to him, but noticed that the noise and the chaos surrounding him was not surrounding her; quiet tranquillity was surrounding her. She watched him roll several times until he lay on his back, clutching his shoulder with his right hand. She willed him to get up, but he did not. She knew this man, she believed. She needed to help this man – to save him. Then she saw there was already something there to save him: a gramophone. It was playing a song sung in a language she did not understand. She allowed its presence to comfort her.

When Elizabeth became aware of her surroundings again, she was in a hospital ward filled with white women – some screaming, some crying, some silent, some looking ahead at nothing, some laughing, some smiling and one of them repeatedly hitting the top of her head with her fist. All of them, like her, were wearing baby-pink tunics and soft pink slippers.

As soon as Calloway Cavendish saw the woman in white, he knew that she was to be his salvation. A white woman walking where she was not supposed to be – the African Location – needed to be saved, and so he saved her. Her feet were bare and bleeding, caked with mud, as was the hem of her dress. Her hands were bruised and her fingernails were broken, smeared with blood and dirt. Her hair was unwashed and matted, flecked with leaves and grass. Her white dress was torn, sullied by reddish-brown soil, so much like blood. Her green eyes were wild and piercing, focused on something in front of her that no one else could see. He would help her. It was so very obvious she needed him to help her, and it felt good to be needed.

When Calloway asked her for her name, she did not give it to him. Instead, she told him she needed to find the giant pair of silver wings so she could give them to the white man. That was when Calloway realised that she was not only in distress, but that there was something wrong with her – something made clear by the fact that her eyes did not focus on him as she spoke to him.

How had she come to be walking down the streets of the Location alone and unprotected? It occurred to him then – and very belatedly – that she had been violated in some way. This would have been the first thought of any man who had seen her in this state, but it had not been his. Why had it not been his? Calloway did not want to consider the answer to that question, did not want to investigate why he was not wired like other men. He opted instead to focus on the redeeming fact that his first instinct had been to be of service to her.

When he asked the dwellers of the Location what had happened to the lady in question, they reluctantly told him she had been roaming the Location for several days looking for a giant pair of silver wings. She had entered one of the stands and started digging into the earth with her bare hands. They understood that she was possessed by a spirit, and so they had let her be and sheltered and fed her when necessary. Someone believed her family was in Ezulwini, and had gone to inform them of her whereabouts.

As Calloway put the woman in his car, he tried not to be too harsh on Africans and their superstitions. Who had ever heard of a white woman being possessed by spirits? He decided it was best to take her to a hospital and have her seen to. As he drove her to Ingutsheni, the sorrow and anguish of her suffering body became a palpable thing in the car. It filled him with a strong desire for forgiveness, so much so that when they arrived at the hospital, the first thing he did was wash her feet.

The first time Dr Clark Dobson saw Elizabeth Chalmers, Calloway Cavendish was washing her feet while she sat before him in a catatonic state. She had not been Elizabeth Chalmers then; she just had been some woman Calloway Cavendish claimed to have found wandering in the Location. You could never be sure with these wealthy men; they got up to all sorts and then went to hospitals or doctor's offices to hide away what they had done. True, Dr Dobson had no knowledge of Ingutsheni Hospital ever having been put to such use, but there was always a first time for everything.

Dr Dobson had become absorbed in the washing of the feet – in the way Calloway Cavendish wiped each foot with a white terry cloth, then placed each one in the iodine-treated warm and soapy water, how he tenderly scrubbed each foot in turn before laying it on a white towel that he used to pat it dry. It was all that care taken that made Dr Dobson suspect that there was an intimacy between the two. He had watched, with practised professional imperturbability, as Calloway Cavendish rested his forehead on the woman's feet and cried.

Although such a situation had never presented itself before, Dr Dobson knew instinctively which questions to ask and which ones not to ask. The hospital was chronically overcrowded, underfunded and suffering through various shortages; it could never hurt to cultivate a benefactor as wealthy as Calloway Cavendish. The story the intended benefactor told the doctor was rather fantastical – he had come across the woman while he was doing some charity work in the Location, and she had told him that she was looking for a giant pair of silver wings she needed to give to a white man.

The story was so outlandish that once Calloway Cavendish had driven away, Dr Dobson had strongly suspected he would never see him at the hospital again, and that he would have a rather difficult time finding out the real identity of the woman with the washed feet, whom he admitted as Patient 925N.

As it came to pass, he was very wrong on both fronts. Calloway Cavendish had visited the hospital the very next morning, and encouraged the doctor to call him by his first name, which the doctor had immediately done. Dr Dobson decided to keep the woman in the hospital for at least two to three months so as to foster the relationship with Calloway. It should be noted here that Dr Dobson did not believe the woman was white; he believed she was Coloured. He decided to keep his beliefs to himself, however, and placed Patient 925N in the White Section of the hospital.

On the fourth day, the woman became very agitated and the implausible things she said confirmed what Calloway had told him. There was a giant pair of silver wings buried somewhere in the Location, and she needed to give these wings to a white man. When asked how she knew this, she said a venerable woman with sagacious eyes had walked on water and told her this was her mission in life – to find the wings and take them to the white man. When it became evident that Dr Dobson did not see the world the way she did, the woman made a frantic but ultimately futile attempt to escape from the hospital, and had to be restrained. Given this display, he was able to provide his diagnosis.

As Dr Dobson was writing the word 'schizophrenia' on the woman's chart and scheduling her for shock therapy, a nurse informed him that there was a man looking for his daughter. Once in the doctor's office, the man gave his name as Mr Chalmers, and after being allowed to see the patient, he confirmed that she was his daughter, Elizabeth Chalmers. According to her father, she was prone to wandering, and this was definitely not the first time she had been away from home, alone and unprotected, for a period of time. The wandering had started because of the music. She loved to dance, you see, Mr Chalmers explained, and followed the music everywhere.

Mr Chalmers helped confirm what Dr Dobson knew to be true: Elizabeth Chalmers was Coloured. Mr Chalmers' light-brown skin was a clear indicator; although, mind you, you found that same colouring in some of your Mediterranean types – your Portuguese and Greeks and what have you. What had convinced Dr Dobson of Elizabeth Chalmers' race was not the colour of her father's skin; rather, it was the lack of discipline and desire for respectability in his outlook on life. What self-respecting white man would let his daughter run wild following the music – probably jazz – leaving her vulnerable to the oft-dangerous whims and desires of men?

He, Dr Dobson, had often noted that there was a certain … weakness of character, a propensity towards frivolity and fornication, in the mixed races. If he could find the time, he would write a paper on the subject. But for now, it was best not to tell Calloway the truth – his generosity might not be as forthcoming if he knew Elizabeth Chalmers was Coloured. With great difficulty, he convinced Mr Chalmers to leave without his daughter, and promised that she would be returned to him once she had been completely cured.

After Mr Chalmers' visit, Dr Dobson drilled a hole into Elizabeth Chalmers' frontal lobe. As the drill cracked through her skull, Dr Dobson was certain that this was the only way she could be set free. But after the procedure, Elizabeth Chalmers was anything but free.

During the time she was in his care, he tried everything – mostly insulin injections and electric shock therapy. He would believe that he had fixed the part of Elizabeth Chalmers that was broken, but inevitably she would mention the giant pair of silver wings and her need to take them to the white man, and they would find themselves right back where they had begun.

Dr Dobson was not a cruel man. He had let the matron of the women's wards talk him into trying out occupational therapy, and so he had the women carry out all sorts of activities: flower-arranging, hair-styling and baking for the women in the White Section, washing the linen for the women in the Coloured Section, and cleaning the wards for the women in the Native Section. He was yet to implement occupational therapy in the male wards. No, Dr Dobson was not a cruel man. If he had been a cruel man, he would have killed Elizabeth Chalmers and the baby she carried. Instead, he had let Patient 925N give birth to the baby girl in the White Section of the hospital, and had had the baby taken to an orphanage before its mother could hold it and form an attachment to it. After the baby was taken away, he had drilled another hole into Elizabeth Chalmers' skull so that she would blissfully forget the baby. No, Dr Clark Dobson was not a cruel man at all.

Calloway Cavendish had been in the balance for most of his life. Somewhere out there there was a scale with his name on it – a scale weighed heavily by that thing he had done as a boy; the thing that had caused a man to be hanged. There had been an African man (Calloway was not the sort to call a man a boy) who had often come to the Cavendish home to deliver parcels. Knowing that Calloway, an only child, must have been lonely in that big house with its big garden, the African man would habitually take a moment out of his day to play with him. They often played hide and seek – there were many places to hide in that big garden. The man had even helped Calloway put the finishing touches to his tree house when his father and the gardener had both proved too busy. Calloway liked this man and considered him his friend – perhaps the only friend he had at that point in his life. The man told Calloway that he had a son of his own, and Calloway felt a child's envy at the time that father and son must have spent happy together.

You have to understand that Calloway and the man played together every time the man came to deliver something. You have to understand that when the man came on that fateful day, without his bicycle or anything to deliver, Calloway joyfully thought he had come just to play. You have to understand that when the man hid in the tree house, Calloway thought it was all part of the game. You have to understand that when the British South Africa Police (BSAP) arrived looking for the man, Calloway thought they were part of the exciting game. You have to understand that Calloway did not immediately read the look on the man's face – as the BSAP dragged him, handcuffed, across the big garden – as the look of one who felt betrayed by someone he had trusted. You have to understand that Calloway only learnt about the consequences of his actions some time later when his parents whispered something about the unfortunate hanging of the delivery boy during dinner. 'He seemed like such a happy fellow … a good sort,' Calloway's mother had whispered. 'Just goes to show, you never can tell,' Calloway's father had whispered back.

The deed irrevocably done, Calloway spent the rest of his life seeking redemption and salvation. Once he was old enough, he poured a considerable amount of his family's considerable fortune into modernising the Location, which is where he assumed the man had lived. He joined and started many charitable organisations geared towards improving the African's lot. Nothing he did made him feel redeemed or saved – until he met the woman in white and washed her feet. And now because of a woman, he felt that the scale was balanced at last.

Who would have thought his salvation would come from a woman – a white one, at that? She had made it possible for him to perform a good act, one he could measure. He looked at Elizabeth Chalmers as she sat in the sterile whiteness of Dr Dobson's office. She wore a baby-pink tunic and soft pink slippers, her hands were folded placidly on her lap, her fingernails cut to the quick, her lips arranged in a benign smile, her eyes staring out at nothing in particular. Her hair had been shorn off and a bandage was wrapped around her head. She looked quiet and peaceful and very different to the wild thing she had been when they had first met.

Calloway watched as Dr Dobson unwrapped the bandages from Elizabeth Chalmers' head and revealed a perfectly ugly scar.

'As you know, the hair will grow back,' Dr Dobson said. 'Soon it will be like none of this happened,' he continued as he began rebinding Elizabeth Chalmers' head with fresh gauze.

'And she will not remember any of it? She will forget completely?' Calloway asked, not quite able to keep the apprehension from his voice.

'Completely,' Dr Dobson said with confidence. He seated himself next to Elizabeth Chalmers and opposite Calloway. 'We used the most modern technique available. It has the best results.'

'And the giant pair of silver wings?' Calloway was almost too afraid to ask.

'There will be no more visual or aural hallucinations for the patient,' Dr Dobson said.

Calloway looked at Elizabeth Chalmers, and part of him missed the light that had shone in her eyes, missed the particular animation of her face, missed the personality that had always bubbled through when he visited her.

'She will come back,' Dr Dobson, accurately reading Calloway's thoughts, assured him. 'Soon it will be like none of this happened.' Had the doctor already forgotten he had just reassured Calloway with those very words?

The two men looked at each other squarely, as though there wasn't a secret between them. But that is, perhaps, what conspirators always do.

Elizabeth was in that place where she was the lady in red waiting for the tall and handsome man to come and sit next to her. She loved the anticipation that was held in the waiting, but she also loved having him sit close to her. Close enough to touch. He always smelled of familiar things that made her feel warm inside. Soap. Sandalwood. Sweet tobacco.

While she waited for him, she motioned to the waiter enclosed in the triangle of the serving station, and he made her coffee – black, hot and strong – in a tall white mug. As she plopped in two sugar cubes and then stirred her coffee, she marvelled at the immaculate whiteness of the waiter's uniform. The whiteness shimmered under the fluorescent lights, and the white cap he wore made him look more like a sailor than a waiter, although she never told him this. She also never told him that the brightness of it all would have made her anxious were it not for the tender yellow of the walls.

As her right hand stirred the coffee, she looked down at the silver teaspoon she held with the tips of fingers whose nails were painted crimson. She wished there was music here. She loved music. But the only sounds were the occasional clink of her teaspoon against the china of the mug, the continuous hum of the two silver coffee urns next to her, and the soft buzz of the fluorescent lights above. She stopped stirring her coffee and watched the steam rise. She wanted to sway her body to the rhythm of a song that only she could hear … a song sung in a language she did not understand … a song she could sing without knowing its meaning. It would be nice to add to the susurration, but she never used her voice here.

She looked at her reflection in the mirror behind the waiter.

Her hair was flaming red, probably that way to match the dress she wore, her frame was leaner and more angular, the make-up making her facial features appear sharper and bird-like – a hawk, perhaps. She did not altogether look like the self she remembered – probably the result of having been in this place, Phillie's, for so long – but she definitely felt like herself: like Elizabeth Chalmers.

She looked down at her shoes: red Mary Janes with a modest heel. Her feet rested on the footrest of the bar stool, and she clicked her heels together twice, then smiled as though she had told herself a private joke. The smile was still on her lips when she raised the coffee mug and took a sip.

The doorbell chimed, letting her know that someone had entered the diner. She did not turn to see who it was because she already knew. It was the third man. The man who sat adjacent to her, and whose face she never truly saw because the brim of his fedora always cast the top half of his face in shadow.

He was not the one she was waiting for.

The third man made a barely perceptible motion with his head, and the waiter started making him a cup of coffee. The third man never lifted his head. He sat with his arms folded on the red lacquered wood of the countertop and allowed himself to sink deep into his thoughts, his body folding in on itself as he did so, the fabric of his blue-grey suit stretching across his shoulders and back. Another almost imperceptible nod acknowledged the arrival of his coffee.

Elizabeth understood his desire for solitude and let it be. She took another sip of her coffee and again longed for there to be music. She had to refrain from tapping a rhythm on the varnished countertop. The air that surrounded her suddenly seemed to be vibrating and pulsating, and she knew this meant that the one she was waiting for was on his way. Sure enough the bell chimed, he took a few long strides, and then sat down on the bar stool next to hers. Near. Close.

She did not look at him, and she was almost certain he did not look at her. What would have been the point of looking at each other when the other was already so very known? She knew, for instance, that he wore a navy-blue suit, azure shirt and navy-blue tie; that on his head assuredly rested a grey fedora with a black band around it; that his shoes were of a comfortable black suede. She knew that he too had hawk-like facial features, and that he did not hide these in shadow. Most importantly, she knew that he smelled of soap, sandalwood and sweet tobacco. She took a deep breath and breathed in these familiar things.

He motioned with his left hand and the waiter went to one of the silver coffee urns and poured him a cup. As he waited, Elizabeth felt their bodies lean in closer and closer until they were *almost* touching. His coffee arrived and his right hand plopped in two lumps of sugar. She smiled at this similarity, and watched as his fingertips found their way around the handle of a teaspoon. She listened to the tinker and clink of the metal against the china and found it to be such a soothing sound.

And so they sat, side by side, forever leaning towards each other but never quite touching, still anticipating.

The man reached into his inner suit pocket and retrieved a sliver of paper that he surreptitiously slid towards her. As she pretended to examine the fingernails of her right hand, her left hand clandestinely inched towards his until her fingertips touched the flimsy paper.

Once the paper was in her hand, she looked down. It always had some cipher on it that she could not decipher, but which she always made an attempt to read because she knew this was where her deliverance lay. As expected, there was a cryptogram, but this time when she made an attempt to read it, she found that she could make it out: E ... Z ... E ...

As Ezekiel, in his military khakis, descended from the train, he felt in his pocket and counted the change – well, all the money he had in the world really – trying to ground himself with something real, something tangible. In the years he had been away, he had allowed himself only one fantasy: in it he saw himself get off a train, feeling lost and looking around him for something familiar. Just as he was about to lose all hope, a woman's voice called out his name, and he turned in time to see Eliza, wearing a red dress, emerge from a cloud of engine smoke. She ran to him and hugged him, and then, smiling and crying, simply looked at him with all the world's happiness. He had seen a similar scene in a film, and had thought that would be just the thing for him. In the film, the hero and the heroine had been just about to kiss when they were engulfed by another cloud of engine smoke, and the words 'The End' were superimposed on the screen.

As he stood on the platform, someone – who would not have touched him were he not wearing the uniform – patted him on the shoulder and thanked him for his service, and he tried to smile in that way that seemed to reassure people. He felt his lips quiver from the effort. Smoke from the train got in his eyes, stinging them with tears he blinked away. He knew that this heaviness inside him was a wanting to cry. His knees began to tremble and the ground grew unsteady beneath his feet. Soon he would have to sit down. But where? He was still in the 'Whites Only' section of the station. He tried to walk on, but found he absolutely had to sit down. It would just be for a moment, he reasoned, and the cold concrete was as good a place as any.

He was sure people would appreciate that a man who had seen the world at its worst felt heavy inside. He began to think of how nice it would be to press his forehead on the cold unforgiving concrete. Just for a moment. To feel unforgiven. Just for a moment. To give in to weakness. Just for a moment. His knees buckled. He saw a flash of white ... but there was no hibiscus hedge for her to emerge from this time.

Ezekiel found them without looking for them. Two houses opposite each other – tiny as all the houses in Thorngrove were tiny – one with the name 'H. Mendelsohn' and the other 'G. Mendelsohn' proudly written on the gates. Ezekiel had learnt that the world was a small place, but surely it couldn't be *that* small. He would have allowed his doubts to let him carry on walking if the two houses had not been the best-looking in the area. He knocked on the door that lay beyond the gate of H. Mendelsohn. He heard a chair scraping the floor and then footsteps. The door creaked open, eyes squinted up at him before widening in surprise and, he was happy to note, joy.

'Ezekiel,' she said, hugging him. He felt instantly welcomed.

'Maria,' he said.

'You're alive! You're alive,' Maria said. 'We thought you were …' She hugged him tighter still.

Henry appeared and beamed beside Maria. 'You've found us at last, De Villiers,' he said as he shook Ezekiel's hand heartily.

Ezekiel gave a slight start – he was still getting accustomed to using his real name.

'We looked for you everywhere. We had long given up hope … and now here you are,' Henry said.

'Here I am.'

'Come in,' Maria said, opening the door wider.

He bowed his way into the room. There was only one window letting in the sunlight. Even sunlight was something that was controlled and governed in this colony. Ezekiel, as he often found himself doing after his return from Malaya, tried not to feel too bitter about it.

'Please sit,' Maria said, smiling from the door as she motioned towards two wooden chairs and a table underneath the window. A vase with a pink plastic flower in it had been placed on the table. So typical of Maria and Henry, Ezekiel thought.

As Ezekiel lowered himself onto the chair and tried to arrange himself comfortably in it, it occurred to him that if this was typical of Maria and Henry, it meant that they lived here together. And this meant that living in the house opposite were George and Eliza. Together. Ezekiel shifted in the chair again ... and again.

It was Maria who sat opposite him and took both of his hands in hers. 'It is really good to have you back. You were so long in returning ... but what does it matter? You are here now and it is such happiness to see you.'

There was not a speck of dust anywhere, and so Ezekiel had to imagine one and flick it off his trousers.

'Where is George?' he asked.

'Work,' Henry said.

'On a Saturday afternoon?'

'He is apprenticing under John McKeurtan, the funeral undertaker,' Henry said. 'Death does not have a weekend or a holiday.'

Ezekiel knew the truth of that statement all too well. He shifted his weight on the chair. He shifted again – he could not put it off any longer. Trying to sound casual, he leaned back in the chair. 'And Eliza?' he asked, but his voice came out dry and scratchy. He cleared his throat. 'And Eliza?'

'Out somewhere. You know Liza,' Maria said quickly. Too quickly.

Maria and Henry shared a look. He tried to read it, but it was gone too soon.

Obviously eager for something to do, Maria got up. Ezekiel got to his feet too. Maria smiled, happy to see he still remembered Mrs Chalmers' lessons. She told him she had found, since being out in the world, that not many men were aware of Mrs Chalmers' lessons, and she felt deeply that the world was a sorry place for it. She was saying words, Ezekiel knew, that would prevent them from speaking about Eliza, who was out somewhere.

'I'll make some tea,' Maria said and, with those words, grabbed her sun bonnet and a kettle. She smiled at Ezekiel apologetically. 'Unfortunately, it will take some time. Water has to be fetched, a fire started.'

'I can chop the firewood and start the fire,' Ezekiel happily volunteered, wanting to be of some use.

'Not while you are our guest,' she said, before leaving the room. As she closed the door, she gave Henry a very pointed look.

Henry sat down and let his fingers tug at the plastic petals of the pink flower in the vase.

'Henry?'

'Please, Ezekiel, do not ask me anything. It is not for me to tell you. You know there are no secrets between us.'

Was there no end to secrets? Ezekiel wondered. Was that what adulthood was all about, keeping secrets?

Maria rushed back in. 'Lucky me. I met Mrs Green, and wouldn't you know it, she had just finished making a pot of coffee. Well, chicory really. So no need to start a fire or boil water.'

Instantly Ezekiel knew Mrs Green did not just happen to be met.

Maria opened a wooden box and produced a tea set. It occurred to Ezekiel that in many ways it was as if Henry and Maria were still playing 'House', except now they were also keeping secrets. She placed a teacup on a saucer in front of Ezekiel. Next, a sugar basin was produced with a teaspoon stuck in it. Then a tin of biscuits. Maria opened the tin. Only two Highlander biscuits left.

'The coffee will be enough for me, thank you,' Ezekiel said.

'Have the biscuits,' Maria insisted.

We're not in need of charity, Henry's eyes warned him. So Ezekiel took the biscuits.

They watched him eat and seemed to take pleasure in it.

The door swung open and the shock of it made Ezekiel stand up abruptly. George in all his glory walked over to Ezekiel, hand outstretched.

'Well, if it isn't Mr de Villiers finally come back to us,' George said.

'George,' Ezekiel said as they heartily shook hands. 'I hear you're working with McKeurtan.'

'Good man. Has an eye for the native women. Little brown McKeurtans everywhere,' George said with a chuckle. 'But a good man.'

'What happened to becoming an archaeologist?'

'Have decided it is better to bury things for future archaeologists to discover. Be the beginning and not the end of something,' George said, obviously having given it much thought.

'You live in the house opposite, I take it,' Ezekiel said. 'May I see it?' Without waiting for a response, he made his way out, very much aware that he was being the badly behaved guest.

It was Maria who opened the door to a room with one window in it. 'Actually, I live here,' she said. 'With Eliza.' It was obvious that this arrangement was in name only.

Ezekiel adjusted to the room quickly. Underneath the window was a sewing machine with a stool in front of it. Another stool was in the right corner of the room, and neatly folded on it was a blanket and a woman's nightgown. Next to the stool was a pair of soft pink slippers, one slightly placed on top of the other. The letters E.C. were embroidered on the slippers. As he bent down and placed the slippers neatly next to each other, Ezekiel said, 'I cannot for the life of me imagine her wearing pink.'

'As you can see, you find us living in somewhat reduced circumstances,' George said, not doing a good job of changing the subject.

'I could be bounded in a nutshell, and count myself a king of infinite space,' Ezekiel said.

'Were it not that you have bad dreams,' George said.

Ezekiel made an attempt at a smile.

'So where have you been?' The question burst from the always curious George.

'Malaya.'

George nodded. 'How was it over there?'

'It was not what I expected.'

George expected more. 'How did you find the world?'

'Not the same as it is in books.'

'Very little out here is like how it is in books,' Maria said, resignedly sitting down by the sewing machine.

Eliza's presence made itself known to Ezekiel when a plum rolled along the floor and came to rest at his feet. She had dropped the basket she had been carrying, and plums were rolling everywhere. Ezekiel bent down to pick up the plum at his feet, but before he could complete the action, Eliza was in front of him, frantically undoing the buttons of his shirt, which she tugged at until his left shoulder was exposed. She looked at the shoulder, or rather the scar on his shoulder, for some time. She ran her thumb over the shiny, smooth surface of the keloid scar. None of it lasted as long as Ezekiel would have liked. Too soon, she stepped away from him.

'You need to go to see Pa. He is waiting for you. He has not been fishing since you left,' Eliza said. She looked into his eyes then, but only briefly. 'You'll go see him?'

'Of course.'

'This Sunday.'

'Yes.'

'Promise?'

Ezekiel had made promises to Eliza he was now sure he could not keep, but he was equally sure that this one he would keep, and so he nodded. What had she ever asked of him that he had not freely given?

And all too soon she was walking away from him and out the door.

Maria, Henry and George were picking up the plums and placing them in the basket. Were it not for this, Ezekiel would have believed he had imagined her. But just to be sure, he bent down and picked up the plum at his feet. He ran his thumb over the shiny, smooth surface of its flesh. He hesitated and then took a bite. Sour ... slightly bitter ... and then ... sweet.

The drive to Ezulwini was pleasant. Chalmers' Place itself looked much smaller than Ezekiel remembered. The house, however, was still charming: cream with an undeniably shiny ox-blood red verandah and stoep; on one side a well-groomed small garden, and on the other, a well-managed orchard; and all around the cacophony of constantly buzzing insects and singing birds.

Out came Mrs Chalmers, carrying a bowl with a wooden spoon in it, her apron spotless. She tried not to cry but failed miserably, and fiercely hugged Ezekiel in a way that let him know she still had not forgiven him for leaving in the first place.

'You'll excuse the mess,' she said, leading him into the spotless house which smelled warmly of something baking in the oven. 'Nothing works. No one capable of repairing anything. You know Mr Chalmers, always in his library. And the ladder needs fixing otherwise how will I decorate the church hall?'

Finally he was to be of some real use, Ezekiel thought, as he happily made his way to the tool shed. His progress was intercepted by Mr Chalmers as he exited his library.

'Ah, Ezekiel, there you are. The fishing rods are in the pantry. You know Mrs Chalmers, always the need for everything to be just so. I'll fetch my gumboots,' Mr Chalmers said. It was as though Ezekiel had never left.

But he had left – and he shouldn't have.

On the water, there was pure and absolute tranquillity. Almost not a word passed between them. If either of them thought back to that day, many years ago, when Mr Chalmers had fished Ezekiel out of the water, neither of them let on.

At some point, Mr Chalmers reached over and gave Ezekiel's shoulder a strong squeeze. 'I think she knew she would one day wander,' Mr Chalmers said. 'And she knew what the wandering would do. She wanted to save you from it ... from the pain and helplessness it creates. Allow yourself to be saved, Ezekiel. Allow yourself to be saved.' And with that, Ezekiel was at last able to let the heaviness inside him out.

Frederick de Villiers had lost his son twice, so he had learnt to be vigilant. When Ezekiel returned from Malaya and informed him he would not be visiting him at the house with its too-big secret, Frederick had first blamed the house; then he had blamed the too-big secret; then, with great reluctance, he had blamed his father; and at last, after an almost unbearable dawning, he had blamed himself. He had let the too-big secret shape his entire life, make him the shadow of a man, mould him into a man incapable of fighting, of defending what was his, of holding on to what he believed in. Frederick realised that, because of the too-big secret, his son would not be coming to visit *him*. While the too-big secret had made him the son that his father could fully appreciate, it also had made him the father that his son could not fully appreciate. If he wanted the relationship with Ezekiel that he did, Frederick knew he would have to change. He would have to learn to fight, defend and hold on.

To accomplish this, Frederick made a point of spending his evenings at Ezekiel's home in the Brickfields' Courtyard. Every day, just before sunset, saw him arrive at his son's house and every day, just after sunrise, saw him leave his son's house. Every day he made sure his son was still there, still alive. For added measure, just to be sure, he decided to spend the entirety of his Saturdays with Ezekiel.

Soon Frederick began to notice things. He noticed that the eyes of the Women of Brickfields' Courtyard followed his son with open curiosity. He noticed that they seemed to take special interest in the three rooms Ezekiel occupied. He noticed that they

155

always asked him if he knew what Ezekiel intended to do with the third room, which they called a 'spare' room. He knew they worried that his need of all three rooms meant he had a family – perhaps substantial, perhaps consisting of a wife and several children – who were waiting to descend upon them.

Most single people and families living in the courtyard could only afford to rent one or two rooms, and squeezed themselves and their worldly possessions into the confined spaces, leaving no room for cooking, sitting, or in any other way enjoying the room; and so they tended to share their cooking, leisure and pleasure (except the most private kind) communally, and they liked to believe that this way of living cheek by jowl with so many things shared was what created their deep sense of community. So much of life was lived on verandahs, on the square patches of dusty earth where several sports were played, in the cooking shed in the middle of the courtyard, in the shared ablution blocks at the back of the courtyard. Frederick knew that the Women of Brickfields' Courtyard feared that the many rooms Ezekiel occupied in comparison to them would make him feel no need to be part of the community.

When Ezekiel, after only a few weeks of washing in the communal ablution blocks, decided to construct a rather ingenious shower at the back of the rooms he occupied, the courtyard women took it as a personal affront and marked rejection. It took them quite some time to appreciate what this development might mean for them.

Ezekiel, being Ezekiel, unwittingly quelled the storm he did not even know was brewing around him by offering to build others their own private bathing facilities. In this all too crowded and confined place, would it not be nice to have a little privacy? The offer so plainly and pragmatically put forward could not help but be seen as extremely attractive. And soon Ezekiel found his weekends were kept busy by the construction of showers and washrooms. He further unwittingly endeared himself to his neighbours by not asking for payment for his labours. As long as they provided all the necessary materials, he was happy to build their facilities. With that particular liberation, the residents were happy to find a hero in Ezekiel. Meanwhile, Frederick did not mind his son's busy Saturdays as long as he knew he was somewhere in Brickfields' Courtyard.

While Ezekiel had been oblivious to the growing resentment of his neighbours, he was very much aware of their growing admiration, and was acutely embarrassed by it. He was a man who did not like to bring attention to himself, and because he walked through the world with an inward focus, he was always surprised when he realised that the world had been paying him attention all along. Desperate not to be seen by his neighbours as what Frederick knew he was – head and shoulders above and by far better than them – Ezekiel took to accepting every social invitation. He joined in their dice and card games, partook in their beer drinks, discussed the politics of the city and the colony, played cricket and soccer on the dusty patches they proudly called fields.

But, of course, there was more to the story of Ezekiel's welcome to the fold than at first met the eye, and the ever-vigilant Frederick knew this. He knew that while the residents spoke their praise of Ezekiel with one voice, there was within that seemingly unified collective, another constituency that wanted something else from Ezekiel: something they made a very poor attempt at keeping hidden, and something Frederick had seen all too clearly from the first.

Now, apart from all his other fine qualities, Ezekiel was a very fetching man, and Frederick had long known that the Women of Brickfields' Courtyard – women of all shapes and sizes, all complexions, all ages, and varying degrees and states of attachment – admired Ezekiel's physical attributes, and wanted a more *intimate* acquaintance with them.

While Ezekiel, with his mostly inward focus, did not notice the looks of longing and appreciation that were constantly directed at him, the women certainly did. They began to imagine rivals in each other, and soon allowed something that was not quite pleasant to steal into their hearts. This not quite pleasant thing crept upwards, found its way into their eyes, and pointed itself like an arrowhead so that when the women looked at each other, they found they could sling arrows even as they smiled.

The cleverly cunning among them, knowing Ezekiel's love for fixing and making things, had been quick to invent problems with the things in their households so that he could attend to them. But because of the overcrowding within their living quarters, they found that once Ezekiel was within their premises, they could not do with him what they desired – regrettably there was no recess that was dark enough to not be illuminated by the wandering eye of a child or the trained eye of a grandmother. The truly resourceful then took to inventing reasons to visit Ezekiel in his quarters when he was alone.

The most determined of these scheming women was Mrs Prinsloo, who always wanted some sugar in her bowl. One Saturday, when Frederick had gone to Lobengula Street to purchase provisions and Mr Prinsloo was off somewhere probably doing exactly what his wife was planning to do with Ezekiel, Mrs Prinsloo had somehow made it all the way into Ezekiel's room, empty sugar bowl in hand. Frederick had luckily returned just in time to find Ezekiel, absolutely oblivious, looking in the kitchen cupboard for the sugar Mrs Prinsloo wanted.

Frederick was genuinely surprised – even knowing how calculating and daring she was – to find Mrs Prinsloo sitting assuredly on Ezekiel's bed, leaning back on her right hand, the almost forgotten empty sugar bowl dangling from her left hand, which rested on her crossed knees. She was wearing a blue chiffon dress with a very low bodice and a skirt that had been re-hemmed well above the knee. Frederick was so shocked by the sight of her that he dropped the parcel he had carefully carried all the way from Lobengula Street.

'Pa,' Ezekiel said, immediately stooping to help pick up the scattered wares. 'Good that you are here. You are just the man Mrs Prinsloo is looking for.' (Frederick sincerely doubted it.) 'She would like some sugar. She says there is a special type of brown sugar you sometimes give her. I looked, but could not find it. She decided to await your return.'

As Ezekiel said this mouthful, Mrs Prinsloo, thwarted by Frederick's arrival, pointed her arrowheads at him; for his part, Frederick, who at that moment also had something not quite pleasant residing in his heart, returned her look of contempt until she stood up from the bed and walked out of the room.

They faced each other on the verandah and Frederick smiled as he slung arrows and said: 'They have stopped stocking the special brown sugar, I'm afraid. So you need never come looking for it.'

He knew she had heard him loud and clear as he watched her walk, empty sugar bowl in hand, back to her quarters.

Frederick had learnt his lesson. He would have to be extra vigilant in future. To achieve this, he placed the rocking chair Ezekiel had made for him on the verandah. He made sure to curtail or end all interactions that took place between Ezekiel and the women who happened to be 'passing by' while the women were still on the dirt path, before they even thought of venturing onto the stoep. His heightened vigilance had rearranged his life to be sure, but it was no skin off his nose, because it ensured that no courtyard woman ever found her way into Ezekiel's room again.

It was not Frederick's intention to turn Ezekiel into some sort of latter-day-saint. He understood all too well the needs of men and women. It was just that Ezekiel was the kind of man who needed a certain kind of woman, and that woman did not reside in the Brickfields' Courtyard. That woman – and of this Frederick was sure, even though they as men had never discussed it – existed in the inward place to which Ezekiel was always drawn. It was she who made Ezekiel unable to see all the longing around him: the soft eyes that followed him everywhere, the love that Mrs Kruger put on the palm of her hand and then rested her chin on as she stood by an open window waiting to sigh at his passing by, the opportunity that Mrs Prinsloo had offered him by sitting on the edge of his bed. Frederick felt grateful to this woman residing in Ezekiel's inward place, whoever she was and wherever in their small world Ezekiel had found her, because she had successfully inoculated him against the wiles and desires of women who plagued and followed him everywhere he went.

However, even as vigilant as Frederick had become, he did not see *the* woman coming. She, like all the other women, must have walked up the dirt path, but she seemed to have materialised out of thin air as she stood there in her emerald-green dress, fur coat, laddered stockings and battered suitcase. It was perhaps because she had taken him completely by surprise that Frederick allowed her to place not just one foot, but both feet, on the stoep.

'My name is Elizabeth Chalmers. I am looking for Ezekiel de Villiers,' she said, climbing the last step onto the verandah.

Frederick found himself actually grateful to Mrs Prinsloo and her empty sugar bowl because had she not ventured too far, he would not have been on the verandah to witness the full glory of Elizabeth Chalmers' first arrival.

Now, although it was very clear to Frederick that Elizabeth Chalmers had come across some very difficult times, he found

160

he liked her immediately. He particularly liked that she was here for Ezekiel and no other man in the Brickfields' Courtyard. He also particularly appreciated that she did not approach the stoep on some pretence, but with her truth firmly in hand. Frederick allowed her to approach further, and as she did so, he noticed the doors of the courtyard homes fly, creak or yawn open as various women exited them so as to get a better view of what was happening.

What was happening was that Frederick was standing up from his rocking chair and offering it to Elizabeth Chalmers, who was graciously declining it, choosing instead to sit on her suitcase. Frederick was far from done with being the accommodating host, and so he offered her what he promised would be a very refreshing glass of Rose's lime cordial, which she accepted. He went into the house and made the refreshments. By the time he returned, Mrs Prinsloo and Mrs Kruger were standing dangerously close to the stoep, and the other women were inching nearer.

It turned out that Elizabeth Chalmers had the same inward place as Ezekiel because she did not realise the danger she was clearly and presently in. She made polite conversation with Frederick while she nursed her lime cordial, and the only thing that kept the women at bay were the arrows ready to be slung from Frederick's eyes. He understood their curiosity and their fear, and knew that they did not stem just from his having allowed her closer than most of them had ever been, but also from the person of Elizabeth Chalmers herself. It was true she was a little worse for wear, and the clothes she wore had seen better days; but an outstanding woman is an outstanding woman, no matter what she wears.

In front of all the courtyard women, Frederick asked Elizabeth Chalmers to follow him. When she stood up, he picked up her suitcase and led her into the lodgings, to Ezekiel's room, and told her that she could wait for him there. It was with great satisfaction that he watched her sit on the edge of Ezekiel's bed. When he left the room, he found that his absence had given Mrs Prinsloo the courage to put one foot on the stoep. He looked at that foot until it found its way back to the dirt path.

In the time he had spent with Elizabeth Chalmers, Frederick knew that she was the woman from Ezekiel's inward place – the kind of woman a man waited and waited for, and did not mind the wait.

It took Ezekiel some time to notice that the expected things had ceased to be expected. The usual eyes that followed him as he walked down the dirt path leading to his home were not there to accompany him. The many-timbral voices that often called out to him in greeting before asking him to help them with this, that and the other – these were silent. Mrs Kruger and her loneliness were not positioned by her window, both lying in wait for him. But it was only when Mrs Prinsloo did not accost him with her always curiously empty sugar bowl that Ezekiel realised that something must be terribly wrong.

Where had all the women gone?

The answer to that question soon revealed itself when he saw them congregated outside his home. His immediate thought was that something had happened to his father. The skaftin dropped from his right hand and the rolled-up newspapers of *The Chronicle* and *Bantu Mirror* dropped from his left armpit. Whether he ran, walked rapidly or flew, he did not know. All he knew was that in no time at all he was making his way through the throng of women gathered outside his home. As he moved between them, the women looked at him with a hostility that was definitely not expected, and something new. It would be an understatement to say that the entire situation was confusing to Ezekiel, especially when he saw his father sitting on his rocking chair on the verandah, looking not only very much alive and well, but also very self-satisfied.

What in God's name was going on?

The situation was made even more confounding by the fact that no one said a thing. His father kept on rocking back and forth, back and forth, back and forth, and the women kept on looking at Ezekiel as though they had discovered he had committed an unspeakable crime. One thing was clear; whatever was happening, he was at the centre of it, and his father was absolutely not giving away any clues as to what 'it' was.

Ezekiel, not knowing what else to do, removed his seersucker Ivy cap and scratched his head, desperate enough to think this act would provide him with the wisdom necessary to understand the situation. And then he saw emerald green leaning against his doorway, and the thing he had not known before suddenly became known.

At long last ... the flash of colour Ezekiel had long been waiting for.

The occurrence he had dreamed of had finally arrived, and although he had prepared himself for both its happening one day and its never happening, now that it was actually happening, he found he was not prepared. He had imagined this moment so many times, but it had never been like this in his imagination – so very real. When he had imagined the happening of this moment, he had seen in his mind's eye something more (and there was no reason to shy away from this word) romantic. He had cast himself as the hero of that romantic interlude. But the in-control hero, contained and courageous, Ezekiel most certainly was not. The woman in emerald green was also not behaving like a heroine. She did not run towards him, but continued to lean against the door frame.

His hands, desperate to do something, dropped the Ivy cap, and without a care, his feet trampled it underfoot as he moved towards the emerald green and reached out to touch the soft and silky fabric. The feel of the fabric on his fingertips reassured him that fortunately this was not something he had conjured up.

Eliza was indeed here.

Her hands were not reaching out to him the way he wanted them to, the way they definitely would have done, if this was a dream he was having. One arm she kept folded behind her back and the other she used to lean against the door jamb.

'I am so sorry, Ezekiel,' Eliza said as her hands found their way to him, touching the coarse blue fabric of his overalls.

'There is nothing to apologise for,' he said.

'There will be plenty to apologise for in the coming years,' she said, as her hands left the fabric of his overalls and touched his face.

That was his undoing, and he found himself on his knees before her, delicately gathering the emerald green of her dress in his hands.

The sound of his father's rocking chair contentedly rocking back and forth, back and forth, back and forth reminded Ezekiel that he had an audience, but he was so exultant in this moment that he did not care.

He looked up and watched Eliza's lips seek his long awaiting.

The Women of Brickfields' Courtyard had been prepared to hate the woman as soon as they saw her standing on Ezekiel de Villiers' verandah, or, rather, as soon as they saw Frederick *allow* her to stand on Ezekiel de Villiers' verandah. To stand on that jealously guarded verandah was a privilege that was not granted to just anyone, and for quite some time, it had not been granted to a woman. Who was this woman and from where did she get her audacity?

It was obvious, just from looking at the woman in her ratty fur coat and silky and satiny emerald-green dress that had been twice mended, that she had gone through some very hard times. It was also evident, just by looking at her, that her hard times had not hardened her as their own hard times had hardened them. The woman was all softness and smoothness around the edges. She would have seemed like sweetness and light had not her green eyes spelled obvious danger.

The Women of Brickfields' Courtyard understood all about hard times, and were intimately acquainted with all the effects of such times: some wore dresses that had over time become ill-fitting, sun-bleached, frayed frocks; some had missing teeth and, therefore, rarely smiled; some had perennially black eyes that looked out on a world that was no longer full of promise; some had bruises and scars on bodies that had become tense with apprehension; most of them had lines of perpetual worry on their faces. The language of hard times was so well known to them that it had long since become their lingua franca.

The women knew their hard times were tied, as all other things

166

in their lives were tied, to men and their fortunes and misfortunes, and that these in turn were tied to a more solid thing – employment in the White Man's Town. The hardest times came when a man was without employment, or when he wanted the element of freedom that came with spending his money in pursuit of his own happiness. Yes, the Women of Brickfields' Courtyard understood all about hard times and were intimately acquainted with all the effects of such times.

Perhaps because of the way she wore her misfortunes, the Women of Brickfields' Courtyard realised that the woman seemed to have gone through an experience that was different from theirs; so, in spite of themselves, they found they wanted to know more about her, if only to somehow use this knowledge against her at a later date.

It was a simple touch that soon turned the women's hatred into envy. They saw Ezekiel de Villiers, ever so gently, reach out to touch the emerald green of the woman's dress; and when they saw this, the grey, brown, blue and hazel eyes of the Women of Brickfields' Courtyard became uniformly green as they witnessed, in the broadness of daylight, Ezekiel de Villiers holding the woman as though it was one of those quiet hours in the night when a man allows himself to love his woman tenderly.

And green the eyes of the Women of Brickfields' Courtyard would have remained had the lady, whom they soon learnt was called Elizabeth Chalmers, not performed some sort of miracle that made them love her.

It should have been obvious from the ease with which she had made Frederick, within seconds of meeting her, fall at her feet – the same Frederick who held women in open contempt and obviously had never felt finer feelings towards the fairer sex – that hers was not the gift of miracles, but the gift of magic – a dark and secret science. Frederick had not only allowed her to step onto his vigilantly guarded stoep – he had gone out of his way to accommodate and entertain her, to show her into Ezekiel's lodgings, which he had always treated like a place so sacred as to be forbidden. And so it should have been obvious, from the way she made malleable someone as formidable and intractable as Frederick, that they, the Women of Brickfields' Courtyard – strong in many ways, but also weak in many others – would be like clay in a child's hands.

Because their first feeling towards her had been the very opposite of love, imagine their great surprise when the love they had not been expecting was suddenly there and strongly felt.

They fell in love with Elizabeth Chalmers because she, like Ezekiel, knew how to do things. But unlike the things Ezekiel did, which made the entire community look and feel good, Elizabeth knew how to do things that made the Women of Brickfields' Courtyard individually look and feel good. In a place like Brickfields' Courtyard, in a town like the City of Kings, in a colony like theirs, it was a rare and precious gift for women like them to feel good about themselves. Elizabeth Chalmers made them all queens. She styled their hair and designed and made dresses that transformed them from the hard-times women they had become into the women they pointed at in magazines: Dorothy Dandridge, Lena Horne, Etta James, Maggie Hathaway, Nina Mae McKinney, Diahann Carroll.

Who would not love such magic? Soon enough, the green left the women's eyes so that when they looked admiringly at their reflections in mirrors, their eyes were grey, brown, blue or hazel once again – and they could clearly see the beauty they had always possessed.

It was this beauty and love that, when Elizabeth started searching for the giant pair of silver wings she needed to give to a white man, made the Women of Brickfields' Courtyard believe that both the wings and the man existed. They saw absolutely no harm in Elizabeth's occasional wanderings; their often constrained lives made them appreciate the desire for movement ... for travel ... for elsewhere. If anyone dared to remind them that once-upon-a-time they would have gladly used such knowledge of Elizabeth against her, they slung their arrowheads from grey, brown, blue and hazel eyes. Elizabeth Chalmers had become a part of them, and they had become a part of her: they were now an intrinsic and integral unit. Together, they were the Women of Brickfields' Courtyard.

When, years later, Elizabeth and Ezekiel were tragically taken by one of the many ways of dying that a war creates, Brickfields' Courtyard had long since been demolished. And yet it was the Women of Brickfields' Courtyard who came from places as far afield as Thorngrove, Barham Green, Newton West, Queen's Park, and Rangemore to mourn them. As they, in their movie-star hairstyles and Sunday best, cooked, washed and prepared for the funeral, their mouths were full of stories – mostly embellished – that they laughed at until there were tears in their eyes. They hardly remembered the same memories the same way, but they all remembered how Ezekiel had allowed himself to love Elizabeth tenderly as though their entire lives were lived in one of those quiet hours in the night.

E ver since she had fallen pregnant, Elizabeth had been waiting for the venerable woman with sagacious eyes, the woman who could walk on water, the woman written as Gagool, to visit her. The woman had told her that she would next visit her when there was life inside her. So when she heard the scratching sound, something sharp repeatedly scraping against the surface of something dry, she knew it was a heralding. Elizabeth was lying in bed, Ezekiel sleeping beside her, his hand resting contentedly on her stomach, when the woman materialised. The woman, upon seeing the gentle way Ezekiel held Elizabeth, did the most unexpected thing: she smiled. It was a most charming and happy smile, the kind of smile one only used among friends – or better still, with family.

'All those years ago, I showed you an ending and it frightened you,' the woman said. 'You tried to save him.'

Elizabeth looked at Ezekiel, and felt sorry for him – for the years of wandering that she could not save him from, and from the ending she knew was inevitably coming.

'Yes, you die together,' the woman said, 'but that is not the ending.' The woman got up off the bed and gestured for Elizabeth to follow her. Elizabeth did as requested. When she looked around her she found that they were not walking through the house, but, rather, through the bush. It was no longer night time but day time, and they seemed to have been swallowed by brittle, blond, far-reaching elephant grass. The woman stopped abruptly and Elizabeth bumped into her.

A very tall and very white man was holding an AK-47 and aiming it at a young man's forehead.

'Tell the man what you will call the child you carry,' the woman said.

'Vida de Villiers,' Elizabeth said.

'Now tell him what you have been looking for.'

'A giant pair of silver wings.'

Without warning, Elizabeth and the woman were standing in a farm compound watching the very tall and very white man build a giant pair of silver wings as a group of people watched him in awe and reverence. Among the people was a girl who smiled – a gap-toothed smile – at the very tall and very white man and looked at him with so much love and pride.

'They are The Fallen Ones and we are The Keepers of the Flame,' the woman said. 'Our paths will always find ways to entwine.'

Again things shifted, and Elizabeth and the woman found themselves on the corner of a busy intersection in the City of Kings. Just then there was a screech of tyres and together they watched, astonished, as a girl in a blue and white uniform went flying through the air. Obviously this was also a time of miracles because the girl was caught, in the nick of time, by a Scania pushcart that was being pushed by a vagabond. The girl had landed on a quilt, but not just any quilt – the quilt that Elizabeth had just finished making for the baby she was expecting – for Vida. It took a moment for Elizabeth to notice that the vagabond was her very own son, her Vida. But before she could feel any definite emotion about seeing her child in such reduced circumstances, Elizabeth saw the girl in the blue and white uniform smile a gap-toothed smile up at Vida, and she saw Vida smile down at the girl. And then without warning the girl was older, standing in front of Vida as he sat with his back against a wall, and she was blocking the sun.

'You need never worry about the boy because the girl will find him,' the woman said, taking Elizabeth's hands in both of hers and giving them a strong and reassuring squeeze. 'Her mother's name is also Elizabeth.'

When Elizabeth looked around her, they were back in her bedroom, Ezekiel was sleeping peacefully beside her, and morning was breaking. Elizabeth felt a love so overwhelming that she leaned over and kissed Ezekiel with this love. 'Endings always give rise to new beginnings,' the venerable woman with sagacious eyes said. And then she was gone.

INTERLUDE

'*E*ndings *always give rise to new beginnings,' the venerable woman with sagacious eyes said. And then she was gone.* I'm writing these sentences when there is a knock on the door. Daisy enters carrying a bowl of peach mangoes. I see the way she sees me in this moment, which is the way I saw myself in the vision the venerable woman with sagacious eyes showed me – sitting by a table in an unbelievably opulent room, pen in hand, lots of paper all around me as I write and write and write.

Daisy places the bowl of guaranteed sweetness carefully on the table on which I write. 'It's not our wish to disturb you,' she says hesitantly. 'But Alfred is beginning to take it personally that you haven't ventured downstairs since your arrival.'

I'm relieved. For a moment there I thought she was going to tell me that the Good Foundation, my mother, Johanna or Mrs Good had called again. 'Alfred?' I say.

'He's the steward, and he is very eager to show you the castle and all it contains.'

'Then I best not keep him waiting,' I say.

Alfred is a very imposing figure in his black and white uniform. Everything about him is impeccable: the parting of his hair at his left temple is the straightest line, his pristine gloves are the whitest white, his starched collars are the stiffest cotton, his cuffs have been ironed into the sharpest edges. He is slightly stooped by his many years of loyal service and the absolute pride he feels in his vocation.

He shows me the finest silverware, china, crystal, tableware, and uses the word 'genuine' often as he allows me to feel the weight, the delicateness, the texture of the objects he puts in my hands. He is a man for whom the realness of things matters. He watches me closely to see if I appreciate what I behold. I must say all the right things about the weight, the delicateness and the texture of the objects because he smiles his approval, and says he is glad everything is to Madam's liking.

He wants me to rest assured that Holdengarde Castle will be able to meet and, perhaps even, exceed the Good Foundation's expectations. People nowadays, he confides, just want to get married – they no longer throw balls or just go out for an evening of fine dining; they no longer just celebrate life and the joy of living. Every event at the castle is a wedding. And now the churches, these new churches that treat God as a commodity (Alfred has been a devout Anglican all his life) want to hold their services at the castle. He understands the castle has to move along with the flow of time, but he also wishes the people of the City of Kings would uphold certain traditions. He is glad the Good Foundation still appreciates tradition.

As Alfred takes me on the tour of the castle – its Great Hall with its impressive furnishings (proud products of a bygone era); its trophy room (where the petrified head of an elephant frightens me, much to Alfred's amusement); its restaurant and boutique hotel (which are both closed for refurbishment); its kitchen (where Daisy, much to my delight, makes me sample a blue cheese ice cream that tastes a million times better than it sounds); its cellar that houses many great wines (which come from both the Old World and the New); its wildlife sanctuary that is home to impala, monkeys and guineafowl (whose temporary truce only lasts for as long as human eyes are upon them) – he tells me of its incredible history.

Built in the first half of the twentieth century by Eastern Cape-born Theodore Garde, the design and construction of the castle was influenced by his time at Durham University where he studied theology and became an enthusiast for all things medieval. So inspired was he by the Middle Ages that he changed his last name to Holdengarde.

Instead of establishing himself in his native Eastern Cape, he moved to the country up north, put together a construction company, and purchased land on what were then the eastern outskirts of the City of Kings. The land was made up of breathtaking white hills, rocks and caves that had witnessed time and its many mysteries and secrets pass by. Holdengarde had one dream, impossible as it seemed: to build a medieval castle on this piece of land, here in the heart of Africa.

When he became the mayor of the City of Kings, he, his wife Maude, and a few workers began constructing the castle from the white stones that were hand-hewn from the rocks and hills. The remarkable towers, turrets and crenellations, the winding passageways and stairways leading to seemingly strange and mysterious places, the curiosity-filled rooms and lounges – these were not built according to any architectural design or blueprint, but from Holdengarde's recollections of Scottish medieval castles. The building of the castle, for which he never sought nor received approval from the council, was painstakingly slow, not only because it was solely done on weekends, but also because Holdengarde often changed his mind and demolished things to better suit his vision.

Upon completion, the Holdengarde family moved in, and the castle became known as Holdengarde Castle. To stay true to his medieval vision, Holdengarde would not allow the castle to have modern plumbing or electricity. Maude had to wait to take advantage of a trip he took to South Africa to have electricity installed in his absence. Other contemporary amenities were only added after Holdengarde passed away in 1948.

Although mostly a well-kept secret, the fortress that was

Holdengarde Castle could not help but attract the imagination of those in the City of Kings who came to know of it. After Holdengarde died and it fell into gradual disrepair, it became home to various squatters and, at some point, a group of Satanists. Local lore had it that a giant pair of silver wings had once been found in the area, and because of this, the Satanists had believed that this was the place where Lucifer had landed when he was expelled from the heavens.

The Good Foundation's Golden Jubilee held at the castle in 1970 had involved a year's worth of concerted effort from the Pioneer Benevolence Society of the City of Kings, the Settler Society's Women's Auxiliary, the Antiquarian Society and the City Council. The entire affair had involved a not inconsiderable amount of sleight of hand. The country was at war and had desperately needed something good to happen; the Good Foundation had overlooked the sanctions against the country and ensured that that something good did happen. However, even that was not enough to ensure that the castle lived up to the glory of its name.

Luckily in 1988, Digby Nesbitt purchased the ruined castle, renovated it into a boutique hotel replete with a restaurant for fine dining, and opened it to the public in 1990.

I tell Alfred that I visited the castle in 1992, during its days of transformation, when it was still something of a ruin. I don't tell him about my first encounter there with Elizabeth. He tells me that I must be impressed by the way it looks now. I tell him that I am. He is pleased. When we part, I feel like I have made a friend in Alfred.

As I make my way back to the Great Chamber, I think of Holdengarde and Nesbitt; I think of Jakob 'Call me Jack' de Villiers; I think of men and the ability they have to realise their visions no matter how fantastic or impossible they seem at first.

I enter the room with its perfect welcome – a bowl of peach mangoes, their scent soft and enticing in the air. I bite into a mango and wonder where Daisy and her impractical boots are.

As if conjured by my thinking of Daisy, I hear laughter. It seems somewhat out of place. Too loud. I carefully open one of the wooden panels and look outside the window. Daisy is talking to a woman, and this woman is laughing and laughing. She places a hand casually on Daisy's shoulder and throws her head back with more laughter. I can't hear what they're saying to each other from up here – things are whispered between them, secrets kept. And then the woman says, intentionally loud, something about the deliciousness of blue cheese ice cream and how devoted she is to it.

She is used to filling space, this woman. She is used to wanting things and then having them. She is used to having the finest things, and because of this she takes the things she has for granted – beautiful things like Daisy, towards whom she leans and then kisses and kisses and kisses. They draw apart and she walks to her parked car. Her step in this world has always been sure.

I am filled with envy and something ugly ... something dangerous ... something that terrifies me. Long after Daisy has walked back into the castle and the easy-laughing, sure-footed woman has driven away, I stand looking out of the window with the thing that terrifies me as my only companion.

Without warning, the room is filled with the scratching sound. Something sharp repeatedly scrapes against the surface of something dry. Letters appear on the replica of Simone Martini and Lippo Memmi's 'The Annunciation and Two Saints'. The writing on the wall reads:

i have shaped into   myself?   come celebrate

I walk to the ornate mirror and disrobe. Naked, I look at the brown splotch above my heart. An inheritance. I, too, have things that belong to me. I should never forget that. But it doesn't stop me from feeling the pain.

Anything dead coming back to life hurts.

As darkness falls, something moves behind me. I turn around, startled. A woman in an English-rose-coloured, high-collared dress with matching parasol and gloves is walking towards me: Anne.

'A heart is a very fragile and delicate thing,' Anne says, as though continuing a conversation we have been having for a while. And perhaps we have. 'You can never stop it from breaking,' she continues. 'That is why it is important to learn how to hold on to yourself.'

PART III

there are so many of those creeping women,
and they creep so fast.

CHARLOTTE PERKINS GILMAN
– *The Yellow Wallpaper*

THE MISBEGOTTEN WOMAN*

1899–1965

---

* Entered the archive as 'Beloved daughter of a pioneer'.

Once upon a time it had been very easy to be a hero.

On the 4th of November 1893, as the British South Africa Company (BSAC) officially occupied Matabeleland, Patrick H. Battison had been part of the colonial force that nailed a BSAC flag and a tattered and battered Union Jack onto a tree that had survived the smouldering ashes of the King's Kraal.

Knowing that the British forces were approaching, the Matabele king, Lobengula, had earlier set fire to his kraal, destroying ivory, gold and munitions before he, along with his people, fled the site, intentionally scattering the inhabitants of his kingdom throughout the land, and thus making the entire business of conquering them rather difficult.

Still filled with bravura, Patrick, who had arrived in the land of the Matabele in 1890 as part of the Pioneer Column, had joined the patrol led by Major Patrick Forbes that had followed after the king to capture or kill him – which, did not matter. What had mattered then was that a new chapter of history was being written, and Patrick Battison was an active part of it. Although Patrick's patrol had returned without the king, they were fêted upon arrival. His patrol fared better than that of Allan Wilson's, which fell to a man on the 4th of December 1893, in an ambush the Matabele warriors had set on the banks of the Shangani River.

Very much a part of the burgeoning colony, Patrick was there on the 1st of June in 1894 when Dr Leander Starr Jameson, outside the Maxim Hotel on Fife Street, declared the occupied place – the City of Kings – a White Man's Town. Patrick was also there in September of that same year when Cecil John Rhodes invited members of the BSAC to the house he had built on the ruins of King Lobengula's kraal. Because Patrick shook hands and had the occasional word with men whose moment in history this was – Cecil John Rhodes, Leander Starr Jameson, Major Patrick Forbes, Frederick Courteney Selous, Sir John Christopher Willoughby, Frederick Russell Burnham – he could be excused for believing that it was his moment, too.

Patrick saw the City of Kings take on new shape and he indeed felt like a king; and, like a king, he was intent on accumulating wealth. To this end, he acquired some land on which to prospect and mine for minerals, and some land on which to farm and husband livestock. It was what they all wanted – these men called pioneers – land and livestock: a comfortable way to start life in the colony, settle down and grow roots. The Matabele king's scorched-earth policy had definitely benefited the BSAC and the early pioneers, as A.J. Davis, publisher of both the *Sketch* and *Directory and Handbook,* would happily lampoon in 1895:

> *Claim rights, loots, and farm rights, appear to be the staple conversa-*
> *tion. Everyone has Rights except the Matabele, a strange reversal of*
> *affairs in Matabeleland. They wander around, receiving their money's*
> *worth by watching the antics of their dispossessors haggling over*
> *their late goods and chattels upon the morning market. They watch*
> *the Auctioneers putting up farms for sale, then claims, and then*
> *loots. They smile inanely at the wonderful performance and have long*
> *'indabas' at their homes, where perhaps one starts to debate 'whether*
> *it is not worth the spolation to behold such wonderful sights free of*
> *charge.'*

Patrick, along with all the other pioneers in the City of Kings, laughed at Davis' observation without questioning the wisdom or foolishness of such an approach. To the victor and all that. As a member of the BSAC, Patrick did not question anything: he faith-fully followed in the footsteps of the Light Brigade, and allowed the natural flow of things to move in their predestined fashion.

Although Patrick was at home in a town where fraternity, bonhomie and earthly delights were fuelled by a seemingly never-ending flow of alcoholic spirits, he found he was in need of still more glory. So when towards the end of 1894 womenfolk were eventually allowed to trickle into the town, Patrick, dreading the loss of the spirit of the bachelor days, and in no need of a wife himself, went to work on the expansion of the Mafeking railway line. He liked that the work itself was unsettled and kept him moving; kept that glory he was seeking just out of reach … always something desired, but not yet obtained.

And then something more thrilling presented itself. In March of 1896, the Matabele, never having seen the humour in having their land occupied and their property looted, decided to attack the now settled pioneers. The First Matabele War had taught them about the mercilessness of the Maxim gun, and so they changed strategies, opting not for battle but for ambushes and raids. Upon hearing this news, Patrick was so excited by the prospect of another battle that for a moment, just a moment, he took his eyes off what he was doing and caused an accident that nearly cost him his leg and put him out of commission for many months. It turned out that he was not destined to take part in the Second Matabele War or to fight alongside General Frederick Carrington and his chief of staff, Colonel Baden-Powell.

When he was eventually able to walk around the City of Kings again, Patrick found it vastly changed. Men he had left merry only a year earlier were either dead or disillusioned. The survivors circled laagers around their fears until those fears became nightmares, and those nightmares became an ever-present, all-consuming dread.

The reality of the constant threat posed by the natives had made murky all that earlier glory; it had changed the tenor of things. But Patrick did not want things to have changed, he wanted them to have stayed the same: he wanted glory still to be a glorious thing. He believed the pioneering spirit should not be something that ebbed and flowed, but something constant instead. It was because of this belief that he did the thing that would change his life irrevocably.

In 1897, not having been able to fight, Patrick chose to do his part by hanging the men who had been caught taking part in what the settlers chose to call a rebellion. Nine Matabele men in all had to be hanged – three for looting and six for spying. A false marula tree, one of the few surviving indigenous trees in the City of Kings, was chosen to be the hanging tree. Patrick set to work: crack and then snap ... crack and then snap ... crack and then snap ... crack and then snap ... crack and then snap ... crack and then snap ... crack and then snap ... crack and then snap ... crack and then snap.

When war broke out in the Mazowe and Goromonzi areas in the north of the colony, those responsible, namely Nehanda Charwe Nyakasikana and Kaguvi Gumboreshumba, were captured and sentenced to be hanged. A decision was made to preserve their skulls as war trophies that would be sent back to England. Patrick did not hesitate to volunteer to sever their heads and travelled all the way to Fort Salisbury to perform the task. He thought it would be so easy a thing to do. It was only when he had begun the business of decapitating bodies: crack ... and then ... snap ... that he realised how difficult a thing it was to do: crack ... and ... then ... snap ... to make a person lose his or her head.

Crack

and then

snap.

But as difficult a thing as it was to do, Patrick found it was a thing he would have to do more than once, because he was soon chosen to be the town's official executioner. There were not many executions to be carried out in a young colony, but every now and again a man, always a native, committed a crime that saw Patrick place the hangman's noose around his neck.

Crack
and then
snap.

While polite society liked having someone to take care of the messier side of creating order and discipline in the colony, it did not particularly like having that someone attend a dinner party, or play a game of tennis, or join a bicycle club. When Patrick eventually stopped wearing a hat – the mark of a true gentleman – and took to drink, polite society decided that the thing to do was to look the other way. When he started singing to himself, polite society took him to an asylum; and when he was discharged, he was told he needed to wear a hat because the African sun was getting to him. He laughed, swearing he would never wear a hat again, but in truth he laughed because he knew they knew why he sang.

He had just left the asylum when a woman stopped him in the streets. Almost frantic, the woman did away with propriety and placed an ungloved hand on his forearm. She explained to him that she had recently arrived in the City of Kings and seemed to have lost her way. She had asked two men for directions before catching on to the fact that they were undesirables. Now the two men, whom she strongly suspected of not being gentlemen, would not stop accosting her. Would he please help her find her way back to the Charter Hotel?

Patrick looked at her and waited for her to notice that he did not have a hat on his head – that he himself was an undesirable. But she did not; or if she did, then she did not care to mind. So Patrick offered her his arm and protection, and together they walked to the Charter Hotel. Polite society looked at them with surprise and wonder, and Patrick realised that he could still have a wife, if he so desired – and he found he suddenly did desire it very much. And that is how Patrick's life took an unexpected turn – because of a case of mistaken identity.

Her name was Victoria, and by the time Patrick left her at the hotel, he knew he would marry her – but that he would not marry her while he remained the executioner of the City of Kings. A few months after their knowing of each other, when Victoria informed Patrick that she was expecting, he knew he would have to change everything about himself; and that for that to happen, he would have to do more than just change his vocation – he would have to quiet the crack ... and then ... snap: he would have to find his way back to being a gentleman. It would not do to be just a man – a poor European man was absolutely no use to anyone in the colonies, and Patrick knew this much to be true. He was going to have to be wealthy. Money took care of many things. Patrick wanted to believe it could take care of the crack ... and then ... snap. He remembered that he had land claims to his name and, just as quickly, he remembered that the more generous members of polite society had offered to take them off his hands soon after he had stopped wearing his hat, and that they had done so quite easily.

The executioner's lodgings were on the outskirts of the town. In his minuscule room, above the washbasin, was a small, tarnished mirror with jagged edges, hanging from a crucifix looped around a nail. He did not own the mirror because he was a vain man; he owned the mirror because he sometimes needed to remind himself that he was still a man. He lit the candle that was sitting atop the basin, and in the poor light, he looked at his reflection. Did he look like a hangman or did he just look like a man – a man who had not taken care of himself in some time, but a man nonetheless? He understood then that when you are told that you are one thing and you believe it, it takes a miracle for you to know otherwise.

Patrick blew out the candle and went to lie down on the thin self-made mattress that was his bed. Next to Patrick's lodgings was the settlement where Coloured wagon drivers who transported people and goods along the Mafeking Road lived while the oxen rested for weeks before journeying back to the Union of South Africa. He knew the area very well from his days of working on the railway line. As he listened to the rabble-rousing of the wagon drivers, he started imagining another life for himself; a life that had everything to do with the road more travelled. All kinds of traffic journeyed along the Mafeking Road.

A new town like the City of Kings was constantly changing as dreams were relinquished and hopes were dashed: people came and went, and the frenzy made things, people, faces, names and old circumstances easy to forget. A place in continuous flux cannot hold on to memory. And on the foundation of this knowledge, Patrick's plan built itself. In a few years he would return as a man who had made his fortune in Kimberley.

On the 2nd of November in the year 1900, somewhere along the Mafeking Road, a mail coach travelling from the Transvaal carrying gold bars worth twelve thousand pounds in an African Banking Corporation specie box was robbed by a masked bandit on horseback, according to the coachman and guard.

The robbery should have been easy enough. Besides the coachman, there should have been the guard, armed and protecting the box with his life. That was what the bandit had prepared for. But none of it went according to plan. Instead of stopping, the coachman galloped the mules as he tried to outpace the bandit on horseback, lost control of the coach, and was thrown over along with all of the luggage. Everything after that was chaos. The guard, who had been sleeping when the whole business began, was so disoriented that he had no time to fully appreciate what was going on when the bandit briefly blinded him by shining the sun's reflection on a mirror into his face. It was the bandit who succeeded in stopping the mules, and he did so just in time, before one of the coach's wheels came off.

When the bandit opened the door of the lopsided coach, he found within it not just a dazed guard, but a Reverend and Mrs Jasper Adair and their five-year-old daughter, Rosalind 'Rosa' Adair. The coachman had taken pity on the young family and allowed them to travel with him as passengers – even though, given his cargo, he was forbidden to do so. The Adairs – a missionary couple who had been left stranded in Mafeking when the ox wagon that was supposed to transport them to Matabeleland did not arrive – had come to the colonies to save black souls, and therefore did not know what to do about a white man whose soul needed saving. They had been told to be afraid of everything in darkest Africa, but had not been warned of highwaymen. They hugged their daughter and did not say a word, not even a prayer, as the bandit left with the specie box.

For the coach travellers, the story ended relatively well, considering. Another coach came along approximately two hours later and found the coachman, the guard and the Adair family, collecting as many of the things that had been thrown out the coach as they could find. They were all alive, but not without worry: the coachman worried about how he would explain the presence of the Adair family to his superiors; the guard worried about how he would justify having been so dazed as to let go of the specie box; the Reverend and Mrs Adair worried that perhaps they should have stayed in the Cape Colony with its long history of civilising missions; the girl, Rosa, worried that they would never find the head of her Victorian doll – she had found its body, but, hard as she had searched, she could not find the doll's head with its pink cheeks, red lips, blonde hair and blue eyes. She could not possibly have known that where it now lay, the doll's head had a lazy eye that looked like it was always winking at you.

The remainder of the journey to the City of Kings happened without incident, except that Rosa noticed that her favourite shawl – the one with her name embroidered on it, the one she had lovingly wrapped around her doll – was missing. She did not have much time to care about the missing shawl because once the mail coach arrived at its destination, the story of the robbery and the subsequent investigation became a cause célèbre for almost two years. The Reverend and Mrs Jasper Adair – who had to re-imagine themselves as heroes, even though they had done nothing besides protect their daughter – became overnight sensations. The Adairs – whether because they loved the attention or because they genuinely feared venturing further into the colony and establishing a mission along the Zambesi River as they were supposed to – never left the City of Kings.

Rosa Adair's photograph was reproduced in *The Chronicle*, at great expense to the newspaper. Her golden curls and blue eyes, although printed in grainy black and white, tugged at so many heartstrings that the photograph was reproduced several times. Rosa received such an embarrassment of Victorian dolls to make up for her close brush with death that she eventually threw away the decapitated doll and forgot all about her missing shawl.

It should be noted here that the Rosa Adair made famous by the mail coach robbery is not the subject of this story. That Rosa Adair lived a very long and happy life. She was considered a great beauty for most of her life. She married twice, was widowed once, and divorced once, after which she took back her maiden name. Her first marriage took her to Bechuanaland. Her second marriage took her to Nyasaland. She had five children whom she loved to varying degrees. Somewhere along the way she became an agnostic, and then an atheist. It was then that she came back to the City of Kings and lived there the rest of her days until she met Jesus on the 18th of April 1980. She died peacefully in her sleep later that night.

The Rosa Adair that this story is concerned with is yet to come into the picture, and for that to happen, we have to return to Patrick Battison's story.

In 1903, Patrick Battison returned to the City of Kings a wealthy man. He told a convincing, if vague, story about the Anglo-Boer War and a chance discovery of diamonds in Kimberley on a claim that he had all but forgotten. Upon his return, almost at the very moment of it, he married Victoria with whom he had been in regular correspondence over the years. Immediately after her wedding, Victoria purchased a chatelaine and a pair of opera glasses, thus announcing to polite society that she had officially arrived. The Battisons and their daughter, Anne, moved to a bungalow house in Suburbs. Patrick and Victoria were regularly invited to dinner at all the best houses in the City of Kings. Victoria played tennis. Patrick joined a bicycle club.

One of Anne's most favourite things was a shawl her father gave her with the name 'Rosa Adair' embroidered on it. It may surprise you that Patrick displayed his loot so brazenly, but he knew that immense wealth often blinded people – both the people who had it and the people who desired it. It may surprise you that Victoria, knowing the story of the Adairs, did not ask questions about the origins of the shawl, but who is to say what was contained in their long correspondence, and that she did not already know the answers to those questions? Something must have given her, an unprotected young mother in the colonies, the confidence to have a child and wait for that child's father to return and marry her. What may not surprise you is that Anne became fascinated with the idea of Rosa Adair.

The Battisons lived happily together until the day a mail coach ran over Victoria after she alighted from a jinricksha and was crossing the ever-busy Selborne Avenue. It was never clear how such an accident had somehow managed to sever her head from the rest of her body, but it did. It is a good thing that polite society was not given to superstition. This, of course, is not to say that Patrick H. Battison himself was not.

Crack ... and then ... snap.

The bottom is easy to find, especially when you are a man not used to being at the top. Patrick mourned his wife, neglected his daughter, gambled voraciously, and speculated widely. But while he was doing all this he promised himself that no matter how far he sank, he would not take to drink. He had a daughter, and while he had delegated her mostly to the care of the Pioneer Benevolence Society of the City of Kings, he did not want her to have to suffer the public humiliation of having a drunk for a father.

The year was 1911, a white woman in Umtali alleged that a black man had raped her, and the City of Kings – no, the entire Union of South Africa – was outraged, so no one noticed when Patrick stopped wearing his hat. A united front was needed now more than ever as evidenced by a widely circulated pamphlet, which had been sent to the city fathers via telegram:

Extenuating Circumstances!
Negro Rapeing of White Women, excused!

SOUTH AFRICA has suffered from the stupidity of many past Governors, playing Skittles with Questions of Vital Interest to its inhabitants.

The most Stupid, if not Criminal, of all these mistakes is the 'latest,' viz., the EXCUSING of Negro Rapeing of European Ladies.

South Africa cannot afford to have its vital interests played with by well-intentioned, but weak, sentimental Governors.

Of course, if Viscount Gladstone wishes to take into his personal service a few Negroes addicted to the gentle pastime of RAPE, we shall have nothing more to say, but we hope he will take them away with him at the earliest possible moment.

Port Elizabeth, January 23ʳᵈ, 1911.   **WILLIAM COLSON.**

It was generally decided, in the City of Kings, that there had to be a petition requesting that the High Commissioner reverse his decision. Patrick, like most of the white men in the city, attended a meeting where the petition was signed by all the men there. All the white men not in attendance were also given an opportunity to sign the petition before it was sent to the High Commissioner. In all, the petition was signed by 560 white men in the City of Kings.

While Patrick could leave the care of his twelve-year-old daughter to the Pioneer Benevolence Society of the City of Kings during the day, in the evenings his only recourse was to leave her with the boys – the cook boy or houseboy – and as no one thought this was a particularly good idea in the current climate, he took Anne with him to the white-men-only meeting.

After that initial meeting, other meetings were called, and Patrick attended them. In those meetings, letters written by an obedient servant were read:

25th January,   11

His Honour the Resident Commissioner,
    Salisbury.

Sir,

UMTALI RAPE CASE:

I am directed to forward you the following copy of a
Resolution unanimously passed at a Public Meeting held in
the City of Kings on the 23rd instant, with reference to the
above, and to request that you will be good enough to trans-
mit the same to His Excellency the High Commissioner –

'RESOLVED, that in view of His Excellency the High
Commissioner's commutation of the sentence of death
recently pronounced upon the native Alukuleta,
alias Valeta, convicted of rape upon a white woman at
Umtali upon the clearest evidence and under circumstances which induced the presiding Judge to inform
the prisoner that he could hold out no hope of mercy,

This meeting of the public of the City of Kings and
district respectfully, but most emphatically, protest against His Excellency's interference with the
course of a law which his predecessors in Office have
recognised should, in the special circumstances of
this country, be most strictly enforced, and they feel
that this course of action on His Excellency's part is
calculated to result in the most serious consequences both in regard to the frequency of the crime and
in regard to provoking the white inhabitants of this
country into breaches of "law and order."'

I have the honour to be,

Sir,

Your obedient servant,

Act. Town Clerk.

After the Matabele Wars of 1893 and 1896, the City of Kings, indeed the entire colony, had not had much need for an executioner

– but there seemed to be a need for one now. The men at the second meeting turned to Patrick. If the High Commissioner succumbed to pressure, which he surely would, would Patrick be willing to travel to Umtali and hang Alukuleta? No better hangman in the entire Union, as far as they were concerned – Patrick Battison did not only hang a man, he decapitated him as well.

After that meeting, Patrick took Anne home, went to a bar – the Bodega – and allowed himself just a little drink, a sip of something, to quiet that sound: that crack … and then … snap.

But all too soon he was at another meeting, listening to the reading of yet another letter from an obedient servant:

Rand Pioneers (Incorporated).

Johannesburg Club Building,
Fox Street,

Johannesburg, 30th. January, 1911.

To
>   HIS WORSHIP THE MAYOR,
>   CITY OF KINGS.

Sir,

At a Special Meeting of the Committee of the Rand Pioneers, Convened this day to consider what action, if any, my Committee should take in regard to the Umtali rape case. It was resolved to forward to you an expression of their deep sympathy with the Colonists, and the offer of their most cordial co-operation, should the need for such arise at any time.

My Committee have always taken and maintained the strongest views on cases such as the one under review. They have but one principle, from which they cannot swerve, and it is that any attempt at rape by a native on a white woman must be punished with death. They cannot accept no such a plea as drunkenness in vindication of the attempt. They feel that their first consideration is for the honour of the Women of South Africa; and nothing that can be advanced by humanitarians or negrophilists will prevent them from insisting that the Native must be taught at all costs, that the person of a white woman is to be held sacred and inviolable.

My Committee have for years past pressed these views on responsible officials, including High Commissioners, Lieutenant Governors and Attorney Generals.

My Committee desire to assure you of their unalterable determination to prevent as best they may the interference of any person or party in carrying out what they deem an absolutely necessary punishment, and the vindication of the rightsof the white race.

In conclusion, my Committee have instructed me to inform you that they have always set their faces against mob law, and have before now intervened to prevent the holding of public meetings where inflammatory speeches might be made; illegal associations formed and measures of retribution adopted, which would cast a slur upon the hitherto well-deserved record of South Africans as law abiding citizens – still, representing as they do, a body who understand the South African problems to a degree impossible to ordinary officials and over-sea idealists, they will continue to insist that their views shall always be fully considered, and are prepared to use pressure to have them carried out when it can be done so legally.

I have the honour to be,

Sir,

Your obedient servant,

Mr Pitts

<u>Secretary.</u>

At this meeting, Patrick was visibly drunk. Luckily, he had found a lonely widow with whom he could leave Anne with in the evenings, so she did not have to witness the embarrassment and disappointment of the other men in attendance.

Another meeting, another letter from an obedient servant:

Office of the Mayor,
P.O. Box 1049, Johannesburg,
20th February, 1911.

The Mayor
of the City of Kings

DEAR SIR,

I have the honour to inform you that at a public meeting convened by me in response to a requisition signed by a large number of enrolled voters of this Municipality to protest against the prevalent outrages against white females by natives, and held at Johannesburg on the 7th inst., the following resolutions were adopted: —

1. This Meeting emphatically declares: —
   (a) That the honour of our womenfolk is sacred and must be protected.
   (b) That the penalty for attempted rape should be death.
   (c) That increased Police Protection is imperative.
   (d) That the gradual elimination of the male native domestic servant is essential.
2. That the Mayor forward copies of these resolutions to His Excellency the Governor–General, all Members of the Union Government, all Members of Parliament and

of Provincial Councils, and all Municipal Councils
in South Africa.

I have the honour to be,
Sir,
Your obedient Servant,

Hofmeyr
Mayor of Johannesburg.

At this meeting, Patrick started singing and disrupted the proceedings. He was not asked to return for another meeting.

The High Commissioner never did succumb to the pressure;
his decision was never reversed.

After a while, life went back to what it had been – whatever that
was – but everything had changed for Patrick. He had gambled
or speculated everything away, he went about without his hat,
he sang in the streets and slept there some nights, but this time
polite society would not let him be: they propped him up, gave
him gainful employment, saw to the education of his daughter.
They did this in part because he had once been wealthy, and
because he was now a father with responsibilities, but they did
it mostly because he was something they had come to value: he
was a pioneer. If the Black Peril had taught the citizens of the City
of Kings anything, it was that a solid community, one with deep
roots, was important.

There is safety in numbers.

So, when Anne Battison started claiming that she was the 'real'
Rosa Adair and that she had the shawl to prove it, the City of
Kings chose not to question her, decided that 'eccentricity' ran in
the family, and took to calling her by that name. By this time, the
real Rosa Adair had already married and moved to Bechuanaland.

Anne was a pleasant girl with a good head on her shoulders and a very kind heart that forgave too many things. Over the years, Patrick had stopped being able to count how many times she had searched the town for him, and found him in some bar or some dingy den or in some dark and dank sanitary lane. She always looked for him and she always found him. She always brought him home – whatever they were calling home that week, that month, that year – *she* never let *him* down.

The truth was that Anne protected Patrick more than he protected her. She saved him from himself – from dying alone, cold, unwelcome and unwanted. Patrick was not sure he wanted to be saved. Did he not deserve to die alone and abandoned, like a thing long forgotten? Regardless of what he thought and felt, Anne would keep saving him. She could not even begin to comprehend his wanting to let go. And so he let her protect and save him, even though he liked the responsibility of staying alive for her more than he liked staying alive.

It was not just Anne who wanted him to stay alive, however; it was the entire City of Kings. And so he took the job that had been found for him at the Avenue Hotel. Of all the many hotels that one could work at in the City of Kings, the Avenue Hotel was one of the best; it was after all, as mentioned in the directory, 'under the distinguished patronage of Their Excellences Lord & Lady Buxton'. Only the most discriminating and discerning denizens patronised the establishment. Patrick knew this because he had been given the position of concierge. To make him look more a part of his environs, and probably also to make people look past his red-tipped nose and bloodshot eyes, the proprietor had fitted him in refined livery that made him look like a former military man – but made him feel like a clown.

Patrick was determined to hold onto the Avenue Hotel job for as long as possible because one of the conditions of the job was that, as long as he had it, the Pioneer Benevolence Society of the City of Kings would pay for Anne's typing classes at Miss C.E. Cardwell's Typing Office on Main Street. Anne also worked at the front desk of the Avenue Hotel on the weekends, and sometimes in the evenings when the hotel was at its busiest.

Father and daughter each occupied a room below stairs, and all their meals were provided by the hotel. They slept in quarters and ate at tables that were segregated from the native employees so that even though they technically lived with many people, in a number of ways, they still had only each other in the world. They had been at the hotel for almost two years when the thing that no one ever spoke about happened.

It was probably because things were going well that Patrick allowed himself to relax, become comfortable and therefore less vigilant – at least that is how he later explained to himself his inability to see The Three Gentlemen From Blantyre for what they really were. He had long since learnt never to trust a man with too much money in his pocket and eyes that never settled on anything, but although The Three Gentlemen From Blantyre were wealthy and shifty-eyed, it never occurred to Patrick to warn Anne about them.

It was not because he had been duped by their top hats, silk cravats and white gloves that he failed to caution Anne; it was because to him, Anne was a daughter and not a young woman of eighteen. And so he did not notice how pretty the good head on her shoulders was, how she always paid extra attention to a particular kind of male customer – young, handsome, single and presumably ready to do what she was ready to do, which was settle down – or when that particular kind of male customer paid her the same extra attention.

Because Patrick did not discern that she was no longer suited to the rather nomadic life he had had them live, he did not detect how she was prone to smile her dimpled smile or bat her lovely eyelashes when the particular kind of male customer leaned forward and whispered something in her ear. In short, Patrick did not observe that at eighteen, Anne was not only a young woman, but one whose type of beauty was not only much sought after, but often used to make a most advantageous match – a match that could make her typing classes unnecessary. Perhaps it was a blessing of sorts that Patrick did not notice any of this, because the truth of the matter was that as soon as this particular kind of male customer realised that the red-nosed concierge was Anne's father, he invariably thought twice about his intentions towards her.

Beyond Victoria, Patrick had never really been good at noticing things about women, but once his daughter started becoming a woman he may have tried to understand them. Another man, another father, would have understood that the girl whom he had haphazardly raised had left girlhood behind – and instead of doing everything in his power to lose himself, he could have tried doing everything in his power to help Anne find herself.

On that fateful day, Patrick had, as always, listened to the crack … and then … snap … and found his way to the Bodega, where he had drunk himself into a welcome oblivion. When the bartender shook him awake a little before eleven p.m., Patrick was not too worried that Anne had failed to come and fetch him because he did not know that earlier that evening, while on her way to the Bodega, Anne had come across The Three Gentlemen From Blantyre.

Although Anne knew instinctively not to trust wealthy men with shifty eyes, she had trusted these three men for several reasons:

they were from such a prominent family that their visit to the City of Kings had been written about in *The Chronicle*; they had been living as guests at the hotel for nearly a month; the older two were close to her father's age; and she and the youngest gentleman – a young man of twenty-one – had been speaking of love for a fortnight and had already had intimate relations. So when The Three Gentlemen From Blantyre had asked if they could join her, Anne had not hesitated in allowing them to accompany her in her search.

In the Bodega, Patrick stood up unsteadily, swerved and stumbled his way to the coat and hat rack, found his hat and coat, and smiled. He was glad to see that he was still wearing a hat, as this meant that another trip to the asylum was not imminent. He put on his coat and hat before he swerved and stumbled his way out of the saloon-type swinging double doors (which took some doing) and into the cold night air.

With the innate and impressive sense of direction that all true drunks have, he staggered his way through the town until he found his way to the front door of the Avenue Hotel, through the foyer, down the stairs, into his room and onto his bed where he plopped face down and snored through the rest of the night – unaware, absolutely oblivious, of the fact that in the sanitary lane of one of the streets he had stumbled along, Anne was creeping with blood on her lips and in her mouth … creeping … creeping … creeping around and over the young gentleman from Blantyre who was fighting for his dear life … and losing.

When the proprietor of the Avenue Hotel shook Patrick awake at ten the next morning, Patrick apologised without knowing what he was apologising for because he had no idea what time or what day it was. He jumped out of bed and made a disorganised show of getting ready. Because he had an audience, he found himself putting both feet into his trousers at once. He remembered to brush his teeth, but forgot to do likewise to his hair. As the proprietor was still in the room, there was no time to shave, and so Patrick's stubbly and dishevelled appearance would have to do until such a time as he could come back below stairs and set it to rights.

The proprietor had watched him calmly, had not rushed him, and had refused to accept his apologies. Patrick began to suspect that there was something wrong. This was the calm before the storm. He was, rightfully, being severed from his position, and the proprietor would only do so once Patrick had made himself presentable and respectable. Patrick reached for and put on his hat and waited for the proprietor to deliver the news.

'If you are ready,' the proprietor said. 'I will drive you to the Private Hospital myself.'

'Private Hospital?' Patrick asked, wondering if the Private Hospital was a place that tried to treat drunks.

'Yes ... the cook – Da Costa – found Anne early this morning. Luckily there were some natives who work for the Sanitary Board collecting refuse and cleaning out slop buckets and chamber pots in the area at the time. They were able to use their wagon to take her to the hospital ... and the young man as well.'

Patrick sat down on the edge of his bed. He could not comprehend what he was being told. 'The young man?'

'Yes. The young man. He is alive, thank God. But barely ... something very unfortunate has happened to him. Very unfortunate, indeed.'

'The young man?'

'Yes. The young man. He is a guest here ... one of the three gentlemen from Blantyre. You know the group. One of them is Sylvester Pemberton.'

'Sylvester Pemberton?'

'Yes, Sylvester Pemberton. But he is not the one that the unfortunate thing has happened to.'

Patrick had had enough of this puzzle. 'Anne – where is Anne?'

'In the hospital. As is the young man.'

'I don't care about the young man.'

'Of course, of course ... quite right. Quite right. It's just that Sylvester Pemberton ... but you are quite right, of course, quite right. It's why I'm here. To take you to the Private Hospital.'

Patrick, still not sure what was happening, stood up unsteadily.

'Such a very unfortunate thing to happen to such a young fellow,' the proprietor said, leading Patrick out of his quarters.

'Sylvester Pemberton?'

'No, no ... the young fellow. The one who had formed an attachment to Anne. That's the thing I cannot fathom. She seemed to like him. She really seemed to like him.'

None of this was elucidating matters. Although Patrick did not know what had happened, he knew it was the kind of thing that would make him lose his hat and start to sing.

The proprietor drove Patrick to the Private Hospital and led him to a private suite. The entire hospital had an overwhelming antiseptic smell that churned Patrick's stomach. He looked at the battered, broken, bruised, bloated and bandaged body on the hospital bed and wondered why he had been brought to this room, and not to Anne's room.

'Where's Anne? You said you were bringing me to Anne.'

The proprietor looked at him and then looked away, and that is how Patrick began to grasp what had happened.

Patrick looked at his daughter lying there. She had black and blue bruises all over her face and body. One of her eyes was half shut. She had bandages on her hands. She looked at him, but did not see him; she looked straight through him. Patrick still had no idea what had happened to her, but he knew that he had let her down. He looked at her bruises – black ... and blue.

'I take it you have some money saved, the Private Hospital ... expenses,' the proprietor said.

Patrick blinked at the proprietor. He was surprised to see how small a man he really was. At the hotel, because he commanded so much respect and deference, he seemed taller, stouter. But here in the hospital room, out in the world, he was a small man. Patrick blinked at him again.

'The hotel will pay for all expenses, of course,' the proprietor said. 'You need not worry about the expense. The hotel will pay … the hotel will pay.'

The hotel had not paid, at least not the way the proprietor had implied it would. The cook, Benedito da Costa, had rallied other members of the kitchen and hotel staff, and they had put together enough money to pay for Anne's hospital bill. The proprietor insisted that he be the one to go to the hospital and pay.

Although the story of what had happened in that sanitary lane on that fateful night was whispered about for many years in the City of Kings, it was never openly talked about, and never reported in *The Chronicle*. When the young man who had had a very unfortunate thing happen to him had left with Sylvester Pemberton and the other gentleman from Blantyre, he had the sympathies of most of the City of Kings.

As he told it, he and Anne Battison had struck up an acquaintance during his stay at the hotel. They had even had intimate relations once or twice before that incident in the sanitary lane. After meeting Anne, he had written to his mother and told her that he had met the woman he would marry. All he had done was accompany Anne to go and retrieve her drunk of a father from a bar, and as soon as the other two gentlemen from Blantyre had left them, she had lured him into the sanitary lane and attacked him like some … madwoman … some … vampire.

The Pembertons of Blantyre wanted the girl put in an asylum. But although he assured them that his sympathies were firmly with them and the young man, the proprietor of the Avenue Hotel explained that the girl's father had already spent a fair amount of time in an asylum, that her mother had died tragically, and that, after what had happened, the girl would be untouchable – she had suffered and would continue to suffer. The Pembertons liked the idea of the girl forever suffering, as their son would also forever suffer, and begrudgingly let the matter rest at that.

For her part, Anne Battison waited. She waited for the City of Kings, for the colony, for the Union of South Africa, to be outraged. She remembered those two meetings she had attended with her father in 1911 – meetings that had been all about the sanctity of the white female body, and how it had to be protected against violation. She had been violated. That young man from Blantyre, whom she had thought she would marry, had tried to force her to do something unnatural in a sanitary lane.

Yes, she had had intimate relations with him twice before, but that had been on the sheets of her bed at the Avenue Hotel – that had been normal, natural. But to have wanted to do something like what he had wanted to do, and in a sanitary lane of all places – in a dangerous, dark, dank place smelling of refuse and shameful things – to have placed his hand on the neck of the woman he said he loved, to have choked and beaten her when she refused to do what he wanted, to have used all his strength to force her down to her knees?

Anne had bit down as hard as she could, and then waited for the outrage.

All Anne got from the City of Kings, from the colony, from the Union of South Africa, was silence. What about the sanctity of *her* white female body? Was she not worthy as other white women were worthy? What was wrong with her? Why was it alright for something like this to happen to her? If something like this had happened to Rosa Adair, *The Chronicle* would have written about it – after all, they had written, week after week, about how nothing had happened to her during the mail coach robbery in 1900.

Anne had grown up looking at the newspaper cuttings of that robbery, kept in a chest by her father. She had Rosa Adair's blonde hair and blue eyes. She had a shawl with the name Rosa Adair embroidered on it. She had, on many occasions after her mother had tragically died, taken to imagining a life as Rosa Adair. Rosa Adair did not have a father who drank, forgot to wear his hat, and sang in the streets; Rosa Adair had the perfect life, the kind of life where even its nothingness deserved to be written about in *The Chronicle*.

When the City of Kings, the colony and the Union of South Africa chose silence over outrage in response to what had happened to her in the sanitary lane, Anne Battison decided to be the real Rosa Adair. Rosa Adair deserved to live every day of her life unmolested.

Although the meeting did not go at all well, Rosa was very happy to have agreed to meet one Edward Halliwell. True, he was something of a disappointment, but he was not an altogether bad-looking man. In fact, if he trimmed away all that wild hair and that ferocious beard, why, he could be positively good-looking. But he was just a man who, like many others in this forsaken place, believed that because they lived the rough-and-tumble life of miners and mavericks, they could be forgiven for eschewing grooming and cultivation altogether.

Rosa knew and understood the men of this young colony very well. They were happier and much more comfortable in the company and camaraderie of other men than they would ever be with women. In fact, that was being too kind; they were completely unsettled by women and their finer feelings and sensibilities, and were therefore prone to do more harm than good in any encounter between the sexes. But even knowing this, Rosa kept agreeing to have lunch with the young men that the Pioneer Benevolence Society of the City of Kings put her in the way of meeting.

Edward Halliwell, Rosa was happy to find, did not have any dirt under his fingernails, so there was hope for him yet. There was nothing that she abhorred more than a man with dirt under his fingernails – the one who had pushed Anne down and held her by the neck had had dirt under his fingernails. But those were Anne's memories, not hers.

Whatever hope there was for Edward Halliwell, it soon became obvious that he was uncultured in the ways of conversation – what kind of man talked about carriages and only about carriages before he became properly acquainted with a lady? What kind of man talked about carriages and only about carriages even when he *was* acquainted with a lady? This talk of carriages was even worse than a man who talked solely about himself and his accomplishments – as the young man from Blantyre had done – because it was really conversing about something that did not matter. But again, those were Anne's memories, not hers.

'My name is Rosa Adair, not Anne. You keep calling me Anne,' Rosa had said, interrupting Edward Halliwell. He must have felt chastened, because after that he had made it a point to show a faint spark of interest in her.

'You surely must agree with me that the automobile is but a fad. Nothing can replace the importance of a horse in a man's life,' he had said.

'Not even a carriage?' she had teased.

He had laughed heartily at that, and Rosa had seen a glimmer of hope. A man who could laugh at himself would be easy to live with. But then Edward Halliwell had gone and spoiled it all, adding insult to injury by not understanding why she had been so upset at the treatment she had received at the New Rhodes Hotel.

'But you are not a qualified typist,' Edward Halliwell said. 'You've just told me that you never completed your course of study. They were well within their rights not to give you the job.

'That is not why they did not give me the job,' Rosa said.

Edward Halliwell shrugged and then fell silent.

Rosa hated his silence. He seemed to have shown interest in her only to cause offence, which was a failing in him she could never forgive. It would not matter how good-looking he might become after he had been tamed because there was no remedy for how very ill-mannered he was.

Rosa wished she could create the fulfilling life she needed to have on her own, but knew that in order to be truly safe in the world, she would always need the protection of a man. Now that her father was in the asylum more often than not, she needed to find another man to protect her. Edward Halliwell was not the man she was looking for.

Almost as soon as the third course had been placed before them, the uncouth Edward Halliwell looked at his pocket watch and suddenly remembered a prior engagement. A new carriage all the way from James H. Birch in Burlington, New Jersey was being delivered to Grieve & Napier on Grey Street, and he had been invited to see it before it went on general sale. He apologised profusely (but not nearly enough), got up, encouraged her to continue the rest of the meal, and then paid the bill without knowing how much it came to exactly. What sort of man did such a thing? A man who lived in the City of Kings and had been irrevocably shaped by the ways of the colony, came Rosa's ready answer.

Mortified, once Edward Halliwell was gone, Rosa saw no reason to stay behind and conspicuously continue eating a meal with only shame as her companion. And so she too arose from the table in time to make it seem as though they had decided to leave together, and that he had gone ahead of her to hail a taxi or call for his carriage. With a forced and frozen smile on her face, she made her way out of the Carleton Café and ran smack into the man – Simeon Simon – who would change her life by providing her with both what she wanted and what she needed.

Simeon Simon was the proud owner of the S.S. Aerated Water Factory. When they had bumped into each other, neither of them had been looking where they were going – Rosa because she had been putting on a pair of long gloves, and Simeon because he was trying to gauge how popular an aerated drink flavoured with passion fruit would be – and this was a good thing because it ensured that Rosa Adair and Simeon Simon found each other.

Unlike all the other men that Rosa had had the misfortune of meeting, Simeon Simon was a true gentleman. On that first meeting, after he made sure she was alright, he removed his hat, bowed so deeply that she saw the top of his silver-haired head, and then apologised to her most charmingly and becomingly before asking her if she would oblige him by joining him for dinner that evening. Even though she could see the ring on his finger, and even though she knew that a Mrs S. Simon was a member of the Pioneer Benevolence Society of the City of Kings, Rosa did not even have to think about how she was going to respond to his invitation.

Sometimes you just know that something is right.

Rosa Adair and Simeon Simon had dinner that evening, and many evenings after that, until he died unexpectedly, but contentedly, on the 17th of February 1920 (which, coincidentally, is the same day that the Grand Duchess Anastasia of Russia was discovered in an asylum after a failed suicide attempt). Simeon Simon died in the bed he had shared with Rosa most nights, in the suite, above stairs, in which he had set her up in in the opulent Grand Hotel. It was a happy ending.

Never, not once, did Simeon Simon call Rosa Adair by the name Anne Battison.

Through Simeon Simon, Rosa Adair came into full being. Even though it was a decade or two after the trend, he turned her into a Gibson Girl: blonde hair piled high on top of her head in a chignon, eyelids in various shades of shadow, dreamy eyes permanently hooded, cheeks rouged into the picture of perfect health, painted lips constantly pouting or smiling, waist warped into wasp-like proportions by an S-bend corset. Rosa Adair was sensational.

Simeon Simon believed that her skin was too precious for plain municipal water, and had her bathe in mineral water he aerated himself and delivered to the Grand Hotel. Rosa would fill the tub with the aerated mineral water and as the bubbles tickled and kissed her skin, she would feel that she was being cleansed, that her old self and all that had happened to it was being sloughed off, and that the many sins that had been visited upon that old self were being washed away. Every day was a baptism.

Simeon Simon, bless his sweet heart, did not stop there. Even though she was his kept woman (and she was well aware that there were other names for women like her, none of them kind), he made sure she was not only seen, but seen with him at the theatre, at the societies, at the clubs. They travelled together by motor car or rail to the Matopos, the Victoria Falls, the Eastern Highlands, the Cape, to all the S.S. Spas that practised and showcased the curative powers of aerated mineral water.

Simeon's wife, Augusta, did not mind this arrangement at all. She had her horses, she had her garden, and she had her grand-children (in that order) to occupy her heart and time. She was made of stern stuff, and was determined that her response would have the right degree of decorum and poise. Butter would not melt and all that. All she asked was that when something truly important – like a governor's visit or a dinner party held by Lord and Lady Buxton – took place, she be the one to accompany her husband. Rosa would have loved to attend these grander affairs, but contented herself with the knowledge that she already had far too many things to be content about.

Simeon Simon bought Rosa actual silk fashions from the Pohoomull Bros establishment, and made sure that McAdie & Innes and the American High-Class Ladies' and Gents' tailors kept her wardrobes bursting with the most elegant attire. He bedecked her with jewels that had been in his family for generations, and bought her a few pieces of her very own – like the diamond tiara with matching necklace and bracelet from W.H. Blackler she wore to the screening of the first picture show in the colony. To keep her entertained, he bought her her own pianoforte, a Bechstein, from Laurence & Cope, which she played very often, but not altogether well.

During her all-too-few years with Simeon Simon, the names of things came to matter very much to Rosa Adair. For instance, a man was a man to be sure, but an Edward Halliwell, or a man from Blantyre, was not a Simeon Simon, and never would be. A woman was a woman to be sure, but an Anne Battison was not a Rosa Adair, and never would be.

So, yes, although the meeting with Edward Halliwell had not gone at all well, Rosa would be eternally grateful to him because he had led her to the man who would make it possible for her to hold on to the part of herself that wanted to survive.

The ever-elusive part of Patrick that wanted to survive had worn so thin that the desire to obtain a rope was strong. It had started when the first letter from the Pioneers' & Early Settlers' Society had arrived at the Avenue Hotel. Crack ... and then ... snap. Patrick had not opened it, but, upon receiving it, had begun to think that it was time to prepare for the ending. By then, Anne had left the hotel. He had waited until it was clear that she would not be returning. When he had recently come across her looking like a very fine lady as she alighted from a carriage, she had looked straight through him; and he had known then, with a certainty that he had not possessed for a long time, that it was time to let go. She had protected him from himself – from dying alone, cold, unwelcome and unwanted – and he had not protected her from a young man from Blantyre. After what had happened to Anne, did he not deserve to die alone and abandoned like a thing long forgotten?

With Anne gone, Patrick got the feeling that the proprietor and the staff at the Avenue Hotel were constantly watching him, suspecting that he was thinking of doing something. So he resigned from the job he had not really done for some years, left his below-stairs lodgings at the hotel, and went to live at the Army of Salvation. Men were allowed to be anonymous, men were allowed to be alone, men were allowed to think of letting go at the Army of Salvation.

However, staying at the Army of Salvation did not stop another letter arriving from the Pioneers' & Early Settlers' Society. How did the Society know how to find him with such pinpoint accuracy?

Patrick wondered. As he had done with the first, Patrick did not open the second letter. He needed to stop the crack … and then … snap before he opened the letter, and there was only one sure-fire way to do that.

He had not been welcome at the Bodega for quite some time, and so he had started going to Scobie's on Selborne Avenue.

Patrick took a swig of his lukewarm and bitter beer as he counted the change in his pocket. Enough for a rope? Not one of reliable length or strength. Might as well get another pint then, he decided. He ordered one and the bartender had no choice but to oblige. The bar had placed, in a very prominent position, a plaque reading 'Right of Admission Reserved', and Patrick knew it was intended to keep derelicts like him away. But as long as he had a hat on his head, shoes – no matter how tattered and worn – on his feet, and a jacket on his back; in other words, as long as he made an effort to look like a gentleman, then the establishment could not refuse him entry or much else, even if it wanted to.

There was a rope, wasn't there? At the Avenue Hotel? Outside the kitchen? A good, strong rope that seemed to be of no use to anyone. If he went to the hotel, pretended to be visiting the proprietor … no … no … he would be instantly suspicious, that one – knew too well how the game was played. There was the cook, Benedito da Costa, a nice fellow, always kind, always asking after Anne … he was the one who had found her in the sanitary lane, wasn't he? Seemed deeply affected by the whole thing. Yes, Da Costa was the man.

Patrick swallowed without tasting the remaining contents of his mug, which was a pity considering that this was probably his last drink. He stood up, patted down his jacket pockets not because he was looking for more change, but because that was what one did when one stood up. He placed his hat more firmly on his head and nodded goodbye to the bartender, who, although he knew who and what Patrick really was, had enough decency to return the nod.

When he left the bar, Patrick was pleased to find that the day had made itself beautiful – mellow sunshine, never-ending blue skies and a gentle breeze. He walked towards the Avenue Hotel at a leisurely pace, secure in the knowledge that there would be no saving him. There was no rush because the exact time of day it happened did not matter anyway.

In the way that the best-laid plans are often interrupted by irrational thoughts, it occurred to Patrick that the rope might no longer be where he remembered seeing it, and so he quickened his pace. He chastised himself for using all the money he had left to buy alcohol instead of rope. Then again, when had he ever been one to make the right decisions?

At the Avenue Hotel, the kitchen staff seemed happy to see him. Da Costa was not there; it was his day off. What to do? Patrick had to think fast. He believed he had left something very dear to him, something once belonging to Anne, in the area just outside the kitchen: would they mind if he had a look? Of course not. They would be happy to feed him when he was done with his search. No, no, that wouldn't be necessary, thank you. He'd already had plenty to eat. Stuffed to the gills, he was. They smiled. He smiled, and then went in search of the rope.

For a moment his desperation would not let him see the rope, and so he searched frantically for it until he found it exactly where he remembered having last seen it. The rope was well twined, strong and of good length. It would do the job very nicely. But once he held its bulk in his hands, he worried about how to smuggle it out of the hotel. Where was a fishing community when you needed it? Plenty of rope in a fishing community ... all those boats. He should know. He had grown up in one. A fishing village in another country, far, far away. There, no one would have looked at him twice if they had seen him walking around with a rope. There, he would not have had to do what he was doing now – stuffing the rope in a khaki paper bag and cradling it in his arms the way he had cradled his daughter when he had first held her many years ago. Had he held Anne as a baby? He was not altogether sure that he had.

Once at the Army of Salvation, Patrick managed to climb the stairs to his room seemingly without a care, as though these were not the last moments of his life. In his room – spartan and clean the way the Army of Salvation liked its rooms to be kept – Patrick took off his shoes, pulled the only chair in the room so that it stood under the cross-beam on the ceiling, and then, after a few attempts, managed to loop the rope around the beam. He tied a secure knot around the beam and then entwined the other end of the rope into a noose, after which he coiled more rope around the beam. Satisfied, he got down and opened the second letter he had received from the Pioneers' & Early Settlers' Society.

The letter hoped it found him in good health. It said it would be honoured if he would join the celebrations to mark the anniversary of the occupation. It said he and other survivors of the 1893 campaign against the Matabele king, Lobengula, were to be the esteemed guests of the occasion. It asked him if he would consider regaling the crowd with his memories of the campaign and of other pioneer activities he had taken part in.

Patrick carefully placed the letter on the table before he stood on the chair in his stockinged feet, passed his head through the noose, and then kicked the chair away.

Crack

and then

snap.

It was unfortunate that when they found him, whenever that

would be, the room would not be as neat and tidy as the Army of Salvation liked its rooms to be. But what was one more regret after a lifetime of many?

B enedito da Costa had been told that he would have to lose his mother. Many in his situation had done so intentionally: losing their mothers allowed them to marry well, to join exclusive clubs, to be considered for promotion and advancement. Benedito had long since reconciled himself to never marrying well, to never being a member of a club, to never being more than a cook at the Avenue Hotel – because he had absolutely no desire to be without his mother, and her easy and free laughter, or her warm and cracked voice that told animated stories as he watched her do the many things that made a life a life.

Benedito knew that he was the exception and that as such, many conjectures were put forward to explain the decision he had made. Some thought him a fool for making what they believed to be the difficult choice; others envied him the fortitude that they lacked in themselves; and others still whispered that he could afford to choose his mother over everything else because he – thanks to his father – already had the privilege of living in the Portuguese and Greek section of the White Man's Town. The truth of it was so simple and prosaic that it seemed to be masquerading as something else – bravery, character, strong will – when all Benedito did in fact was love his mother. Love will do that to you. It will make you do the unexpected thing.

It was this love that made Benedito, on his days off, wear his best suit (on this day that was to change his life forevermore, he chose a brown one that had been tailored for him by Morum Bros), buy the best stewing mutton from the Dundee Butchery opposite the Palace Hotel, and take a jinricksha all the way to the Location, to a rondavel that was polished with cow dung, thatched with elephant grass, and filled with the deeply satisfying smell of wood smoke and heavenly earthly things, where his father would cook a mutton curry – his mother's favourite meal – and Benedito could allow himself to feel the full weight of his parents' love for him.

No, Benedito was never going to lose his mother. However, this is not to say that his heart had not made room for another woman. It had. His father, seemingly not knowing this, worried that Benedito would be a forever bachelor, and had taken to introducing him to families on Lobengula Street. Benedito found his father's desire to marry him off interesting, to say the least, since his father had resisted all machinations to get married and was a forever bachelor himself. Benedito did not know that his father, whose eyes saw everything and missed nothing, understood that sometimes you love the right wrong woman and that that love is in many ways fulfilling, but not always easy to bear. Benedito did not know this about his father because fathers and sons talk of many things, but rarely talk of the heart of the matter.

And so Benedito thought that the things he kept – the crown of her head, the blue of her eyes, the turn of her nose, the curl of her lips, the sound of her laughter, the taste of her skin, the feel of all her soft places, the memory of her scent, the dip of her waist, the music of her voice calling his name – were secrets safely tucked away in a place that only he knew. Anne Battison. She allowed him to walk the earth, raise a trail of dust in his wake, and hold onto the promise of a future – all the while knowing that Rosa Adair was evermore beyond his reach.

His mother, whose eyes saw everything and missed nothing, told him that hope was a thing that didn't kill, and that love was a malleable and unbounded thing that could stretch itself infinitely as well as fit itself into the tiniest crevice. It was as he was listening to his mother say these words that the news of Patrick Battison's passing found him. The news, he was informed, had not been able to find Rosa Adair with the same ease.

There were certain things Benedito was capable of that he had long ago stopped trying to explain or understand. Like the night he found Anne in the sanitary lane, he had known, as soon as only two of The Three Gentlemen From Blantyre returned to the hotel, that something had happened to her. Knowing this had allowed him, somehow, to see her crawling over a body in a sanitary lane – blood on her mouth, throat and hands. He did not think of the body – he thought only of saving her. Now, all he knew was that he needed to be the one to tell her about Patrick, because the news of a parent's passing needed to be handled with delicate tenderness. Knowing this allowed him, somehow, to see her walking along Abercorn Street. So, without ceremony, he took leave of his parents, whose eyes saw everything and missed nothing. Benedito was in such a rush that he did not see the smiles on their faces as they watched their son run out of the dusty yard towards the future that had always already been predestined as his.

For the rest of his life, Benedito would not be able to say with any great certainty how he got to Abercorn Street that day. One minute he was running out of his mother's yard, and the next thing he was bumping into a couple walking along the street. Although he tipped his hat to them, he did not verbalise his apology because just then he had seen Anne, and she was looking like the epitome of beauty itself.

The man he had bumped into cursed under his breath and mumbled something about the colonials that his wife had heard many times before. And then, after closer inspection, the man pronounced: 'A touch of the dago, I suspect,' as though that explained everything. For her part, his wife looked at the rushing figure of Benedito da Costa and said out loud, 'I wonder.' For good measure, she repeated the phrase 'I wonder' as she and her husband witnessed a reunion. The couple were Archibald and Agatha Christie. I will leave it to the reader to decide for themselves whether or not this encounter in any way led to the penning of *The Man in the Brown Suit*. I know what I think.

osa, wearing an English-rose-coloured, high-collared dress with matching parasol and gloves stood in front of the shop window of the Pohoomull Bros establishment on Abercorn Street, trying to decide if she needed a new dress. Mrs Augusta Simon had been very generous after Simeon passed away, and, as well as paying for Rosa's suite at the Grand Hotel, gave her a monthly allowance. As it turned out, butter could melt after all, and Rosa was extremely grateful for this.

She had witnessed the precipitous journey to the bottom when women in her position lost their benefactors: the runs in stockings that even the careful application of colourless nail varnish could or would not stop; the dresses that first showed their age, and then showed that they were no longer in fashion; having to use lipstick for rouge, or worse, constantly having to pinch your cheeks to get the same temporary effect. But none of those humiliations compared to the open resentment and scorn the women of the City of Kings heaped on the woman who unexpectedly found herself alone and unprotected – every snub was calculated and orchestrated to be deeply felt.

'Anne?' said a voice, interrupting her thoughts.

As she had done since re-christening herself, Rosa ignored the voice.

'Anne?' said the voice, moving closer.

And then she saw him reflected in the shop window that held her reflection. She would have known and remembered that profile, that face, that aristocratic nose anywhere. But most of all she remembered how gentle and tender he had been when he had found her ... found Anne ... in that sanitary lane. How careful he had been when he picked her up. She remembered how Anne had clung to him. Even in that moment, when she had known what men really were, Anne had clung to *him*: Benedito da Costa.

'Anne?' he said, as he took off his hat.

She knew what he had come to tell her even before he started to say it. Her father, Patrick H. Battison, pioneer, was dead.

It was she who went to him. 'He should have been there for me,' she said.

'I know,' Benedito said.

'He should have protected me.'

'Yes. He should have.'

'He broke my heart,' she said.

'And yet you managed to hold on to yourself,' he said.

Although it was a thing highly frowned upon by polite society, there was no law against public displays of affection in the City of Kings. So when Benedito da Costa put an arm around Anne Battison and comforted her in front of the shop window of the Pohoomull Bros establishment on Abercorn Street, he was, technically, not breaking any laws; and neither was she when she rested her head on his shoulder.

Sometimes you just know that something is right.

'Please take me home,' she said.

And he did.

Benedito took her to the Portuguese and Greek section of town.

Polite society had plenty to say about the choice Anne Battison had made, but they trusted that this relationship would go the way of her other affairs – have some tragedy befall it, and then end. Polite society continued to think this even when Anne Battison became pregnant and had a baby girl who was christened Mildred. Polite society continued to think this when Anne Battison attended the Prince of Wales Ball in 1925 with Benedito da Costa. Polite society continued to think this when Anne Battison and Benedito da Costa officially married in 1927. Polite society continued to think this when Anne Battison-da Costa died in 1965 and her official obituary simply read: 'Beloved daughter of a pioneer.' Polite society is nothing if not self-preservative, and that is why it let something happen in the City of Kings that it should not have – because letting it happen was so much easier than acknowledging what was really happening.

INTERLUDE

The woman with the easy laughter and the sure foot is back. I try to ignore her hereness, but find myself looking out of the window again, watching them. This time there isn't that much laughter, and this makes me almost happy. Daisy shakes her head – a denial, a refusal – and takes a step back, away from the woman. The woman reaches out to touch her, the act just shy of being desperate and aggressive.

Someone clears their throat right behind me. Startled, I turn around to find Stevens standing there. He doesn't look at me; he looks out the window, and doesn't bother to hide the look of triumph on his face. He carries a silver tray in his hands, and on it is a bottle of hand sanitiser and a packet of surgical masks. The government wants everyone in the country to start wearing surgical masks and sanitising their hands, he explains.

Feeling like an unwilling conspirator, I close the wooden panel so that neither of us can look outside the window. I accuse him of not having knocked on the door, of having entered the room without having been granted entry. He calmly tells me that he did indeed knock; several times, in fact, and upon receiving no answer, thought that perhaps there was something wrong with me. He was particularly worried because I haven't been eating well lately. He is glad to find that all is well with me.

I don't like his closeness. It's too familiar. He looks at me and smiles. He is offering me something that's not held in his hands, but in his smile – in the curl of his lips. I walk away from the window and go to sit by the table and prepare to write, even though I have nothing to write. Stevens follows me and places the surgical masks and hand sanitiser on the table. He lingers, hovering above me.

He has been here many times before: offering a guest the thing promised by the curl of his lips. He is a handsome man, and I am a guest whose longing he has just witnessed. He expects easy passage.

I thank him for the things he has brought me, and inform him that I would like to get back to writing. He nods his understanding and continues to smile. He places the tray underneath his arm and walks away undefeated, sure that my resolve won't always be so strong. There is a sharpness to him that finds it easy to cut through things. I watch him walk away. He wears very sensible shoes.

I've made a fool of myself. I've wanted something that isn't mine to have. Now Stevens knows my secret, and he is the sort of man for whom another's secret is both a commodity and a weapon. He'll find a way to use what he knows against me. I'm sure of it.

I stand up and go to lock the door, suddenly afraid. I place a chair under the door handle.

I'd planned something with a very different outcome. Several days ago, I'd expected Daisy to come and perhaps apologise for the laughter, for disturbing my writing. I'd intended to rebuff her overtures of professional cordiality by telling her that I didn't appreciate interruptions when writing, and to make her realise that in that very moment of apologising, she was disturbing me again. I was hurt by her actions, and so she had to be hurt by my actions.

But Daisy hadn't come to apologise. She'd sent a tray of delicious food with a note saying she understood that I was in the middle of writing and wouldn't appreciate interruptions. My only recourse for revenge had been to send back trays of delectable food, barely touched. And, of course, the longing part of me hoped that Daisy would worry because I was eating so little, and would come and check up on me. When she did so, I'd find another cutting remark to hurl at her. It was important to me that Daisy *feel* something because of me.

But Daisy hadn't come.

There's a knock on the door. I must've been lost in thought for quite some time because the sunlight in the room has shifted. There's another knock, more persistent this time. Someone turns the doorknob, jiggles the lock. This time the knock on the door makes a banging sound. My name is called from the other side of the door by a voice I don't recognise. There's a rush of footsteps. A jangle of keys. A whispered exchange. And finally, a familiar voice.

'Madam?' Daisy says through the door. 'Please open the door.'

I stand up to do as she asks. Hadn't I put a chair under the handle? When did I remove it? I open the door. On the other side of the door, two men I've never seen before stand with Daisy, Alfred and Stevens. They all wear surgical masks underneath the eyes that stare at me.

One of the men asks me if I'm alright, and when I don't immediately respond, both men walk past me into the room. They seem to be searching for something. They look under the bed, in the bathroom, in the wardrobe, on and under the table for the thing they're searching for. They don't find it.

Daisy and Alfred have entered the room. Stevens continues to stand outside the room.

The man who spoke first turns to me and asks me if everything is fine. I nod. He asks me if I'm sure. I nod again. He doesn't seem entirely convinced. He looks me up and down, tells me that I don't look well. I tell him I'm fine. He still doesn't seem entirely convinced.

He asks me if I'm being mistreated in any way. I make the mistake of not answering immediately and instead asking who they are. The man doesn't answer my question, but asks me again if I'm being mistreated in any way. No, I tell him. I've been treated tremendously well. I'm enjoying my stay at the castle. He doesn't seem entirely convinced. Perhaps I sound too happy, and happiness is not something that can be believed of me.

'As you can see, she's absolutely fine,' Daisy says. 'She's just been busy writing.'

The second man, the one who hasn't said anything so far, looks at Daisy with venom in his eyes. He looks at her from her newsboy cap to her high-heeled boots, and asks her what she is supposed to be.

'Something you can't have,' Daisy says. There is venom in her eyes as well.

They stare each other down – adversaries long before this moment.

'Daisy?' I say, lost.

'It's alright, Madam,' she says, still looking at the man. 'These men are with the Organisation of Domestic Affairs. They received a call from the Good Foundation, and now they are here to check on your wellbeing.'

As though Daisy hasn't spoken, the man who has been asking me questions informs me that the Good Foundation *and* the Good Family are worried because they have not heard directly from me in weeks – ever since I arrived at the castle. Their attempts to communicate with me have yielded no results. The castle staff have repeatedly made promises that I would communicate, and these promises have not been kept, and no explanations have been given. The Good Foundation *and* the Good Family fear that something untoward has happened to me, and they have asked the Organisation to come and investigate.

'As you can see, I'm fine,' I say. 'I've just been busy writing.'

The man still doesn't seem entirely convinced and wants to know why I haven't communicated with the Good Foundation *and* the Good Family. Haven't I been receiving their messages?

'I have,' I say. But that's all I can say because I can't explain why I haven't responded to these messages.

The man tells me that with the world in the situation it is in, communication is key.

I nod my agreement. 'I will communicate with them soon,' I say.

The man obviously thinks I can do one better. He takes out his phone and calls a number. He tells whoever is on the other end that they've found me alive and well, and there's nothing to worry about. That's the expression he uses – alive and well. He's very friendly on the phone, much friendlier than he's been in the room. He hands me the phone.

Johanna is on the other end of the line. She is relieved (she doesn't use the word 'happy') to hear that I'm alright. The virus is spreading its tentacles across the world. Everyone is worried. She and A.J. have had to cut short a trip to the Velaa Private Island in the Maldives. There is talk of suspending international air travel. I definitely do not want to be stuck in Africa at a time like this. I need to come back home. I can always return to the castle in a few months and continue preparing for the centennial celebrations once the world has righted itself again. Johanna says all this, and then repeats the phrase about the tentacles. I make no commitment to a return, but she seems to hear one. She tells me that my mother and the children miss me.

The Three Good Children – two boys named after famous men and a girl named after me.

Johanna cannot wait to see me soon.

I, choosing not to lie, bid her farewell, and hand the phone back to its owner.

The two men only seem to feel out of place once they've completed their mission. They make me promise to communicate regularly with the Good Foundation *and* the Good Family. I nod, not wanting to commit to the promise verbally. Convinced at last, they make their way out of the room. Daisy and Alfred follow the two men out. Daisy turns to me and smiles before closing the door and leaving me alone in the otherworldly opulence of the Great Chamber. I let her smile give me comfort.

And to think I thought I wanted to hurt her.

What did I think she needed to apologise for? It's not her fault that her life is already on its own trajectory towards a desired destination. It's not her fault that this is simply a point of convergence for us as she uses the light she carries to illuminate my own darkness. It's not her fault that where once *Everything was brightness, or dark* now I understand that there's light in the darkness and darkness in the light.

All is twilight as I watch what has become familiar turn into chiaroscuro all around me. Daisy has done this. I feel a sense of comfort. I know that my time here is fleeting, but the place has long felt like home. I find that I want to be held at this point of convergence forever. And so I let myself be held … captive.

When I smell the scent of cheap tobacco in the air, I welcome the visitation: Sethekeli.

There's nothing captives fear more than loneliness.

PART IV

*But I was soon up; crawling forwards on my hands and knees,
and then again raised to my feet—*

CHARLOTTE BRONTË – *Jane Eyre*

THE FORGOTTEN WOMAN*

1877–1939

---

* Entered the archive as Settie Muhambie.

Queen Lozikeyi had stated it as a by-the-way thing, but Bathabile Mahlabezulu knew to take it seriously. If the baby that Bathabile was expecting was a girl, then she would be named Fulatha – after King Lobengula's mother, who had died during the civil war, along with Mwaka Nxumalo and many of King Mzilikazi's indunas. Queen Lozikeyi, although formidable, was often generous, and she was being very generous with the giving of the name. Fulatha: Bathabile liked the name for the baby she already knew was a girl because she had seen her in a vision.

Since King Lobengula had loved his mother, Bathabile thought that maybe her Fulatha would remind the king of something of his mother that he had lost and wanted to cherish, which would then make him treasure her daughter as well. Bathabile worried for the child she was carrying because when she looked into the child's future, all she saw was a crooked line whose crookedness ran into the next generation ... and the next ... and the next ... and the next ... and the next.

Bathabile knew that, in addition to being generous, Queen Lozikeyi was being strategic. The position of a queen was always precarious in the Matabele Kingdom; to survive, it was imperative to create strong alliances. The Mahlabezulus were a long line of seers and healers who used their vast knowledge to ensure that there was always equilibrium in their world. It might seem like a small, almost insignificant thing on which to focus your knowledge, but humans are inherently greedy, and greed is inherently destructive; therefore, these seers and healers performed this most vital function.

True, the Khumalo Kings – Mzilikazi and his son Lobengula – had created very strong ties with the Mahlabezulus to ensure the proper governance of their rule. But it is often the case that when a man becomes accustomed to his power, he invariably begins to imagine he is responsible – through his own ingenuity, prowess and intelligence – for what he has. A gentle reminder here and there occasionally proves necessary, and so Queen Lozikeyi had said in her by-the-way manner that Bathabile's baby would be called Fulatha.

Bathabile herself was the product of such strategising on the part of a queen. Queen Loziba, King Mzilikazi's wife, had known that anyone who settled on this land would do well to curry the favour of the Keepers of the Flame – a mixed people made up of the autochthonous San and a succession of various Bantu groups who had migrated or expanded into the region from the Leopard's Kopje to the Mapungubwe Kingdom to the House of Stone Kingdom to the Butua Kingdom to the Mutapa Kingdom to the Rozvi Empire, and now the Matabele Kingdom of Mthwakazi – who steadfastly guarded the territory and its secrets. To this end, Queen Loziba had arranged a union between a Mahlabezulu and one of the Keepers of the Flame; and this had resulted in Bathabile.

Unfortunately, Bathabile had not been fortunate enough to have an arranged union. So she had made a match for herself, marrying one Sola Mhambi, a very handsome man who turned out to be useless and disappointed her at every turn. When she found herself carrying his child, she was grateful to Queen Lozikeyi for the generosity of her attention.

All was well. But just as Bathabile was preparing herself for a future that she would like – one in which her child's life created a straight line – she had a vision that threatened that future in so complete a way that it terrified her. In her vision, she saw Sir Bartle

Frere send Captain Patterson, Mr J. Sergeaunt, and Thomas, a missionary's young son, as emissaries to King Lobengula. There was also a man called H.R. Haggard who had wanted to accompany the men, but the government of the Transvaal, for which he worked, could not spare him. In his stead, Haggard had sent his two servants, whom he called Khiva, the Bastard Zulu, and Ventvogel, the Hottentot.

Of course Bathabile had seen a few of these men who came from over the land and across the waters, but none of them had ever done the curious thing Captain Patterson, Mr J. Sergeaunt, and Thomas, the missionary's young son, did in her vision: while they were perfectly capable of walking upright, they chose instead to crouch and then creep and then crawl as they made their way first to the precious stones that glimmered in the distance, and then to the giant pair of shimmering silver wings that lay beyond. Their quest for riches had turned them into half-broken things.

'Watch out for izethekeli,' Bathabile warned the king and queen when she next had an audience with them. 'They are not to be trusted.'

The year was 1877 and King Lobengula had already had quite a few encounters with izethekeli. He nodded slowly before asking: 'Did you ever see a chameleon catch a fly?' Bathabile knew it was a rhetorical question, and therefore did not respond. 'The chameleon gets behind the fly and remains motionless for some time,' the king continued, 'then advances very slowly and gently, putting forward first one leg and then another. At last, when well within reach, he darts his tongue and the fly disappears. England is the chameleon and I am that fly.'

'I understand that we cannot stop the march of time, Your Majesty,' Bathabile said. 'But we are mere custodians of this land. Others have come before us and others will come after us. A king's rule is like the mist, but some things do not belong to time or man.'

'You speak of the silver wings?' Queen Lozikeyi said.

'I do.'

'But surely these men from over the land and across the waters will be like all those who have come before them – they will know not to interfere with what they cannot completely comprehend,' King Lobengula said.

'I'm afraid they will simply erase what they cannot completely comprehend,' Bathabile said.

'But you cannot erase the past,' the king and queen said simultaneously.

'If they know this, then their actions do not show it,' Bathabile countered politely. 'They have a way of recording things that makes erasure seem possible.'

The king and queen looked at each other, wanting to believe that such a thing was impossible, but also afraid that it was completely possible.

'Their greed knows no limits,' Bathabile said. 'They will take not only the precious stones, they will also find a way to take the giant pair of silver wings. They may take other things they do not fully appreciate as well.'

'Take them where?' Queen Lozikeyi said.

'They have created something invisible. This invisible thing will make it possible for them to take things that do not belong to them, acknowledge that they have taken them without the owners' permission, and openly display them for all to see.'

'What you speak of is theft. Who openly displays a stolen thing?' the king asked.

'The invisible thing they have created will make them believe that those they have taken things from will never have the power to take back what was taken from them.'

'A person always has the power to take back what rightfully belongs to them,' the queen said.

'They will use the invisible thing they have created to deny that such power exists.'

King Lobengula understood the import of what Bathabile had told him, but he could not be seen to have come to a decision after talking to two women – no matter how intelligent and formidable those women were – and so he called an indaba with his indunas.

When the visitors – izethekeli – arrived, the king received them well, and when they expressed a desire to go to see the Zambesi Falls, the king sent twenty of his people to serve as bearers. Sometime during the twelve-day journey, before the party arrived at the falls, Captain Patterson, Mr J. Sergeaunt, Thomas, the missionary's young son, and Haggard's two servants, Khiva and Ventvogel, died after drinking water from a poisoned source. None of Lobengula's bearers were affected by the water.

Bathabile was not sorry for having warned the king and queen. She knew that these men and the many others who would come after them wanted the land, the precious stones and metals, the cattle – all the things that made a man wealthy. Once they had acquired their wealth, they would think they had been so favoured because of their ingenuity, prowess and intelligence. When they saw the giant pair of silver wings, they would ask all the wrong questions: Who had made them? When had they been made? How had they been made? It would never occur to them to ask why they had been made in the first place; and so there would be nothing to remind them that the world was ancient, and they were but mere mortals walking the earth.

When H.R. Haggard – the man who had been meant to be one of the visitors but had not been because the government of Transvaal could not spare him – heard what had happened to his friends and servants, he decided to avenge their deaths by recording what he had not witnessed, but could re-imagine. He wrote a book called *King Solomon's Mines*. In that book, by some alchemy, lives and circumstances transformed: the Matabele became the Kukuana; King Lobengula became King Twala; Captain Patterson became Captain Good; Mr J. Sergeaunt became Sir Henry Curtis; Khiva remained Khiva; Ventvogel remained Ventvogel; Haggard himself became Allan Quatermain. Whereas Haggard never saw Bathabile, Quatermain saw a woman he knew to fear, and he wrote this woman as Gagool.

Fiction became fact. Fact became fiction. The line was forever blurred.

When Bathabile had her baby girl, she did not name her Fulatha after the king's mother, because, curiously, Haggard had written a character called Foulata whose eyes were made large by her never-ending sorrow and love for Captain Good, a man who definitely did not deserve her affection. Bathabile decidedly did not want such a life for her daughter, so she named her Sethekeli after Haggard himself. Sethekeli: the visitor who had not come to visit the king, and had thus lived to write about her and her people in a way that she would somehow have to undo even in the presence of the invisible thing that had been created.

Sethekeli Mhambi watched King Lobengula set fire to his Royal Kraal. As all the long-familiar things began to smoulder, she tried to understand what was going on, but could not. They were at war with the men who came from over the land and across the waters, she knew that much. But why did the king have to reduce their world to ash? When they returned, all they would find would be ruins, and they would have to build something new from the ashes. Sethekeli did not understand why they had to let go of the long-familiar things.

Earlier, there had been the packing of the king's belongings into three wagons. Then the women, children and the elderly had taken the things they could carry, and, led by Queen Lozikeyi, they departed following the wagons. Now the king's warriors in their leopard skins and ostrich feathers, carrying their shields and assegais, and chanting their rousing war songs, were heading in the opposite direction to the one that the women, children and the elderly had taken. The warriors were flanked at the front and the rear by those of their ranks who carried Martini-Henry rifles.

Sethekeli's father, Sola Mhambi, was one of the warriors, even though he had begged the king to let him go with the women, children and the elderly – ostensibly to protect them from whatever lay ahead. It had not helped matters that her mother had informed her father that she foresaw his non-return from this particular war. Many called her father a coward, but Sethekeli thought he was brave; brave enough, at least, to be willing to march towards his certain death.

Of course her father wasn't going to die. It was just her mother's

245

back-to-front way of making sure he did the right thing. Wasn't it? He would fight with all his might to prove her wrong. Wouldn't he? Sethekeli had many questions and no one to ask because the person she would have asked – her mother – was currently standing in the middle of the kraal, watching the king dig up something with his own assegai and bare hands. Sethekeli had never seen the king kneel before, and so she was acutely aware that her eyes were witnessing something they should not. Out of respect, she looked away.

Her eyes, as they often did, chose to look at her most favourite thing: Bopha, her future husband. He stood with a group of the king's most trusted warriors, guarding the king's Martini-Henry rifles. He looked as he always did: tall, dark, handsome, broad-shouldered, confident and brave. He had been made with purpose like an arrow. Who would not love such a man? So one evening, when he had waylaid Sethekeli as she walked back from the river and given her a necklace he had made himself, she had taken it in her stride. Of course she was going to be his wife. Had there ever been any doubt?

Her brother Dingindawo, who had the uncanny ability to destroy all her happy moments – first by being born a boy exactly three years after she had been born a girl, and therefore taking up all their mother's attention; and thereafter by appearing every time Sethekeli was trying to have a private moment of joy – came to stand next to her. 'He will marry other women, you know—' he began before Sethekeli punched him in the stomach without looking at him. She thought she saw Bopha chuckle at this, and she was pleased. The number of women Bopha married after her did not matter because she knew she would be his favourite wife: she would make sure of it.

'You are not good at sharing things,' Dingindawo said, as though he had read her thoughts. 'Mother says you are a handful and will continue to be a handful even after you are married.' Before she could respond, he walked over to the group of warriors who were waiting for the king, and made a great show of being able to talk to them in a way that Sethekeli could not. Why did he always have to interfere with the good things in her life? Dingindawo said something that made the warriors – especially Bopha – laugh, and Sethekeli felt betrayed. Bopha should know better; she would teach him to know better.

Sethekeli looked back at the king and her mother just in time to see them remove a giant pair of silver wings from the ground. Her mother collected the wings in her arms with the tenderness and delicacy that women's hands often reserved for newborn babies. Sethekeli had thought seeing the king on his knees was the most extraordinary thing she had ever seen, but the sheer beauty of the shimmering wings surpassed even that. And then she watched in stupefaction as her mother started to glow and then burn bright as though there was a fire within her – and that fire made her a precious and beautiful something. It was over so soon, Sethekeli almost believed she had imagined it.

The king and her mother exchanged some brief words before the king left, followed closely behind by his retinue of trusted warriors. Bopha, her future husband, who was now trailing at the tail-end of the warriors, waved at her; with her heart thumping in her chest, Sethekeli waved back. 'Sethe. Remember,' was all he said. 'Sethe.' She had never allowed anyone to shorten her name before, but now, hearing the diminutive from Bopha's lips, she felt she liked it very much. 'Sethe'. She could already hear him calling her that upon his return. Because of the happiness of the moment, it never occurred to her that what she was witnessing was actually an ending, and so it was with great joy that she watched Bopha disappear on the cusp of something beautiful.

As Sethe observed her mother and her brother walking towards her carrying the giant pair of silver wings, she wondered how much of what was going on Dingindawo understood. Had he also witnessed their mother's ephemeral glow?

'I know you are both very curious, so I will tell you,' Bathabile said. 'I am now the Keeper of the Flame. I need to find a safe place for the wings. They belong in the white stone caves, but it is not safe for them there at this time. And that is all I am going to tell you, because that is all you need to know.'

Sethe knew she came from a long line of seers and healers, but at fifteen going on sixteen, she had never had a vision or healed anyone. She had to ask, 'Will I also one day be the Keeper of the Flame?'

'You are a handful now, and men will always be your weakness,' Bathabile said, as she and Dingindawo carefully wrapped the giant pair of silver wings in cowhide. 'I'm afraid it's just crookedness for you.'

Sethe did not like the sound of that – handful, men, crookedness. All she wanted was for Bopha to marry her, and for her mother to tell her that she too would be the Keeper of the Flame.

'What do you think of the wings?' Bathabile asked.

It was a test, Sethe knew. Most things her mother said to her were a test. 'They are really big.'

'Is that all you see?'

'They are lovely.'

Her mother looked at her long and hard and then said, 'If I had asked you about Bopha, you would have had so much more to say. You would have recited an entire poem.' Bathabile shook her head and sighed.

Sethe had failed her mother again. There was something, some *way* she was supposed to be, and she wasn't that way. She had known this about herself ever since the white splotch had appeared on her chest above her heart. Her mother had started treating her differently after she saw it. Sethe had been a toddler then, and had believed she would one day succeed in making her mother look at her without shaking her head and sighing. It was probably time to stop hoping for something different where her mother was concerned, Sethe sadly acknowledged.

Once they had finished wrapping them, Bathabile and Dingindawo carried the silver wings, and Sethe carried her family's bundled belongings. She wasn't even trusted to touch the wings. It was only when they started walking away from the only home she had ever known that Sethe realised the finality of everything she had witnessed that day: the many departures, the burning kraal, the retrieval of the silver wings ... they were never coming back to the long-familiar things. This was an ending. She noticed something else. Everything all around them was burning, and yet the smoke was not affecting them. She wanted to ask her mother how this was possible, but was not ready to prove herself a disappointment again; by now, as a seer and healer, she was supposed to know these things without having to be told.

After walking a long, long time, Sethe, Bathabile and Dingindawo crossed paths with a column of men who came from over the land and across the waters. They travelled on horseback, wore coats, carried rifles and looked forward as if they knew exactly where they were going – not at all like visitors, who always looked uncertain and stopped to ask for directions. Sethe had seen enough of these men in her time not to be impressed by their sheer number. But while the men and their number did not impress her, she was much taken with the brass buckles on their boots. The men galloped on without giving Bathabile and her children a second look or thought; it was as though they could not see them.

The men were headed towards the rising smoke of the King's Kraal, hoping to find something there that they would not – a king and his warriors ready to fight. When the first of the men on horseback arrived at the kraal, there was much hooting and shouting – the sounds of celebration and victory – and so it is quite possible that they had always meant to find a ruin. They gleefully and triumphantly trampled over the ruins of another man's kingdom, and then nailed two tattered cloths onto a half-ruined tree.

'Do you know why we say another man's wound is never to be laughed at?' Bathabile asked rhetorically. 'It is because history has a way of repeating itself. But never in the ways that we think it will. Every ending is another beginning, to be sure. But every beginning also anticipates its own ending.' And with that lesson delivered, Bathabile and her children continued on their journey.

It should be mentioned here – because there won't be another appropriate place to mention it – that Bathabile had been right about Sola's fate in the war.

The final destination for Bathabile and her children was the place that had once been the reserve of the king's queens, where they had cultivated and harvested crops. This was where some of the women, children and elderly people who had left earlier had settled. Bathabile and her children set about making a home among them. The giant pair of silver wings was safely buried in their homestead. With that done, everyone allowed themselves to feel settled as they awaited the return of the king. As long as the wings were safe, all would be well. That was how it had always been.

The legend goes as follows: Four women went in search of water. In order to make this journey possible, the women transformed themselves into splendid, silver-winged creatures who could fly. They landed on the breathtaking white hills and rocks that were home to many caves. With the arrival of the women, the hills, rocks and caves began witnessing the many mysteries and secrets that time produced. The earth was still so new and soft that to this day, you can still see the footprints of the four women on the rocks on which they landed.

Since these silver-winged creatures were women, they found that they could create life; and while they searched for water, they made the first humans – the people of the white hills, rocks and caves. These humans loved and respected the earth and all the other living things the four women had created so much that they lived in perfect harmony with everything around them.

However, even though they were happy with what they had created, the women still had not found water, and so they decided their search would perhaps be more successful if they travelled in different directions. One went to the north, one went to the east, one went to the west, and one stayed in the spot where they had landed and awaited the return of the others.

The one who went to the north found fire. She loved fire so much, she started creating life with it. The humans she created adored her silver wings, and so she let them take a few feathers so that they could share in their splendour. But, naturally, some feathers were bigger than others. The humans she had created each wanted the biggest feathers for themselves. They started fighting one another. The woman gave them more feathers. The humans continued to fight. She gave them all her remaining feathers. They continued to fight. She gave them the unfeathered wings. They continued to fight. When she tried to intervene, they told her she needed to grow another pair of wings. When she could not, they ignored her and continued to fight. Time passed, and still they continued to fight. They began to forget the original source of the feathers. When the woman tried to remind them, they told her she had never had a giant pair of silver wings – what human had ever had wings? They called her a madwoman for ever thinking she had had them. She died soon after, heartbroken and alone – not understanding the thing she had created.

The one who went to the east found the purest air and used it to make the finest humans. She wanted them to appreciate beauty so much that they lived only for it; and so she created many wonderful things. The fine humans she had created did indeed appreciate beauty – they dug up and plundered the earth in search of it, and when they found it in precious stones, they were happy, but not satisfied, because they knew that her silver wings were the most exquisite things in the world. And so they conspired to kill her so they could have her wings for themselves. One day they attacked her and when she fell on her knees, they removed her wings, taking care not to damage them, but intent on hurting her. Broken, first she crouched, then she crept, then she crawled, then she died. When she was dead, they buried her and built a shrine for the wings, which they worshipped. From then on, they killed anyone who refused to worship the giant pair of silver wings.

The one who went to the west did indeed find water, but having found it, she decided it was too precious a thing to let others know about, and so kept its discovery a secret. She drank water, she bathed in water, she swam in water. She did not even create anything that would share the water with her; she loved water that much. Then she decided to live in the water, and when her feathers started to fall off – she did not care. And when her wings stopped working – she did not care. She was in water, surrounded by it everywhere, and that was all that mattered. She died alone, but selfish and happy. She was, perhaps, even happier in death, because her body sank to the bottom of the water and forever became a part of it.

When the one who had stayed behind heard tales of what had happened to her fellow silver-winged creatures, she decided there was a lesson in all of this she needed to share with the first humans. The silver wings had great value, but only if humans saw them for what they really were – something impossible made possible. She told them that before they became silver-winged creatures, the four women had simply been women. As women, they had gone in search of water many times, but could only get so far on foot. They decided they needed something that would enable them to transcend their limited abilities: flight seemed like the only viable solution. And so, with no model to follow, they did the impossible and made wings: wings that worked, wings that were capable of flight. The wings were the result of their belief in themselves to make possible the impossible.

The surviving silver-winged creature told the first humans they would always have to be vigilant, always ready to protect themselves from the warring and plundering humans who, in turn, would travel over the land and across the waters looking for more people to fight and more things to plunder. She too would die and leave behind her silver wings. Once they saw them, the greed of the warring and plundering humans would make them want to take the silver wings and possess them. The first humans had to make sure that the wings always remained in the land of the breathtaking white hills, rocks and caves. This would not be an easy task because the warring and plundering humans had learnt to be cunning and devious. She could not stress too strongly how vigilant the first humans needed to be.

When the surviving silver-winged creature who had come in search of water died, the first humans put her giant pair of silver wings in a cave, and appointed a Keeper of the Flame to guard and protect them. It was always to be remembered that the first humans – the people of the white hills, rocks and caves – were the true custodians of the silver wings, and that without the wings there to inspire them, the people would stop believing in themselves and their capabilities.

The legend goes as follows: Four women went in search of water; and because of the wisdom of one of them, impossible things can still be made possible in this world.

When, months after King Lobengula had burnt the King's Kraal, the surviving warriors returned without the king, it took the Matabele quite some time to appreciate that they had been defeated. At first, the former warriors and the men without a king put their heads together and tried to think of how best to move on, but then word reached them that Cecil John Rhodes – the man who had at first come in the guise of a friend before he turned conqueror – was building his own house on top of the ruins of the King's Kraal. Furthermore, the BSAC was taking over the administration of the country and its people on behalf of a faraway queen named Victoria. Queen Victoria proved rapacious; she wanted all the things that made men wealthy and powerful: the land and the people and the livestock and the precious stones and the minerals.

The invisible thing that Bathabile had foreseen was now all around them, turning them black as it turned the visitors white. Whites were superior; blacks were inferior. Whites had more than was necessary; blacks had barely enough. Whites created the laws; blacks obeyed the laws. Whites had power and property; blacks had subjection and abjection. The country they had belonged to was put together with other countries, and together these formed a single entity called a colony, whether they liked it or not. The colony was, of course, run by the whites. The invisible thing made this seem like the natural or normal state of affairs. The invisible thing called this progress.

The Matabele men, as black men, were left with very little they could still consider their own, and so they had very little choice but to allow themselves to be co-opted into the white man's world as labourers. Although defeated, the people were not altogether broken, and they knew that they would live to fight another day. To this end, Queen Lozikeyi secretly started collecting ammunition for Martini-Henry rifles, Winchester repeaters and Lee-Metfords.

While the men went to work as labourers, the women continued building pole- and dagga-thatched huts, raising children, cooking meals, washing clothes, making baskets and brewing beer. But now with the changing economy and the growing number of labourers, those women who were unattached started charging for these comforts of home. The network of thatched huts spread, and a new settlement was born. The white administration called it the Location.

It was this flourishing settlement on which Patrick Fletcher – BSAC member, civil engineer, government surveyor, and partner in the survey firm Fletcher & Espin – turned his back as he, in the early months of 1894, planned the White Man's Town using a very rigid grid. The new town spanned vertically from what would be King's Avenue to what would be 14th Avenue, and laterally from what would be Lobengula Street to what would be Borrow Street. Each street was divided into stands that Messrs Napier & Weir of the BSAC could sell for the upset price of 30 pounds. And because Fletcher's back was turned to Sethe, he did not see her standing on the other side of what would be Lobengula Street, watching him.

Since Sethe had absolutely no idea what he was doing, she was convinced that Fletcher, with his obsession with straight lines, was a madman. She wanted Fletcher to turn around and see what her people were building as well – the beautiful thing that the Location was becoming – but the white man's eyes were not for beauty to see.

Once Fletcher's plan had been mapped out, the actual job of building the White Man's Town could commence. First, there had to be the space clearing. The former warriors and the men without a king, Bopha among them, were called to perform the arduous tasks of felling indigenous trees, removing felled trunks, digging up stumps, removing living things by their roots, and casting off and carting away no longer living things. Second, there had to be the levelling of the field. The former warriors and the men without a king stomped on and stamped down whatever remained until the surface of things was deceptively smooth. Third, there had to be the building of the new settlement along Fletcher's very rigid grid. The former warriors and the men without a king built roads and erected pole- and dagga-thatched huts and square brick structures with thatched roofs, using both old and new knowledge. Some of the materials could be sourced locally, but other materials had to be brought over several hundred miles via the Hunter's Road or Mafeking Road by ox wagon, and then transported by various porters to the specific stands that were their final destinations. Last, there had to be the occupation of the buildings. The former warriors and the men without a king carried furniture, fixtures, machinery, odds and ends, bits and bobs to the newly built buildings; some of these objects had travelled over the land and across the waters and seen a world that the men carrying them never would.

It was a lot of work, and soon other men, equally defeated, equally black, started trickling in from other parts of the colony – and in some cases, from other colonies as well – which was a godsend, since there was no shortage of things that needed to be done in the White Man's Town. These men all needed places to stay, and since the town they were building was not meant for them, they made their way to the ever-prospering settlement that Fletcher and the other white men had turned their backs on – the Location – where the women made them pay for the few creature comforts that were to be had.

The Location became a place where anything went, and Sethe loved it. She loved its haphazard nature. She loved that it made sense of itself without any need of a map. She loved best of all that it was zigzagged right through with crooked lines. Crookedness: Sethe found it was not something she feared after all. She decided that a crooked line was the best kind of line because it allowed mistakes, compromises and external influences to shape it. What was true of a line was also true of a person. She looked at the White Man's Town, this place that she, as a black woman, was not allowed to enter because black women were thought to be diseased, lazy, stupid and promiscuous – and therefore both a danger and a nuisance. She felt a strong desire to disrupt its order. With this desire, she saw her first vision: her child, her grandchild, her great-grandchild, even her great-great-great grandchild, all of them creating crooked lines where straight lines should be. Sethe smiled to herself as she came to understand that before a thing arrives, it is always foretold.

But as Sethe was finding much to love, the Matabele men were beginning to feel the last vestiges of their control slip away. In 1896, some of these former warriors and the men without a king, using the ammunition that Queen Lozikeyi had so wisely collected for three years, attacked the very town they had built in what the white men called a rebellion, but was really Umvukela, the Second Matabele War. Using Martini-Henry rifles, Winchester repeaters and Lee-Metfords alongside their trusted assegais, knobkerries and battle axes, these former warriors and the men without a king showed that building the White Man's Town, being governed by the BSAC, being taxed for continuing to live on what was their land might have broken them, but not completely.

Bopha, the arrow, was one of the men who took part in the battle. He fought so valiantly – with the might with which he had fought the First Matabele War – that when the war ended in 1897, he wanted to carry on fighting. The only person left for him to fight was his wife Sethekeli – he had long since forgotten that he had once called her Sethe and asked her to remember.

Sethe saw in Bopha not an angry man, but a man in pain – an aimless man. He had been moulded from boyhood to become a warrior, and now he was just a sharp and pointed object that had no true target in sight. He was still tall, dark, handsome, broad-shouldered, and Sethe still loved him. But his confidence had given way to fear of further defeat and humiliation, and his bravery had turned itself into a fist aimed at her. Bopha had always been meant to be glorious, but he had been made inglorious by the invisible thing the visitors had created. It was because she loved him and felt pity for the thing he had become that Sethe killed Bopha in his sleep, while he still had something of the true warrior left in him, before he became truly lost. It was a kindness on her part.

Edmund Haliburton found himself waiting in the queue at J. Garlick – Wholesale Merchant and Direct Importer, which was not really how he had imagined he would spend his first months in the colony – standing around and waiting. He had envisaged himself constantly occupied and industrious as he ran around prospecting for gold in a place called, of all things, Eldorado: pegging off the area that would be his to mine, signing documents that would establish the land as his, filling his hat and his pockets with gold nuggets. But, instead, here he was in the City of Kings, in the section known as the White Man's Town – standing around and waiting.

The waiting had begun long before he arrived in the colony. His intention had been to sail for the Cape soon after his twenty-first birthday in 1900. The year 1900 seemed like one for new beginnings and adventures, but the Anglo-Boer War had not abated as he had hoped it would; in fact, it had intensified and continued, and so he had had no choice but to wait – to put off what, at that moment, his heart desired most. As soon as he had heard of a place called Eldorado, all he had wanted was to get to it as soon as possible and begin exploiting it. It had been his idea to make his wealth quickly, return to the British Isles, and thereafter live the life of respectable comfort and luxury to which he felt particularly suited.

But then the war and the waiting had happened, and Edmund had had to find an outlet for all the pent-up potential energy his dream had created in him. For lack of a better thing to do, he found a sweetheart and together they dreamed of a time when Edmund's future feats would bear fruit and much fortune. Edmund, who, for whatever reason, made friends easily, made friends easily with a group of young men who were similarly inclined: all of them were thinking of going to the Cape Colony and finding more exciting ways to become men there than their fathers had ever had at home. Some, like Edmund, were thinking of going to the newer colony further north; some wanted to settle in the colonies permanently; others, like Edmund, wanted to explore and exploit, and then return home. They all agreed that you were given only one life, and that you had to make the most of it, by God.

Edmund was rather relieved none of his friends spoke of Eldorado, choosing to speak instead of the tried-and-tested possibilities Johannesburg and Kimberley had to offer. It occurred to him that perhaps Eldorado was not a well-known destination, and while Edmund was a very good friend, he was not so good a friend as to divulge his true destination. He pretended to be solely interested in making a go of things in the City of Kings or Salisbury. Was it not a gentleman's prerogative to never make known the entire truth about anything? Some of his friends not patient enough to wait out the war, joined it – one of them died, and the others lived to tell the tale.

Just when the war seemed as though it would never end, it did – on the 31st of May 1902. Edmund bought a ticket for his passage to the Cape on the 15th of June, a first-class ticket on the Union-Castle Line. He had enough time between the war ending and his sailing away to propose to his sweetheart, and write her two not altogether bad but not altogether good poems about love, blossoms, sunbeams and moonbeams, which she told him she would treasure until his return as a made man.

Once he arrived in the Cape, it took an inordinate amount of time – a near lifetime, it seemed – to reach the colony to the north. The long ocean voyage was followed by a very long ox-drawn wagon journey, which was followed by a very long train ride, and then a short but bumpy horse-drawn carriage trip that took him to the dusty and minuscule clearing that very proudly called itself the City of Kings. Edmund looked at the town with its neatly lined and arranged streets that had on them a scattering of burgeoning businesses, and he knew that had he been planning on staying on, he would have found a lot to disappoint. Fortunately, he was moving on, and so he pitied all the men who had had no other ambition but to settle there. He remained optimistic as he headed over to Tattersall's Hotel, which turned out to be 'replete with every comfort' as advertised. He decided to stay in the City of Kings for a week in order to get his bearings.

The City of Kings, although small, was bustling but not particularly lively, as it had been made sombre by the passing of Queen Victoria, the monarch whose vision had brought most of them there; and the more recent passing of Cecil John Rhodes, the hero of every man in the colony. It had been Edmund's dream to meet Cecil John Rhodes, but he had to content himself with going to see where the great man had been laid to rest on the Matopos Hills. He found nothing wrong with spending his brief time in the town thus, for is it not every man's dream someday to meet his childhood hero or speak to a real-life legend – so as to know what exactly could be made possible in a man's life?

When his week in the City of Kings came to an end, Edmund had his hair barbered to perfection by A.J. Frost himself, had a satisfying meal at the Duke of Abercorn, and then went to board a Zeederberg passenger coach, the first of several coaches that would take him via a meandering route to his final destination: Eldorado! The circuitous trek was rather lengthy, but this time he did not mind; he had already waited years for this moment. He did not feel the haircut was a waste of money and time because he wanted to make a good first impression on the place (not its people, but the place itself). He knew that most did not try with mining towns, allowing themselves to arrive ragged and unkempt, their wild eyes searching only for the thing that would bring them wealth. Edmund felt if he respected the place, it would respect him in return and make his endeavours prosperous. It is a well-known fact that very little logic holds sway during a gold rush.

Because Edmund had prepared himself for a place filled with gold, he could not even begin to be disappointed with the Eldorado that he actually found. There were no streets, let alone any paved with gold. There were just broken men leaning heavily on their dashed and disappointed hopes and dreams, littering the small scraggle of earth that had been entirely different in their imaginations. Edmund found himself confronted with a choice: he could choose to be broken alongside these fellow dreamers; or he could return to the City of Kings. At least there something was growing ... forming ... taking shape. Without knowing how he managed it, Edmund found his way back to the City of Kings. He had absolutely no idea of how best to proceed; his mind, so full of sumptuous visions before, did not know what dreams to dream next.

When he had first arrived in the City of Kings, he had made sure to steer clear of the friends he knew had settled there, lest they pry Eldorado out of him; given the size of the place, this had been no easy feat. Now, upon his return from the very opposite of a place of gold, he sought his friends out, pretending to be newly arrived. They received him warmly, and, perhaps guessing at his truth, told him of their own clandestine forays to Eldorado and their subsequent disappointments. They assured him that all would be well because the City of Kings was a place suited not to mining, but to business – maybe even industry on a large scale. They were determined to stay on and make a go of it. With the City of Kings being such a popular option, Edmund at first thought he would do something different; go to Kimberley and Johannesburg, perhaps. At least there the existence of diamonds and gold were known facts. However, the more he listened to his friends and to the City of Kings itself, the more he began to hear a different kind of calling within him.

He could start a business ... no, he *should* start a business. But what kind of business? He began to feel restless, and that restlessness saw him move from Tattersall's Hotel to the Grand Hotel (perhaps living there would provide him with a grand idea). Still idealess and fearing that he would squander his savings living so extravagantly, he moved from the Grand Hotel to the Sussex Hotel, and from the Sussex Hotel to the Central Hotel, and from the Central Hotel to the Caledonian Hotel. During all that unsettledness, he had been offered several options, and some ideas of his own had flittered through his mind, but the one that held more promise than the others was the idea of starting a kaffir truck business – everyone said it was the quickest way to make money in the colony, as there were so many natives in the land, and none of them very discerning.

The missionaries were doing an excellent job of converting the natives, if not necessarily from their heathen ways to Christianity, then definitely from their more primitive forms of consumption to a more civilised commerce. For example, the missionaries had created enough shame around the idea of bared skin to make the natives start buying clothes of European manufacture; therefore, any man who found himself in this line of business soon found himself making a killing. Of course, it was not supposed that one would continue selling kaffir truck for the rest of one's life; no, that would not do at all. Once enough money had been made, then one could diversify into more respectable businesses.

Edmund came to reason that if he could not exploit the land in order to make his fortune, then he could at least exploit the natives:

which was why and how he came to be standing where we first found him, waiting in line at J. Garlick – Wholesale Merchant and Direct Importer, which was advertised in the directory as having 'kaffir truck in large variety'. There were just two people in the line: Edmund and a young native woman wearing a miscellany of African and European attire. Edmund supposed that once he was in the business, he would be responsible for creating such abominations himself.

The young woman was standing at the counter and negotiating something in her native language with the shopkeeper, a Mr Robert Patterson. Edmund supposed he would also need to acquire a smidgen of the native language in order to get by. He did not feel altogether comfortable with this, but needs must. The young woman had put a sack containing many rattling things in it on the countertop, at which point the shopkeeper had looked cursorily in the sack, then retrieved a can of Borden's Eagle Brand Condensed Milk from the shelf behind him and placed it on the counter. The young woman had a lot to say to that. A lot. She had obviously bartered whatever was in her sack for the can of condensed milk, and was now negotiating her way towards a better exchange. You learnt how to read things very quickly in the colony – you had to. In the short time he had been in the City of Kings, Edmund had become adept at reading European-native relations.

Edmund supposed he had every right to cut in front of the young woman. It did not do to have a white man be seen to be waiting behind a native – not even in a kaffir truck store. What did this young woman mean by keeping a white man waiting? Edmund tried to use this line of thinking to sum up the courage to supplant the young woman, but it was obvious, from the way she carried on and on, that she was not aware of Edmund's presence. Edmund liked to think that had she been aware, she would not have carried on in this manner.

Mr Patterson seemed amused and ready to indulge the young woman even further, and while this should have irked Edmund, he decided to use the time this exchange provided him to inspect the kaffir truck. The clothes all seemed to be of inferior quality: indifferently made and the colours garish. The trinkets – and there were many of them – all seemed paper-light, and quite a few were already tarnishing. There seemed to be no craftsmanship or pride in the manufacture of these goods. This was the quality of things that he would have to sell in order to make it in the colony. The entire business seemed rather vulgar and not a little sinister; and to take his mind off this, Edmund chose instead to imagine how rich such poor stuff would have made him by the time he returned to his sweetheart in four, maybe five years.

When Edmund once again paid attention to what was happening at the counter, he saw the happily defeated Mr Patterson reach for another can of condensed milk and put it on the counter. The young woman jumped up and down in excitement, and that was when Edmund noticed she was wearing a pair of women's lace-up boots with brass buckles affixed atop each boot for no apparent reason. Edmund refused to believe that anyone would design such an incongruous shoe, and concluded that the young woman had placed the buckles there herself. He had heard about the natives' love for shiny things.

Now that the second can of condensed milk had been placed on the counter, the young woman triumphantly plopped a can in each pocket of her Little Lord Fauntleroy jacket. Satisfied, she turned around, and Edmund found himself looking at a very pretty smile on a very prepossessing face.

And without warning, everything in his world was suddenly wrong.

Edmund was not altogether sure of himself as he watched the smile on the lips of the lady petrify. She was evidently shocked by what must have seemed to her to be Edmund's sudden appearance.

It took Edmund a very long time to notice he was staring at her – and that she was staring back at him. Both of them seemed unable to move, and looked, for all intents and purposes, terrified of what they had discovered in each other. .

And then the petrified lips moved, and Edmund found himself liking the huskiness of her voice once it was directed at him.

'She asks to pass,' Mr Patterson said, translating what the lips had said. .

Edmund realised he was blocking her way to the door. Before he moved out of her way, he tried to contain all of her in one glance, but found he could not. He heard her husky voice fill the store again, and before Mr Patterson could translate, Edmund somehow managed to move his body, which, in that moment, seemed too bulky, out of her way. His eyes followed her out and were blinded by the sunshine that lay beyond the doorway.

He had no idea how long he had been standing there, looking at the doorway through which she had just exited, when he heard Mr Patterson politely clear his throat. Edmund struggled to bring his senses to his present surroundings.

'She is quite the character, isn't she?' Mr Patterson said, amused. He was a man who had obviously seen all kinds of everything in the colony.

'I beg your pardon,' Edmund said, his voice sounding both angry and afraid. There was an implication in what Mr Patterson had said that Edmund did not appreciate.

'Nothing,' said Mr Patterson, still smiling. He was removing the contents of the sack that *she* had left behind – ten empty condensed milk tins. Edmund counted them as Mr Patterson placed them under the counter.

'You can get two cans of condensed milk for ten empty tins?' Edmund asked, incredulous.

'You can if you are Sethekeli,' Mr Patterson said as he took some coins out of his own pocket and placed them in the till. The exact price of two cans of condensed milk, no doubt. He was still smiling as he carefully folded the sack.

Edmund looked at the expression on the older man's face, and could not help but wonder if there was some … understanding between Mr Patterson and the lady. Edmund had been in the colony long enough to know that, out of sheer necessity, these things happened. But he could not imagine the lady and the fullness of her bottom lip …

What in God's name was he doing? Why even begin to imagine such a thing? Edmund chastised his mind into focusing on the business at hand, but found it very difficult. As an antidote, he tried to remember the particular curl of his sweetheart's lips, which he had found so alluring.

Mr Patterson cleared his throat again. 'And how may I be of assistance this afternoon?' he said.

Edmund was happy to be asked so direct a question. Directness gave him a purpose, and he strode to the counter, but once there, all he could think was that he was now standing in the spot where she had stood a second … a minute … an hour ago. Time no longer seemed to him to be the trusted thing he had long known it to be. *Snap out of this foolishness, man*, he reprimanded himself, banging a fist on the countertop and surprising both Mr Patterson and himself with its force.

'I am thinking of starting a kaffir truck business,' Edmund said, leaning on the counter slightly, the way that she had … he really needed to stop this.

'You and every other young man in the colony,' Mr Patterson said, sounding bored and somewhat disappointed.

'I am told it is the best way to establish oneself in this town,' Edmund said.

Mr Patterson looked at Edmund for a long time before opening the flap of the counter and exiting the shopkeeper's enclosure. He walked past Edmund, beckoned for him to follow, and led him onto the sun-blinding and dusty street. They both squinted as Mr Patterson gestured the length of the street, at all the shops that had mushroomed there. 'What is missing?' he asked, pointing to the storefronts.

Edmund looked and looked, and all seemed as it ought.

'Alright, perhaps not what is missing but what is not there,' Mr Patterson prompted again; and again, Edmund looked and looked, but could not see what was not there.

'Look at the signage, man!' Mr Patterson said, sounding not a little exasperated.

Edmund saw it then. Most of the shop signs had been written in a slapdash way that simply stated the name of the business, and did not in any way attempt to attract potential customers.

'You see it now, don't you?' Mr Patterson said.

'Yes ...' Edmund said slowly and a little uncertainly.

Mr Patterson smiled and headed back into the store, with Edmund following him.

'That is what I would do if I were still a young man,' Mr Patterson said.

'Signwriting?' Edmund asked tentatively.

'Signwriting,' Mr Patterson said. 'Sooner than they expect, all those businesses will be overwhelmed by a growing population and competing with each other. They will need to stand out – and you can help them do that.'

It was Edmund's turn to smile; and that was how a rather unlikely friendship came to develop between the two men.

Edmund found, upon further consideration, that the idea of a signwriting company really did appeal.

He forgot all about the lady with her cans of condensed milk and unnecessarily buckled shoes – until the following night, when he dreamt about her. He woke up as soon as she appeared, and so he was not able to tell if it had been a dream or a nightmare that had roused him. He did not understand himself. What was he up to? He had never, not once before seeing her, given any thought to native women. He had rightly assumed they would have absolutely nothing to do with his life, and although he must have seen some since his arrival, he did not remember doing so; they had not left a lasting impression. And yet here was this particular native woman refusing to be forgotten.

As Edmund tried to fall back to sleep, he realised why he remembered this particular native woman. Of course! It was because she was all wrong. Walking around with brass buckles where they shouldn't be … with a husky voice that came out of such soft features … with the fullness of a lower lip – no, he could find nothing wrong with that fullness. He tried to recall his sweetheart, her softer and finer features, the liberties she had allowed him to take with her person – but none of it worked. It got to the point where he was afraid to sleep.

Surely this was madness. There was no way that he could be … it did not bear thinking about … mentioning … articulating.

T heir worlds were so far removed from each other that they need never have met again for the rest of their lives. But as it turned out, Mr Patterson had a daughter recently arrived in Natal, and he wanted to visit her to ensure she settled in well. Mr Patterson would be gone for three months at least, and he wondered if Edmund, who had no other employment, would mind keeping the store in his absence.

Edmund – and it must be known that this was the only reason he agreed – wanted to give the man who had given him such a brilliant idea something in return, and so he put off ordering the materials for his signwriting company, and temporarily stood in for Mr Patterson as shopkeeper.

The first time she arrived, it was a Thursday, just before midday. She did not make it past the entrance, but turned around and left as soon as she realised it was not Mr Patterson behind the counter. Did she even remember him from before? Edmund found himself wondering. Was she reacting to the fact that it was him, or was she reacting to the fact that it was not Mr Patterson? For whatever reason, Edmund found he really wanted to know the answer to this question.

She came back again, twice, both times on a Thursday and both times before midday. Again, as soon as she saw him there, she halted in the doorway. On her third visit, he tried to beckon her in, but she ignored the universally acknowledged gesture and left. Every time she walked away, he felt that she was rejecting him, a feeling he steadfastly refused to examine further. On the fourth Thursday she did not come at all, and Edmund rather surprised himself by feeling dejected for the remainder of the day.

What exactly was going on with him? What exactly was it that he wanted?

The next time he saw her was on a Monday, and the unexpectedness of her appearance – her sudden presence at the door – made something within him give way. She did more than just look at him briefly and then walk away; this time she made a series of sounds. She was saying something to him. He beckoned for her to come in, but, as she had done before, she ignored his gesture. She made a frustrated sound and walked away. Well that was progress – of a sort, was it not?

Unlike all the other times she had walked away, this time she came back soon after. She was not alone. She had with her a young native man who was wearing a fine-fitting suit. As soon as he saw the young man, Edmund found himself rising from his stool. Who on God's green earth was this man, and how had she found him so soon, and why had he agreed to do her bidding so quickly? She put a hand on the young man's forearm, and Edmund found himself stepping out of the shopkeeper's enclosure. What was he going to do? he wondered, as he walked towards them.

She was saying a long series of things to the young man, who listened with a patient smile before translating for her in perfect English: 'The lady wishes to enquire as to the whereabouts of the gentleman who runs this store.' The young man's perfect English riled Edmund. Who was this young man? And where had he learnt to speak so eloquently? And besides, it was so very obvious that the 'lady' had said much more than that.

'Tell her that whatever she wants, she can buy it from me,' Edmund said, sounding not a little angry. The young man hesitated before relaying the message, and Edmund took the opportunity to say, 'Would you like me to repeat that?'

'No. No, sir. No need to repeat it,' the young man said with a graciousness that further irked Edmund. He then turned to the lady and said a lot of things, most of which Edmund was sure he had not said. She tried to give the young man the sack full of what Edmund knew to be empty tins of condensed milk. The young man refused to take the sack from her. She said a lot of rapid-fire things that Edmund was almost certain were directed at both him and the young man. She made to approach Edmund directly, but the young man quickly stayed her by placing a hand on her shoulder. More was the pity.

The young man approached the counter himself, reached deep into his pockets, and retrieved what Edmund would have considered loose change, but which he knew was precious money to the young man. The young man placed the money, almost reluctantly, on the countertop. There was only one reason a man would sacrifice the things that were dear to him for a woman.

Edmund went to stand behind the counter and pushed the coins back towards the young man, who looked at them confused. The young man with the fine-fitting suit was not the only man in J. Garlick's capable of grand gestures. 'I know she pays with empty condensed milk tins. I will accept what is in her sack as payment.'

The young man looked at Edmund and frowned, not sure how to proceed. 'That is an arrangement she has had with Mr Patterson for the longest time. You need not accept it,' he said. It was Edmund's turn to frown: what was the young man trying to tell him? The young man leaned cautiously across the counter and said, 'She has ten empty tins in that sack, sir. She will be expecting two cans of condensed milk.'

Edmund was even more confused. What exactly was the relationship between the young man and the lady?

The lady obviously did not like the conspiracy she was

witnessing. She had a lot to say about it, and it was obvious from the look on her face that none of it was good.

'I am only standing in for Mr Patterson,' Edmund said as he brought down two cans of Borden's Eagle Brand Condensed Milk from the shelf. 'I cannot change the rules of the game.'

The lady understood enough of the exchange to make a sound of pure delight. The sound made something in the pit of Edmund's stomach somersault deliciously. That something fluttered again as she made her way to the counter with her sack. He was on very dangerous ground. The look on the young man's face, as he put the coins back in his pocket, confirmed it. This was treacherous territory indeed.

'Tell her those buckles don't belong on those shoes,' Edmund said, trying to find his way to higher and safer ground.

'She knows,' the young man said, and his expression promptly closed off.

Now why should that something in the pit of his stomach choose to somersault again at the news that she was *intentionally* doing something she knew to be wrong?

The lady in question was too busy placing the empty tins on the counter and the full cans in the sack to pay much attention to what the two men were doing. Having laid her hands on what she had come for, she was now eager to be gone. She grabbed hold of the young man's wrist, and started leading him away. Edmund felt many emotions, the most dominant being jealousy. And then, completely without warning, she looked at him and did the most amazing thing: she smiled that pretty smile that he remembered all too well, and that had visited him on far too many nights. Edmund felt his lips also curling up and returning the gesture. She looked at him for a moment longer, her own smile no longer certain – and then they were gone.

When they next came, it was that following Thursday, just

before midday. Twice in one week – that was something Edmund had not even known he could wish for. The lady walked all the way to the counter and the young man lingered by the door. She was not carrying her sack, and she did not look altogether happy as, with the daintiest fingers Edmund had ever seen, she placed a few coins on the counter. She looked back at the young man standing by the door, and he nodded slightly.

Not knowing what else to do, Edmund started to reach for a can of condensed milk. He quickly determined that there were enough coins for at least three cans.

'No, sir,' the young man said. 'She is here to pay for the cans she took last time.' Edmund did not know what to do. Had he not made it clear that the tins were payment enough?

'You have to watch out for this one, sir. She will fleece you and take everything you have, if you let her,' the young man said, walking towards the counter. Edmund was confounded. 'My name is Dingi,' the young man said. 'And this is my sister, Sethekeli.'

Edmund found himself trying to say her name, and failing. 'Settie ... Settie ... Settie.'

S uddenly, he was there.

Sethe was very sure he had materialised out of thin air. One moment she was talking to Umphathi (which is what everyone who lived in the Location called Patterson), and the next moment she turned around, and there was this giant standing right in front of her – in broad daylight. His skin was as white as snow, his eyes were a cold and hard blue, and his hair and beard were a flaming red. He looked like he was about to breathe fire down on her.

And for what? Because she chose to barter instead of using money to purchase her condensed milk? What business was it of the giant's anyway how she went about her business? But they did make it their business, didn't they – to find everything wrong with the way her people did things. They seemed to think they knew everything – as though there could never be anything left to learn. She did not much care for these people who came from over the land and across the waters, but she did, unfortunately, have an insatiable need for their greatest invention: condensed milk. It was her only weakness, and the only reason she interacted with them.

She was still waiting for the fire that would come. Did giants breathe fire? Or was it that they crushed humans and left them half broken? No, no, it was that they were lonely and captured pretty women and took them to their caves where they held them captive, wasn't that it? They probably did all of the above. Giants could do whatever they desired, couldn't they? But whatever giants did, this particular giant did not do anything to her; he just stood staring at her, making it very clear that he did not approve of her in some way. Did he want her to return the two cans of condensed milk?

As though she would ever do a thing just because he wanted it done.

Well, he had words, didn't he? So why didn't he use them? Whatever the giant might have said would have been useless, of course, but Sethe was still disappointed when he did not speak, and chose instead to stand before her, crushing his poor hat in his hands. She was curious as to how his voice might sound. It would be a nice detail to add when she later regaled her family and friends with the story of this encounter. Sethe was known the Location over as an impressive mimic of the white man. At a beer drink, there was always the moment when she would puff out her chest, clench her fists, bow her legs, stand tall or crouch low (depending on the size of the man she was imitating), thrust out her neck and speak nasal nonsense syllables, to the delight of those gathered there.

But no sound came out of this giant's mouth; he just stood there blocking her way and disappointing her, until she was forced to be the one to speak. She asked Umphathi to tell the giant to get out of her way if he knew what was good for him. Umphathi translated, and Sethe was convinced he had not told the giant what she had said, but had politely asked him to give her room to pass, which the giant did.

At the next beer drink, when the time came to regale the crowd with her latest encounter with a white man, she realised there was not much of a story to tell. There was a red-headed movable giant and he was silent – what kind of story was that to tell? What good was a white man to her if she could not impersonate him and make a parody of their encounter?

She continued to do with her midweek what she had, for the

longest time, done with her midweeks; she went to Umphathi to barter the empty condensed milk tins she had gathered from all over the Location for one or two cans of Borden's Eagle Brand Condensed Milk. The only difference was that now when she did so, she thought of the giant and his long look of disapproval. If she had any luck at all, she would never see him again – and Sethe believed she had plenty of luck.

Then one day, Umphathi disappeared. Just like that. And the silent giant took his place. Just like that. His presence made it impossible for her to enter the store: what would be the point since he so obviously disapproved of bartering? She had hoped his being there was a temporary arrangement. It was not. Week after week he would be there, wouldn't he? Sitting or standing between her and the thing she wanted most in the world. Why did he have to be there? Why couldn't he be somewhere else? Why wouldn't he return to whatever mystical and mythical realm he had come from? And then, probably thinking her a fool, he had taken to beckoning her into the store as though she had been born without the good sense to steer clear of giants.

Just when Sethe was beginning to despair of ever again having a can of condensed milk she did not have to pay actual money for, her brother Dingindawo had, like a dream come true, returned home from his studies in the Cape.

A brief interruption is needed here to explain how Dingindawo came to be a young man who wore fine suits, spoke good English, and studied in the Cape. It was a truth universally acknowledged in the colony that where there were natives there were missionaries, and so it did not surprise anyone when several churches sprouted outside the Location. Sethe had followed Bathabile's advice and ignored the missionaries' presence. Dingindawo swore he had tried to do the same, but that some woman had tricked him into entering a church. Before he knew it, he was receiving Jesus Christ as his Lord and

Personal Saviour, attending church, calling himself 'Dingi', and receiving a European education that eventually took him to the Cape. Bathabile was so devastated by this turn of events that she refused to allow anyone to speak of it.

Although ordinarily Sethe would have downplayed her brother's return and done her best to ignore him, these were extraordinary times. How many weeks had she already gone without condensed milk? So many that it was a crime. Dingi's education had taught him something of the white man's tongue, so perhaps he could convince the giant to accept the empty tins in exchange for condensed milk. Sethe was at this point so desperate that this plan seemed good enough. For his part, Dingi had missed his sister and her many forms of mischief while he was away, and so he was happy to help her.

But they did not head out to J. Garlick's for quite some time because first there was a huge celebration lasting several days in Dingi's honour. After the celebration, Dingi had to showcase what he had spent so many years learning from the white man. Once they had seen his wonderful penmanship, fourteen men had asked him to write a letter that they wanted delivered to the mayor. Dingi was definitely not the only one in the Location who could write; quite a few people could make those markings that the white man seemed to set so much store on, but everyone agreed that no one else could make the markings as beautifully as Dingi did. Apparently all those years receiving a white man's education had been worth it. As the fourteen men dictated the letter, many people came from all over the Location to watch Dingi write it:

11th Nov. 1903

To the Mayor
City of Kings Town Council
City of Kings

We, the undersigned for and on behalf of the residents
of the City of Kings Native Locations, and by their special
request, desire to pray Your Councillors' sanction, and approval
to the formation of a Native Vigilance Board – members of such
Board to be elected by the residents of the Locations.

The object of such Board, will be to look after the
wants of the people generally, to report on the state of the
Locations, to lay their grievances before the authorities, in
fact to do everything appertaining to furthering their interests.

We are well aware that we have a Location Inspector,
and hail his presence among us with utmost respect and think
that he will be greatly benefited by the formation of such a
Board.

Lastly, we desire to assure You Sir, that Your
petitioners are animated alone by a desire to advance the
interests of the Native residents of the City of Kings
in accordance with law, notwithstanding rumours to the
contrary.

We have the honour to subscribe ourselves

Your most Obedient Servants

After the fourteen men had signed the document and the ink had dried, the paper was carefully placed in an envelope already addressed to the mayor.

On the day Dingi went to deliver the letter, in what would turn out to be a fool's errand, Sethe accompanied him all the way to J. Garlick's. She never ventured beyond Umphathi's store because she did not like the White Man's Town with its straight lines and sharp angles. There was a cutting edge to the town that never let her feel as safe or as settled as she liked to feel in the spaces she occupied. The only thing that softened the city's edge was Borden's Eagle Brand Condensed Milk.

While her brother went to deliver the letter at the municipal buildings, Sethe went to Umphathi's store and tried to explain to the giant that she was bringing someone who would talk to him in a language he understood, but the giant just looked at her, uncomprehending. Why did he have to be so frustrating? How on earth was he able to sell wares to people when he did not understand them or what they wanted?

When Dingi came and asked the question that she wanted to ask, the giant surprised her twice over: first, by having a booming voice that sounded as though it were coming from the depths of a gourd; and, second, by being unexpectedly understanding and generous. He actually gave her two cans of condensed milk. Two! And accepted her empty tins as payment. Umphathi would have made her haggle and haggle and haggle before giving her the second can. She had smiled at the giant in appreciation, and he had smiled back.

It was that smile that did it. It changed and illuminated many things.

Sethe looked at the giant with his white skin, water-blue eyes, fiery hair, booming voice and big hands, and watched him transform into a man in front of her very eyes. The many things that made him should not have made him worth looking at, but they did not make him otherwise – and without warning, things that should not have made sense at all, made all the sense there was for Sethe. For the first time in her life, Sethe was afraid – afraid of a man in a way she had not been afraid of a giant.

It was that smile that did it. It made another kind of dreaming possible.

Some of what she was thinking must have betrayed itself, otherwise why wouldn't Dingi allow her to enjoy her booty in peace? Why did he keep on insisting that the giant-man was a young man, and Umphathi was not, and so the things she could do with the one, she could not do with the other? As though the age of a man really mattered in such matters. Sethe had lived long enough in the world to be wise to its ways – *she* hadn't spent all her adult years with the missionaries thinking only of Jesus Christ.

Dingi was insistent that she pay the young man what was owed; and, believing that he had some power over her, forbade her from ever again bartering with white men, especially the young man at J. Garlick's. Sethe allowed her brother to take her back to the giant-man. She paid him half what he was owed, just in case he decided he wanted payment in full and would necessitate her having to come back again.

And then, quite unexpectedly, the giant-man said her name, or at least he tried to. 'Settie,' he said over and over as though it already belonged on his tongue and was a part of him. Now why did he have to go and do that?

The next day, Sethe went back to Umphathi's store and did not take her brother along with her. What she was about to do did not need any translation.

Sethe stood in the storeroom of J. Garlick's in her undergarments and watched a giant-man crumble at her feet. He did not go down alone, but took her with him until she heard her name escape his lips and fill the room like a presence ... something breathing fire ... Settie.

Edmund's friends understood more about what was happening at J. Garlick's than Edmund probably did. At first he thought nothing of it when his friends first took to filling his days with the amusements of their set: there was the tennis to be played on the Grand Hotel courts, there was the shooting to be had at the range as a member of the Rifle Club, there were the boats to be sailed on the Maleme, Mtshelele and Toghwana dams and on Lake Matopos, there were the horse races to be spectated at the Turf Club, there was the golfing to be endured at the Golf Club, there was the badminton to be valiant about at the King's Athletic Club, there was the cycling to be exhilarated about at both the Cyclists Union and Amateur Athletic Association (Edmund could not help but be a bicycle enthusiast, and had bought two bicycles – a Raleigh and a Sunbeam – from C. Duly & Co). As though all this activity was not enough, his friends also ensured that he was a member of several societies – the more meetings they held, the better.

It was when the ever-changing woman became a constant that Edmund cottoned on to what his friends were really up to. Lately there was always an extra woman at their gatherings and activities; never the same woman, but always an extra one. The presence of the ever-changing woman let Edmund know that his friends knew about Settie. All of this busyness was just to ensure that he did not hire a jinricksha or ride one of his bicycles across Lobengula Street, beyond the White Man's Town and its control, something he had taken to doing ever since Umphathi's return. He had also taken to calling Patterson Umphathi, and that is how his friends knew the extent of his malady.

But even that did not prepare them for what came next.

Edmund sent ten fine-looking Aberdeen and Brahman oxen to Settie's mother, Bathabile.

Edmund's friends were appalled. Edmund was trying to undertake a customary marriage right under their noses, and the ten remarkable oxen were meant as a bride price. They acknowledged then that the thing they had thought was under control was very much out of control, and dangerously so. This personable man who was their dear friend was in great and grave danger of taking things too far and letting the side down.

The meeting at the Gentleman's Club was their latest and most direct intervention. Mackintosh pulled him aside and told him that he did not have to give up the girl, not entirely; he could keep her and others too if he liked, but the time had come for him to make the right and proper choice. When it became obvious that Edmund had no intention of making the right and proper choice, Mackintosh had no other option but to break the news to him. 'She already has a man. Da Costa is his name. They've been together for years now.'

Edmund did not believe him. Not his Settie. There couldn't be another man. Not for her. He would – threat or promise, Edmund would never know which he had intended to convey because at that very moment he lost consciousness.

His friends, in a desperate attempt not only to get him away from Settie but also to cease her importance in his life, had bought Edmund a one-way ticket to the Cape. While Mackintosh had his private word with Edmund, the others plied him with his favourite whisky, one glass of which had been doctored with a high dose of a barbiturate. Once Edmund was unconscious, they deposited him in the first-class cabin of a train that was going to the Cape, and told the conductor not to let him off until the final destination. They removed his wallet, his pocket watch, his silver cigarette case and anything else on his person that he might be able to exchange for ready money and use to make his way back too soon. They gave these to the conductor and instructed him to return them to Edmund only when they arrived in the Cape. Before they left, they put a letter in Edmund's breast pocket.

As luck would have it, travelling on the same train was a pretty nurse called Daisy Hancorn-Smith. Edmund's friends took to her instantly, and tasked her with giving Edmund a dose of Veronal if he proved too determined to return. As luck would have it, thankfully, she did not have to.

When Edmund woke up, the train was entering Mafeking. In his breast pocket, he found the letter written by his friends. It explained that he was becoming something of an embarrassment, and that they were giving him a chance to pull himself together. The letter went on to say that there came a time in a man's life when he had to have his fill and move on to more appropriate pursuits, and that that time had come for him. They appreciated that he believed himself to be in love, but they hoped that the smell of the ocean would remind him of home, clear his head, and make him see and seek allurements elsewhere. If he came back affianced or, better yet, married, then they would be very happy for him, and gladly welcome him back into their ranks. If he came back too soon and returned to his old habits, they would be left with no choice but to have him visit the asylum – for his own good. There was such a thing as a taking a thing too far. The most important issue was that he get well, and soon. That is what the letter said: 'get well' – as though he had an affliction of some kind. It closed with the usual fond valedictions.

His friends had placed a photograph within the folds of the letter. At first the photograph confused Edmund. It showed a man with an aristocratic nose: moustachioed, proud-looking and upright. On the man's knee was a toddler-aged boy. The man and the boy meant nothing to Edmund. Was this his friends' way of telling him to start a family? He turned over the photograph, which was stamped Mackintosh Studios, and found written there the words: Bartolomeu da Costa and son. Da Costa? He vaguely remembered Mackintosh saying something about a Da Costa ... And then he remembered fully. He flipped the photograph over and looked at the toddler. There was so much of Settie in that face that he could not deny the truth. Edmund let the train take him all the way to the Cape.

He had been brave when falling in love, but found he could not be brave when trying to fall out of love.

Edmund bought a first-class ticket on the Union-Castle Line, returned home to his erstwhile sweetheart, married her, had two sons in quick succession, moved his family to the City of Kings, and started his signwriting business – Haliburton & Sons Signwriters Extraordinaire. In many ways it was a good life, which is not to say that Edmund did not occasionally venture beyond Lobengula Street with a can or two of Borden's Eagle Brand Condensed Milk in the basket of his Raleigh bicycle.

Bartolomeu Aurelio Benedito da Costa – like his namesake who had sailed forth from Portugal at the beginning of the sixteenth century – was born with the taste of adventure firmly placed on his tongue. His earliest memories were filled with the sound of the ocean calling out to him and wanting to make him her very own. However, as a young child, every time he walked to the ends of the earth, where the ocean's water lapped onto the shore, the water would gently kiss his toes and then recede, refusing to take him with her … but always leaving him with the promise of tomorrow.

Bartolomeu came from a long line of lascars. The boast of the family was that there was no port anywhere along the Indian Ocean where you would not find a Da Costa. Another boast was that wherever there was the British East India Company, there was a Da Costa. But the real pride of the Da Costas was that since the sixteenth century, they had been more at home on water than they were on land. At thirteen, after a few rejections, and after the British East India Company dissolved in 1874, Bartolomeu began to worry that the boast would end with him – that for him, the ocean would always hold a promise that it would not keep. Imagine having a name like Bartolomeu Aurelio Benedito da Costa – a traveller's name if ever there was one – and not being able to travel?

Thankfully, luck is always changing. In Bartolomeu's fifteenth year, he walked to the shore, and this time when the ocean's waters washed over his toes, they did not gently kiss but strongly pulled and pulled and pulled, refusing to recede without taking him along. In this way, he knew that the ocean had loved him with the same desperate fervour with which he had loved her all these years. The pull directed him to a merchant ship that was recruiting seamen, and he was immediately hired as a lascar. The promise of tomorrow had been kept. His destiny realised at last, the adventure of his life could begin.

He let the ocean carry him wherever it wanted, or, rather wherever the British needed to go. Apparently there were people somewhere in the world called the Zulus, and they were fighting against the British. Then there were people somewhere in the world called the Boers, and they were fighting against the British. Then there were people somewhere in the world called the Burmese, and they were fighting against the British. Then there were people somewhere in the world called the Sudanese, and they were fighting against the British. It seemed to be what the British did best: meet people and then fight with them. The British and their love of fighting kept Bartolomeu travelling for many, many years.

These British wars needed a steady stream of soldiers, weapons, machinery and material to fuel them. Bartolomeu never fought in these wars himself, but he helped transport whatever was necessary to fight them. While labouring on ships for very little pay, Bartolomeu got to see the world: so many ports, so many shores, so much beauty, so much devastation, so much death, so much life – and a world of ocean. He took in all the sights and sounds, the languages, the politics, the cuisines, the cultures, and made his own map of the world – a map that could fit in the palms of his hands and make the world something he knew intimately.

Belonging to an always-moving and forever-changing thing – that was the only true freedom to be had.

Bartolomeu imagined himself growing old as most seamen grow old: weather-beaten, a little rough, a little hard, somewhat colourful, and full of memories. He never entertained the possibility of settling down and starting a family of his own. As he grew older, he began to see, then understand, and then know the importance of women in the larger scheme of things; but no woman he met could make him love her more than he loved his first mistress, and until the day she washed him up on some distant shore, she would always have his heart. It was all very romantic, he knew, but that was what the ocean did to a man; it made him believe no other thing would ever dare to be so beauteous in his eyes.

So it has to be said that when he first saw her casually sitting on a table, he did not readily appreciate the danger that lay in looking at her too closely. It was only later, having stolen a moment away from the gruelling work, lying on deck, looking at the stars, listening to distant gun and cannon fire, and feeling a yearning he had never felt before, that he apprehended, too late, what was happening to him. He reached into his breast pocket, retrieved the postcard secreted there, struck a match, and there she was in the flickering flame – regal and utterly resplendent – the Grand Hotel, located somewhere called the City of Kings. She was still in the process of being built, and he wanted to be part of the making of her. The yearning he felt was a deep desire to make his life somehow intertwine with hers. He secreted the postcard in his breast pocket again, and knew that while he had been on many voyages, his life's real journey would only truly begin at the Grand Hotel.

Bartolomeu Aurelio Benedito da Costa was thirty-nine years old when, during yet another war between the British and the Boers, he sailed away from the life he had always thought would be his. He did so in fitting fashion on one of the ships of the Deutsche Ost-Afrika Linie. For the first time in his life aboard a ship, he was just a passenger. He – proud not to be in steerage – travelled third-class on a ship that took him from the Suez Canal, across the Indian Ocean to Dar es Salaam, German East Africa. From here he took a dhow all the way to Beira. In Beira, he did something he had never done in any of those other ports and shores; he ventured farther inland. For the last leg of his journey, he took the Beira Railway Line to Salisbury.

'**B**artolomeu Aurelio Benedito da Costa of Goa,' Bartolomeu said, when the young clerk at the immigration office in Salisbury asked him for his name and nationality. It definitely helped that he had spent more than half of his life on various British merchant ships. His English – he had been told many times – was very good.

The clerk looked at him for a long time, and judging by the twitching of his mouth, seemed to be deciding on whether or not to laugh before he said: 'So you want me to believe you are what? Portuguese?'

'No,' Bartolomeu answered, although he was not sure he had understood the question. What was all this business about him wanting the young clerk to believe something? What was it about his name and nationality that could possibly be about belief?

'So you don't want me to believe that you are Portuguese, then?'

Bartolomeu was beginning to worry that the too-neat desk of the clerk masked the workings of an addled brain. 'What I am is not a matter of belief, sir. It is just who I am.'

'You think you can find your way this side of the colour line? Sorry, my friend, not a chance,' said the clerk.

'Colour what?' Bartolomeu asked. Were they even having the same conversation?

'Colour what? Colour what?' the clerk said, mimicking a voice that Bartolomeu realised was supposed to be his. 'Colour line. Colour. Line. You think that just because we are a new colony, everything is topsy-turvy, do you?'

This was now getting ridiculous. 'I believe you asked me for my name and nationality, sir, and I provided both. I am Bartolomeu Aurelio Benedito da Costa, and I am from Goa.'

'Says here you travelled on the Deutsche Ost-Afrika Linie. The Deutsche Ost-Afrika Linie is a German shipping company. I suppose the next thing you'll be telling me is that you are German.'

Was it the young clerk's intention to perplex him? Bartolomeu wondered, because if it was, then he was succeeding – exceedingly well. 'I am Goanese,' he said, holding on to the conversation that made sense.

'Enough of this,' the clerk barked. 'I know an Indian when I see one, and what you are, my friend, is an Indian. You are definitely not Portuguese.'

When had Bartolomeu said he was Portuguese? Could it be that the young man did not know that Goa was a Portuguese colony? He had worked on enough British ocean liners to know that the British, very often, could not see the world beyond their empire. 'I am Goanese, sir,' he said, hoping that an explanation would be useful. 'And Goa is—'

'Let me make this more manageable for the both of us,' the clerk said, no longer finding humour in any of this. 'I have here four options. I will call them out. When you hear the option that describes you, say "yes" and I will put a little tick – like so – next to the option. Understood?'

It seemed straightforward enough, and so Bartolomeu nodded.

'Good! Now we are getting somewhere,' the clerk said. 'Are you an Asiatic?'

'Yes.'

With a flourish, the clerk put a tick next to the word 'Asiatic'. 'Not so difficult after all,' he said, satisfied.

Bartolomeu was looking at the paper and noticed that their exchange was not over. 'I am also European and African,' he said.

He really thought he was being helpful. The clerk did after all seem invested in ticking the right boxes.

As it turned out, what Bartolomeu had said had not been helpful at all. The clerk was apoplectic.

'What do you mean, you are European *and* African?' he spat.

Bartolomeu started to explain about Goa, and centuries of his family traversing the Indian Ocean.

The clerk did not have time to entertain any of it. 'You cannot be European *and* African! You can only be one or the other.'

But Bartolomeu knew what he was. 'Sir, I am Goanese.'

The clerk stood up, and Bartolomeu was sure that he intended to strike him. But Bartolomeu was a tall man whose body had mostly known hard work; he knew he was not an easy man to strike. Indeed, the clerk thought better of it and sat back down. He ran exasperated fingers through his hair until something else occurred to him. 'Are you Coloured?'

Of the four options on the paper, that was the one Bartolomeu did not know and therefore could not be. He shook his head.

The clerk looked at him with eyes that had become pleading. He looked defeated as he said, 'So you want me to believe that you are what? Portuguese?'

'If that is what you need to believe, sir, then yes,' Bartolomeu said, wanting to put the young man out of his misery.

The clerk pulled out a sheet of paper, placed purple-brown carbon paper over it, and then put another sheet of paper over the carbon paper. He wrote Bartolomeu's name, nationality – Goanese – and ticked the space next to the word 'European'. He seemed to want desperately to write something else, but had no other choice but to carry on with the form. He asked for Bartolomeu's date of birth and filled it in. As he filled out the rest of the form, his hand kept on returning to the word 'European' and hovering above it. At last, he scribbled 'of Portuguese extraction' and, seeming somewhat appeased, handed the copy to Bartolomeu. 'Welcome to the colony,' he said. He seemed happy, if not with the encounter itself, then certainly with the fact that Bartolomeu was finally leaving.

'Thank you, sir,' Bartolomeu said as he received the paper. He did not appreciate, until later, the importance of the thing he held in his hands.

Bartolomeu boarded a train in Salisbury that took him to the City of Kings. All in all, it had been an arduous journey and one that did not immediately seem worth it once he saw the town for the first time. The City of Kings was a town that was still birthing itself, and as such had very little to recommend it. Why give such a sneeze of a town such a lofty name? Bartolomeu wondered. He very much doubted that such a town could contain the grandness that was at that very moment secreted in his breast pocket.

He made some enquiries as to the whereabouts of the Grand Hotel. Although sceptical, he followed the directions he had been given, and sure enough, there she was in all her majesty on Main Street and 9th Avenue. Bartolomeu actually found himself on the ground and weeping, so overwhelmed was he by her absolute splendour. She was worth the sacrifice of being in the City of Kings. She was worth thousands of ocean voyages; she was magnificent. His strongest desire was never to leave her.

When Bartolomeu sought employment at the hotel as a builder, he was informed that he could be part of the Grand Hotel as one of the many Indian waiters the hotel had in its employ – the manual building of the hotel was reserved for Africans. He accepted the job and was soon wearing the red fez cap that, according to the hotel, was an essential part of being an Indian waiter. Bartolomeu wore the red fez cap for only a fortnight before the hotel proprietor 'discovered' that he was European, informed him that he could not employ him as a waiter – a matter of wages, you understand – and took back the cap. Bartolomeu did not have enough money to stay in the hotel as a guest.

He found himself in no-man's land – neither this nor that, or too much of this and not enough of the other.

A few men with whom he had worked as lascars had travelled to the City of Kings before him, and several had even settled there. One of them, Gopal Naidoo, had been classified as Asiatic, and because of this, he had been able to establish a garment and fabric store on Lobengula Street. He suggested Bartolomeu do the same. He made him see that their experience on the Indian Ocean could actually make them very wealthy men in this landlocked colony that was eager to feel connected to the world.

Bartolomeu had never thought about being a wealthy man. He had never thought of owning his own business. He had never thought of having people work for him. The Location, Gopal Naidoo informed him, was full of possibilities. So Bartolomeu found his way to the Location, where he established an eating house, and prepared to become a wealthy man.

One day, a woman who had placed brass buckles on boots that did not need them entered his eating house. Bartolomeu had been to many ports and had been with many women in those ports – those women had provided stability in his always-moving and forever-changing world. This woman was different. He could tell, just by looking at her, that she would not provide him with stability. She would be like the ocean: something that could not be contained, that enthralled him with its ever-flowingness. She would be like the ocean: sometimes calm, sometimes tempestuous, never predictable. She would be like the ocean: lapping onto the shore, gently kissing his toes and then receding, refusing to take him with her, but always leaving him with the promise of tomorrow … and the eventual pull … pull … pull.

He smiled at her, and she smiled at him. Some things did not need language in order to be fully appreciated.

The aroma that filled the air had been too tantalising to ignore, and so Sethe had faithfully followed it. She had never smelled anything quite like it, and knew that whatever it was, it would be the most sumptuous and scrumptious thing she had ever tasted. She zigzagged her way through the Location until the aroma led her into an eating house. She had come for something delicious to eat and she did eat – eventually – once she was able to look away from the mesmerising green eyes that had beheld and then welcomed her.

While those green eyes held her, all the things that Sethe thought she knew and understood about herself ceased, and she became a different kind of possibility. When Sethe left the eating house that day, she knew she was now walking on a path that was very different from the one she had been walking on all her life – and that she had no desire to turn back. She knew she was creating a crooked line.

After that first encounter, she made frequent visits to the eating house, telling all who were curious how wonderful the food was there. The eating house soon became very popular, although none of its patrons sang its praises the way Sethe did. 'You should try the mutton curry,' Sethe would recommend with enthusiasm as she left the eating house. The people waiting to be served would take her recommendation, eat the mutton curry, enjoy it – but ultimately be a little disappointed because their experience was evidently not as transformative as Sethe's.

A very short time after meeting the proud-looking man with the mesmerising green eyes, Sethe's body fattened and rounded as it prepared itself to birth a child. Joyful as she was, she did not think there was anything wrong with a widow falling pregnant, but others in the Location did. As you did not quarrel or fight with a pregnant woman because that would bring undue bad luck on the innocent child, those in the Location – mostly the men, trying to hold on to a modicum of tradition and control, and the married women, trying to hold on to a modicum of respectability – who had a lot to say about a pregnant widow held their tongues. And so Sethe happily prepared for the baby inside her to enter the world the way she had entered it, the way her mother had entered it, the way her mother's mother had entered it. Yes, she supposed, the way even Dingindawo had entered it.

Everything was going according to Sethe's plan. As soon as her labour pains began, she sent word for her mother and a midwife to come and deliver the baby. However, while her mother and the midwife were getting ready for the delivery, Bartolomeu arrived, allowed himself to see things he had no business seeing, picked Sethe up and drove her all the way to Memorial Hospital in his jinricksha. As she bumped along in the throes of labour, Sethe told Bartolomeu, or, rather, the back of his head, exactly what she thought of him, his green eyes, his mutton curry, his jinricksha, his coming all the way over the land and across the waters just to be a thing for which she had absolutely no use.

Later, as she lay in the foreign surrounds of the maternity ward in the Native Section of the Memorial Hospital, Sethe watched Bartolomeu – much to the consternation and chagrin of the hospital staff – carry and coddle the baby he had not allowed a peaceful passage into this world. 'He is the one I have been waiting for without knowing it,' he kept saying over and over again. She watched as the baby enclosed Bartolomeu's index finger with his tiny hand. She watched as Bartolomeu sank to his knees and wept while still holding the baby in his arms. Maybe the ride in the jinricksha had not really been that bumpy, Sethe decided. And she was sorry for what she had said about the mutton curry – it really was the most-best-tasting thing she had ever eaten.

'Ibizo,' Sethe offered softly.

The gratitude in Bartolomeu's eyes when he looked at her brought tears to her own. 'My name is a traveller's name. Too cumbersome. He will be more settled than I ever was. Benedito ... the settled part of me. Benedito da Costa,' Bartolomeu said, before placing the baby in Sethe's arms.

'Benedito,' Sethe said, as she held her impossibly perfect baby for the first time. Benedito opened his mouth to wail, and before he could even finish making the sound, his lips clasped themselves around Sethe's areola, and he drank and drank and drank. He raised a small hand and touched Sethe's face as his green eyes looked at her – the curious creature that had created him – in wonder. Sethe appreciated then why Bartolomeu's knees had buckled and sunk him to the ground. 'Benedito.'

There is love, and then there is love.

It had been hard and often difficult for Bathabile Mahlabezulu – seer and healer – to adapt to rapidly changing times, and now here she was at last preparing to go to a world that would make more sense to her. She lay on her side on her favourite reed mat, which had been made by her daughter and given as a gift. The pattern of brown concentric circles that ran through the mat did not do so uniformly. Crookedness, always at play in her daughter's life.

As Sethe stuffed sweet-smelling tobacco in Bathabile's long and curved smoking pipe, her mother, with sagacious eyes, watched every move she made closely, and although Sethe knew her mother was weighing all the decisions she had made as an adult – judging and finding fault with them – she allowed herself to feel loved. She now knew that a mother's love need not be perfect in order for it to be deeply felt.

'You do not even know what you have created,' Bathabile said, her voice hoarse.

Sethe shook her head and sighed. Their dynamics had shifted. 'You have just never seen what is possible for me.'

'So bountiful and beautiful a thing,' Bathabile said.

Sethe frowned. Could it be that her mother was paying her a compliment? She handed the stuffed and lit pipe to her mother, who did not take it.

'You will have to smoke it for me from now on,' Bathabile said.

Sethe took a drag from the pipe, and in the dimness of the room, she saw her mother's radiant smile.

'You know, when I gave you your name, I didn't mean for you

301

to be so very welcoming to *every* visitor,' Bathabile said, and then laughed. It was a joyous sound that made Sethe chuckle as well. 'They did not see you coming. Not one of them. Not one of them,' Bathabile laughed and laughed, coughed, and then stopped laughing. 'It is a very rare thing for a woman. To be something so totally unexpected.'

Sethe took a drag from the pipe and began to understand. The bountiful and beautiful thing she had created was her own life: her own self.

'The courage to be your peculiar type of being ... to be your true self ... is a precious gift. You need to know that. You need to know it for yourself. You need to know it for your son. You need to know it for his children and his children's children. You can only make something an inheritance if you treasure it,' Bathabile said, and then paused for so long it seemed as though she had said all she wanted to say. 'Mine has been a long existence,' she eventually continued. 'So much has changed, some of it irrevocably. I have witnessed both the change and the inability to change back to what once was. Some things ... of necessity ... have been broken. But I have done what I was put on this earth to do; I have kept the giant pair of silver wings safe. One day they shall be returned to the white caves. But that is not my job to do. My job is done.'

Sethe started thinking about how best to take the giant pair of silver wings to the white caves. The white caves were in the White Man's Town. If she enlisted the aid of Bartolomeu and Edmund ...

'You need not worry yourself about that,' Bathabile said, reading her daughter's thoughts. 'There is a beautiful one yet to be born and she will know when the time is right.'

'She will know to take the silver wings back to the white caves?'

'She will know to give the silver wings to the white man,' Bathabile said, reaching out a hand to her daughter who in turn held her mother's hand firmly.

Sethe took a drag from the pipe and admitted to herself that she was confused, and that she shouldn't be confused. All this confirmed her long-held suspicion. 'I am not a Keeper of the Flame, am I?' she asked.

But Bathabile had already spoken her last words. Sethe watched as her mother glowed with enough light to illuminate all the dark places of the world.

V.E. Thomas, Location Superintendent, held a letter in his hands from the city fathers and looked out of his window at the sprawling chaotic expanse that was the Location. The letter from the city fathers told him, in no uncertain terms, that he was being terminated from his job. As he had been embezzling money from the Location coffers for years, he had been expecting to receive such a letter. In fact, he was rather surprised it had taken them so long to ferret him out. But even so, he still thought he was the best person for the position; the only white man who fully understood what the job really entailed.

He could not help but wonder if the letter writers knew that nothing in the Location was as it seemed. Nothing. He wondered if the letter writers knew that most of the natives who were allegedly self-employed and employers of other natives – as carpenters, shoemakers, wood hawkers – were actually just a floating population of black men who had not been fortunate enough to find day-time work in the White Man's Town. These men did not consider themselves unfortunate, however, because they had found many ways to be in the night time, and that was the reason they stayed on in the Location and refused to return to their rural homes – for these many ways of being.

He wondered if the letter writers knew that most of the Indian owners of jinrickshas and taxis plied a respectable trade only during the day and indulged in a very different kind of trade at night time, when, under the cover of darkness, they ferried mostly female passengers to Lonely Mine and Hyde Park, which both lay on the outskirts of the City of Kings.

He wondered if the letter writers knew that some of the unmarried native women in the Location were making a very healthy living being ferried to Lonely Mine and Hyde Park.

He wondered if the letter writers knew that most women in the Location, even the married ones, earned money by making available the comforts of home: providing accommodation, cooking meals, washing clothes, brewing beer, and, when the occasion called for it, sharing the intimacy of their reed mats.

He wondered if the letter writers knew that the eating houses actually doubled as gambling dens in the evenings. The Location never slept; it was always teeming with life, bustling with energy, toying with danger.

He wondered if the letter writers knew that all of this activity was lubricated by the toh ... toh ... toh ... that could be heard when you passed by certain huts. Toh ... toh ... toh ... the sound of the homemade distillery.

He wondered if the letter writers knew that there were only two sources of power that mattered in the Location – the Superintendent's Office, and the group of matriarchs whose huts lay at the centre of everything, and had been in the Location before it was the Location.

He wondered if the letter writers knew that of these two sources, it was not the Superintendent's Office that had the most power and influence.

Most of all, V.E. Thomas wondered if the letter writers knew that at the heart of it all was one Sethekeli Mhambi, who, though seemingly small in stature, was the most formidable presence in the entire Location. She lived an outwardly very simple life that belied the sheer immensity of her wealth, power and influence. She had a hand in everything that was anything: the eating-houses-cum-gambling-houses, the self-employed natives who were not just self-employed natives, the jinrickshas and taxis that operated a very different kind of trade at night, the young women who were not in the Location waiting to get married. But she was known best and loved most of all for her homemade brew whose toh ... toh ... toh only began after she had added the contents of a can of Borden's Eagle Brand Condensed Milk to the mix.

He wondered if the letter writers knew that there was a very delicate balance in the Location, an ecosystem that worked wondrously well because it had been left alone to thrive for the longest time; and that with the slightest shift in that balance, the centre would not hold – not just the centre of the Location, but the town itself – the colony even.

He wondered if the letter writers knew that whomever they chose to replace him would have to have an incredibly delicate touch, and the sensibility to tell them only the things that they needed to know.

For years they had relied on V.E. Thomas to tell them about the Location via his monthly reports; and when they had come to visit, they had seen exactly what they had been meant to see. These were the same men who, for years, had not seen fit to map the Location, or even hint that it existed immediately west of Lobengula Street where the White Man's Town ended. V.E. Thomas loved the myopic insularity of these men – the city fathers – because under their watchful governance, the Location had had no choice but to be cosmopolitan and robust and wonderful.

V.E. Thomas laughed to himself. What was he thinking? Of course the city fathers knew exactly what went on in the Location: some of them partook of it; some of them profited from it. But when you are part of a staged production, there comes a point when you forget that you are all just acting. V.E. Thomas folded the letter from the city fathers and placed it in his pocket. He sat down to write his last report as Superintendent, and made use of the language of the theatre they had created.

Report of Location Superintendent re
PROPOSED NATIVE VILLAGE FOR MARRIED NATIVES

To The Town Clerk   6/7/22

Sir,

I have the honour to forward a report on the above
subject.

To my mind it will need very careful consideration,
and I am very doubtful if there will be sufficient numbers
who would take up occupation of acre plots, under such
conditions as would have to be imposed. The idea would be
to make the new location a model one, and not allow it to
develop into a native kraal, because, I take it, the object is
to try and uplift the native and give him an opportunity to
live as like the white race as possible.

The position should be as near to the town as possible and
at such a distance from the present location as to make it
entirely separate. The Medical Officer of Health once told me
that he had a place in view somewhere near the Rifle Range.

I would suggest that the site be properly surveyed, laid
out in plots and roads, and each plot fenced when taken up
for occupation. That each occupant be recommended by some
person of standing, or the Native Commissioner. That only
bona fide marriedmen be accepted, and, if married under
native law, only one wife be permitted, and to strictly bar
polygamists. Each occupier build his own house, to be of such
design as approved by the council.

The rent would need to be such as would cover sanitary
arrangements, and water. I consider that £1. per month
would not be out of the way. Apart from the fact that natives

307

occupying these plots would necessarily be in receipt of substantial salaries, they ought to be able to acquire some profit from the ground.

That ground be set aside for educational and religious purposes.

That the place be called the 'Municipal Location Extension', and the regulations of the present location be made to apply to it, together with certain amendments which would be considered.

That it be under the supervision of the Location Superintendent who would visit it daily, and at such other times as he thought fit, to see that good behaviour was maintained.

That a Native Constable be in residence there.

I consider too much importance cannot be attached to supervision. It is my experience that the educated native needs more discipline than the raw native. He has reached that stage of his existance, which one might term half broken, and he might take the wrong step which leads to crime and fornication. This invariably happens, as is perfectly obvious to those who have to deal with them. The real reason is, because of their superiority over other natives, they have been allowed to have moreprivileges than are good for them.

I would also suggest that before any steps be taken applications be called for by asking the Native Department and missionaries to advertise the project to such natives as would take up occupation of these plots.

I have an alternative plan, which I think would be more successful in the present bad times. There is about half the population in the location there was this time last year, due to erection of new compounds for railway boys, and the reduction of native employment generally. Therefore, there is ample room, and, as the place is being surveyed on straight lines, I think suitable stands of 100 ft. by 80 ft. could be laid out and made, what one would term a suburb, to accomodate the better class native. In fact, every class could be segregated, namely, married natives, single men, coloured people, and Indians. When better times arrive and the population returns the other scheme can be considered.

I understand that the real complaint among these educated natives is, that they are afraid to bring their wives to the location, owing to its bad reputation and the class of native residing there. Well, the worst offenders are these men whose wives are away, and if their wives were here they would not be tempted andthe single girls would have less temptation from the married men. Besides this, the married women would set an example to the single ones, and so improve the general tone of things, also, they would keep their husbands in order.

The location is bounded by eight churches and schools of different denomination, so that the location with such surroundings is an ideal place for those who wish to lead a virtuous and pious life.

The educated native has less idea of cultivation than his brother who has been brought up in the reserves, in fact, there are very few natives who would profitably cultivate an acre of ground. Therefore, I think, they would be just as well off on a piece of ground 100 ft. by 80 ft. and I am of the opinion that if such stands were suitably fenced and a brick house built they would be very attractive.

I have the honour to be, etc.,
LOCATION SUPERINTENDENT.

FOR FINANCE COMMITTEE MEETING 26/7/22.

C. Hollier, Acting Location Superintendent, believed in the power and veracity of first impressions, and one Settie Muhambie had made such a very bad first impression that he knew that she would forevermore be a thorn in his side. Things had started off well enough. He had sent word telling all the people who had built and/or owned pole- and dagga-thatched huts in the Location to come and see him – the Location was modernising, and only square brick houses would be allowed to stand.

He had set a particular date and time for the meeting. So he was surprised when a woman who wore brass buckles on laced-up boots, a mishmash of African garb and European finery, and smoked a long and curved pipe – looking for all intents and purposes like a madwoman – came to visit him in his office before the day of the meeting. C. Hollier thought the woman was understandably eager to live in modernised housing, and welcomed her enthusiasm even as he refused to meet with her. It didn't do to have natives visit the Superintendent whenever they wanted to. They had to understand from the first that he was a very busy man. They had to understand that he was not like V.E. Thomas and the other Superintendents who had come after him – men who hadn't held down the job for long because they had allowed themselves too much ... familiarity with the natives.

C. Hollier's assistant, Constable Manyika, knew how to put people in their place. He was respectful and gentle about it, but he knew how to make people recognise the importance of the office of Superintendent. C. Hollier appreciated how adept and successful the constable was at escorting people out of the building. This woman with her brass buckles, higgledy-piggledy attire and her smoking pipe was the first failure in this regard. Constable Manyika removed his cap both in deference and apology, and told C. Hollier that the woman, whose name was a long succession of nonsense syllables to the superintendent's ear, refused to leave until she had spoken to him. C. Hollier told the constable to instruct the woman to leave, but the constable just crushed his cap in his hands.

'What is the matter, man?'

'Nothing is the matter, sir.'

'Then tell her to leave.'

'But she is Sethekeli Mhambi, sir.'

'I don't care if she is the Queen of Sheba. Tell her to leave.'

The woman obviously understood enough of what was transpiring and stormed out of the office, leaving the sweet scent of cheap tobacco in the air.

'See, Manyeeka? Nothing to it,' C. Hollier said. He thought he had scored a victory, but he soon found out how wrong he was.

The date and time for the meeting came, many attended; the woman with the brass buckles, hodgepodge fashion, and smoking pipe did not.

A date was set to start modernising the Location. Another meeting was called. Some men attended; the women did not.

A date was set to start demolishing the old pole- and dagga-thatched huts. Another meeting was called. No one attended.

'It is all because of Sethekeli Mhambi,' Constable Manyika said, refusing to look his superior in the eye. 'You will need to go and talk to her, convince her that what you are proposing is a good thing.'

The very idea was so preposterous that the Superintendent almost laughed. He remembered the woman's brass buckles, muddled dress sense and smoking pipe. He remembered how incongruous – no, ludicrous – no, ridiculous, she looked. She was absolutely mad if she thought she was on equal footing with him. Mad! 'I will do no such thing!' he declared.

C. Hollier went ahead and started demolishing the huts and building the square brick houses.

And then this happened:

THE BANTU WOMEN'S LEAGUE GRIEVANCES:

I.   The houses that are built by the Council at the Location here do not agree with our men's wages.

II.   The Beer Hall in the Location ruins the Bantu nation and causes starvation to our children.

III.   Where are the helpless old women in the Location to go to if their houses are being broken down.

IV.   Why should our strangers' Registered Certificates be kept in the office, and they do a piece of work each time they go for them.

V.   Why should we be stopped from gathering dry wood from the veldt.

VI.   Why does the Government not value our marriage.

VII.   There are girls at the Location who are under nobody's control how do they get their living.

VIII.   We should be granted free schools for the fatherless children in order to keep them from being savages.

signed.   R. Manylh.

SECRETARY:

The pamphlet was followed by this letter:

Women's League   Nov. 22 1929

To the town Council and the Clerk   City of Kings Location

Sirs

We strongly protest against the treatment excercised upon us, by the council to break down our stands without giving us any notice, by taking our previlages of building our own houses. The previlage which was given to us by the council that we should build proper modern houses. Now we have started to build the houses which we put in a line according to the rule of the council. But we find to day when we are busy building we are stopped to finish them. We sincerely ask the council whether this is the British traditional system of ruling its subject race. If so it is very hard for us Bantu who look upon Europeans as our guiding fathers. But in this case our minds have been agitated by these treatment. We want to know whether the council has changed the rule that we should not have stands in our location any more. Please give us a definite answer so that we should know what to do and where we are.

We are sirs your obedient and humble servants
The Womens League

Martha Ngano President

Mrs Lobengul Chairman

Louisa Guqu Secretary

The letter from the Women's League was followed by this letter:

Plot 89. Location

30th Nov. 1929

To The Town Office

Sirs

We beg to inform you that we strongly protest against the treatment exercised upon us by the council to break down our houses without giving us any notice, by taking all our previlege which was given to us by the council in the past, of building our own houses in a modern European style of building as the council is intending to take all our stands and houses. We sincerely ask the council to compensate the owners of the stands and houses according to their expenses, but in this case our minds have been agitated by this treatment. We hope this will be well understood. The houses we own in this Location have already cost us a tremendous sum of money for rent from the council, besides the expenses of building houses which have also cost us a tremendous sum of money. To stop the trouble please give us our expenses fully when you compensate us; then we will be saisfied providing that the condition of the Location is improved according to the modern standard of living. We are the Bantu workers who are living in the City of Kings Location.

Thanking you in anticipation
Your obedient servant
Sirs
On behalf of the workers
Sergeant Masotsha Ndhlovu
General Secretary I.C.U
Vice Chairman Job M Dambutjena

C. Hollier could not believe what was happening. It was as though the natives did not know that what was being done was for their own good. They seemed to think they could be trusted to handle their own affairs. Did they not understand what it meant to be a colonised people? When he handed the latest letter to the constable, the constable had the audacity to look impressed. These people!

'She is very clever,' Constable Manyika said.

'She?'

'Sethekeli Mhambi.'

'Not that again.'

'If I may, sir. You see, the Bantu Women's League and the Bantu Worker's Union do not approve of the Sethekeli Mhambi's of the world.'

Who cared about the intricacies and animosities of native lives?

'They do not like the type of … economy that Sethekeli Mhambi has created in the Location.'

C. Hollier thought he heard something in that he could take advantage of. 'Go on,' he encouraged.

'But now she has found an issue that puts them all on the same side. She is clever. Very clever.'

C. Hollier gave up. 'What do you suggest we do?'

'You will need to go and talk to her, convince her that what you are proposing is a good thing.'

'I was afraid you would say that.'

'And, sir. You may have to entertain the possibility that you will not be able to convince her,' Constable Manyika tentatively added.

So that is how C. Hollier went to visit Settie Muhambie in the very thing he wanted to talk to her about – her unsuitable lodgings.

C. Hollier liked to think of himself as a very understanding man. He had humbled himself. He was prepared to convince a woman, of all things, that all he wanted was something right for her and her community. It should be stated here again that he was a very understanding man. But even the most tolerant man could not have borne what happened next.

Settie Muhambie, in all the glory of her jumbled person, stood arms akimbo in the doorway of her dilapidated hut, and watched him and Constable Manyeeka approach. And then, her eyes on him specifically, she bit into a strawberry. A fresh strawberry! C. Hollier, Acting Location Superintendent, could not remember the last time he had eaten a fresh strawberry: and here was this woman with brass buckles where there shouldn't be eating the freshest of strawberries. How did she even know what a strawberry was? This could only be an open act of aggression on her part.

C. Hollier decided there and then that he would demolish her monstrosity of a hut if it was the last thing he did. And he would have done so immediately, had not the Lady Doctor arrived in the Location at that very moment.

C. Hollier did not understand anything about the Lady Doctor. He did not understand why she chose to be a doctor when she was a woman – a very pretty one at that. He did not understand why she wanted not only to work, but live in the Location. He did not understand why she wanted to treat venereal diseases, of all things. He did not understand why she wanted to treat venereal diseases in both men and women. He did not understand why she did not see the wrongness in everything that she undertook.

C. Hollier did not understand anything about the Lady Doctor. He did not understand how she could refuse his offer of marriage: not once, not twice, but thrice. He did not understand how she could choose to be that most undesirable of things – a spinster. He did not understand how she thought she could survive being unmarried and unprotected in the colonies. Most of all, he did not understand how she could strike up a friendship with Settie Muhambie – even after he had told her what sort of woman she was.

And Settie Muhambie – how was she able to make everyone who was not supposed to love her, love her?

On the 1st of September 1939, during the umpteenth screening of Charlie Chaplin's *The Gold Rush* at the Location Bioscope, Sethekeli Mhambi died. She died laughing. Coincidentally, the 1st of September 1939 is also the day that Elizabeth Chalmers made her determined entry into the world, a month or so early. I leave you to make of that what you will.

It is surprising, given how grand an event her entire life was, that no one remembers Sethekeli Mhambi today. Well, maybe it is not so surprising when one considers that the City of Kings has repeatedly chosen to honour and reward respectability and conformity over independence and individuality, especially in a woman; and has an easier time remembering great men than it does great women. Even so, while she was alive, anyone who was worth knowing in the City of Kings knew that there existed among them an incredible woman named Sethekeli Mhambi.

Sethekeli Mhambi's funeral was a huge send-off. The men who had been turned black by the invisible thing were in attendance. The women who had been turned into providers of many forms of comfort were in attendance. The members of the Bantu Women's League and the Bantu Workers' Union were in attendance. Some of the city fathers were in attendance, and one of them, who had personally and particularly prospered through his association with Sethekeli Mhambi, even promised to have a street in the Location named after her. Both Edmund Haliburton and Bartolomeu Aurelio Benedito da Costa were in attendance, and spoke at the funeral: it was very obvious why they spoke. Her son, Benedito da Costa, was in attendance, and spoke about a loving mother, while his wife, Anne Battison, stood by his side. The Lady Doctor was in attendance, and spoke about the importance of friendship.

The only person who was conspicuously not in attendance was C. Hollier. For years, she had refused to allow him to tear down her home. It was the home that she and her mother had built as the Matabele waited for a king who would never return. She had repeatedly told him that she had no intention of modernising a place rich with such history. Therefore, C. Hollier intended to take the occasion of her funeral to demolish the only remaining eyesore in his now neatly ordered and modernised Location. Victory would finally be his.

But when it came down to it, he found he could not do it. He could not raze the hut of his nemesis. He looked at the pole- and dagga-thatched hut that offended every sensibility, and he could not bring himself to erase it from the face of the earth. He gave himself time: a day ... a week ... a month ... a year ... many years – and he could not do it. He began to find solace in the fact that every time he looked out of the window of his office, the first thing he saw was a ramshackle hovel. Time and the elements gradually made the hut cave in on itself; and still he could not do it. He could not knock it down. The hut became a monument. To what? He was never sure.

When many years later, on the eve of C. Hollier's retirement, Calloway Cavendish, a man of considerable wealth and generosity, came to the Location with great ideas to modernise it even further, C. Hollier encouraged the endeavour as long as Calloway Cavendish understood that the last remaining pole- and dagga-thatched hut was never to be touched.

Calloway Cavendish obeyed the wishes of C. Hollier while he was the Location Superintendent. As soon as C. Hollier retired, Calloway Cavendish demolished the decrepit hut, dug up the ground on which it stood, and in so doing, made a discovery of life-changing proportions – the kind of discovery that most men only dreamed of making: he found a giant pair of silver wings.

Calloway Cavendish could not believe the grandeur of those wings.

He remembered the woman in white – Elizabeth Chalmers – and what she had said about a giant pair of silver wings. He remembered other things that he had learnt to keep to himself. If only he had believed her about the giant pair of silver wings. If only he had known that he was the white man she had been looking for.

Calloway Cavendish could not associate the giant pair of silver wings with the Location at all. He could not associate them with the City of Kings at all. He could not associate them with the colony at all. The giant pair of silver wings were too lovesome for all of that. They needed to be somewhere where they would be properly appreciated. They needed to be somewhere where the right questions would be asked and answered. Who had made them? When had they been made? How had they been made? He had heard of a missionary somewhere along the Zambesi River, a John B. Good, who was doing a great deal of trading in artefacts, and whose family owned a museum. That's where the giant pair of silver wings belonged; with someone who could really value them.

It never occurred to Calloway Cavendish to ask why the giant pair of silver wings had been made in the first place.

PART V

*Now at last I know why I was brought here
and what I have to do.*

JEAN RHYS – *Wide Sargasso Sea*

THE ANONYMOUS WOMAN

1985–PRESENT

I look at the stacks of paper with my chicken-scratch on them. A manuscript. Something that seemed so impossible for me. A history. A story about misremembered, misbegotten and forgotten women – women who are kindred. A gift from Bathabile. Bathabile who was written as Gagool.

Here I am at the end of Sethe's crooked line.

The now familiar scratching sound fills the room. Something sharp repeatedly scrapes against the surface of something dry. I watch as the following words are etched on the wall opposite me:

won't you celebrate with me

The urge to see Daisy, to share with her what I've done, what I've accomplished, stands me up and propels me forward.

For the first time since arriving at the castle, I decide to venture out of the Great Chamber on my own. I notice that the door creaks when you open it, that the stairs squeak when you step on them, that sound echoes easily and freely on the stone walls. This is not a quiet castle.

Voices carry. I follow them.

'If she is really here to prepare for the celebrations, then why does she spend all her time in her room writing?'

'And what could she possibly be writing that requires no break?'

'At least the Good Foundation and the Good Family called here looking for her – otherwise I would be doubting that she is connected to them in any way.'

'She is not normal. Do you think she is normal?'

'She still has not communicated with the Good Foundation or the Good Family. Even after the Organisation's visit. Why?'

'How could you possibly know that?'

'I just do. I have my ways.'

'If the Organisation has to come here a second time ...'

'Guests are so inconsiderate. Always leaving a mess for us to clean up.'

'She is not normal. Do you think she is normal?'

'Ah, Madam,' a familiar voice says behind me. Daisy. She opens the door in front of which I stand, listening. 'Here you are,' she says, gesturing for me to enter the room before her. 'I take it you're here to discuss the menu for the centennial celebrations,' she adds.

I have no choice but to enter the kitchen; it is filled with people I don't remember having met before. They all wear surgical masks and their eyes look at me with no allegiance. I realise too late that I should have done more to get to know the staff. Daisy follows me into the room.

'I know the Good Foundation wants the menu to be seventies-themed to honour the Golden Jubilee,' Daisy says, continuing to save me. 'I have some ideas I'd like to share with you. But, first I think we should go to visit that artist I was telling you about, the one who can construct a commemorative sculpture.' Daisy leads me out of the kitchen. Mission accomplished. 'I'm sure Evans will be more than happy to drive us.'

I smile at the staff as I leave. Their eyes do not smile back. I really should have done more to get to know them.

There is a man building a stairway to heaven. I don't see the man, I just hear him tinkering somewhere in the clouds. The stairway, made up of scrap metal and found objects, is quite a beautiful thing to behold, impressive and imposing as it winds its way heavenward.

A woman called Matilda, and a man called Stefanos, stand next to Daisy and me. We all strain to see beyond the clouds.

'He has not come down for days,' Matilda says.

'It is good that he has found something to keep him so busy,' Stefanos says. 'Otherwise he would spend all his time waiting for death.'

'I was going to ask Vida to make something for the Good Foundation's centennial celebrations. But I see that there is no point in doing so,' Daisy says.

Matilda and Stefanos seem to agree with her.

'Vida?' I say. 'Vida de Villiers?'

'Yes,' Daisy says.

'You know about Sir?' Stefanos asks, excited.

'Of course she knows about Sir,' Matilda says, still looking at the clouds. 'Everybody knows about Sir. He's a world-famous artist.'

I smile, very glad not to have to explain how I know of Vida.

'The day suddenly is so full of promise,' I say.

Daisy looks at me and smiles. 'Where would you like Evans and the day to take you to next?'

Without hesitation I say, 'I'd like to see where the Lady Doctor is buried.'

'The Lady Doctor?' Daisy says.

'Yes. She was very kind to me when I was a child. Gave me love when I needed it most.'

Daisy nods, seeming to understand more than I have said.

Finding a tombstone in an overpopulated cemetery when you re-member only vaguely where the person you are looking for is buried is not an easy thing to do. But I'm lost with Daisy, so the search seems effortless. As we walk around the maze-like Athlone Cemetery, I tell Daisy about the Lady Doctor, about 'All Kinds of Everything', about Beetham's Larola, about the short-lived guar-anteed sweetness of my childhood.

In the telling of the story I haven't made room for my father, so imagine my surprise when I stumble upon him. Literally. My father's name, date of birth and date of death on a headstone. A modest thing of grey with letters etched in black marks his final resting place. He shouldn't be here. In my mind he is still running away from me, from the thick texture of my hair, from the fullness of my lips, from the unexpected duskiness of my complexion. But as he is not running towards something, he is aimless, lost – a man with no direction, blinded by fear. In my mind, he is still carrying a fractured idea of himself and his contribution to the world to destinations unknown in his Peace, Love and Understanding van. He shouldn't be here.

I only realise how much I hate this man who is my father when I kick the headstone with so much force that a part of it lifts off its foundation. Flimsy, worthless thing. I don't know how long I have been kicking, how long I have been screaming words that make no sense even to my own ears, how long Daisy has been holding me tightly, tightly … tightly. Tighter still. Until I stop.

'He shouldn't be here,' I scream. 'That's my father, and he shouldn't be here. He should be somewhere feeling broken about

326

what he did to me. He doesn't deserve to be here resting in peace.'

Of all things, at this moment, I want Daisy to understand me: to really know the person she holds in her arms.

'He made me feel so unwanted ... He named me after his mother, whose name means clear and bright in Italian. But then I changed. In his eyes I was no longer clear ... I was no longer bright ... I was no longer something he could completely comprehend. And so he left. But he didn't just leave. He told me I didn't deserve his mother's name.'

That, it turns out, is not his only crime, because there, etched in black, under his date of death, are the words that lie to the world: 'Beloved Son, Husband and Father.' He was never beloved. Not to me.

'It was such a pleasant day,' I say. 'So full of promise.'

'It is still a pleasant day,' Daisy says. 'It is still full of promise. Don't let him take that away from you.'

Evans is more than happy to drive Daisy and me around the city. He comes from a long line of builders, was a builder himself before he became the castle's driver, he informs me. We drive past the Portuguese Club on Jacaranda Avenue, and I wonder if Bartolomeu and Benedito were members there.

'Four generations of builders,' Evans proclaims proudly. Daisy has obviously heard all this before. She relaxes into her seat and takes in the passing city. 'We built this city. Brick by brick.'

First he drives us to the buildings he thinks I might remember – Meikles, Haddon & Sly, F.W. Woolworth – although none of them still serve as department stores, they retain some of their former glory. When we drive up what used to be called Abercorn Street, I see Anne standing in front of the Pohoomull Bros shop window in her English-rose-coloured, high-collared dress with matching parasol and gloves, her hair piled high in the style of a Gibson Girl. I see Benedito, in his tailored brown suit, carefully approaching her with news of her father's passing. I see them embrace openly in a city not accustomed to such displays.

As we drive past the African Life building, Evans tells me that his father built it in 1954, the same year Evans was born. Thirty-five years later, Evans himself built the towering National Railways building that, for years, was the tallest building in the country.

I don't want this journey to end, and so I say: 'Please may you take me to Lobengula Street?'

'Lobengula Street?' Evans chuckles. 'What do you know about Lobengula Street?' But even as he says this, he is making a turn that accommodates my request.

Lobengula Street is an impossible thing to describe – you feel and experience it. It is the throbbing heartbeat that provides the city with its pulsating rhythm. It is the place where the city chooses to collide. I see Sethe standing on the other side of the street, watching Fletcher meticulously map out the White Man's Town on his rigid grid, his back turned to her. I see Sethe turn and go to create a different kind of reality in the Location. I see Edmund riding his Raleigh bicycle across Lobengula Street – two cans of Borden's Eagle Brand Condensed Milk in the basket of his bicycle – eagerly leaving the White Man's Town behind him.

And then I see it. Rusted as all street names are here. S Muhambie Way – marking the main artery that leads into the Location from Lobengula Street.

'S Muhambie Way!' I exclaim. 'It must be named after Sethekeli. It must be.'

Both Daisy and Evans look at me uncomprehending.

'Have you ever heard of Sethekeli Mhambi?' I ask.

They have not.

But other things are possible.

'Do you know where Brickfields' Courtyard used to be?' I ask, wanting to see where Elizabeth and Ezekiel reunited. 'I know it was demolished a long time ago, but do you know what suburb was built in its place?'

'Brickfields' Courtyard?' Evans says. 'I'm sorry. I've never heard of it.'

'It doesn't matter,' I say. And it doesn't. What matters is that there was once a Brickfields' Courtyard, and Elizabeth found her way to it – and to Ezekiel.

Evans drives to the place he says breaks his heart the most: the Grand Hotel. Nothing remains of the turn-of-the-twentieth century building Bartolomeu saw on a picture postcard a passenger had casually left behind on a table; the building he fell so much in love with that he travelled over the land and across the waters just to see it; the building that had been responsible for making him a European 'of Portuguese extraction'. What now remains of the Grand Hotel is the façade of the modernised building that was erected in the latter half of the twentieth century, an edifice with none of the sheer grandeur of the original. The entire area has been turned into a twenty-first century shopping centre.

But Evans is not one to focus on a broken heart, and so he drives us to the National Art Gallery, which resides in Douslin House. 'My great-grandfather built this beauty in 1901. It was called Willoughby's Building then. My great-grandfather took me on a special trip to the city when I was still a boy in shorts and showed me the building, which had changed its name to the unremarkable-sounding Asbestos House. He said that this wonderful structure was the testament of what he had done with his life. As soon as I saw this building, I knew that I would be a builder too – I mean, just look at it. A thing of such beauty can only inspire more beauty.'

Evans allows himself to take it all in as though seeing it for the first time. A Haliburton & Sons Signwriters truck drives past. 'That day, I remember a BSAP officer asking my great-grandfather for his pass,' Evans continues. 'When he said he didn't have one, the officer told my great-grandfather to leave, because the White Man's Town was only for able-bodied men. The words were meant for my great-grandfather and for me. But the officer was too late. I already knew, as my great-grandfather surely did, that the city belonged to him as much as it belonged to anyone else ... As much as it belongs to me. This magnificent building gave me that realisation.'

I look at the city – really look at it – and know that this, out of every place in the world, is where I belong.

D aisy says she and her team are open to staying true to the 1970 Golden Jubilee menu – Course One: Mini Quiches, Scotched Eggs, Pineapple and Cheese Skewers; Course Two: Beef Carpaccio; Course Three: Chilled Cream of Watercress Soup; Course Four: Caviar Mousse served with Cucumber Slices and Toast Rings; Course Five: Waldorf Salad; Course Six: Grilled Rainbow Trout with Lemon Butter; Course Seven: Chicken Roulade; Course Eight: Mint Sorbet; Course Nine: Beef Bourguignon; Course Ten: Cheese Log and Cheese Fondue with an Assortment of Breads, Crackers and Vegetables; Course Eleven: Black Forest Cake; Course Twelve: Mini Highlander Biscuits served with Coffee – but she feels the original menu, impressive though it was, doesn't quite seem to fit the occasion somehow.

'Perhaps it was too much a product of its time,' I say.

Daisy looks at me, somewhat relieved. 'We could be *inspired* by it,' she says. 'To do something we could call "Around the Continent in 20 Bites". A tasting menu. Smaller plates full of the distinctive flavours of this continent. Where we will use as many local ingredients as we can,' she adds. She hands me a notebook. She has obviously given this a lot of thought.

'And if I'd chosen the 1970 menu?' I ask.

'Something told me that you wouldn't.'

The notebook is filled with notes – recipes, places where the ingredients should be sourced, and diagrams of how the food should be plated. I notice that the first note – 'start with Grandma's signature dish, the perfect welcome' – was jotted down on the day of our first correspondence. While I was thinking of escape, Daisy was thinking of welcome.

'So the menu will consist of things like Ghanaian Jollof Rice,' Daisy says. 'Njera with Doro Wat, Lamb Bunny Chow, Fried Fish with Plantain, Curried Goat, Boerewors with Chakalaka, Kale in Peanut Sauce, Baobab Cheesecake, Malva Pudding, Madagascan Vanilla Ice Cream with Amarula Poached Fruit. And on the adventurous side, Ostrich Steaks, Braised Rabbit, Crocodile Tails and Venison Stacked Sliders.' A part of Daisy has come alive, her enthusiasm is so infectious that I can already taste and smell her wonderful creations. I have never experienced anything like it. I have never known anyone like her.

Dear reader, I think you have known from the first that this is it for me. Even the easy-laughing, sure-footed woman can't take away what I feel.

For the first time since coming to Holdengarde Castle, I have the courage to get in touch with the Good Foundation. I inform them that we need to start finding accommodation for the invited guests. I check to see how far the shipment with the giant pair of silver wings has travelled; I am happy to hear that it is somewhere in the middle of the Atlantic Ocean. There is no turning back now. I excitedly tell the Foundation about the menu Daisy has planned.

The Good Foundation does not quite share in my zeal. It is happy to hear from me, happy that things are going well, happy that preparations are underway ... but Daisy's menu seems too ... exotic. It may be best to stick to the original plan and simply replicate the 1970 menu, which aligns more with the tastes of the invited guests. Having got that out of the way, the Foundation informs me that the Good Family thinks I should return home. The Good Foundation agrees with the Good Family in this regard. At a time like this, the family has to be together. Anything I am doing at the castle, I can do more effectively at the Foundation. If it so happens that the celebrations cannot be held this year, which seems highly likely, a contingency plan has already been proposed: the Good Family will create a residency for African journalists who live under despotic regimes that do not allow for press freedom. They believe this is what John would have wanted. Besides, I definitely do not want to be stuck in Africa at a time like this.

I tell the Good Foundation that even here in Africa, everyone is armed with surgical masks and hand sanitiser. The Foundation questions the quality of these things and their source of origin. It will go ahead and buy me a plane ticket. I can always return to the castle in a few months to finalise preparations when the world has righted itself once more – if the celebrations are indeed to go ahead. I make no commitment to a return, but the Foundation seems to hear one.

I realise there is no use in escaping if you don't let your captors know that you've escaped.

Needing something else to do, I tell Daisy that she and her team can create a few dishes from her tasting menu, and we can have a party for the staff as a gesture of my appreciation for their hospitality.

I'm aware that this is soon talked about as my farewell party among the staff.

I realise there is no use in escaping if you don't let your saviours know that you've escaped.

F eeling that an ending not of my choosing is imminent, I've taken to following Daisy everywhere. Like a puppy sick with longing, I watch her joke, haggle and barter with farmers, hunters and service providers. I watch her give instructions in the kitchen and gently correct where they have not been followed properly. I watch her share sundowners with Alfred and Evans, and good-naturedly listen to their memories of the good old days. I watch her be the most brilliant thing I have ever seen.

I know my presence everywhere is obstructive. I'm aware that the staff tolerate me because I'm a guest, and, more important, because I work for the Good Foundation. I'd hate to think that Daisy merely tolerates me as well. I'd like to think we're making our way towards friendship, even as I yearn for something more.

On the day of the party for the staff, there's a lot of commotion in the kitchen. Daisy is making a veritable feast. She seems both excited and anxious. She takes especial care with a dish she calls Chicken and Dumplings – Grandma's Way.

Later in the day, a car arrives, bringing with it guests. Daisy's family. Her mother, her father, her grandmother and her grandfather. They help each other out of the car, they help each other walk, they lean on each other, and yet they seem to be people without age and weariness. Wearing a surgical mask and thoroughly sanitised, Daisy hugs her parents, but it's her grandparents who get the full force of her affection. She showers her grandparents with kisses, masks and all. They don't endure this, they welcome it, rejoice in it, revel in it. Daisy exchanges the newsboy cap on her head for the fedora on her grandfather's head. Her grandmother, mother and father look on indulgently. This is how it has always been between them.

I see Daisy growing up in this family. I see them standing back and watching her, letting her go forward, letting her explore, letting her find who she wants to be. I see them actively preparing the space for her to do so. I see her looking back at them during moments of doubt and uncertainty. I see her relaxing into the knowledge that they're still there, that they will always be there. I see her venturing further ... and further still ... until she is completely who she wants to be. She, but her way.

'I don't understand why you always have to wear such high-heeled boots,' her mother says, breaking the spell. 'They can't be good for your feet.'

'And I don't understand why you always have to wear a uniform and carry that messenger bag,' Daisy responds.

'You two,' her grandmother gently chides.

'Is the food ready?' her father asks.

Her grandfather chuckles and adjusts the newsboy cap that now finds itself on his head. 'Watch out for this one,' he says to me, using his walking stick to point at Daisy's father. 'He'll eat you out of house and home if you're not careful.' The kindness in his eyes makes him an instant friend. Just like that, I'm pulled into their orbit. I offer him my hand and he lets me help him up the steps leading to the entrance of the castle. 'My greatest fortune in life has always been letting women lead me where they will,' he says with another chuckle.

In the castle, Daisy's grandparents prove to be very popular.

'Is it true that you're the only man alive who knows what happened to Emil Coetzee?' Stevens asks Daisy's grandfather.

'What does someone as young as you know about Emil Coetzee?' Daisy's grandfather asks as he sits down.

He has an immediate audience. Stevens is joined by Evans and

Alfred, and they all have questions for him that he is very happy to answer – glad that his mind is still capable of holding onto memories.

Daisy leads her grandmother to the kitchen, where she makes her try the Chicken and Dumplings dish.

'You make it even better than I ever did,' her grandmother says after sampling it. She gives me some to taste as well. It does indeed taste wonderful.

'That's not true,' Daisy says. 'I will never make it as well as you do.'

Her grandmother places her hand on Daisy's cheek. 'That's just the love talking,' she says.

Daisy's father is meanwhile helping himself to the Doro Wat, and the Curried Goat, and the Chicken and Dumplings. In the end, Daisy has no choice but to usher us all out of the kitchen.

The family, staff, and I – the only guest – have the feast in the Great Hall. The food is divine. The conversation is lively. Conviviality. I'm a part of something. I'm so happy, I think I smell the scent of Beetham's Larola and cheap tobacco in the air.

'Do you know who my daughter is?' Daisy's mother says, addressing me directly for the first time. She opens her messenger bag and retrieves papers that she hands over to me. They are newspaper clippings of Daisy in a chef's uniform in France, Italy, Japan. The Daisy in the clippings is smiling next to other chefs. There are quite a few of her on her own in front of a restaurant somewhere in the world. Starred reviews. A lot of praise. But the smile in the 'on her own' clippings is no longer what it once was.

'Mum!' Daisy says, snatching them from my hands.

'What?' her mother responds. 'This woman needs to know what you're capable of. She's probably sitting there thinking you're lucky to have the Good Foundation's business. She needs to know the Good Foundation is lucky to have you cater their affair.'

'What she needs is to enjoy the meal,' Daisy says, handing her mother the clippings.

'I'm well aware of your daughter's talents,' I say, trying to win her mother over. I'm not so sure I succeed.

'She goes everywhere with those clippings in her bag,' Daisy's grandfather says to me, a twinkle in his eye.

'I'm a proud mother.'

'Sometimes she stops complete strangers at the store and shows them those clippings,' Daisy's father says as he reaches for more njera.

'You all talk as if you know another woman in the City of Kings who has a Michelin-starred chef for a daughter. Imagine where she would be if she hadn't come back for that undeserving woman—'

'She's here with us now, and we're all enjoying this moment together,' Daisy's grandmother says, and the subject is brought to a wise end.

This is family, the way it should be – tender in the middle, rough around the edges, but always homing towards a shared love.

When they leave, it is like they have taken something essential with them.

Daisy's grandfather makes me promise to visit them in Krum's Place once the world has righted itself. I fully intend to keep that promise. It feels good to have something to look forward to.

I help Daisy with the clearing of the table. A newspaper clipping had fallen, unseen, to the floor. Daisy finds it and bends to pick it up.

'My mother thinks I came back for the wrong reason,' Daisy says, looking at an image of her younger self smiling back at her.

I hear the easy laughter of a sure-footed woman.

'But the truth is, I came back for them. I think I came back for the right reason.' Daisy looks up at me, and that's when I notice that she's crying. I kneel down next to her and hold her.

'I don't ever want to lose them … I know I cannot hold on to them forever. But I never want to lose them. I don't know what I'd do if I did.'

I hold her tightly, tightly … tightly. Tighter still. Until she stops.

T he time has come for me to be truly brave. I call my mother.
'I am not coming back. It was never my intention to return,' I inform her.

She is silent. For a long time.

I am not really sure what kind of reaction I was expecting.

'As a baby, you preferred the Lady Doctor to me,' my mother eventually says. 'She had a house – a cottage, really. I had a van. When she held you for the first time, you refused to come back into my arms. Cried. Made such a fuss. Like I wasn't your mother.'

What can I say to something I do not even remember?

'You thought your life would be much better with her. You made yourself impossible for me … for your father … all so that you could live with the Lady Doctor. You should have seen how happy you looked when she came to take you away from me. You looked like you were being saved.'

My life, our relationship, begins to make sense to me. 'You've never forgiven me for that,' I say. 'For something I did as a child.'

'You do not know what it is like not to be wanted. To be rejected.'

I realise that for my entire life, my mother has only been able to see and hold on to her own pain.

'I found my father's grave at Athlone Cemetery,' I tell her. 'He died many years ago. Soon after we left.'

She is silent again.

'I wasn't looking for him,' I say, feeling that ever-present need to explain myself to my mother.

'You were looking for the Lady Doctor's grave.'

'Yes.'

'Did you find it?'

'No.'

'I was not her first choice, you know. She came to the orphanage many times. She was really interested in a girl called Charmaine. Blonde hair and blue eyes. Charmaine and I were the same age, the oldest children in the orphanage. The Lady Doctor was advancing in years, and made it known that she thought the other girls were too young. She needed to be taken care of as much as she needed to take care of someone. Charmaine died of an illness that took her with no warning. But the Lady Doctor really needed to adopt, and so in the end she had no choice but to adopt me.'

'I see,' I say.

'No. You do not. You do not see. It was not the first time it happened to me. A young couple in desperate need of a child had come before her. They adopted me when I was still a baby. They chose to overlook the circumstances of my birth. Like you, I was born with blonde hair and blue eyes. Like you, I changed physically when I became a toddler. Luckily, not as much as you, but still enough. They did not know what to do with the change. They chose not to overlook the circumstances of my birth then, and returned me to the orphanage. Just like that, I became an unwanted thing.'

'Oh,' is all I can say.

'You do not know what it is like not to be wanted. To be rejected,' my mother repeats, following her own train of thought.

'My father—' I start to say.

'*I* kept you. I have kept you close to me through everything. And now after everything I have done for you, after all these years, you tell me that you are not coming back … that it was never your intention to return.'

'Mother—'

'You do not know how to appreciate what you have.'

341

'And what do I have?'

'You have me. You have three children. You have the Good Family. You have us. You have a family. I gave you a family.'

'Surely you must realise what my life's been like there.'

'You think it is easy for us? It is not. You are not easy. We never know what you are thinking, what you are going to do, and when you are going to do it.'

'It's not the life I wanted.'

She is silent again. Again, for a long time.

'I hear you have been writing,' she says with a sigh.

'Yes.'

'About the woman in white?'

'And others. Yes.'

'I know the woman in white is my mother. I know the exact circumstances of my birth,' my mother says.

It is my turn to be silent. For a long time.

'So you listened to what Gagool had to say?' my mother says.

Of course. Bathabile must have appeared to my mother at some point and told her about the giant pair of silver wings.

'Her name was not Gagool. Her name was Bathabile,' I say.

'The world is not kind to people – women especially – who see things differently,' my mother says. 'I tried to stop you from going down the path you are currently on.' She sounds resigned. 'With all my might, I tried.'

I remember her trying, trying with all her might, until I was black and blue ... until my wrist was broken ... until I associated writing with pain.

'I have tried to save you all your life, and you have fought me all your life.'

Black ... and blue.

'You have chosen to listen to a fiend and somehow expect good to come of it,' my mother says.

Black ... and ... blue.

'It is nothing to be proud of. A lineage of madwomen,' my mother says as much to herself as to me.

My mother is capable of many things. She is particularly good at culling, hollowing things out, removing what is inside.

It is a bloody business.

But apparently I am capable of many things too.

'They were not mad. They were just women,' I say.

'Well, you are on your own now,' my mother says, affording herself the final word.

Our connection is severed. The line goes dead.

But I no longer feel that I am on my own.

Holdengarde Castle is shutting down. The country is shutting down. The world is shutting down. But before all that happens, there will be a wedding.

I put on my best dress. I want to impress. I want to be seen.

The wedding is ostentatious. Everything glimmers. The smiles are bright. The laughter rings true. The happiness seems real. I try to feel welcomed by it all. The theme of the wedding is ebony and ivory. I am wearing a red dress. Many people look at me. Their eyes are curious, but not unkind.

I hear a member of the castle's staff explain my presence. 'She's a guest. Works for the Good Foundation. Yes, *that* Good Foundation. The Foundation will be having its centennial celebrations here at the castle, later this year.' Murmurs of approval and nods of appreciation are sent my way.

Daisy is busy making sure everything the bride and groom wanted and paid for is exceeding their expectations. She is wearing the colours of service – black and white – which should make her blend in with the ebony and ivory of it all, but she does not. It is the way she wears the black and white that separates her – makes her stand out. The bowtie knotted around her neck is something I want to pull loose.

Someone clears his throat next to me. I turn to see Alfred sitting at a table at the periphery of the action. He gestures to the chair beside his. Feeling grateful, I sit down next to him.

He runs his gloved fingers over the silverware – not sterling silver, but stainless steel. He flicks a finger on the stemware – not crystal, but something made to look like it. He unfolds the swan centrepiece – not cotton, but a thick cotton-like paper that can be easily disposed of after the wedding. None of these things have to find a home for themselves in the newlyweds' house; none of them have to witness what happens to the couple and their professed undying love after this day.

'The flowers are real,' Alfred says, as his thumb and forefinger rub the petals of the lilies arranged in a vase on the table. 'At least there is that.' Having found the silver lining, he looks at me. 'This is what we have come to. We only know how to approximate what we would really like to be. We are rich in many ways, but our tongues do not know how to speak of what we truly have, and our eyes are not for beauty to see.'

I place a hand on his shoulder.

He pats my hand and attempts a smile. 'You are one of the really good ones,' he says. 'I do not think they make them like you anymore.'

'That's supposed to be my line,' I say.

We laugh, and then we sit there for quite some time. My hand still on his shoulder, neither one of us made uncomfortable by the prolonged gesture.

The wedding party goes to the dance floor. A waltz begins. Over the speakers, Engelbert Humperdinck sings 'The Last Waltz'. The wedding party dances. The guests clap, whistle and ululate their appreciation. The master of ceremonies encourages the guests to join in the dance.

Alfred's body sways slightly to the tune of the waltz, his feet tap the beat.

'May I have this dance?' I say.

He looks surprised, and then he smiles. 'That would make this old man very happy,' he says. 'They really do not make them like you anymore.'

We make our way to the dance floor. I regret the decision only briefly. I'm not a good dancer, and here I am making this a fact known to everyone at this gathering. But there isn't much time for regret. Alfred is an accomplished dancer, and he carries me along with great ease as he dances towards his memories, towards his youth, towards sterling silver, towards genuine crystal, towards one hundred per cent cotton. His body even forgets to stoop as we dance and dance and dance.

In life, you should always let the music take you where it wants to.

I'm aware that we are being watched, that all eyes are on us. The wedding party has stopped dancing and is now looking in our direction. We have become spectacle and entertainment. But I don't care because Daisy has stopped her busyness and *she* is watching *me*. Finally.

I know that if I ask her, she will let me loosen her bowtie. Actually, I know that I won't even have to ask.

Someone laughs. A loud, forced laugh. Too loud. I see the easy-laughing, sure-footed woman. She is sitting next to a man – one of the men from the Organisation who came to the Great Chamber. She laughs at what the man is saying, but all the while she is looking at Daisy.

And Daisy is still looking at me.

The music comes to an end. The guests clap, whistle and ululate their appreciation. The applause is thunderous. The spell is broken.

Alfred and I come crashing down into the reality of the moment. He bows nobly and I think I curtsey clumsily before we walk away from the dance floor. It's best to let such occurrences be brief and swiftly relegated to glorious memory.

Alfred heads to his quarters, and I head up to the Great Chamber.

I pace the floor in hope or despair, I cannot tell which – until there is a knock on the door. I open it. Daisy stands on the threshold. Sleeves rolled up. Waistcoat unbuttoned. Hands in her pockets. The bowtie is still knotted around her neck like she knows exactly what I plan to do with it.

'I didn't have to imagine you,' Daisy says as she crosses the threshold and enters the room. Her body is making its way towards mine.

Some part of my brain – a very small part – still remembers language. 'What?' this small part asks.

'I didn't have to imagine you the way you had to imagine me,' she says.

I cannot make sense of anything except her long lashes, her full lips, her still-knotted bowtie.

'I saw you in a magazine once. You're "That Girl".'

'Oh,' I somehow manage to say. 'There were many "That Girls".'

'That may very well be,' Daisy says. 'But you're the only one I remember.'

I would love to revel in this knowledge, but Daisy is kissing me, and I am kissing her, and there are so many other things to revel in, to luxuriate in, in this moment – the feel of her bottom lip between my teeth, the long column of her neck, the effortless unravelling of her bowtie.

I feel a certain kind of power. I have a certain kind of courage.

I use this power and this courage to ask Daisy: 'The laughing woman. What was that?'

'The end of something,' Daisy says.

It is as though Daisy's lips, hands and fingers already know me. I love being already known.

It is a forever-hungry thing that I feel. A hot-to-the-touch thing. A breathing thing. Alive. I feel alive.

B ad news arrives the morning after. Stevens comes carrying it on a silver tray. He bangs on the door until I open it. He looks over my shoulder and sees Daisy getting dressed. His eyes are cold and calculating above the surgical mask.

'The bosses will not be liking this,' he says to Daisy, ignoring me.

'Let them not like it,' she says.

'No fraternising with the guests. Strict policy.'

'That's never stopped you before,' Daisy says, coming to stand next to me.

Stevens, still not looking at me, his eyes still cold and calculating, offers Daisy the piece of paper on the tray.

'What's this?' she says, taking it.

'Read it,' Stevens says.

Daisy starts reading. Stevens looks at me then. He looks triumphant. I know from his look what that piece of paper is: my plane ticket.

Daisy has stopped reading, but she still holds the paper in her hands. She looks at me, and then hands me the paper. I cannot read her look.

'Alfred has called a meeting for all the staff,' Stevens says.

Daisy nods. She attempts a smile and then leaves with Stevens, closing the door behind her.

I look at what I hold in my hands. It is not a plane ticket. It is a letter. The letter reads:

To Whom It May Concern:

I regret to inform you that my daughter, a guest at the castle, is not altogether well. She has a history of mental illness and has, on occasion, been violent. She has caused great harm to herself and others. I am worried for her safety and yours. She suffers from visual, aural and olfactory hallucinations. Not so long ago, while under psychiatric care, she told her doctor that she had befriended a woman named Isabella Van Wagenen. Isabella Van Wagenen (also archived as Isabella Van Wagener) was born Isabella Baumfree (also archived as Isabella Bomfree and Isabella Bomefree). Later, after she claimed to have heard the Spirit of God tell her to preach the Truth, she renamed herself Sojourner Truth. Sojourner Truth was an abolitionist and a champion of civil, human and women's rights. She died in 1883.

I love my daughter and only want her health and happiness. But unfortunately she can no longer be trusted to do what is best. She has three wonderful children who need her. The Good Family only wants her to get better and stronger. We have repeatedly encouraged her to come back home. This has been in vain. She has not used the plane ticket the Good Foundation sent her. We now need your help. Borders will close soon. Flights will be cancelled. She needs to be put on the next available flight. You may need to use force. You have my permission to do so.

Sincerely.

The happiness that was recently felt will from now on be a thing of the past. A memory. But I will not allow this letter to break me. I will not fall, not this time. I will not crouch. I will not creep. I will not crawl. I will not become a half-broken thing. I will continue to stand.

Voices climb walls and make their way into my room.

'What kind of mother leaves her children behind?'

'I always knew she was not normal.'

'She needs to go.'

'We cannot find ourselves on the bad side of the Good Foundation or the Good Family.'

'We can always call the Organisation. They will be happy to handle this.'

'I am happy to throw her out.'

'I always knew she was not normal.'

I must do something.

I look around the Great Chamber. My eyes rest on the replica of Simone Martini and Lippo Memmi's 'The Annunciation and Two Saints'. I look at the olive branch that the Archangel Gabriel offers to the Madonna. I look at the way the Madonna shrinks away from him, recoiling with both distrust and disgust, not wanting what he has to offer, not wanting that olive branch and what it symbolises. If that olive branch is removed, then the Madonna can go back to reading her book and carry on with her life.

It takes a lot of effort to move the four-poster canopied bed, but I do. My fingernails start chipping away at the olive branch. I know it would be more comfortable if I was in a crouching position, but I will do this standing. I will not crouch. I will not creep. I will not crawl. Not this time.

When they come to take me away, they will find me with my fingers aching and bleeding, but the olive branch will be gone. I am victorious. I sit on the bed and wait for the footsteps I hear on the stairs to enter the room.

Daisy walks in. She is alone. She has not brought Alfred, Evans or Stevens to force me out. She is going for something gentler. She sits next to me on the bed. She notices the blood on my hands, and goes to the en-suite bathroom. She comes back with a bowl of water, a towel and a bottle of antiseptic liquid. She sits next to me and places my hands in the bowl. The cloudy, antiseptic water is warm even as it stings.

It is too kind. Too soft. Too gentle. This goodbye. I do not deserve it.

'Stevens and most of the other members of staff will be leaving over the next few days,' she says without looking at me.

'Because of me?'

'Because the government will soon restrict movement and travel. Those who want to be with their families at a time like this need to be with their families.'

It is not too subtle a hint.

Daisy removes my hands from the warm water and begins to dry them with the towel.

'Alfred and Evans will stay. A castle always needs to have people in it.' She looks at me then, and smiles. 'We've talked about it and decided you could stay here – if you so wish. Alfred and Evans will need a guest to look after, otherwise they may very well go mad.' I can see that she regrets the word as soon as it comes out of her mouth, but she doesn't apologise for it. I am grateful to her for that. In this moment, I am grateful to her for many things.

'What my mother says about me is the truth,' I say. 'I do have a history of violence.'

Having cleaned my hands, Daisy turns over my left wrist. We both look at the ugly keloid scar there. Daisy runs her thumb over it.

'Hurt and heal,' she says. 'It is what we do.'

I look at Daisy, who does 'she' her way. I lean over and kiss her.

I am still in the castle.

Somewhere, crossing the waters, there is a shipment making its way to me. In that shipment is a giant pair of silver wings. I am on a mission that needs to be fulfilled. Me.

I look in the mirror at this woman on a mission. Finally I see her, the one who has always been formless, blurred, indistinct, undefined: I see her clearly. I look at her *long slim legs*, her *small and narrow feet*, her *capable clever hands*, her *mass of dark hair, standing out from her face like a halo*, hair that can sometimes be *shaggy* and *grizzled*. I touch her face, my face, *small and oval*. I touch my lips, full and plump. I look into my green eyes; something inherited from Bartolomeu Aurelio Benedito da Costa. I smile. It is the wonderfully warm and self-assured smile I remember from the dream-memory I had in the attic an entire lifetime ago now. A smile full of promise.

I look at myself and realise that I am no longer this misshapen, malformed, half-broken thing. I am what I have been for a very long time: *tall, dark and majestic*.

My name comes to me in that moment. My name. My very own. Bathabile has long had a name to give, and I have long had a name to receive.

Daisy joins me. She stands beside me. I tell Daisy my name. She smiles at me before she says it. She feels it on her tongue, tastes it on her lips, breathes it into the air, and makes it a living thing.

My name. A living thing.

Daisy has come to say goodbye. She is going to join her family in Krum's Place. She puts something in my hand. Origami. Tender

354

yellow paper folded into the shape of a swan. She encourages me to open it.

Everything that was broken has forgotten its brokenness
– Mary Oliver

Daisy holds me tight and kisses me. She will return to the castle when the world rights itself again.

But for now we stand together in front of the mirror.

This is me, and here I am loving and being loved.

A ship is finding its way to safe harbour.

There will be a time after this.

won't you celebrate with me
what i have shaped into
a kind of life? i had no model.
born in babylon
both nonwhite and woman
what did i see to be except myself?
i made it up
here on this bridge between
starshine and clay,
my one hand holding tight
my other hand; come celebrate
with me that everyday
something has tried to kill me
and has failed.

– Lucille Clifton

ARCHIVAL SOURCES

BLG 3/18 – Umtali Rape Case

BLG 3/96 – Location, 1924

BLG 3/142 – The Prince of Wales Visit, 1924

BLG 3/195 – Kaffir Beer Brewing, 1926

BLG 3/242 – Location, 1927

BLG 3/311 – Beer Brewery – Native, 1928

BLG 3/356 – Vawdrey Case, 1929

BLG 3/373 – Location Matters, 1930 *(see pages 361 to 365)*

BLG 3/408 – Rickshas, 1930

BLG 3/344 – Location Sub-Committees Report, 1929–1930

BLG 3/465 – Native Eating House Matters

BLG 3/501 – Unemployment, 1931

BLG 3/502 – Unemployment Issues, 1931

BLG 3/629 – Coloured School – Applications, 1932

BLG 3/630 – Coloured School Advisory Committee, 1932

BLG 3/696 – Kaffir Beer – Illicit Brewing Of, 1932

BLG 3/710 – Native Malingerers

BLG 3/713 – Native Assaults on European Women, 1932

BLG 3/725 – Coloured Community Service League, 1933

BLG 3/762 – Fortieth Anniversary Celebrations, 1933

BLG 3/763 – Fortieth Anniversary of Occupation Day Celebrations, 1933

Davis' Bulawayo Directory and Handbook of Matabeleland, 1895–1896

Davis' Bulawayo Directory and Handbook to Matabeleland, 1899

Papers Relative to the Coloured Community 1950–60 – Reverend Reuben Frederick 'Rufus' Green

Rhodesia Directory 1911, 1912, 1913, 1914, 1915

Rhodesia Directory Including Beira, P.E.A, 1918, 1919, 1920, 1921

Rhodesia Directory 1939, 1950

All listed archival materials are housed in the National Archives of Zimbabwe, Bulawayo.

Report of Location Superintendent re

PROPOSED NATIVE VILLAGE FOR MARRIED NATIVES.

To the Town Clerk.   8/3/2?.

Sir,

I have the honour to forward a report on the above subject.

To my mind it will need very careful consideration, and I am very doubtful if there will be sufficient numbers who would take up occupation of acre plots, under such conditions as would have to be imposed. The idea would be to make the new location a model one, and not allow it to develop into a native kraal, because, I take it, the object is to try and uplift the native and give him an opportunity to live as like the white race as possible.

The position should be as near the town as possible and at such a distance from the present location as to make it entirely separate. The Medical Officer of Health once told me that he had a place in view somewhere near the Rifle Range.

I would suggest that the site be properly surveyed, laid out in plots and roads, and each plot fenced when taken up for occupation. That each occupant be recommended by some person of standing, or the Native Commissioner. That only bona fide married men be accepted, and, if married under native law, only one wife be permitted, and to strictly bar polygamists. Each occupier build his own house, to be of such design as approved by the council.

The rent would need to be such as would cover sanitary arrangements, and water. I consider that £1. per month would not be out of the way. Apart from the fact that natives occupying these plots would necessarily be in receipt of substantial salaries, they ought to be able to acquire some profit from the ground.

That ground be set aside for educational and religious purpose

That the place be called the "Municipal Location Extension", and the regulations of the present location be made to apply to it, together with certain amendments which would be considered.

That it be under the supervision of the Location Superintenden who would visit it daily, and at such other times as he thought fit,

I consider too much importance cannot be attached to supervision. It is my experience that the educated native needs more discipline than the raw native. He has reached that stage of his existence, which one might term half broken, and he might take the wrong step which leads to crime and fornication. This invariably happens, as is perfectly obvious to those who have to deal with them. The real reason is, because of their superiority over other natives, they have been allowed to have more privileges than are good for them.

I would also suggest that before any steps be taken applications be called for by asking the Native Department and missionaries to advertise the project to such natives as would take up occupation of these plots.

I have an alternative plan, which I think would be more success-ful in the present bad times. There is about half the population in the location there was this time last year, due to the erection of new compounds for railway boys, and the reduction of native employment generally. Therefore, there is ample room, and, as the place is being surveyed on straight lines, I think suitable stands of 100 ft. by 80 ft. could be laid out and made, what one would term a suburb, to accomodate the better class native. In fact, every class could be segregated, namely, married natives, single men, coloured people, and Indians. When better times arrive and the population returns the other scheme could be considered.

I understand that the real complaint amongst these educated natives is, that they are afraid to bring their wives to the location, owing to its bad reputation and the class of native residing there. Well, the worst offenders are these men whose wives are away, and if their wives were here they would not be tempted and the single girls would have less temptation from the married men. Besides this, the married women would set an example to the single ones, and so improve the general tone of things, also, they would keep their husbands in order.

The location is bounded by eight churches and schools of different denomination, so that the location with such surroundings is

The educated native has less idea of cultivation than his brother who has been brought up in the reserves, in fact, there are very few natives who could profitably cultivate an acre of ground. Therefore, I think, they would be just as well off on a piece of ground 100 ft. by 80 ft. and I am of the opinion that if such stands were suitably fenced and a brick house built they would be very attractive.

I have the honour to be, etc.,

(Signed) T. E. Vawdrey.
LOCATION SUPERINTENDENT.

FOR FINANCE COMMITTEE MEETING 26/7/22.

Bulawayo
11th Nov 1903.

To the Mayor
B'wayo Town Council
Bulawayo.

We, the undersigned for and on behalf of the residents of the Bulawayo Native Locations, and by their special request desire to pray Your Councillors sanction and approval to the formation of a Native Vigilance Board—members of such Board to be elected by the residents of the Locations.

The object of such Board, will be to look after the wants of the people generally, to report on the state of the Locations, to lay their grievances before the authorities, in fact to do everything appertaining to furthering their interests.

We are well aware that we have a Location Inspector, and hail his presence among us with utmost respect and think that he will be greatly benefited by the formation of such a Board.

Lastly, we desire to assure You Sir, that Your petitioners are animated alone by a desire to advance the interests of the Native residents of Bulawayo in accordance with law, notwithstanding rumours to the contrary

We have the honour to subscribe ourselves
Your most Obedient Servants

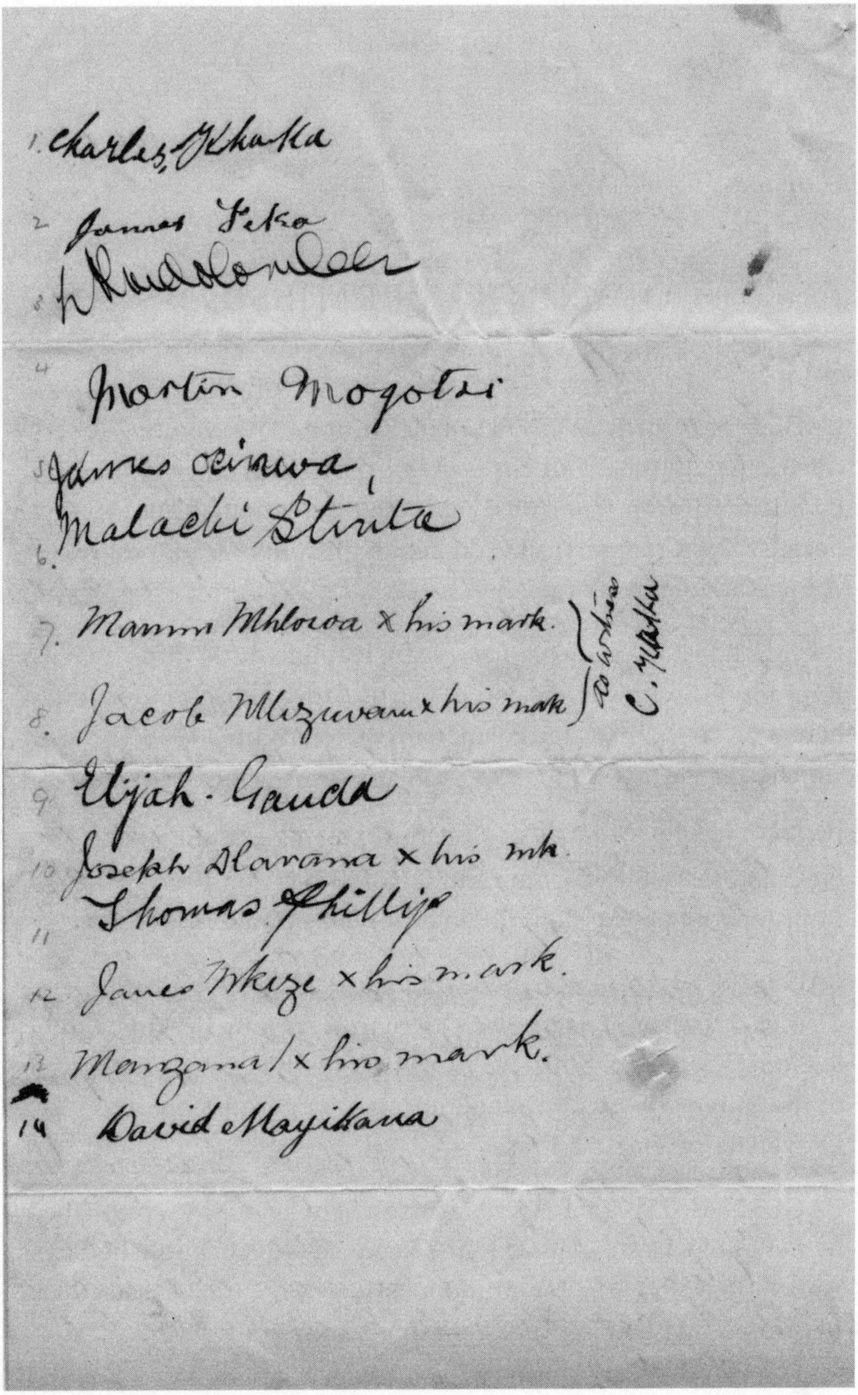

1. Charles Mkhaka

2. James Feka

3. Mhudolomdea [illegible]

4. Martin Mogotsi

5. James Ocimawa

6. Malachi Stinta

7. Mamma Mhlowa x his mark.

8. Jacob Mlizwana x his mark

To witness C. Mkaka

9. Elijah Gauda

10. Joseph Dlavana x his mk.

11. Thomas Phillips

12. James Mkeze x his mark.

13. Monzoma x his mark.

14. David Mayikana

COPYRIGHT PERMISSIONS

SELECT BIBLIOGRAPHY

Barnes, Teresa. *'We Women Worked So Hard': Gender, Urbanization and Social Reproduction in Colonial Harare, Zimbabwe, 1930–1956.* Portsmouth: Heinemann, 1999.

———. *'"Am I a Man?": Gender and the Pass Laws in Urban Colonial Zimbabwe, 1930–80.' African Studies Review* 40.1 (1997): 59–81.

———. *'The Fight for Control of African Women's Mobility in Colonial Zimbabwe, 1900–1939.' Signs* 17.3 (1992): 586–608.

Brontë, Charlotte. *Jane Eyre.* London: Penguin Classics, 2006 (first published London: Smith, Elder & Co, 1847).

Burke, Timothy. *Lifebuoy Men, Lux Women: Commodification, Consumption and Cleanliness in Modern Zimbabwe.* Durham: Duke University Press, 1996.

Geschiere, Peter. *The Perils of Belonging: Autochthony, Citizenship, and Exclusion in Africa and Europe.* Chicago: University of Chicago Press, 2009.

Greenland, Chris N. *The Other – Without Fear, Favour or Prejudice.* lulu. com, 2010.

Haggard, H.R. *King Solomon's Mines.* Dover Thrift Editions. Mineola: Dover Publications, Inc., 2006.

Hawkins, F. 'The Reminiscences of Charles Quinche (1900–96): A Bulawayan of Swiss-Ndebele Parentage.' *Heritage of Zimbabwe* No. 36, 2017.

Jackson, Lynette. *Surfacing Up: Psychiatry and Social Order in Colonial Zimbabwe, 1908–1968*. Ithaca: Cornell University Press, 2005.

———. '"Stray Women" and "Girls on the Move": Gender, Space, and Disease in Colonial and Post-Colonial Zimbabwe' in *Sacred Spaces and Public Quarrels: African Cultural and Economic Landscapes*, Ezekiel Kalipeni and Tiyambe Zeleza (eds.), 147–167. Trenton: Africa World Press, 1999.

———. '"When in the White Man's Town": Zimbabwean Women Remember Chibeura,' in *Women in African Colonial Histories*, Susan Geiger, Nakanyike Musisi, and Jean M. Allman (eds.), 191–215. Bloomington: Indiana University Press, 2002.

McClintock, Anne. *Imperial Leather: Race, Gender and Sexuality in the Colonial Contest*. New York: Routledge, 1995.

McCulloch, Jock. *Black Peril, White Virtue: Sexual Crime in Southern Rhodesia, 1902–1935*. Bloomington: Indiana University Press, 2000.

Pratt, Mary Louise. *Imperial Eyes: Travel Writing and Transculturation*. 2nd ed. New York: Routledge, 2007.

Schmidt, Elizabeth. *Peasants, Traders, and Wives: Shona Women in the History of Zimbabwe, 1870–1939*. Portsmouth: Heinemann, 1992.

———. 'Patriarchy, Capitalism, and the Colonial State in Zimbabwe.' *Signs* 16.4 (1991): 732–756.

———. 'Negotiated Spaces and Contested Terrain: Men, Women, and the Law in Colonial Zimbabwe, 1890–1939.' *Journal of Southern African Studies* 16.4 (1990): 622–648.

Stoler, Ann Laura. *Carnal Knowledge and Imperial Power. Race and the Intimate in Colonial Rule*. Berkeley: University of California Press, 2002.

Vaughan, Megan. *Curing Their Ills: Colonial Power and African Illness*. Stanford: Stanford University Press, 1991.

West, Michael O. *The Rise of an African Middle Class: Colonial Zimbabwe,*

1898–1965. Bloomington: Indiana University Press, 2002.

White, Luise. *The Comforts of Home: Prostitution in Colonial Nairobi*. Chicago: University of Chicago Press, 1990.

ACKNOWLEDGEMENTS

Helen Moffett, editor extraordinaire – we crouched, we crept, we crawled, and now we are standing – thank you so much for the incredible journey.

The amazing women at Picador Africa – Terry Morris, Andrea Nattrass, Zodwa Kumalo-Valentine, Jane Bowman, Ayanda Phasha, Shakti Pillay and Nkanyezi Tshabalala – there is so much to thank you for, but most of all I would like to thank you for making such a wonderful home for this novel.

Fourie Botha, once-upon-a-time publisher and now maverick agent, thank you for believing in my work and championing it from the very beginning.

Jenefer Shute, ever brilliant and insightful, thank you for the reader's notes that helped guide the way.

Dumisani Ndlovu, thank you for giving us permission to use your beautiful painting: in the mysterious magic we inhabit, it anticipated the story I was yet to tell.

SIPHIWE GLORIA NDLOVU is a Zimbabwean writer, scholar, and filmmaker. She is a 2022 recipient of the Windham–Campbell Prize for Fiction. Her debut novel, *The Theory of Flight*, won the Sunday Times Barry Ronge Fiction Prize in 2019. Her second and third novels, *The History of Man* and *The Quality of Mercy*, were shortlisted for the Sunday Times Fiction Prize. After almost two decades of living in North America, Ndlovu has returned home to Bulawayo, the City of Kings.